Judy Johnson has a special interest in creating fiction from little-known but compelling aspects of Australian history. Her writing has won many prizes, including the Victorian Premier's CJ Dennis Award in 2007 for her verse novel, *Jack*.

The SECRET FATE *of* MARY WATSON

JUDY JOHNSON

FOURTH ESTATE • *London, New York, Sydney* and *Auckland*

Fourth Estate
An imprint of HarperCollins*Publishers*, Australia

HarperCollins*Publishers*
Australia • Brazil • Canada • France • Germany • Holland • India
Italy • Japan • Mexico • New Zealand • Poland • Spain • Sweden
Switzerland • United Kingdom • United States of America

HarperCollins acknowledges the Traditional Custodians
of the lands upon which we live and work, and pays respect
to Elders past and present.

First published in Australia in 2011
by HarperCollins*Publishers* Australia Pty Limited
ABN 36 009 913 517
harpercollins.com.au

HarperCollins*Publishers*
Macken House, 39/40 Mayor Street Upper
Dublin 1, D01 C9W8, Ireland

A catalogue record for this book is available from the National Library of Australia

ISBN 9780732292508 (paperback)

Cover design by Darren Holt, HarperCollins Design Studio
Cover images: Woman © Yolande de Kort/ Trevillion Images; Rocks by Sara Winter/
Getty Images; all other images by shutterstock.com
Typeset in Historical 12.5/17 pt by Letter Spaced

*For Rob
and my children*

MARY WATSON'S TANK DIARY

(copy of an original document held in John Oxley Library, Brisbane)

Left Lizard Island September 2nd, 1881 (Sunday afternoon) in tank or pot in which bêche-de-mer is boiled. Got about three miles or four from the Lizards.

September 4. Made for the sand bank off the Lizards but could not reach it. Got on a reef all day on the look-out for a boat, but saw none.

September 6. Very calm morning. Able to pull the tank up to an island with three small mountains on it. Ah Sam went ashore to try and get water as ours was done. There were natives camped there so we were afraid to go far away. We had to wait return of tide. Anchored under the mangroves, got on the reef. Very calm.

September 7. Made for an island four or five miles from the one spoken of yesterday. Ashore, but could not find any water. Cooked some rice and clam-fish. Moderate S. E. breeze.

Stayed here all night. Saw a steamer bound north. Hoisted Ferrier's white and pink wrap but did not answer us.

September 8. Changed the anchorage of the boat as the wind was freshening. Went down to a kind of little lake on the same island (this done last night). Remained here all day looking out for a boat; did not see any. Very cold night; blowing very hard. No water.

September 9. Brought the tank ashore as far as possible with this morning's tide. Made camp all day under the trees. Blowing very hard. No water. Gave Ferrier a dip in the sea; he is showing symptoms of thirst, and I took a dip myself. Ah Sam and self very parched with thirst. Ferrier showing symptoms.

September 10. Ferrier very bad with inflammation; very much alarmed. No fresh water, and no more milk, but condensed. Self very weak; really thought I would have died last night (Sunday).

September 11. Still all alive. Ferrier much better this morning. Self feeling very weak. I think it will rain today, clouds very heavy, wind not quite so hard. No rain. Morning fine weather. Ah Sam preparing to die. Have not seen him since 9. Ferrier more cheerful. Self not feeling at all well. Have not seen any boat of any description. No water. Near dead with thirst.

DEPOSITION OF ROBERT WATSON

(copy of an original document held in John Oxley Library, Brisbane)

I am a *bêche-de-mer* fisher residing at present in Cooktown and belong to the firm of Fuller and Watson. I have recently resided at Lizard Island and first went to reside there in 1879. I built on Lizard Island a dwelling, smoke and storehouse, and cultivated a small portion of the island.

I was married on the 30th May, 1880 to Mary Beatrice Phillips Oxenham [sic]. Subsequent to our marriage we resided on the Lizard Island, and since. In March last year (1881) my wife went to reside in Cooktown pending her accouchement and returned to the island about the end of June last, being then the mother of a male child born on the 3rd June.

On the 1st September, I left with my partner Fuller, taking our boats to fish northward on a six-weeks' cruise.

About the end of October while fishing at Restoration Island, I was informed that the Aborigines from the mainland had attacked the island and that my wife, child and two Chinamen who were left on the Lizard Island in charge were missing, and my houses sacked and property all destroyed. Upon my immediate return to Lizard this report was confirmed by personal observation. Since the 7th November last I have been untiring in my search for traces of my wife and child, assisted by the police and Harbour authorities and others, amongst the islands and coast land between Cooktown and Cape Melville.

From information I received I visited No. 5 Island Howick Group this morning in the Government Schooner *Spitfire* accompanied by Harbour-master Fahey and the Inspector of Police. On this island I found the remains of my wife and child.

I recognised the body of my wife, although in a state of decomposition, by her clothing, a leather belt she wore round her waist and her hair. I also produce a ring — I remember its being made by a Chinaman in Cooktown and subsequently placed by me on the third finger of her left hand on the occasion of our marriage. The ring I now produce I took off her finger this morning and recognized it as the one placed by me on her finger on the occasion of our marriage.

I also identify a revolver found in the vicinity of the body as the one left by me on Lizard Island in the beginning of September last. A box containing clothing, jewellery and two one-pound notes, half sovereign and silver, also her diary, I identify as our property.

The diary in which is recorded in pencil the

circumstances attending my wife's departure from Lizard Island, I recognize as her handwriting. I recognize the remains of the child by its clothing found on it and in the vicinity. The child's name was Thomas Ferrier Watson.

I also recognize portion of an iron tank in which I found the bodies of my wife and child on No. 5 Howick, as that I used for a *bêche-de-mer* boiler on Lizard Island — also two paddles which I picked up near the boiler and identified.

I also saw the remains of a Chinaman lately in my employ named Ah Sam. I saw them on the island in the vicinity of my wife and child. I recognize them to be those of the Chinaman from the peculiarity of his hair, the clothing and contents of his box — and identify a rifle found alongside the body as one left by me with my wife on Lizard Island. I believe that my wife, child and the Chinaman, Ah Sam, died from thirst.

I make this statement from circumstances related by my wife in her diary which records I recognize as her handwriting.

Sgd. Robert Watson

Taken and sworn before me on board Government Schooner *Spitfire* this 24th day of January, 1882

Sgd. B. Fahey, Water Police Magistrate

It's peculiar the assumptions we all make. For instance how, in a diary, the truth bone's connected to the hand bone. But those experts at smuggling, the Chinese, know how accommodating anatomy can be. They dig up their dead relatives, then send the bits and pieces home to Canton Province in large earthenware jars. The fact that no customs official cares to dig through the contents for contraband doesn't mean the gold nuggets aren't there, tucked in snugly between the bones.

In hindsight, I'd rewrite my ending. Specifically, I'd correct that small but telling error in the tank diary. It was October, not September, when Ah Sam, the baby and I left Lizard Island. You might think it a trivial point. But it seems to me the kind of clue that an eagle-eyed observer could well home in on, suspecting things are not exactly as they seem.

The cynical might well advise: Don't believe everything you read.

I would prefer to put it this way: The truth lies waiting to be uncovered.

Brisbane

Autumn, 1879

1

Keen observation is a skill that the homely find useful.

From the secret diary of Mary Watson

12TH MAY 1879

Strange what you might find in the Positions Vacant column. For instance: Dutiful daughter for life-wrecking father. Young ladies with expectations of a benevolent family life, or even a respectable name, need not apply. Good luck with your interviews, Papa. For my part, I'm applying for a new life. I just hope it doesn't ask me for references.

Mid-afternoon, a mild Brisbane autumn. A cat's tongue of cloud laps at the sun. The spilled milk tips down the shopfronts of Edward Street. My boots crunch through the toffee wrappers of a thousand fallen leaves.

I stop at the two-storeyed Ulster Hotel. Mrs Menzies, proprietor of the boarding house where I'm staying, told me I'd find Mr Wilson inside. In my jobless state, I desperately need to convince him he won't find a better governess for his offspring anywhere between here and Mount Isa.

A horse and buggy are drawn up outside. His? The suspension's seen better days, and the trap hangs low at the back. The horse's elastic has gone at the neck; the bristly head droops as though the knacker's yard has been whispering sweet nothings in its ear for months.

A man in dirty overalls holds a young boy in britches above his head. The boy has a chimney brush in hand, clearing away the cobwebs under the verandah ceiling. My eyes fix on the man's damp armpits.

'Excuse me. Could you tell me where I might find Mr Wilson? Of Witterby Downs?'

Two pained blue eyes peer through the boy's legs. The braces jiggle as he lifts the top half of the acrobatic act over his head then onto the ground in front of him, dodging a pair of wiggling boots in the process. A patch of dirt mars the boy's left cheek. A caul of web adheres to a spot on the side of the man's head.

'In the bar, miss,' he says. 'But you'd better hurry if you want to talk to him. There'll be a poker game upstairs shortly and you've no hope of getting any of the men's attention then.'

He looks at my face and I'm aware of what he sees. I've had eighteen years to get used to the landscape, after all. My maternal grandmother's eyes set too far apart. Hooded lids like half-closed envelopes on two grey letters. The square jaw and big ears of some long-lost uncle. I scratch a cheek with a finger too thick to be ladylike. Mine are man's hands, useful for scraping the hairs off a scalded pig. One day I will make some farmer a wonderful wife etc, etc.

'No hope,' he repeats, after his perusal. 'In fact, you could cut your own throat and then lie in the middle of the table and the men would deal the cards right over the top of you.'

'Well,' I say, 'there go my plans for the day.'

The fellow seems nervous. His fists open and close, and he won't hold my eye. He keeps glancing at the pub door, then looking away, distracted. But I've no time to analyse his mood. I need to find Mr Wilson before the poker game starts.

The air inside is stale and hoppy; old beer soaked into rugs that haven't been aired. Tradesmen and dock workers chat and smoke quietly in the corners. Near the window opening onto the street, several better-dressed men sit leisurely, nursing pints of ale. Only one man props up the bar, his back to me.

'Mr Wilson?'

He turns. Veteran of a travelling boxing troupe, if ever I've seen one. Short, stocky, thick-necked, caught in a meat press as a child, perhaps. It's hard not to feel the discomfort of all that bulk, crushed down into five feet nothing and bulging outwards at each seam. My first thought is: dumb and apeish. But there's some cunning lurking behind his protruding eyes.

'Not every day a young lady comes looking for me.' He winks exaggeratedly and licks a fleshy bottom lip.

'Mary Oxnam,' I say, but don't offer my hand. 'Mrs Menzies tells me you may be looking for a governess.'

I'm going through the motions now. My instincts have already made up their mind.

'Ah, the sweet widow Menzies. She'd be missing her husband by now, don't you think?'

Sweet? I think of the old harridan floating into the kitchen this morning while I sat at the table peering at the Positions Vacant columns in the *Brisbane Courier*. I'm not sure what I found more alarming about her: the white hair piled high on her head in a snowy mountain, or the dark pupils of her eyes, like two climbers who had fallen from the alps above and turned black from frostbite, their picks still in hand, as she enquired, ever so delicately, about: 'the small matter of the board that's owing today, Miss Oxnam!'

'No, I don't think she's missing her husband at all,' I reply. 'He did, after all, leave her a debt-free establishment with which to practise her considerable business acumen. And, from what I can gather, she's been attracting the avid attentions of several gentlemen of a certain age, with less-than-certain resources for their dotage.'

My eyes are drawn to a frayed patch on Mr Wilson's stretched waistcoat. 'Is that your horse and buggy outside, sir?'

'Yes.' He blinks. 'Why do you ask?'

'No reason.'

I calculate the extra information. If he intends to play poker upstairs, he must have ample money to bet. But no money, it seems, for a decent mode of transport, nor a new waistcoat. Neither dumb ape nor slimy opportunist; rather, a classic case of habitual gambler. As if to prove it, his fingers twitch around his glass, those bulging eyes stray to the stairs.

He smiles with his thin top lip. 'Matter of fact, Miss Oxnam, I am looking for a governess for my two children. Think you might fit the bill?'

'How much would the job pay, Mr Wilson?' No use trying to sniff the honeysuckle without first beating out the bees.

He picks up his beer and takes a swallow.

'Depends,' he says. 'There are always bonuses to be had with duties above and beyond the call, if you know what I mean. But, at the start, let's say two shillings a week.'

Big spender. I could make that much cleaning, and would rapturously prefer to.

'And Mrs Wilson?' I enquire politely.

'Sadly, gone to heaven, with the angels.' The thick bottom lip pushes out in melancholy.

'And the eunuchs,' I add, flicking an imaginary speck of dust off my collar. 'How restful for her.'

I'd thought the far-off gaze meant he was, in spirit, already in the card room above. But his ears are still open, it seems.

'You've a smart mouth, Miss Oxnam. Yes, indeed, smart as paint.'

But I've done no real damage; his tone has a gleam to it. The heavy brows lift and I realise then what the bulging brown gaze reminds me of: weeks-old cowpats; cracked and dry on the surface, with smelly slop just underneath.

He glances at the clock on the wall. 'There's a poker game upstairs. Come up and watch, why don't you? We often have an audience of appreciative ladies. I'll even buy you an ale and lemonade. And, afterwards, we'll talk some more. Happens to be I like a spirited filly.'

I hear the implied appendage: more fun to break her in.

He gestures to the bartender to bring me a drink before I have a chance to refuse, then hefts his bulk off the stool. I pick up the cool glass when it arrives, deciding I've nothing better to do for the afternoon. The sweet widow Menzies is doubtless lurking about my room, looking for something she can pawn to pay for my supper tonight. And if I can't be a player, I can at least be entertained. Poker is serious business, and a good spectator sport for those who understand it. But as for the job, Mr Wilson of Witterby Downs can take his gambling habit, his two shillings a week and his half-dead horse and ride off into the sunset without this spirited filly tied to the backboard.

Pipe smoke has bullied the air clear out of the room. Five fine leather-padded chairs are positioned around the poker table. Wooden ones skirt the walls on three sides; on the fourth, French doors open onto the verandah. The muffled clip-clop sounds of Edward Street trot in. Two women in their thirties perch like crows on their seats. They've been watching me since I came in the door, whispering to each other. They probably think I'm Wilson's fancy piece. The thought's so disturbing I need a long swallow of my drink. Bubbles hit the back of my throat too quickly and I suppress a cough.

I nod to the man I spoke to outside, under the awning. He's leaning against a heavy wooden post, a foaming glass in hand. His small companion has disappeared, and he's exchanged his overalls for tan trousers. The piece of cobweb still clings to the hair above his left ear. He doesn't acknowledge my gesture; looks away, as if he doesn't want to be noticed. Strange. I hadn't thought to offend him; hadn't really had the chance with the few words we'd exchanged.

I take a seat against the wall opposite the verandah, ignoring the now pointed looks of the women. Minutes pass, and another six spectators arrive. Three are men, neatly dressed, as if they'd like to be considered players should someone drop out from what's obviously a well-established circle. Two of the three seem easy in manner. Only one, a tall fellow, sixtyish, with bushy, grey-white sideburns, strikes me as having enough tension in his shoulders to be a part of the inner sanctum. Sure enough, he takes his place at the poker table. The other men take seats together near the wall to my left, separating me from the whispering women.

Wilson takes his spot across from Sideburns and scoots his

chair forward until the padded barge of his belly nudges the pier of the table. His bearing is confident, probably too casual. Afternoon sun falls amber in a column on the wood in front of him as he stacks his chips. It's a bit early for such an act — he reminds me of Papa: always that projection of relaxed confidence, right through until almost the end, when the liquor has spoiled his judgement and his more sober opponents have scooped away the last of his stake. That's when things got nasty. An angry Jack bouncing out of his box, fists flailing.

Two more players arrive. One is at least as short as Wilson, and fatter, but much more meticulously attired. I christen him Dandy for his gold silk cravat and his greasy little moustachios. He purses his lips and fidgets as he takes the chair opposite Wilson, next to Sideburns. The other fellow stands near the French doors, looking out onto the street, his wide back to me. His blondish hair is cropped short, his pale bone trousers and blue shirt neatly pressed. He's tall, holds his body steady. He seems self-assured, relaxed.

Some movement or noise turns Wilson's attention towards the door. He startles slightly, a wallaby smelling a dingo on a far ridge.

I twist my head slightly. Not a dingo filling the doorframe; more like a bear. He must be six foot tall, with shoulders so broad and straight they could be used as a try square. A long, black beard hangs halfway down his chest. But it's the steady intensity of his dark eyes that has every man in the room suddenly skittish. My own gaze turns away, but I'm curious to know who Blackbeard is. And why he commands so much nervous attention.

The tall player by the verandah turns, exchanges a glance and a nod with Blackbeard. They're not equals, that much is clear, but this man's closer to being so than any other contender in the room. The deference is there — superficially, at least. But I detect the frayed edge of something else beneath the surface of his green eyes that interests me. Not to mention the fact that he's very attractive. Clean-shaven, fair-featured. I judge him to be forty, perhaps. His skin is biscuit-brown, and that blondish hair, seen front on, has gold flecks in it.

Handsome must feel my attention because, mortifyingly, he catches my careful inspection. He nods. The ghost of a smile lifts the right side of his mouth, ending in a fold of skin. The line remains for a while after the smile recedes, suggesting he's almost always vaguely amused. Or, perhaps, chronically cynical.

I grin stupidly in response, then hide the bottom half of my face in my glass as I take another drink. Not only mortified, but an idiot, it seems.

Blackbeard's big strides, meanwhile, have eaten up the space between the door and the poker table. He sits with his back to the verandah, puts a booted ankle across his knee. Then strokes his beard, slowly. He, too, has noted me. Those bottomless black eyes pin me for a moment, then move on without betraying any readable impression.

Cobweb draws a thin, burlap curtain over the opening in the French doors. Handsome walks around the table and sits with his back to me, facing Blackbeard, Wilson on his left, Dandy to his right. Sideburns, between Blackbeard and Dandy, takes a long swallow from a large glass of whisky and smiles nervously without making eye contact with his opponents. Cobweb sits near the wall, several seats to my right. He stares resolutely ahead, but I get the distinct impression he'd rather stand. Wilson glares at him briefly, then reaches for the deck and shuffles the cards.

The players ante up, the poker game begins, and no one seems relaxed any more.

Especially the continental Dandy. I'd noticed him wince when Blackbeard walked behind him. Now his forehead's sweating. Of course, it could be the fact that his waistcoat's too tight. A donkey track of buttons strain at their holes as they twist over his belly.

The game is five-card draw, and it's played mostly in silence. Sideburns has started well, and Dandy isn't doing badly either — he may be a fop, but he's hard to read under the sweat and the fidgeting. He has a strong French accent; I should have guessed. Wilson is a rock — he plays few hands, and, when he's in, it's with strong cards. Blackbeard's been unlucky early on. Handsome's back is to me and, without seeing his face, it's difficult to tell how he plays. All five of them are clinical. This is a serious game.

The ante is ten shillings, and the pots so far have run up to eighty pounds. It's exciting to watch, but worrying. No ... discouraging. So much money, and they're playing with it as if it doesn't count. I know quite well how the game works. I could play. I could win. Just one pot would take me a long, long way. But you can't bet what you don't have. Damn Mrs Menzies. There's enough for three years' lodgings just sitting on the table. Minding Wilson's horrors for a month would barely make the ante for a single round, and there's no pretending that his 'bonuses' would make a difference. I seethe and simmer, cross and uncross my ankles. If Papa was in my position, he'd try to bluff his way through a losing hand. But I've seen what that leads to.

The bet's gone around the table twice. When it comes to Blackbeard, he raises by ten pounds. No one moves for a moment. Sideburns folds, then Dandy. Then Handsome. Wilson hesitates, then lays down his cards. Blackbeard gathers up chips worth eighty-six pounds, ten shillings. Without having to show his hand.

He would've been fifty pounds down, but his patience brought it all back.

An hour later, my eyes want to close in the warm room. The game drones on in chip clicks and monosyllables. Sideburns is on his third glass of whisky, and it's starting to show. Dandy and Blackbeard are holding their own. Wilson's been fortunate of late, but Handsome's struggling with bad luck. Good hands at the wrong time, plus he lost a tough head to head with Wilson: both men had drawn to a flush, but Wilson's was King-high to Handsome's Queen.

It's Blackbeard's deal. The pot is right, and he distributes the cards. All in for the draw. It's probably nonsense, but I'm trying to read Handsome from the back and something about the set of his shoulders makes me wonder if he hasn't just had a nice surprise. When the bet comes around, he raises. I look to see how Wilson responds. He glowers at his cards, then looks up for the briefest second. But not at Handsome, and not at Dandy either. I glance to the right. Cobweb has his chin buried in his chest but, for an instant, his eyes meet Wilson's. I look back to Wilson, just in time to see his scowl change into a resigned smile. He folds.

Blackbeard folds too, without looking up. Sideburns raises five pounds. Dandy folds. Handsome sees the five, and raises another five. Sideburns hesitates, a bit unsteady, and calls, laying down Jacks and Sevens. I can't see what Handsome shows, but Sideburns' face says it all. I've seen that expression of righteous suffering before … years of it. His judgement is gone with the whisky in his glass, but he still blames the cards. Why is it every loser reminds me of Papa?

I glance back to Wilson. This time he's smiling, and again he looks up at Cobweb. Just for a second, but enough to alert me.

I lean back in my chair, eyes half-closed, stretching my neck as though it's stiff from holding one position. What I really want is a better view of Cobweb. Yes, he would be able to see Handsome's cards ... if Handsome isn't careful how he holds them. Sitting two seats to my right, Cobweb also has clear sight of Wilson's face, and vice versa. And he seems more alert and attentive than he should be. The game's been trundling on for some time, the air's close and tepid, yet he holds his arms across his chest as if he were cold.

Suddenly alert again, I re-involve myself with the game. Three hands, pass, four, five ... but Handsome's cards are ordinary. He plays a head to head with Dandy for a smallish pot, wins with something I can't see but it leaves Dandy scowling down at a pair of Queens. Six hands, seven ...

And then it happens. Blackbeard and Dandy have folded on the bet after the draw, but Handsome raises ten pounds. Wilson ponders for a moment before his eyes dart to Cobweb. Instantly I look right, but only with my eyes. The man's arms are still folded across his chest, but this time his chin is lifted. He's almost looking down his nose at the game.

Wilson sees the bet, and raises another ten. Handsome sees the bet, and calls.

'Tens and Eights,' he says calmly.

'Too bad,' Wilson counters. 'Three ducks.'

Now I'm interested. And angry. I didn't like Wilson from the start, and it's almost a personal affront that he'd take advantage of

Handsome. Now that I'm on to them, it doesn't take long to make sure. Cobweb's chin up means Wilson stands a show of winning; chin down means he should fold. Their system is almost certainly more complicated — I notice that sometimes Cobweb's left arm is over his right, sometimes right over left; sometimes his hands cup his elbows; sometimes his fists are balled. I can't make out what messages Wilson might be sending to Cobweb, if any; I can see his face, but not enough of his hands to make a judgement. Still, I don't need the details.

They're clever; they don't make eye contact except when Handsome's involved in the betting. Cobweb might sometimes be in a position to see Dandy's cards, but not often, and too much communication would make the others around the table suspicious.

I watch the two conspirators for three more hands just to make perfectly sure, then decide it's time to powder my nose. As I pass Handsome, I graze his back with my arm. He turns, irritated, those green eyes already stirred up by his inexplicable losing streak.

'Terribly sorry,' I murmur, 'there's not much space to move in here.'

I point with my eyes first to Wilson, then in the general direction of Cobweb. It's all I can do. I can't hesitate without giving myself away, but as I turn to go I see one of Handsome's eyebrows hitch.

'Not at all, miss,' he says. I walk casually downstairs.

Five minutes later, I return. The men are tamping their pipes; in between hands they've ordered another round of drinks. I walk to my chair. Cobweb hasn't moved. Wilson doesn't look up; neither does Handsome. Dandy mops his damp face with a monogrammed silk handkerchief. Sideburns tries manfully to look sober, without success. Blackbeard leans back, comfortable in his chair. We exchange the briefest of glances, and a slight crinkling around his eyes hints at the possibility of a smile. I'm sure he knows. He's probably known what was going on from the beginning. He knows, and now he knows that I know too.

I look up again. Blackbeard's smile is gone and his eyes are cold. Dreadfully cold. He's thinking of something else.

He's looking at Cobweb.

2

The ability to bewitch a man must be delightful,
but it's infinitely more practical to settle for gratitude.

From the secret diary of Mary Watson

Wilson's not sure how or why the wheels have fallen off his clever plan, but he looks disgruntled when the game finishes and he counts his somewhat reduced pile of chips. Still, he's finished ahead. Handsome recovered somewhat, but has probably dropped fifty pounds overall. Dandy has done well, and Blackbeard has broken even. The big loser, predictably, is the inebriated Sideburns, who makes light of his losses with the kind of forced bonhomie that's just waiting for the wrong word, or wrong look, to turn viperish.

Wilson has forgotten all about our follow-up conversation, which suits me admirably. He knows something went badly wrong, and isn't clear about how much trouble he might be in. I didn't notice Cobweb leaving, but I imagine he's shaking in his boots somewhere private. He'd paled like a feverish frog under the fangs of Blackbeard's stare.

The spectators depart for the bar. I'm about to follow them downstairs when I feel a hand on my shoulder. I turn to find Handsome's face inches from my own.

'Percy Fuller,' he offers, then lowers his voice, brings his face close enough that I can smell his cologne: a mix of pine needles and warm male. 'But please call me Percy. I owe you a favour. How did you know?'

Some small spring tightens in my chest and then lets go with a pleasant ping. I step back a little.

'Mary Oxnam. Please call me Mary.'

I hold out my hand and he takes it. His is dry, with calluses on the palm. I look down. He wears no wedding ring.

'The eyes, of course,' I tell him. 'Once you know what to look for, it's obvious.'

He tips his head a little to one side. 'An observant girl, aren't you?' It's a rhetorical question. 'Pardon my curiosity, but how would you know about card sharping, Mary Oxnam?'

I think of lying, then wonder what would be the point. I won't see this man again, and fabrication requires more energy than I can muster. It's been a long afternoon.

'I've had a lifetime's apprenticeship.'

He looks quizzical.

'I've watched my father's failed attempts to extract money out of his customers and business colleagues in any number of illegal ways. Rigged poker games were the least of it.'

'I see.' An extra string pulls tight in those green eyes. 'Customers?'

'He's proprietor of the Red Lion pub in Rockhampton. And before that, many other ventures. He's not a particularly competent cheat, which led to a lifestyle that is ... Peripatetic is probably the word.' My throat feels dry. I need another drink.

'Even with a family to look after?'

'My father never lets a small thing like responsibility slow him down.'

'Where are you from originally?'

'Cornwall. My family came over from Truro two years ago on the *City of Agra*. And you?'

'London,' he says, but somehow I doubt it. There's something slightly askew about his accent. 'These days I operate a sea-slug-fishing station on Lizard Island with my partner, Bob Watson.'

'Sea-slug fishing!'

'Let me guess. You've always imagined it's a dirty business that no self-respecting gentleman would lower himself to.' He seems more amused than offended.

'Something like that, I suppose.'

He looks briefly over my shoulder, then brings his gaze back to mine. 'Look, rather than standing here making the place look messy, will you come downstairs with me for a drink? We'll find a quiet corner table. You're an interesting person, Mary, scambuster extraordinaire. And there is the small matter of the favour I owe you.'

The pulse at my throat won't let me say no. I look around. The room has largely emptied.

By the time we reach the bar, Wilson has gone. Blackbeard's in the corner talking to a middle-aged man who was not in the group upstairs. Dandy has taken a seat at a table under a window across the room, as though to get as far away from Blackbeard as possible. He, too, has company: a man dressed in grubby trousers and a worn shirt. One of the two ladies from upstairs is engaged in conversation with Sideburns, who apparently had enough money left to buy another big glass of whisky. Cobweb has disappeared.

'Taking your inventory?' Percy mutters near my ear.

I smile slightly. 'It's habit. The world can't pull the wool quite so easily over my eyes if I'm watching what everyone is knitting.'

He guides me to an empty table next to a shaft of fermenting light near a window. Dust motes have lazy fits inside it. I look at the clock on the wall: four thirty. His hand is light under my elbow. I quite like the sensation.

'Interesting that you think the world has a special balaclava with no eyeholes just for you,' he says, laughing and indicates a stool. 'What will you drink? They tell me a shot of absinthe can lead to high levels of enlightenment.'

'I think I'll stick to my lowland deductions rather than risk madness,' I say. 'Ginger ale, thank you.'

Percy heads off to the bar for our drinks. I sit on the stool and look around. Blackbeard catches my eye and nods.

I'm not sure what mischief is in me, but I stand and walk over to his table. The man he's speaking with sees my approach and sits back abruptly, as though someone has hit him. Blackbeard's hooded expression doesn't change.

'Mary Oxnam.' I offer my hand. 'I just thought I'd introduce myself.'

Blackbeard looks down at the offending object on the end of my arm and, for a moment, I think he won't take it. But finally he lifts a long, black sleeve and touches my fingers with his own.

'Samuel Roberts,' he says. His voice is low and deep, as self-contained as the rest of him. Like something long settled on the seabed, undisturbed by currents or surface ripples. 'Pleased to make your acquaintance.'

I'm determined not to lower my eyes in submission, but the effort is considerable. He apparently never blinks.

'Interesting poker game, wasn't it?' I comment.

He doesn't answer. His face is a mask. After a few long seconds, there's nothing to do but turn and walk away. I take two steps, and his deep voice taps me on the shoulder.

'You've a sharp eye.'

I turn slowly. 'So have you.'

The man with him flinches — on my behalf, no doubt. Apparently I deserve compassion for my ignorance of beast-in-lair protocols.

Samuel Roberts makes an odd sound. Of amusement, I assume, but it's hard to tell. Acoustics on the seabed are somewhat distorted. It could be just a shifting of sand in his throat.

I walk away for good this time, satisfied with the exchange. He knows there is at least one person in the room who is not frightened of him.

Percy stands stock-still near our little table, two drinks in hand. I ignore the thunder brewing on his forehead and sit.

He puts the drinks down, reaches into his shirt pocket for his pipe and a plug of tobacco. He tamps the leaf into the bowl, inspects it, puts the stem to his mouth, then lifts his eyes again.

'How do you know the Captain?' he asks.

'I don't know him. But the way everyone was reacting to him upstairs, he's obviously someone important. I wanted to meet him. That's all.'

There's a small flare, then a wet, popping sound as he draws in. A smell of plums on the turn and splinters reaches my nose. He shakes the match out and drops it on the table. He's looking at his drink, not me.

'I may as well be hung for a sheep as a lamb,' I say. 'Who is he?'

Percy takes the pipe out of his mouth and inspects it. 'I thought you said you introduced yourself. Didn't he respond in kind?'

'I know his name. But who is he? What's the nature of the kingdom he lords it over?'

Smoke escapes in a small worm from the corner of his mouth. He takes a swallow of beer.

My foot is tapping the floor and it takes an act of will to stop it. Suddenly, I'm excited again. And wary. Without meaning to, I've managed to start a conversation with people who have real money. One of them owes me a favour. Time to be careful. And clever.

'Samuel Roberts is a steamer captain. Out of Townsville.'

'Oh? What cargo does he carry?'

'Back in the heyday of the gold rush, prospectors and their packhorses to Cooktown. Nowadays, as the gold's almost done on the Palmer and diggers are trying their luck at the new seam in New Guinea: food, medicine and mail to Port Moresby.'

'That can't be all,' I say, incredulous. A mere commercial courier wouldn't command so much respect.

Percy takes a sip of his beer. Looks off into the middle distance. 'He occasionally brings in Kanakas from the islands too, I believe. Recruits to work in the canefields.'

'I see,' I say, though I don't. 'What's the name of his boat?'

'*Blackbird.*'

I try to stifle a sudden laugh, and fail. 'He names his boat *Blackbird*, and he uses it to run Kanakas! He's obviously not blackbirding. Or maybe he is, in which case ... My word, he must be a very powerful man. People in high places must owe him a great many favours.' Something new occurs to me and I feel my eyes widen. 'Maybe his cargo is opium. Or illicit gold.'

Percy's green eyes turn malachite. 'I think your wild speculations have jumped the fence in your head. If I were you, I'd swallow them before any more escape.'

He's right; I'm too eager, and I'm playing what advantage I have badly.

'Yes, I'm sorry. I do lead with the mouth, I'm afraid.'

'I think the root cause is the nose,' Percy says coolly. 'I imagine it's not the first time you've inserted it in other people's business.'

'You didn't mind too much when I inserted it in yours upstairs,' I say. 'Are you serious about owing me a favour?'

'Yes. Of course.'

Time to raise the stakes.

'I need a job. Do you know of anything on offer?'

'In Brisbane?' he asks slowly, as if leaving himself time to think something through. 'Or ... elsewhere?'

'Anywhere away from landladies with pickaxes in their eyes.'

A *pardon?* expression crosses his face, but I don't try to explain. He looks at my hair pulled tightly back in its bun. My plain face.

'How old are you, Mary Oxnam?'

'Eighteen.'

'Going on thirty,' he adds with a wry smile. Then, suddenly, 'Why are you here?'

So he sees me, and raises again. I'm in the game! Now ... will the truth serve?

'Here in Brisbane, or here in the pub?'

'Brisbane.' Impatient. He knows I'm stalling. Time to show my hand.

'Before leaving home, I went to the registry office for a copy of my birth certificate so that I could apply for work as a teacher.' I think I see a look of doubt on his face and find myself saying, defensively, 'I'm quite well educated. I went to school in Truro and I read a lot of books.'

'I didn't suggest otherwise,' he drawls. 'You seem impressively intelligent.' The silent *for a woman* finishes the thought. Pity. I hoped he'd be somewhat different from the other men I've met.

'Anyway, the surname on the certificate was my mother's maiden name. My father hadn't bothered to marry her until after I was born.'

'Hard luck.' He clucks his tongue. 'Must've been a bit of a shock. But no reason to toss yourself out into the big, wide world with all its wilful wool-pulling. That would only make knitting your own garment that much harder.'

He won't let me bluff through this. I look into his eyes, weighing up how much I should say. May as well be hung for a sheep as a lamb, indeed.

'If that were all, you'd be right,' I tell him. 'My father is a drunk, Percy. He'd been sober since we arrived in Australia. I thought he was resolute about making a new start. But one of the creditors he thought he'd left behind in Cornwall turned up at the pub. Papa fell off the wagon, got into an altercation. Landed in gaol. He's always been something less than honest. Clumsily so, most often. With a tendency to use force first, reason last. I was of age, so I left. It's as simple as that.'

Of course it wasn't simple at all. But there are some things I wouldn't tell a friend, let alone a stranger. And in any case, I've given him the information he wanted. Will it be enough?

Percy's bottom lip creases as he thinks about this. 'What state is he in now?'

'He's dry again, or so my mother's letter tells me. Being locked in a cell like a common criminal gave him a jolt. How long his sobriety will last is anyone's guess. There's nothing for me in Rockhampton either way.'

'He doesn't want you home again?'

'No.' I lean across the table towards him. 'The point is that I have no intentions of going back. You will have inferred that my money is almost gone. I have an avaricious widow on my back for board. I'm desperate for employment, gainful or no.'

He looks at me steadily. 'You're not serious about the last part, of course.'

I shrug, trying for insouciance. 'Breaking the law is not really my line. But if I were inclined that way, trust me, I could make a good fist of it. I won't fail the way my father has failed. I may be without means at the moment, but I won't be for long. I'm not useless by a long shot.'

'I didn't imagine for an instant that you were.'

Seconds stretch. He sips his drink. I'm very much in the dark, but the longer he thinks, the better. Up to a point. If only I had a clue about how he earns a crust! Enough to play poker for pounds, not pence. I don't believe for a minute he's wholly and solely a slug fisherman.

'Can you play the piano?' he finally asks.

'Yes, actually.' An unusual question. I wish I knew where he was headed. 'Why?'

He points to the table where Dandy and his careworn companion are having their conversation.

'That's Charley Boule. He runs an entertainment salon — French Charley's — in Cooktown.'

'You mean a brothel.' No. He can't be serious. That's not much better than Wilson's offer.

He smiles. 'A rose by any other name. Charley's been putting the word around that he needs a piano player.'

'Cooktown. I read the papers. Wild blacks in the bush, wild whites in the town. Blackmail, thievery, murder ...'

'Comes with the climate.' He's still looking over my head towards Dandy — that is, Charley Boule. 'Gold scratchings, alcohol and sultry weather don't mix well, true. But it's the sort of territory that breeds … opportunity. In a way that Brisbane, say, might find a trifle challenging.'

'I didn't mean to imply that I was opportunistic. I merely suggested I would be adept at creative interpretations of the law, should I be that way inclined.'

I groan inwardly. Fool! Who else but me could pluck, stuff, truss *and* cook my own goose in a mere few words.

'And I didn't intend to imply you have criminal tendencies. I merely observe that the marriage of a sharp mind to an open environment like Cooktown is likely to produce fair offspring in the form of … new ideas.'

His own phrasing has more than a whiff of the artful dodger about it. But how can I say what I'm thinking without jumping a gun he hasn't so much as loaded?

I glance over at the Frenchman in his too-tight waistcoat. 'Cooktown is so very far away. And I've heard that everything is twice as expensive up north. How would I survive, let alone avail myself of these so-called new ideas, on the few shillings a week I'm likely to make playing piano?'

Two streams of smoke ride the humph noise he makes with his nose. 'I see. Your desperation has its conditions.' One sea-cracked finger plays with his bottom lip. It's a nice lip, not fleshy like Wilson's, nor tight as a drawn-shut purse like Charley Boule's, nor carved of rock like Samuel Roberts's. 'All right,' he says. 'I'm not particularly interested in improving the quality of Boule's entertainment. I do, however, sometimes pay for information. Useful information. Cooktown is the gateway through which all captains and crews must pass to reach the far north reef passage. And French Charley's is often the first port of call for them when they reach Cooktown. A skilled observer can learn a good deal in a short time if he ... or she ... pays appropriate attention. Such as you demonstrated upstairs. If you prove reliable, and discreet, you'll do quite well. Nothing illegal *per se.* Comings and goings, arrivals and impending departures, perhaps the occasional overheard conversation. The region's shipping is ... of interest to me.'

'Why would a sea-slug fisherman be concerned about boats passing through Cooktown?' My mouth opens involuntarily as a whole new slew of pennies drops into the slot. 'You're the one involved in smuggling. That's what you do with your lugger when you're not catching sea-slugs.'

He bends forward conspiratorially. 'Yes. You're on to me. I bundle up young girls who talk too much, smuggle them north and straight into the arms of fat Mandarins in Shanghai. They pay a good price and, incredibly enough, once they take possession they even remove the gags. Maybe it's because they're deaf from all those firecrackers.'

I give him what I hope is a withering look, then glance at the Frenchman again. He's noticed the attention we're paying him and, for a second, my eyes lock with his.

'Just one more question,' I say. 'Do you work for, and therefore would I, ultimately, be working for, Samuel Roberts?'

'You don't need to know that.'

'I do,' I insist. 'I need to know where my loyalties lie.'

This is a reasonable request and he must know it. Being aware of who the big boss is doesn't make me any the wiser about the business.

'All right then. Yes.'

So one piece of the puzzle resolves, at least.

'Would I also be working for Mr Boule — in the same line of business, I mean?'

'That's more than one question. But, no. Not if you know what's good for you. Roberts doesn't tolerate divided loyalties.' There's something ironic twitching around his mouth. 'You play piano for Boule, that's all.'

The room's emotional temperature has dropped several degrees. I don't dare look over to Roberts's table again in case he somehow knows what we're discussing. In case he's staring at me with that same frigid malice he turned on Cobweb upstairs. But now, at least, I know the hierarchy of their mysterious business. Percy is an underling of Roberts's, and I would be an underling of Percy's. And Charley Boule is very firmly out of the picture. That is, If I Know What's Good For Me.

I realise then it's not quite enough information to allow me to sell my soul, no matter the wages.

'Why would it be traitorous for me to have dealings with Charley Boule? Who is Samuel Roberts working for?'

Percy puts his glass down firmly on the table and makes to stand. 'No. If you can't manage your curiosity by knowing when to turn it off, you're no use to us.'

I put my hand out to stop him. 'Wait. I'm sorry. But don't you see? The kind of intelligent observance you want from me is at odds with your request that I just blindly follow where I'm led, like a donkey. I won't do anything against my scruples. If you ask me to trust and be trusted, you have to give me more. If I were to hand over my unswerving loyalty for less, then I wouldn't be honourable enough to rely on, would I?'

I'm not sure that my tortured argument makes sense, and, by his crumpled forehead, neither is he. But it seems to do the trick.

He chews his bottom lip lightly with his teeth. 'Are you loyal to the Empire?'

'Of course I am.' I'm indignant that he has to ask.

'Then you are, in principle, already loyal to Roberts and to me. That is all I am at liberty to tell you.'

I nod 'Good enough. And Charley Boule is a Frenchman. Therefore ...'

'Enough political sleuthing!' The shutters come down in his eyes. 'Boule has his own fish to fry, and plenty of pans to do it in. He minds his business. You and I take care of ours.'

'Yours being the sea-slug business.' I emphasise the last three words and his eyes flicker with annoyance.

'Quite. You'll need to report to me: who is in port, what cargo they're carrying, what they happen to chat about when they've a few drinks under their belts. There will also be notes that you'll receive and then pass on. Everything will resolve when you are in place. But one last warning before you commit yourself. You won't survive very long if you don't learn to pull on your own reins. This is not so trivial as a poker game.'

I nod with my lips compressed. I'd make the motion of buttoning them together with my fingers, if I didn't imagine it would annoy him further.

'Do you or do you not want the job on the terms I've laid out?' he asks.

Something behind my ribs feels trapped. The wings of my bravado under a fly-swatter? It's not too late to back out. I can find another job. The risks are high, my chances uncertain.

But I'm excited. These are the cards I've been dealt and they're good ones. If I fold, Mrs Menzies still wants the week's board. If I win, I need never kowtow to the likes of her again. Do I trust myself to open my mouth now? What will I say? *Thanks, but penury is safe and I'm used to it?*

I undo the voice buttons. 'Of course I want the job.'

'Well, come and I'll introduce Charley Boule to his new piano player.'

'What if he doesn't think I'm suitable?'

'My impression is he hasn't exactly been overrun with applicants.'

I straighten my collar. Take a last sip of my drink. He has one more point to make.

'Boule can be persistent, but your loyalty and discretion are everything. Your eyes and ears belong to Roberts and me. If I find out you're making a bit more pocket change on the side spying for him ...'

It occurs to me that Charley Boule, having seen us talking, might feel he's being manipulated into hiring me. But Percy seems so sure I'll be welcomed with open arms I dismiss the thought, for now.

I take a step. He puts a clamp-like hand on my arm.

'I'm not quite done, Mary Oxnam.' His voice is an inch from my ear. 'Don't go over my head to the good captain.' His eyes flit in Roberts's direction. 'You report to me. Do you understand?'

'Anything else?' I ask tightly.

He reaches into his pocket and extracts a pound note. 'To pay your landlady.' He holds it out.

I slip it into my purse.

'I could enjoy being a kept woman,' I say flippantly, but he's already turned away.

Cooktown

Spring, 1879

3

*Half a year in the wild far north
is good tutelage for any number
of unsavoury careers.*

From the secret diary of Mary Watson

8TH NOVEMBER 1879

Eight o'clock on a Saturday night at French Charley's, and the place is jumping like spring fleas on a stray dog. Smoke haze. Flashing thighs. Disgruntled prospectors back from the Palmer River. They have no fire in their throats other than heartburn from fermenting possums, grubs and boiled grass, and all are drinking steadily, not fussed that the rum's been doctored with laudanum and plug tobacco. Prostitutes in unlaced corsets bend over their tables like swaybacked mules. The room around them shimmies and sways with its cheap velvets and tinny chandeliers. The fool's gold of paid companionship.

I'm wrist-deep in Strauss, my feet pumping the piano pedals. My mind's eye's riding a bicycle away from this place. I watch the dream-like scenery bounce by: a scattershot of gold-diggers, a thousand black snakes, ten thousand gum trees, each with a wild Myall hiding behind it. And over the lot, the great, dripping damper of the sun.

Dimly, above the music and noise of conversation, I can hear the hollow, knuckle-on-bone thumps of a fist fight out in the street. I don't stop playing. Don't bother turning. It's a nightly occurrence. It could be grog, a woman or a gambling debt that threw the first punch. Cooktown generously encourages all three preoccupations. Twenty hotels with a liquor licence, twenty more sly-grog shops, three opium dens, ten joss houses, countless gee fah and pak-a-pu shanties. And then there's greed, holding both pockets closed while simultaneously trying to pick someone else's. If all else fails: the wet season squatting over the chamber pot of the town is reason enough for a punch-up.

Charley Boule's garlic breath drags me back to the present, plants me firmly on the hard seat in a wide room brittle with the girls' lacquered laughter. He's apparently noticed my spirited playing. 'Pianissimo,' he murmurs in my ear.

As usual, my suave French employer wears his too-tight waistcoat. It's a vanity he won't relinquish despite the sultry weather and the risk of torsion in his vital organs. A swollen swamp of cognac and rich sauces gurgles in the cauldron beneath the material.

'What does it matter if I thump the keys?' I ask. 'No one's listening anyway.'

The blood's sunk from the diggers' eardrums to what's between their legs. And the girls' attention is in the same general area: just a little left of centre, in the pocket where the nuggets are.

Charley clicks his tongue. 'Subtleties of culture, *chérie*. They escape you entirely.'

'Not entirely.' I look sideways at him. 'Not much escapes me, Charley. What will happen to that prospector? The one your two standover men dragged outside half an hour ago?'

'They are my friends and protectors,' he says mildly, inspecting his fingernails. 'Name-calling is not nice. Did your mother never teach you that?'

He places a damp hand on my arm. I look down to a garish gold ring. Nails clipped on a perfect horizontal; the ugly knobs of knuckles half an inchworm's length away. I shake him off.

'So that's why you threw him out, because he was calling you names? Let me see. French sack of bilgewater was one, wasn't it? And what was it he said he would do after he'd run you through with a knife? Feed scraps of your Froggy hide into the stamping machine you sent him out to the goldfields with.'

He sighs. 'Efficient, those little ears of yours. A pity they do not work for me.' He smoothes his moustachio on one side and then the other.

Percy was right. Charley is persistent, and patient. I've been testing a theory over the last few weeks; amplifying my insolence with every night that passes. He accepts it all, showing remarkably little irritation. He wants something from me, all right, and he's prepared to wait for it.

'You have my fingers,' I say, a delicate injury in my voice. 'Why would you need my ears?'

He looks down at my big hands. 'Ah, yes, your fingers. Alas, they appear the most useless part of the animal, if your playing is anything to go by. Do not gossip about the prospector, *chérie*. A slight misunderstanding, that is all. Charley Boule, in his generosity, tries to help those less fortunate. Such charity always backfires on the selfless.'

'Of course.' I nod, as though a curtain has parted. 'It's a translation problem! Now that you've pointed it out, it seems so obvious. You see, what you call charity in France, we call loansharking here in Australia.'

His face goes an unflattering shade of pink, but he doesn't explode. 'I do not understand your ridiculous expression. Stop pounding those keys like a wounded kangaroo. This is a salon, not a dance hall.'

'Yes, Charley.'

I obediently slow the pace, turn my eyes back to the piano, so that he'll walk away. My little experiment in stretching a Frenchman until he snaps has been interrupted by something more important. I've just seen one of Percy's contacts in the periphery of my gaze. A crewman who almost certainly has a note for me.

Charley waddles off. The gaunt-looking sailor approaches the piano. Nothing untoward in that. Many do, requesting a favourite tune. I keep playing as though I haven't noticed him. Wait for his words.

'Do you know the *William Tell Overture*, Miss Oxnam?'

'Yes, indeed,' I say. 'But my favourite is *Life is a Dance*.'

'Ah, yes,' he sighs. '*Das Leben ein Tanz oder Der Tanz ein Leben*.'

'Indeed. So much better than *The Last Waltz*, wouldn't you say?'

The preliminaries have been dealt with.

'Do you have something for me?' I relax into the music, turning the page of the score with a snap of paper.

'Yes.' And then louder: 'I've so enjoyed your Strauss, Miss Oxnam. Please accept a tip.'

His right hand reaches across the top of the piano and a few pennies clank into the change dish perched there. He steadies himself with his left hand, which drops a folded paper behind the upraised keyboard cover. He doffs his hat and moves away.

I've finished my shift, having unobtrusively collected the note from behind the keyboard cover. Now I'm following the patches of gaslight along Charlotte Street. On my right, a decaying drift of jasmine. On my left, warm exhalations: hops, sweat and damp smoke coughed out through the mouths of open hotel doors. I dodge lewd suggestions, bold hands. Even plain girls are pretty in the drunken dark. Outside the Great Northern, a quick sidestep saves me from yet another fight tumbling into the street, the jerky dance spurred on by a string-pulling crowd in the doorway.

I slip across the road towards the night beyond the town. Charlotte Street is muddy from recent rain. I do my best to avoid the worst of the puddles, holding up my skirt in one hand. A yolk-yellow moon hangs low in the cloud-sling of the sky, and a light breeze brings to my nose a whiff of the lavender oil I've rubbed onto my skin to deter mosquitos. But the Mediterranean can't compete for long with the tropics' sweet rot and cloying jasmine soon muscles in again.

How romantic it sounds: a secret tryst at midnight, on the banks of the Endeavour River. I'm to meet a handsome man, as I do every month on the eighth. Pity it's work and not play. Even so, I smooth back my hair, bite my bottom lip to bring some colour to it, as though he'll be able to see me in the dark.

I scramble down the bank. Debauched sounds of cursing and laughter follow me, faint ghosts of themselves, tearing voice-strips off the edges of the air. In the distance, beyond the river and over the ocean, a purple razor of lightning is sharpening itself, back and forth, on the leathery strop of the horizon. The night turns sickly white for a brief moment, then blackens again. On that edge between cold light and nothingness, between dark trees and the cream between them, I think I see movement to my right. I'm used to Percy's — or are they Samuel Roberts's? — spies. They follow me constantly. My room at the boarding house is searched regularly. The vase I keep on my writing desk to check has been moved minutely when I've been out. At least three times, probably more. But whatever evidence of betrayal they're looking for, they won't find it.

I pass the massive bauhinia tree where I leave the coded notes I'm given at French Charley's. I presume one of Percy's elves descends to spirit the mysterious missives away, decode them, and pass them on to another elf like myself. The maw in the side of the bole gapes threateningly. I never stick my hand inside without imagining a snake curled up in the dark, ready to strike. And yet the routine has become, if not monotonous, then predictable.

Tonight, I go further. Small twigs and leaves crack under my boots. Fruit bats rustle overhead, squeaking. They make me think of funerals in the rain. Each of them a rat-faced undertaker shielded by a black umbrella of wings. I shiver just a little when I feel a hand on my arm.

'Mary.' A familiar if disembodied voice.

I turn. The bowl of his pipe glows red, a single fevered eye.

'Percy.' I smell his pine cologne, say the first thing that comes to mind. 'Is one of your men following me?'

'Maybe.' He's calm. 'What of it?'

Should I ever need evidence of how small a cog I am in the machine …

'What do you have for me?' he asks.

We sit together on a log, close to the river. I can hear the slow pant of water on the bank. I keep my ears open for the stealthy plod of crocodiles, feel the bark beneath my thighs dig in.

I tell him what gossip I've heard over the past month. About the captain of *Desperance* meeting with one of the town's corrupt businessmen down near the docks while his packhorses were loaded. A delivery of hundred-years-old eggs from China to Charley's three weeks ago in the middle of the night. Percy says nothing. He stretches out his long legs and listens, his pipe resting in the corner of his mouth. I mention Charley's lucrative sidelines: his small-time smuggling rackets through the far north reef passage; his habit of supplying destitute diggers with the means to go into the goldfields and work a claim, followed by extortionate demands when they come back into town. Lately, though, they come back with only scratchings. It's getting harder for Charley to extract his pound of flesh.

'Hmm. Keep an eye and ear on Boule's grand plans,' Percy says. 'Roberts particularly wants to know if he's planning another gold-prospecting expedition to New Guinea.'

'Another?'

He shifts a little on the log. As though I'm on the other end of a seesaw, I have to adjust my feet on the ground or else be tipped off.

'He funded an expedition earlier this year. Sent a schooner loaded with experienced prospectors and equipment north to Port Moresby. Apparently some missionary had found alluvial gold about forty miles inland, and Boule thought he would get in on the ground floor. Make a killing.'

It sounds like something Charley would do. I've heard him and his cronies at night in his backroom, speculating about the white colonisation of New Guinea. Nothing on a small scale, of course: Charley wants to revive the lost utopia of Louisiana. Sees himself relaxing on a verandah, sipping sloe gin delivered by a dusky, bare-breasted maiden, while the tamed natives work in his sugar plantations.

'What happened?' I ask. 'Did they hit a lucrative seam?'

'No. Dysentery and malaria put the kibosh on the whole operation. But Boule won't give up so easily.'

Something puzzles me. 'Didn't you say Captain Roberts took medicines up to the new seam in New Guinea? Surely there was quinine available? Why would Charley's prospectors contract malaria?'

'Just because a medicine's available doesn't mean that it's *available*.'

'So Captain Roberts withheld the medicine from Charley's men?'

'You'd have to ask Roberts about that. I'm not particularly interested in the business in New Guinea. My focus is on something else. But I know enough to say that Roberts wants to keep Boule away from anything north of Cape York.'

No use asking questions about the 'something else' he's interested in. I'll just get the speech about loyalty, repercussions and the dangers of curiosity. Again. So I latch on to another comment that he made.

'You say I'd have to ask Captain Roberts about Charley and New Guinea, but I can't, can I? You've told me not to approach the man.'

'I told you not to go over my head,' he corrects me.

I see it as a minor difference. Not that I've had to restrain myself to any notable degree — I've only seen Captain Roberts twice in the past six months. Once in French Charley's, much to Charley's discomfort. And once down at the ASN Company's wharf as I was passing, his huge black head bent forward as he listened with attention to a man I didn't know. I tried to catch his eye as I passed, but failed. He was clearly deep in thought about something, lifting the bottom of his long beard up with one hand, then letting it sink again; as though weighing a handful of seaweed.

'I'm not permitted to know about the new venture, of course?'

I don't expect an answer. But fortune favours the brave, and I sense tonight the string has been loosened slightly on Percy's pouch of secrets.

'One thing at a time,' is all he says.

The sky rumbles in the distance, and there's some teeth-edge energy in the heavy air. We'll get a storm before very much longer.

I remember the note then and reach into the pocket of my dress for it. Percy takes it from me. Our fingers connect, briefly. He slips the paper into the top pocket of his shirt.

'You're doing a good job, Mary.' I wonder if I imagine a slight reluctance in his voice. 'Roberts is happy with your performance.'

I flush all the way along my cheekbones. One more try, I tell myself, and then I'll give up — until our next meeting, at least.

'I could be more useful. If only I knew a little more about what to listen for.'

I'm not sure what I expect from him, but it's not what he says next.

'It seems, against my better judgement, that you will. And sooner rather than later.'

My pulse speeds up. I must stay calm. This is my chance at promotion.

'How so?'

He breathes out deeply. Empties the tobacco from his pipe with a few taps on the log.

'I'll be out of town and touch for a while. The man responsible for the decoding of our communications has turned out to be … unsatisfactory. Roberts says you will take his place. Provisionally, of course. There will be an increase in wages to three pounds a week.'

'Thank you. I mean, that's wonderful.'

My mind gallops. I've had a vague suspicion of who the man might be: the skinny, copper-haired fellow who regularly visits French Charley's with more money in his pockets than seems reasonable for a prospector in these difficult times. He dresses too well, washes too often, and his hands are too smooth. I've caught him staring at me on several occasions.

'What happened to him, your code man? Why isn't he up to scratch?'

Percy ignores both questions. His silence falls into the cracks between storm birds calling, the thunder's tumbler of rocks turning in the distance, and the far-off funfair of the town. The warmth I felt moments ago unravels and I shiver. I recall something I've tried not to think too deeply on: Brisbane, the morning after the poker game; the cheat I'd nicknamed Cobweb on the front page of the *Brisbane Courier*, found floating face down in the river off Kangaroo Point.

'Did someone kill him? You, or Roberts? Like the cheat in the poker game back in Brisbane?'

It's as if I haven't spoken.

I take a deep breath, turn to him in the half-light of the emerging moon. It throws his features into relief. His face is still handsome and amiable. Even when lightning swathes come and go, wrapping him like a mummy, unwrapping him. He could kill me now. Dump my body in the river, and no one would even come looking until tomorrow night when I didn't turn up for work. By then the crocodiles would have had their fill.

'Do you know what a grille is?' he asks.

'No.'

'It's a piece of metal with boxes cut out of it. When it's held up against a note that has the same dimensions, these boxes correspond to words on the page. Those words are the message.'

He hands me a piece of burlap. I can feel a hard rectangle beneath it.

'You will continue to receive notes. Take them back to your room and decipher them using the grille. Memorise the message, then burn it. Be sure to disperse the ashes. Henceforth, you will come to the wharf at ten o'clock every Saturday morning. Inspect the Chinamen's fish baskets. A man will approach you. He wears a dirty white neckerchief. He'll ask you, conversationally, which fish you think you might buy that morning. You will tell him you fancy the flathead. He will suggest the flounder because of the brightness of its eyes. You are then to recite the message verbatim. Do not look him in the face, and he will not look at you. I leave it to you to ensure that bystanders don't overhear you. Repeat the message until he leaves; he won't go until he's memorised it or he feels it is unsafe to continue. If he tells you that none of the fish are any good, you may take it to mean something untoward has happened and you should not speak at all. You will then try again the following Saturday. Do you understand?'

'Yes.' But my head is spinning. 'When will I see you again?'

'In about six weeks time.'

He pulls something from his pocket and hands it to me. Pound notes by their feel.

'Do a good job and there'll be more where that came from. Oh, and another thing.' He stands, dusts off his trousers and looks down. 'If you value your life, don't lose the grille.'

'Is that what happened to your other decoder?' Cotton wadding's jamming up my throat. 'Did he lose his grille?'

But I'm talking to myself. His back is to me, walking away into the night.

4

From the secret diary of Mary Watson

9TH NOVEMBER 1879

The next night is a long one and I'm glad when my shift is over. I negotiate the obstacle course home without incident. The boarding house has tall windows and a breezy verandah. In my stuffy room, I coax the lantern to a panting flame. Strip off. Dab my mosquito bites with a piece of rag soaked in the pale-blue sear of meths. I've just unlaced my boots, taken them off and slipped on my nightdress, when there's a squeal outside the window.

I peer through a gap in the curtains. By the soft flutter of gaslight, I watch a man's bare backside jerking up and down in the middle of Charlotte Street. Two fists thump half-heartedly above it. The fists belong to Nicole, one of Charley's girls. I can tell by the high, shrieking voice. She's on her back on the sodden ground, petticoats around her waist. She's forgotten the refined French accent Charley's schooled her in and swears in fluent Sydney Sailor. 'Ah, get orf, ya fucken robber! Ya promised ya'd pay me first!'

I drop the curtain, pull a flannel from the drawer, sprinkle it with a wet forest of eucalyptus oil and hold it to my forehead. The smoke and cheap scents at Charley's always let loose the nibbling mice of a headache behind my eyes. I catch a glimpse of my image in the dressing table's glass. My mother's platitude rises like a bloated fish. *Don't judge the quality of the linens inside by the rough wood of the glory box.*

Quite right, Mama. In fact, I decided some time ago that it's better to be clever than pretty. Faces fade. Figures fall. But, unlike a slackening money-box between the legs, what's between the ears keeps on paying dividends. Unless, of course, the head is held beneath the water for long enough, puts in the other little voice that followed me home from my meeting with Percy last night. Then the cleverest brain in the world is no help.

I give myself a mental shake. This is not a good time to have an attack of the vapours. Silence outside. The two have finished, it seems. I snuff out the lantern.

On the last edge before sleep I hear another noise. A thin scream. Then a gurgle, like a penny whistle trying to make music in the rain. A heavy thump. Something pushed with a hiss-crush against the bushes a few doors down.

I don't light the lantern again. I cup my hands like a viewfinder on the cool glass. Nothing.

The wood whinnies at the frame as I lift it. I'm downwind and the smell that wafts through the window is straight from Papa's first job in Australia: the Maryborough boiling-down works. But the body sprawled awkwardly in the dirt four yards away isn't destined for anything as useful as meat cubes. Copper hair, illuminated by gaslight as it falls across his forehead. Eyes wide open. Throat cut from ear to ear with something ragged. A broken bottle?

It's him. The man I thought might be Percy's decoder.

I pull the window down again, hard. It shudders the glass. I knit my hands together and sit, tense and upright, on the bed.

It can't be right. Nobody's fears come to fruition quite so easily. The clunky foreshadowing of our discussion last night, and now the corpse!

No. It's anybody but him. Or if it is him, then he's not the code man. That's the part I got wrong. Just one of those strange synchronicities my Cornish third eye is attuned to.

Deep breaths. The mad trotting in my chest eventually slows.

No one will collect the corpse until dawn. That's when Inspector Fitzgerald does his rounds.

To calm myself, I project the night forward six hours. See the first sluggish flies, and a blood-streaked show on the horizon. Fitzgerald scratches his backside. Piles the body onto his cart, careful not to smear his boots with blood. His horse twitches in the comparative cool. A few minutes later, he's waking Müller, the butcher. There's Müller, his umlaut firmly in place even so early in the morning. His German-sausage torso fills the doorway. They manoeuvre the body into the room-sized meat safe. Dump it with a thud, like a gourd tossed on a stone floor. The corpse stares with glazed eyes at the goat carcasses hanging above it.

Fitzgerald asks Müller if he knows the man. Müller fetches his glasses, mended on the right-hand side with string. Peers more closely, shakes his head. Or maybe he nods.

What will happen after that? A half-hearted investigation, probably. Fitzgerald will wander over to Blotch, the undertaker. Blotch will agree to knock up a cheap coffin (as though he ever makes any other kind). Blotch, in turn, will send word to the gravedigger.

It's working. I wipe the fluff off an aniseed ball from the nightstand drawer and pop it in my mouth. The shiny blackness melts like medicine, with the help of a worrying tongue.

Eight o'clock the next day and already the air's heating the sun's iron on the blue-hot stove of the sky. In a few hours, clouds will pile log on log, and the silver-snake smell of rain will uncoil from the centre of the woodpile. But that's for later. Now, a light onshore breeze sneezes through the open window. The curtains billow, then settle. A blowfly operates its small saw in the corner.

The corpse is gone. I checked at 6 a.m., saw only a faint stain. Drag marks in the dirt. Then I fell back into bed and a trouble-free sleep.

A hollow beat in the distance — the Good Templars are heading this way. Heaven-bent on collaring the drunks when they spill, top heavy with hammering heads and empty pockets, into the stoic heat outside the Commercial Hotel. If I don't get up and close the window, tambourines will hiss like crazed ducks at the sill.

I throw the covers aside. Walk over, only half-awake. I see Inspector Fitzgerald across the street.

'There you are, my lovely,' he says.

He's not talking to me, but his dog, Virgin Mary, who's lying under a bauhinia tree in the shade. Fitzgerald has the stoop of a tall man used to carrying the heavy monkey of his conscience on his back so he never has to look it in the eye. His loose braces hang frayed down either side of his trousers as he bends to place a bowl of water on the ground. He's an animal lover, I'll give him that. It's just the blacks he hates with an itchy-trigger-finger passion.

'Inspector,' I call. 'The man near the bushes?'

I point in the general direction of where the body had lain, and realise suddenly I'm standing in full sight of the street in my nightdress, hair still in a sleeping cap. No matter, I suppose. Compared to the dress of the prostitutes in town, I could be off to join a nunnery.

Fitzgerald turns and lifts a hand in greeting. The water in the Endeavour River behind him belches blue, then flattens.

'A gold-stealing blow-in from Dead Dog Creek. Reginald Bawly by name.'

By the faint slurp-clack in Fitzgerald's voice, I can tell he still hasn't worn in the new set of teeth he bought last month, for a guinea, from the London Dentistry Institute in Melbourne.

'How did you find that out so quickly?'

He stares over the water for a minute. It's still murky from yesterday's storms. The breeze carries that weedy stink of crushed shell and iodine. He looks back, shields his eyes, and quenches my last faint spark of hope in the competence of the local constabulary.

'Can't take credit for sleuthing. The lair sunk himself. Went from one drinking hole to the next last night, boasting he'd seen Jack Wilson bury his stash of nuggets, and dug it up when Jack came into town to stake his claim. The Kangaroo Court, or part thereof, must have caught up with him sometime through the night. It's a good survival tip: keep your bleedin' mouth shut or you'll end up with a bleedin' throat.'

My mind underlines that ragged wound.

'Who did you talk to?' I ask. 'Are you sure that's the whole story?'

It could be tiredness, but I feel a pressure between my brows, my third eye peering intently.

'Several men I doubt you know,' he says, mildly offended by my lack of faith. 'A slug fisherman, Percy Fuller, and others.'

A sick tingle moves downwards from my chest.

'Did you know him before, this Reginald Bawly? Was he renowned for usurping other men's claims?'

'I know nothing about him really,' he says. 'But I've no reason to question local opinion on the matter.'

At least, not if it involves a skerrick of real police work. There's nothing else to say. Fitzgerald assumes my feminine sensibilities have been violated by the night's events.

'Don't take it to heart,' he says. 'This part of the street was just nearest to hand. Left him there as a public example of what happens to thieves, I shouldn't wonder.'

'Of course,' I say dully. The informative part of the conversation is over.

He hitches up his braces over a stained grey singlet. 'You hear the latest on the Myalls?'

'No. What about them?'

'Speared a white prospector down at the Deighton. Poor beggar wandered into camp with the shaft still in his thigh. They pulled it out and put a mustard poultice on the wound, but he's a dead man walking. Infection. You know they dip the spear tips in putrefying corpses?'

'No, I didn't know that.'

'My boys and I are riding out today to shoot up the camp. You watch yourself. Don't wander on your own after dark. Spearing's the least of what they'll do to a white woman.'

My ears wake up a little at this. Does he know I sometimes go walkabout at night? I will have to be more careful in future.

If I wonder how many blacks it takes to throw a single spear, and why a whole camp needs to be shot up, I keep my thoughts to myself. Leave criticism to the couple of native sympathisers in the *Brisbane Courier*. They're far enough away not to choke on a cloud of contempt.

'No, I won't wander,' I say. 'I'll stay safely in town with all the upright European citizens. And if any other deceased appear in the general vicinity, I'll mind them until you get back.'

He's oblivious to irony. 'You've got pluck, young Mary.'

I give up. He clearly couldn't care less about a murder committed by a white man in town. He's already galloping through the tinder-dry bush, crashing through rivers, the hot scents of sweaty horse and revenge in his nostrils. The monkey of his conscience hanging on to his back like grim death; a sackful of innards bouncing up and down.

The Templars are almost on top of us. I dress behind the closed curtain. My eyes dart, nervous birds, to the place where I've hidden the grille. Between the third and fourth chapter of Wilkie Collins's novel, *Hide and Seek*.

There's a stone of dread settled deep in my stomach. How do I avoid the same fate as Copper Hair? How do I prevent myself from making the same mistake?

I don't even know what it was he did wrong.

5

From the secret diary of Mary Watson

11TH NOVEMBER 1879

Seven o'clock and I'm yawning already, playing another tedious Mozart set, when Charley approaches me.

'What is it?' I ask. 'I've barely skipped a beat all night.'

'Why do you assume, *ma chérie*, that I wish only to admonish you? I am most grateful to you for telling me about Nicole and her client in the street.'

I'd also told him about the dead man near the bushes, but he was, predictably, more interested in possible damage to his salon's reputation.

'Did you talk to her?' I ask. 'Perhaps it's a case of species confusion and she thinks she's a dog. They fornicate in the middle of the road all the time.'

The moustache turns: a worm tickled by a feather. 'I have talked with her, yes. And she will behave. Unlike your tongue.' He looks down at me from his not-so-lofty height, more in sorrow than anger it seems. 'When I find that whetstone you sharpen it on, I intend to throw it into the sea.'

'Is that what you came over to tell me?'

'*Non.*' He straightens his cravat. 'There is a man I think you will like to meet. He has just arrived, and as it is almost time for your break…'

So Charley is playing cupid. Why?

'You mean, a potential suitor? Exactly what kind of a man would I meet in a place like this? And who appointed you village matchmaker anyway? Or perhaps you have changed my duties without telling me and I must now entertain male clients?'

Charley drags up a sigh from some well of long suffering. 'I do not change your duties. I do not think you are suited to being a hostess.'

'True,' I say, thinking of Nicole. 'My tongue may be honed, but my baser instincts are clearly not up to the task.' A frown pulls at the skin between my eyes. 'What mischief are you hatching?'

He holds a hand to his heart. 'I am distressed you think so little of Charley Boule.'

'I'm nineteen,' I say. 'I can look after myself. I don't need you to drag men out of the gutter on my behalf. If you want to help me, increase my wages.'

Never mind the extra money from my second job neatly stashed in a tin hidden behind my dresser. One useful thing I learned from Papa: it doesn't do to let the truth get in the way of a good argument.

His eyes are glinting as he rests his arm on the piano top. I feel sorry for the material of his shirt when I see the sweat in his armpit. 'All the more reason to find yourself a *beau* — improve your financial security.'

Something near the door to the street attracts his attention. 'Turn your head,' he says. '*Je vous présente:* Captain Bob Watson, a sea-slug fisherman from Lizard Island.'

I sit a little straighter on the stool. Watson is Percy's partner in his 'legitimate' business. I've seen him in here a few times, drinking quietly by himself. He strikes me as awkward in company, unsociable, a closed book. And he never disappears upstairs with any of the girls. If he doesn't want a woman for the night, why does he come here? And why would he want to meet me?

Of course, there is that other critical question. How might it serve me to meet him?

Charley answers at least one of my queries. 'He observes you playing. He thinks you to be a nice girl.' His tone suggests the poor man's in for a rude shock. 'He asks Charley Boule to make an introduction. He has taken a little shine to you.'

It seems unlikely. But not impossible, I suppose. I'm probably the only virgin for a hundred miles in any direction.

I turn to glance at Captain Watson. He is paused just inside the doorway, hat in hand, like a cartoon of a destitute farmer. Gilt dust from the porchlight fizzes around him. He surveys the room. Its mirrors and velvets. Charley's girls flitting from table to table in their unlaced corsets. His head is suddenly still. So is Laura's, over in the corner. He looks away. She skips to a noisy table and plops herself extravagantly onto a surprised prospector's lap.

'He's short,' I tell Charley. 'And old. I'm not interested.'

It isn't strictly true. I have nothing against older men. They are far more intriguing than silly boys my own age. Take nineteen-year-old Heccy Landers, for instance — one of Charley's barmen, who makes no secret of his admiration for me. Hopeless, gangly, innocent Heccy with his painful stammer. Percy is forty, after all; and Bob Watson seems only five years his senior, if that.

Think, Mary. Think.

Watson runs the sea-slug business with Percy on Lizard Island. What could I learn about Percy and his doings by talking to him? I haven't time to ponder the possible repercussions. But what harm could come of a conversation or two? I won't lead him on, exactly. Just be friendly. Get him talking.

'Why are you trying to push me towards him?' I ask Charley. I have no intention of letting him off the hook too easily. 'Where would you find another piano player if I decide to run off with a man? I'm not so bad with Mozart and Strauss. Why are you so keen to get rid of me?'

'Some nights, only so-so,' he mutters. 'Some nights your rancour sizzles on the end of your fingertips like a match held too long. Unattractive for any woman. But for you ...'

His voice trails off and he consults the book of hopeless cases in his head for a possible precedent. His mouth puckers. The moustache looks suddenly less like a worm and more like a curled-up dead possum.

I wish I'd been the one to shoot it.

Ten minutes later, I'm on my break. I dry my palms on the front of my long skirt as Charley makes the introductions.

'Captain Watson, please be acquainted with Miss Mary Oxnam. She plays piano, sometimes *passablement,* here in my salon.'

Watson responds with an awkward greeting. He's a Scot. There's no mistaking the snare-drum vowels vibrating off his tongue. My father hates all Scots. Even more so if they're

Catholic. I find myself wishing that Bob Watson is a Pope-lover, just on general principles.

The kerosene lamps on the wall toss a small star into each of Watson's eyes, and, at the same time, turn his face cadaverous. He steps forward into the more flattering aura of a dozen smoky cigar-ends. I notice his receding hairline: the tide pulled back on his skull, exposing the pebbles-and-shell mulch of discoloured skin. A few sandy hairs cling bravely to the shoreline.

'Captain Watson,' I say.

He reaches out a hand riddled with jaundice-yellow corrugations. His fingers are sharp with calluses of horny skin from salt water and weather. There's a sudden fluttering fume of feathers in my nostrils. Cold, wet paddles on the back of my neck. A goose walking over my grave.

He asks, do I feel chill?

I shake my head. I don't know why I'm reacting this way. My intuition doesn't usually let me down. Why is it warning me off?

It could be just that he appears slightly sinister. There's something persistently askew about his face, even when the light plays fair with the shadows. A rough scar runs from his right cheekbone to his lip. Skin puckers at its top edge, as if, having braced itself for the initial blow of knife or axe, it never relaxed again. It makes the eye above it appear intent, like an eagle's. The left eye, held in a loose pouch of skin, seems less aware and more approachable.

I look into his left eye and smile.

Charley slips discreetly away.

Watson's fingers move like caterpillar legs around the brim of his hat. 'I'm going back to the Lizard in a week. Could I see ye again beforehand? Have a drink, or take a stroll?'

An inelegant man. Absurdly direct, obviously unskilled in social niceties. Reticent, I'd guess, to a fault, and beyond. But an industrious hitch tightens under my ribs. Like the future picking up the stitch of the present. I don't know what to make of it, but at least the goose is gone.

'I can see no harm in it,' I tell the ravaged side of his face. I explain that I have half an hour's break now. We can go for a short walk down by the river if he likes. Although the mosquitos are voracious. And I've heard there's been trouble with the Myalls. I ask him if he thinks they'll come into town, then look briefly beyond the open door, where night's fallen like tar.

'Aye. Maybe under the cover of darkness.' He wonders, with a raised eyebrow, if I have some lavender oil.

'Is that the frontier's new defence against the natives? I'd better tell Inspector Fitzgerald. He's still using rifles.'

His laugh has something gritty in it.

I fetch the small bottle from under the bar. We rub oil into our arms, our throats and faces. I accidentally smear a little into my eye — a sensation as though it's been doused in carbolic acid. I blink and blink until the sting is washed away. The other eye waters in sympathy.

'Just the oil,' I sniff, and pull my handkerchief from my sleeve.

We wend our way outside. The lamplighter, Albert Ross, is almost to the far end of Charlotte Street. Where we're standing is already aflame. A whiff of gas. The spit and fizzle of small insects drawn in. Beyond Dooley's Sailmakers, the night is a solid wall of darkness: like the hood of a camera. Easy to conjure a set of all-seeing eyes inside it.

'The blacks won't come into the lit street,' Watson tells me, as if I've spoken.

'Have you had trouble with the Myalls too, Captain Watson? On your Lizard Island?'

'Call me Bob, lass. I'll feel like yer father otherwise. As I should, no doubt — I daresay I'm almost the same age.'

He waits for a compliment, but I don't supply it.

'No real trouble,' he goes on, talking about the blacks. 'Just aggravation. I don't know that they're Myalls. Could be any local tribe, really. They land on the far side of the island, light their fires and howl round them at night. Why the Lizard, I don't know — the only pickings are leathery goannas they could get anywhere on the mainland.'

A lightning leash flashes above us. A minute later, the thunder-dog on the end of it growls.

'Perhaps they're after the iron around your slug station,' I say. 'Don't they make their spears with it?'

'Aye. The tips, at least. They've not figured out how to heat and forge it, but they're canny wee buggers, banging and grinding away on wet sandstone till they get a passable shape.'

We're almost to Chinatown. The sultry breeze reeks of gunpowder, soy sauce, ginger and, faintly, the thick syrup of opium. A firecracker puts in its tuppence-worth down near the waterfront. A yelp of surprise, then the splash of waves.

The approaching storm ups the ante. A brilliant zigzag. Then a stack of wood falls on the floor of the sky. Like most loners, Bob doesn't know how to start a conversation. Or how to sustain one — once he's started talking, he can't stop. He regales me for nearly the length of Charlotte Street with tales of woe and worry from Lizard Island: gory accidents to his crew, encounters with pirates, the rough justice he's dealt out to would-be swindlers, troubles with the blacks. He rabbits on as if I'm not really there. Only a sudden burst of fat, lukewarm raindrops saves me.

'We'd better go,' he says at last. 'Before the downpour.'

We turn back for French Charley's. Fortunately, the rain holds off, though thunder continues to grumble overhead and occasional flashes set the busy street in stark relief. Aside from reinforcing my poor opinion of the sea-slug trade, I've learned nothing of use and my break is almost over. At the first sign of a gap in his monologue, I interrupt.

'It just sounds so worrying for you, Bob. But you're not alone on the island, are you? You have back-up against the natives? You have a partner, surely?' My voice sounds suitably breathless.

'Oh aye, Fuller. Percy Fuller,' he says in a flat tone.

'Does Mr Fuller go out fishing with you every time?'

I hope I've struck the right tone: *I'm so interested in you. I want to know every trivial detail.*

'No. He owns his own lugger, *Petrel*, and keeps his own crew. Kanakas and tame black boys. My lugger's *Isabella*. Another fisherman, Porter Green, is on contract and works on *Isabella* with me. Fuller and I split the catch, but I'm thinking of changing that, seeing as he spends so much time gallavanting around instead of fishing.'

'Oh, dear.'

I leave a substantial gap for further disgruntlement and he fills it.

'Aye. I told him straight: I'll buy ye out, but ye'll not be my partner if ye don't pull yer weight.'

My mind ticks over. Peculiar that Percy's decided on slug fishing as a cover for his real business. This upcoming project of his and Roberts's must somehow be accommodated by the trade.

Or perhaps the fishing is irrelevant and it's Lizard Island he has an interest in.

French Charley's and my piano are only minutes away, so I decide to risk a few more questions.

'You must get a lot of sea traffic past your island, Bob?'

'Oh aye.' He nods in the dark. 'Seems there's always a steamer or schooner passing, north and south. We have a signal hill with flags to send messages to passing ships should there be the need.'

'Really? How very interesting.'

Something's tingling on the tip of my perception. Something to do with Charley Boule. When nothing resolves, I have to conclude that my third eye has a cataract from all the smoke in the salon. Never mind. There's time. I'll figure it out.

When we reach the front verandah of the bar Bob falls silent. I can tell he's desperately trying to think of a way to justify a second assignation. In the pause, I hear a mechanical clicking noise coming from somewhere on his person. I mention it, and he looks slightly abashed. He pulls two battered silver balls about the size of human eyes from his right trouser pocket, rolls them around in his palm.

'Medicinal balls. I bought them from Wang Fe down on the waterfront six months ago. Now I can't leave them alone.'

'What are they supposed to do?'

I've been inside the herbalist's lean-to, seen the spiders in bottles, chunks of dried starfish, row on row of curiosities he grinds into powder and then expects his gullible patients to swallow. Metal balls seem fairly tame.

Bob tells me they're to calm him when he's nervous, amuse

him when he's bored, help him think when he can't concentrate. His eyes dart away.

'Which are you now? Nervous, bored or flighty?'

'Nervous. I want ye to like me.'

I tell him baldly, 'I'm not one of Charley's girls. I won't go upstairs with you for a handful of gold dust.'

'Why would a man bother with the preliminaries if that's all he wanted? Truth is, Mary, I'm a peaceable, solitary fellow.'

I glance at the evidence to the contrary — at least, to the 'peaceable' claim. The scar. The sinewy muscles just under the skin. *Click, click,* go the balls.

'Aren't you going to say it?' I ask. 'What's a nice lass like you doing working in a place like French Charley's?'

'A man ought to mind his own business. I just have one question for ye.'

'Yes?'

'What's a nice lass like ye doing in a place like French Charley's?'

I laugh at his weak attempt at humour, and watch him relax. It isn't pretty, his smile, but better than the alternative. The lack of symmetry in his face is exhausting if taken at a single gulp, but I gaze at it front on, albeit briefly. Lightning from behind my shoulder opens a scar across both his eyes. I think of Mary Shelley's monster. I slap at a mosquito on my forehead. Inspect the blood smear and wings on my fingers. In the dark it's just a smudge.

'There's always the odd one that develops a taste for the very thing that's supposed to repel it, isn't there?' I muse.

'Ye strike me as an odd one yerself, Mary Oxnam. Are ye attracted to things that should repel ye?'

I think of Percy. 'Yes,' I confess. 'Often.'

I glance down the street briefly; see the line of bawdy houses, gambling dens and assorted pits of iniquity, known in generous circles as the vibrant heart of the far north.

'You can stop fiddling with your medicinal balls, Bob. I do rather like you. And one day I'll be bold enough to ask how you got that scar. But right now, there's a storm coming and I must get back to work.'

6

Connections are shy creatures.
Sometimes they only announce themselves
in the middle of the night.

From the secret diary of Mary Watson

21ST NOVEMBER 1879

It's been ten days since I first met Bob. We've been for a few more strolls in that time, and now he's gone, sailed back to his island. I've learned nothing more about Percy's new venture. Heard little of interest between Bob's alternate bouts of self-pity and self-aggrandisement. But last night, as I lay awake, tossing and turning in the heat, the puzzle pieces came together. Bob Watson. Charley Boule. Lizard Island. Of course! It's time to interrogate Monsieur Boule.

French Charley's. Ten minutes before opening time. A stale urine smell in the air mixed with hops, barrel sherry and a splash of sweet-pea water. I'm standing in the doorway and feel the slide of silks and satins as half-a-dozen girls flounce past me. I open my mouth to stop Laura; I want to ask her how she knows Bob Watson. Their shared look, just after I first saw Bob standing in the doorway at Charley's the night we met, implies a history. But she's gone before I manage the words. In any case, I have other, more pressing matters to attend to.

'I need to talk to you, Charley.'

My boss is at his makeshift bar, his back to me. He's mixing his seasonal cocktail: Yuletide Mule. Never mind that Christmas is a month off. He'll decant it into jugs and put one in the middle of each table. With its Scrooge's nip of brandy, slurp of industrial alcohol and tingling sprinkle of gunpowder, it has a kick that keeps on kicking. For a fee.

Heccy Landers, my not-so-secret admirer, bends his ungainly bones over three-dozen bottles standing in the stone trough, spilling more than he's filling. This evening, it's beer and moselle mixed together. The bottles will be recorked and passed off as champagne. Heccy must have heard about Bob and me walking out together. He looks extravagantly miserable, from his red hair down to his boots, every time he glances over his shoulder. Typically, Charley's more concerned with the splash of profits down the drain than the slow leak in Heccy's heart.

'*Mon Dieu*. Wake up, stupid boy!'

Nicole jostles past me. Her make-up is thick enough to mortar bricks. She's riding high on a wave of heat and resentment. Her mouth opens and the log of lipstick breaks into splinters. Here it comes: a gem from the almanac of whores' wisdom.

'That Watson fella, ya watch 'im. I know yer up yerself, my girl, but some men'll pull the life outa ya regardless, like a tapeworm.'

'You've missed your calling, Nicole. An image like that, you should've been a poet.'

'Insultin' me ain't gunna help. Just this, Miss Prissy-Britches. I seen his type before. Lookin' po-faced, like they'd rather go to church than have a poke in the bushes, then turnin' into animals when ya get 'em alone.'

'Well, you'd know all about animals.' I look her up and down.

This provokes a smirk; the red smear forming an exaggerated bow as she returns the favour. Her eyes run over my cream blouse and long beige skirt, her contempt glittering. 'Yer jealous of me face and figger. Can't blame yer for that. But men arcn't too fussy, and I'm tellin' ya somethin' for nothin'. Blokes like Watson leave serious bruises.'

'Nicole, I am jealous, dear. I've always wanted a career like yours. Remind me how the promotions go? First a salon. Then a pub. Then down among the Chinamen. Then the hospital. Then an unmarked grave.'

'Stop fighting or I'll put you both in a hessian bag and throw you in the river, like the squawling cats you are,' Charley says, without turning.

'I'd rather have my own bag,' I say coolly. 'I might catch something, otherwise.'

Nicole sticks her tongue out of the side of her mouth. She looks remarkably like a cud-chewing cow. I tell her so.

Charley intervenes again. 'Nicole, go and open the front door. Mary, start playing the piano. It is what I pay you for.'

Nicole flounces away, buoyed by the many petticoats she'll take off later in the night for some drunken prospector at the rate of one handful of gold dust apiece.

'I said I want to talk to you,' I remind Charley.

'And I say go to work. Come to see me on your break.'

'Louise. Out of the way!' Charley holds both hands palm up in exasperation. Louise, the resident carpet snake, is unruffled. Leisurely she flows, like a patterned river, between his legs, then curls into a fat Cumberland sausage in her favourite spot just under the trough's drainhole where the slow drips of alcohol ping off her skin.

'I know why you introduced me to Bob Watson,' I say.

This works. Heccy looks up, startled. Charley exhales noisily through his nose.

'Come to my office.' He takes off his apron and folds it neatly.

He closes the door behind us. There's a rich, mahogany silence, at odds with the chaos outside. The phantoms of fine cigars and snifters of cognac have made soft, expensive connections with the rosewood table. He opens his polished case and pulls out a cigar. He takes the key from around his neck, bends over and unlocks the drawer that holds his float of bribery money, paid to customs officers on duty when one of Charley's special deliveries turns up on the dock. He extracts a gadget that looks like a walnut crusher. Nips the end of his cigar and reaches for his matches. He neglects to lock the drawer again, and I infer he's distracted.

'This could wait,' he says.

'I don't think it *can* wait, Charley.'

The sky's bucket upturns on the roof and I have to bide my time for a few seconds until the first deafening gush becomes an ordinary deluge.

'I've heard you, when I clean up the tables at night, talking with your cronies in here. Knight, that underling of the customs sub-collector; Douglas from the telegraph office. And Müller, butcher and under-the-counter trader *par excellence*. It's not the price of sausages you're discussing.'

'What exactly have you heard, *chérie?*'

'Nothing specific.'

His eyes relax back in their hammocks of fat.

'It's difficult to make out every word through the symphony of moans and bedsprings coming from upstairs. Tell me, do the girls get paid more for melodrama?'

He taps his nose. 'Every man likes to feel he is a stallion.'

'More ass than stallion if you ask me.'

'But no one does ask you. You are, how you say, left on the shelf?'

'Spare me your sparrow pecks.'

'Stop wasting my time. Say what you must.'

'I've heard you speculate about the prices of gold and opium. Passing steamers. Drops in the ocean in kerosene tins in the middle of the night. Knight's an important man to consult on matters of avoiding import and export duty, isn't he? And what does Douglas bring to the party? Did I hear something about telegraphic codes? A Playfair cipher? I imagine you think you have it all covered: sea, air and ground?'

'You have no shame,' he tells me. 'Listening at keyholes. You insult not only Charley Boule, but the protector of our lawful oceans and the guardian of our vital communication channels.'

'What's Müller?' I ask. 'The feeder of our hungry bellies? Overacting, Charley.' I tap my own nose. 'There's no one eavesdropping on this conversation.'

He lowers his outrage a couple of notches, but keeps a firm hold on his paranoia. 'How can you be sure? That stupid boy Heccy lurks around corners, ears like little mice with pieces of cheese: nibble, nibble. Perhaps you two are in collusion.' He twists his ring around so that its showy face is to the front. The action seems to calm him. 'I speculate about many things. Why would I not discuss customs matters with Knight when it is his gainful employment? He has many interesting stories: the crate of eggs not full of yolks and whites, but liquid opium, discovered when the sub-collector decided to have a cooked breakfast one morning. Gold nuggets hidden in ginger jars full of human bones.'

'I'm not interested in your stories of greedy Chinamen.'

'As for Douglas and Müller, I complain about the cost of postage to the first, and with the other I discuss the quality of meat supplied to my restaurant.' He lifts an ornate brass letter opener off his polished desk and runs his finger along the blunt blade, then tilts it this way and that. A single ray of late-afternoon sunshine throws off a spark of fire as it hits its surface. 'None of this is your concern.'

'When were you going to approach me?' I ask.

The rain has tapered off to the odd pin-drop: a pine tree shedding its needles on the metal roof. The humidity still simmers like rank stew.

'About what, *exactement*?' His face twitches, but minutely.

'Lizard Island. It's got a hill with a lookout and signal flags. Ships passing north and south have nowhere to hide. How handy it would be for you to have an ally on the island. Perhaps even a business partner. With the reefs so treacherous, and with so many other boats about, it would be almost impossible for smugglers to rendezvous without someone *in situ* to guide them. Or warn them.'

Thirty seconds of silence is broken only by the room's heart beating: Charley's nautical clock, each tick dragged along by the cocked spring before it.

'Why would I suggest such a thing to you?' he asks eventually. 'To you, so upright, so lawful. You would not consider it for a minute.' His eyes throw out their sticky strings, waiting for me to fly closer.

'Not even for a second,' I reply.

He snorts, then does a complete about-face.

'I change my mind about Watson. He is not a good match for you.'

'And why would that be, Charley?'

'He is not to be trusted. Some men ...' He shakes his head. 'They are no good with women.'

Nicole's strident voice comes back to me. *Blokes like Watson leave serious bruises.*

'You were happy enough to hand me over to him when you thought it might serve your own purposes.'

'He is too old for you, and he has a history.'

'What sort of history?'

He stares at me for a few beats. 'It is ... delicate. There is sometimes a little rough-house with the girls ... and Watson is more keen than most in this. He had an obsession with Laura. She accepted extra money for his ... eccentricity ... when the other girls would not.' He leans back in his chair until the leather squeaks.

That explains the look I saw pass between Bob and Laura in the salon. And as for Charley — I feel unreasonably hurt by his blatant manipulations.

'You wouldn't have said a thing about this, would you, if I'd agreed to be your accomplice? You would have had me become a beaten wife. But since I've said no, you've reached the conclusion that a fair-to-middling piano player is better than none at all.'

He stands abruptly, causing the chair to bounce back, and paces over to the window. The twilight outside is the colour of a three-day-old contusion. I can't see his face, and he knows it. That alerts me to be suspicious of whatever he comes up with next.

'Watson has stayed away this last year. I think he has calmed himself, perhaps. Maybe he is ready to settle down.' He turns back around, fiddles with his watch chain. 'But I think it is better to be safe than sorry, *non*?'

'I don't believe you,' I say, my mind working rapidly. 'Why don't you go to Bob Watson directly with your scheme? Or have you already, and he turned you down? I don't know why anyone would. You would be the perfect partner in business: loyal, protective, selfless.'

'Sarcasm does not become you, *chérie*.'

'And a complete lack of human decency doesn't become you, Charley. But it seems we must both bear our faults.'

His voice drops several degrees in temperature. 'My business dealings with Bob Watson are pocket change. He has carried the odd package or two on his lugger for me, that is all.' Another sigh. 'His capacity for risk is somewhat ... limited. He does not see the more expansive picture, as I do.' He pauses, examining his fingernails. 'And perhaps you *aussi*?'

He's testing the water again. Given Percy's warning in Brisbane, I know it would be more than my life is worth to go swimming.

'I'm nothing like you, Charley,' is all I say. 'Was Bob ever interested in me, or did you convince him that I was a desirable catch?'

Charley shrugs. His cigar has gone out: further proof of his underlying agitation. He inflames it with another match. 'Think of it as one of my cocktails coming together. A pinch of influence from one place; a *soupçon* from another. Ask instead why Watson comes to Cooktown fishing for a wife.'

'Any old wife?'

'So much the better if young. He has a weakness for girls.'

The last of the élan slides away, and I see his true face. He draws deep on his cigar until its red core bristles, then blows smoke upwards into a small cloud above his head. He carefully extracts a piece of tobacco from the tip of his tongue and studies it.

'All right. I buy in,' he says. 'It is, after all, nearly the time of year for Christmas pudding and parlour games.' He rubs his cheek in exaggerated contemplation. 'Why you, as a wife, for Bob Watson?' He walks over to the window again. Looks out at the sodden street. The wheel ruts in the road are full of thin mud. They'll stink sullenly when the sun comes out. 'Men outnumber women four to one in this town. Who else would he marry? A whore?'

I'm almost to the door when his voice hooks me back. 'A little bit of knowledge is like gunpowder — best kept dry in a locked box, *non*? I know that you have been receiving notes and passing them on to someone. I am not stupid.'

I stand still but don't turn.

'Who is to know, or care, what you are up to if you return the favour of a blind eye with a couple of small errands?' he goes on.

'Errands?' I spin slowly to face him.

'A respectable girl does not draw suspicious attention. Your boss asks you to deliver a missive here and there. You do so, like any dutiful employee.'

'You have nothing to blackmail me with, Charley.'

'You are right, of course.' He shrugs. 'All I could do is speculate out loud. Expose you before anything comes to fruition.'

I meet his eyes calmly. 'The difference between you and me is that what I know of your activities is not vague supposition but, shall we say, *fait accompli*. I imagine the harbourmaster would not be above making a retrospective arrest.'

He's calm. 'A couple of small errands, that is all. How do you say … chickenfeed.'

The hard tinkle of breaking glass, followed by a female caterwaul comes through from the kitchen.

'What now!' His belly is through the door well before the rest of him.

I follow close behind, but not before I've passed his open drawer, retrieved a five-pound note and slipped it down the side of my boot. Call it annoyance money for putting up with him.

The door snicks shut as I leave.

7

*All of life is a code. One only needs
the right grille to decipher it.*

From the secret diary of Mary Watson

The edge of the bed at midnight seems a fitting perch. The mattress squeaks as I turn sideways to smooth the note flat on the covers. The lamplight's steady. It's my nerve that's faltering.

Dearest Mary,
No time to write a long letter. They say no man (or woman)
is an island, and that was brought home to us all on Aunt
Jane's birthday. The event was a triumphant signal of the
family's success, not to mention her own sweet nature. Every
man in town paid his respects. Even the Chinaman at the
laundry donated a huge fish for lunch, which was gone in
ten minutes. Uncle Jonathan was tipsy and fell into the bush
near the house. I'm searching for words to describe the fun.
Hope you're still keeping well.
Cousin Eleanor

I rest the grille on top of the page. The message resolves, far too easily it seems to me.

No island signal man? It *must* be Lizard Island they're referring to. There is no other strategic position along the coast with such an advantageous bird's-eye view of the passage north and south. That great lumbering reptile of rock seventy miles north of here, the water surrounding it fairly fizzing with every ambitious smuggler's intentions. That's why Percy has placed himself there, working as a sea-slug fisherman. I'm positive of it now.

I fill my cheeks with air, then exhale noisily. It's the signal hill that's the magnet, of course. For Charley Boule, for Percy, and, it seems, for Captain Roberts. But who is the Chinaman? Roberts and Percy must want him as a signaller for their upcoming operation. But why him particularly? And why would he have gone bush? So as not to be found?

Drunken cursing just outside my window startles me back to the job at hand. I pull the empty chamber pot from under the bed. When the paper's burned, I'll moisten the ashes with water from the bedside jug. In the morning, I'll tip it into the lavatory trench behind the boarding house. No danger of forgetting the message. I'm too riddled with curiosity for that.

Dry-mouthed, I light the note at the lamp and hold it over the chamber pot as it burns. The smoke seems far too pungent for such a small piece of paper.

It's more the size of someone burning a bridge behind them.

Ten o'clock on a coruscating Saturday morning two weeks later. I look up and down the shimmering dock, basket in hand, searching for Dirty White Neckerchief. But he's not leaning his angular frame casually against a pylon, smoking. Nor standing on the crooked wooden slats at the end of the pier staring out to sea, the hot breeze fiddling his brown hair. The harbour smells of oil, the salty-leather of seaweed cooking in the sun. The fish stalls for European customers are crowded, the catch of the day lined up like silvery exclamation marks. The tables for Chinese buyers are a witch's larder of fins, roe, sea grapes, and slimy fish eyes piled into the single socket of a blue-rimmed dish. Sun throws a slab of steel at the water, where the raw material is reorganised and thrown back as rippled blades, making my eyes water. Beyond the pier to my left, two men drag a dirty crab-pot along the muddy edge of the river. Behind me, on Charlotte Street, Harry Browning, proprietor of Victoria Stores, throws a saddle over his horse and reaches under its belly to secure the girth.

I shoo away a heat-drugged fly. It's a quarter past the hour. Where is he?

The work has been easy so far. I've arrived at ten precisely each Saturday with the word-for-word recital of the note I've burned ready inside my head. Two more notes have been passed to me since the first, each one, in substance, emphasising with increasing urgency the need to find the elusive runaway Chinaman. It seems he's destined for the position of signaller on Lizard Island. I must also assume that he doesn't want the job.

Up until today, the script has gone exactly as Percy said it would. After our banter about the relative merits of the fish on offer, Dirty White Neckerchief and I wander casually around the dock as if going about separate business. Briefly, we're close enough for me to play my unobtrusive part in our game of Chinese Whispers.

But what am I supposed to do now?

At eleven o'clock, I give up. Unease stirs my stomach for the rest of the day. If he's finished up like Cobweb and Percy's last note decoder, I don't want to know. Captain Roberts's mysterious business tends to turn poisonous for his minions. There is no other conclusion to draw.

Bad things happen when people know too much.

8

Luck is indeed the residue of design.
A pity design can be so easily tampered with.

From the secret diary of Mary Watson

6TH DECEMBER 1879

Saturday night, nine thirty. French Charley's, like a sickening carousel, throbs with laughter and movement. I can't block it out, but neither can I focus on my playing. The morning's drama is too fresh. Dirty White Neckerchief's failure to make our rendezvous is still thumping the piano keys in my head. Riley Robinson, the town's oldest ex-prospector, slides into the chair next to me, cradling a beer. Seventy and toughened to ox-leather, he's the only man who comes to French Charley's just for the music — and only then, Charley says, because he's half-deaf and doddery. But Riley is neither deaf nor senile. He's a kindred spirit ... in an uncomfortable way. He sees and hears far more than most.

Usually, he minds his own business. But he clicks his tongue when I mention my walks with Bob Watson. It's true these outings are endurance events. I feel sorry for Bob's graceless attempts at courting. And slightly fond of him, in the abstract way one is fond of a lame duck trying to swim towards a piece of bread whilst going around in circles. I've amused myself during his broguish babble by making a study of his habits. The clink of his medicinal balls, which have a language all their own. The way he holds his hat in front of his trousers, then rides the boundary of its brim with his fingers. How his scar twitches when he doesn't want to answer a question I've posed. The whole rusty machine of his social skills cranked up on each occasion by his nerves. He must, I tell Riley, be very lonely to put himself repeatedly through such an ordeal. That, or he is quite enamoured of me.

Riley runs a withered hand over his jaw. Puts the glass to his mouth. One beer lasts him all night. He swallows, and his wrinkled Adam's apple drops down the shaft of his throat like an underground miner with his protective hat on sideways. Comes back up again. He licks the foam off his upper lip.

'Dirty business, slugs,' he says. 'Men go slugging when there's nothing else left for them.'

My nostrils twitch. Someone in the darkened corner is smoking an opium pipe.

'Gold prospecting's hardly the employment of gentlemen,' I say. 'Besides, Bob and his partner own the station on the island. A business like that could expand in all sorts of ways: trochus, pearl shelling. One found pearl is worth a fortune.'

I don't know why I'm defending Bob's profession. It's not him I'm interested in, after all, but Percy and the island. At the moment Bob's just the closest I can get to either of them.

'Grand plans of expansion, eh? Does Watson know you've already mapped out his future?'

I let this pass. 'What do you know about him? Is he a murderer, a rapist, a pillager? In these parts that would add up to a run-of-the-mill chap.'

My tone is light, but Riley answers seriously.

'There was some talk of a woman a year back. Disappeared under strange circumstances. His woman, they say. Though he wouldn't want to claim her, I'm sure.'

I run a sweaty finger under the high collar of my blouse. There'll be a reddish ring left on my skin when I get undressed tonight, as though someone began to garrotte me and then lost interest.

'A wife? And what do you mean he wouldn't want to claim her?'

'Not exactly a wife. It was before he got that partner of his — Fuller. Before they took over the station from Bowman.'

He's avoiding my eyes. I wish the drugged air would do better work of loosening his tongue. Cause him to lay his reticence down on a soft divan and relax into mind-expanding gossip.

'Who's Bowman?' I ask, hoping to bring him back to the topic by roundabout means.

He takes another swallow of his beer. 'Bowman built the station, the curing shed and the house on the island. The woman went missing from the goldfields, though. Watson did some commercial travelling for a while — pencils, bamboo racks and what not. Ask Inspector Fitzgerald. Me, I keep my own counsel.'

'You must think Bob was involved in her disappearance or you wouldn't have mentioned it.'

He shrugs. 'Lots of things happen on the goldfields. And it's not my place to comment. It's something to do with the Lizard, though, I'll wager.'

'Lizard Island. What, is it cursed?' I laugh.

He pulls back a little more into his shell. 'All I know is bad things happen there. And the wild blacks are drawn to it, like a fingernail to a scab.'

'You said Bob's woman went missing from the goldfields. Is it a kind of moving curse, then?'

He ignores my dismissive tone. 'The past casts lengthy shadows.' He opens the lid of a metal spittoon, then clicks it shut again without using it. 'You more than anyone should know that.' His gaze is suddenly overbright and I turn away from it. 'Fancy the idea of hitching up with Watson, do you?' he asks.

'Don't be ridiculous, I hardly know the man!'

He rubs a grimy thumb over his glass. The condensation smears. 'He doesn't usually come to Cooktown so often. Reckon he *must* be sweet on you. If you don't feel the same way, you should let him know. Soon.'

'Yes, Riley.' I give him a sideways, dutiful-daughter glance.

One of the girls in a darkened corner shrieks like an exotic bird. The sound cuts through the chattering jungle of the dim room. I finish playing the last few notes of Chopin, then stop for my break. I stretch my fingers and pull the cover down. I love that moment when it slips so neatly into place. Like soothing a fractious animal; the bared set of key-teeth covered up by a polished brown lip. The background noise in the room is suddenly an octave louder.

'How did you meet Watson in the first place?' Riley asks.

'Charley introduced us.' I tilt my head over my shoulder to where *le raconteur* is in a deep and heavily gesticulated conversation with some harried-looking man who probably owes him money. Charley untangles himself long enough to frown at me, then look forcefully at the piano. I point to the clock on the wall in return.

Riley brings my attention back. 'What's that scheming so-and-so up to this time?'

'Who knows?'

He peers at me intently, the skin around his mouth tightening. 'You know, Mary, there are some things beyond even your cleverness.'

'Charley's not beyond me,' I say. 'I may not be able to glean the particulars of any given contrivance, but I know the way his mind works.' It helps to have had the example of a scheming father all my life. 'He's just a petty shyster,' I add, scratching the top of one foot with the other through my boot. 'Blasted mosquitos.'

'I'm not talking about Boule. Time will take care of him. He can't dodge the guillotine forever.'

His voice and eyes have boiled down to their essence. 'I have some money. Why don't you take it? Go home to your family.'

'Thank you, Riley, but home is backwards,' I tell him.

'What's wrong with that? Death's in the future.'

'Don't say that to a Cornish girl!'

'You still have time to back out,' he says.

'From what? Another walk?'

He sniffs audibly. 'I'm not as old or as foolish as you think. I watch and I listen. I'm like you in that way.'

I give him a smile and head for the door, through the breathless heat of too many bodies. On the verandah, I take a deep lungful of what passes for cool night air in the tropics. Riley's a cagey old coot, but far too morbid. I pull the threads of his words from the velvet dark around me. Death? Not for me. Not now; not soon. And when it happens, it won't be Bob Watson or his island that will get the credit. Look at Cooktown. If ever a bone's had a target to point at! And I've managed to survive here.

9

*When your predecessors have all lost their heads
on the chopping block,
it's wise to heed the warning
of a scratchy throat*

From the secret diary of Mary Watson

Something's changed in the bar when I come back from my break. No immediate sight or sound alerts me, rather it's my sixth sense twanging. I look up and realise what my intuition already knows. He's sitting alone in the corner, a fresh beer untouched on the table, his arms folded across his chest. Dressed in black.

Captain Roberts holds my eye. Fondles the pet of his beard.

I try to swallow, walk slowly to the piano. It's no good. I still feel his attention: through the material of my dress, between my shoulderblades, digging deeper, through skin and muscle, reaching the spine, making it vibrate like some ghastly xylophone. My fingers are full of stuffing. I lift the lid and sit, start playing automatically. I hear the music from a long way off. What does he want? What have I done?

After a few moments I realise I can't go on until I know. I take a deep breath, wipe my palms on my skirt, close the lid, turn, and meet his stare. His head kinks almost imperceptibly towards the door. He stands and stalks into the night. It's clear that I'm ordered to follow. Two men I've never seen before peel off the far wall and follow him out. Bodyguards?

I quickly scan the room. Charley's nowhere to be seen. Hiding in his office, probably, his usual obnoxious bravado headed down the nearest rabbit burrow. Heccy Landers is behind the bar, polishing a glass with a rag. He frowns as I walk past. I plaster on a smile so brittle it's a wonder my face doesn't crack. The worry deepens on his face.

'Ma-Ma-Mary?'

I put a hand up to still his question. Place one foot in front of the other until I'm through the door.

Outside, the air is warm and fragrant, the texture of talc. Voices bubble out from inside Charley's, breaking into faint fragments the further I move away from the safety of illumination, the security of a crowd.

Roberts steps into the alley adjacent to the salon. His two human guard dogs follow obediently, scanning the street as they move. They're watching me, too. I hurry to catch up, my heart a few gallops in front of me. The narrow corridor leads to the back of the Federal Hotel, where a door has been left open. A faint mulled-pear light shines from inside. Roberts's thugs take up position either side of the door, but not before peering over my head and down the alley. Roberts is walking up the stairs, not bothering to check if I'm following. It's an effort to lift my legs. At the top, he takes a lantern from its peg on the wall and steps into a small, dimly lit room. I follow him in.

Roberts positions the lantern on a pale wooden writing table near four tatty smoking chairs. Dead cockroaches lie on their backs on the hearth of a disused fireplace. The air smells of dust, neglect and the wild, wet-paper stink of mouse droppings. A piece of flypaper dangles from one corner of the ceiling with a dozen desiccated victims stuck to it.

He chooses a chair facing the door; the dry leather breathes out noisily as he sinks into it. He lifts his big feet onto an upended crate. My eye fixes on his left boot. It will need to be resoled soon; there's a worn patch the size of a shilling at the ball. I remain standing, but he doesn't speak, doesn't gesture for me to sit.

'I wish you'd just get it over with,' I say finally.

He doesn't respond. Just steeples his forefingers, taps his lips. I glance back towards the door. He doesn't seem to mind if it stays open. I take that as a hopeful sign. But if he doesn't blame me for the morning's disconnect, then I don't know what purpose his silent stare would serve. He might be waiting for me to explain.

I meet his eye. 'Permission to speak freely?'

One dark brow rises minutely as he thinks about this. 'Permission granted.' There's a flicker of amusement deep in those black eyes. He's mocking me. 'Have a seat, Mary Oxnam.'

I sit. Carefully. In the chair furthest from him, back to the door. My mouth opens and all the nervous energy tumbles out. 'The man who is supposed to receive my messages — Dirty White Neckerchief. He wasn't at the dock this morning.'

'You mean Collins.' It isn't a question.

'Nobody told me his name.'

'Do you always do that?'

'Do what?'

'Caricature people with nicknames?'

'Sometimes. At the poker game back in Brisbane, I did it to all of you. Charley Boule was Dandy. The older man who drank too much was Sideburns ... and so on. The man who passed messages to Wilson was Cobweb because of a piece of web stuck to his head. I guess shoddy grooming turned out to be the least of his worries, didn't it?'

I didn't mean to add that last sentence. Not quite. I lean back in my seat. The stiff old leather squeaks.

'What name did you have for me?' he asks.

'Blackbeard.'

'Not original. But apt, I suppose.'

'Are you a pirate, Captain Roberts?'

'On occasion, when it's necessary.' This said without pause, and casually, as though I asked him if he was a member of the polo club. He threads those large fingers together on his lap. 'I know Collins wasn't there this morning. He's had an accident. He won't be your contact any more.'

'What sort of accident?' I can't not ask.

'A low branch knocked him off his horse, I believe. Act of God.' He pauses, watching me. Before I can think how to respond, he asks, 'What was the message you had for him?'

'*China man not found replace.* I think a question mark may have been intended after the last word. The grille didn't align perfectly.'

I'm not sure whether to believe him about Collins, but I don't have time to think about it now. If ever there was an occasion to keep my wits about me ...

'I see.' He stares into the fireplace.

Dare I say anything? As usual, my mouth decides before my brain has thought it over.

'I don't mean to interfere, but surely this reluctant Chinaman is not the only signaller you could get for Liz ... I mean, the island?'

Too late to pull back the word. Nowhere in the notes was Lizard Island specifically mentioned. And the Chinaman's role was only hinted at obliquely.

'There are many islands around here. What makes you suspect it is the Lizard?'

The voice is silky, non-threatening, but something about the stillness of his head is more alarming than if he'd yelled the words in my face. He's testing me. If I say the wrong thing now ...

'Charley Boule introduced me to Bob Watson. Charley thinks that if Bob and I get married and I go to live on Lizard Island, I might signal boats for him. His own smuggling operations no doubt require some such communication. I made it plain I'm not interested, of course,' I add hastily. 'But Bob and Charley put Lizard Island and its signalling hill in my head. And, of course, Percy works on the Lizard with Bob. So when an island and a signaller appeared in your notes, I put two and two together ...'

I'm trying to make it sound as though anyone would draw the same conclusion with the information at hand. But his eyes have hardened.

'It never occurred to you, I suppose, that it's not part of your job to consult your abacus?'

Roberts is attempting to stare me down. And succeeding.

'Back in Brisbane, I thought you'd make a good poker player,' he says. 'But you're too impetuous. You haven't quite got your timing right. Perhaps it's your age.'

I don't answer, just attempt to look chastened. I can't work out if I'm off the hook or on it.

'I'm not surprised Boule's approached you,' he continues. 'He's incapable of relinquishing short-term profit for long-term gain.'

Having just had my fingers burned, I don't dare fire him up

with another question, but I find his comment puzzling. What long-term gain might Charley be missing?

Roberts pauses again, as if weighing the risk of explaining himself. Or of letting me wander around Cooktown with too much impetuosity at the tip of my tongue. His next words do nothing to clarify my position.

'As for the Chinaman, he's not hiding from us. There's a lynch mob of his own kind after him. He robbed and killed a Chow shopkeeper. He knows what will happen if they catch him. He'll be pinned by his ears to a tree for a few days, until they've agreed on a suitable punishment.'

'That's barbaric.'

Something snags in the back of my mind. A wanted poster I've seen plastered in a few shop windows. I didn't take much notice of the Chinaman's face, as it was in profile, but his raised hands left an impression. Veined and knotted, ugly fingers with long nails like chicken's feet. So that's why he had been so difficult to locate.

'It's nothing compared to what's meted out to thieves and murderers in China,' Roberts says. 'They behead them in the town square. Then the crowds dip their money in the blood as it gushes out of the neck. It's supposed to be lucky.'

'Depends on whether it's *your* head that's been disconnected, I'd think.'

My nerve is returning; I wouldn't have thought two minutes ago that I'd do anything but stare dumbly at him. But curiosity hasn't quite killed this cat … so far, at least. I risk another one of my nine lives.

'Why would you want a man who's on the run to work for you on the Lizard?'

'What better reason for him to co-operate? He's delivered from vengeful compatriots and put in a safe haven in the middle of the ocean. It's not just that he can't escape. He can't even want to.'

'I see.' His last remark reminds me of my own situation. 'What am I to do now, Captain? Who do I pass the messages on to?'

He grabs his beard under his chin and tugs on it like a bell rope. 'That part of your job has come to an end. You can go back to the same surveillance work that occupied you when you first came to Cooktown.'

'So I'm being demoted?'

He scratches his cheek above the beard. 'Did you think you would rise through the ranks in measured increments and then end up with a nice fat pension? This is not the Civil Service.'

I feel my shoulders sink. He's right, of course. There's nothing civil about this business. And not many of his employees, I would imagine, need to worry about saving for their old age.

'I was hoping my loyalty might count for something,' I say.

'It does. There's a direct correlation between your loyalty and the state of your health.'

The sense of foreboding that started this morning with the absence of Dirty White Neckerchief, and reached a breaking point when Roberts appeared in French Charley's, is back. I know enough to see a lessening of my duties as a very bad sign indeed. Roberts and Percy will soon have their base on Lizard Island. The small-time intelligence I can supply from Cooktown will be of only peripheral interest to them. At best, I'll be ignored, left to languish, playing piano in a brothel. At worst, I'll outlive my usefulness altogether.

What are my options? Would they let me go now? Could I walk away? Even so, I'd only have enough money to get back to

Brisbane, where I might live frugally for six months. Then, back to where I started. No prospects. No future.

I take a shuddery breath. I have to talk myself back into the game. I've risked so much, come so far. I'm still as good a player as any of them. My motto in Brisbane when talking to Percy comes back to me: *may as well be hung for a sheep as a lamb*. I hold my sweaty hands together in front of me.

'Captain Roberts, what if I could position myself on Lizard Island? I could be your signaller.'

He's relaxed, not taking me seriously. 'And how exactly would you propose to do that? Get out the lampblack? Disguise yourself as one of the Kanaka crew on Watson's lugger? At least the Chinaman, if he ever materialises, will pass as a servant.'

'I told you that Charley Boule introduced me to Bob Watson. Bob's fond of me. More than fond. If I married him, we would live on Lizard Island. But not to signal for Charley; to signal for you. What could attract less suspicion than a dutiful wife, helpmeet to her husband in his sea-slug-fishing business?'

'You would go so far for mere money?'

'I'm not un-fond of Bob,' I say, a trifle defensively. 'And there's nothing mere about money to me. It means a new life. A new start. If I continue to prove my loyalty, that is. I assume it would be a well-paid position?'

'Oh, indeed. It's risky work. For which I naturally pay a generous stipend.'

'All the more reason, I would think, not to entrust such an important task to a nervous Chinaman who's stupid enough to murder a countryman in a much-too-public way.'

Roberts puts one finger to his temple. His black stare dares me to falter.

'What would you do when your job on the Lizard was finished?' he asks. 'Would you stay with Watson?'

'Would that matter to you?'

'Probably not. But if you mean to go and start this new life of yours, it would be an extra complication. You'd have an irate husband trying to track you down.'

I project as calm a demeanour as I can manage. 'You'll allow I don't let much get past me? Bob Watson has a chequered history with women. He would just chalk up the loss of another to experience, I think. One more disappointment to feel bitter about. How many sensible marriages are built on romance, anyway?'

I can feel the pulse beating at my temples. It's as though someone far older and more cynical is putting the words in my mouth. How could I possibly know how Bob would react if I left our hypothetical marriage? I hardly know the man. And what of me? Could I really accomplish such a charade? Could I live with Bob? Go to bed with him? That strange, two-sided face sweaty and intense above me ... Am I really setting the bar too high? Or am I perversely setting it too low? Maybe I've convinced myself that real contentment with a man is not the province of a homely girl like me, and I must orchestrate the future on my own terms. There's enough truth in this to make me feel squeamish.

I realise that Roberts has been talking and, for the first time since I met him, I haven't been hanging on every word. I must sustain a firm argument with this man, whether or not I'm convinced, myself. He'll see even the smallest hesitation, and discount me because of it.

'Marriage? I've never been locked up in that particular institution, so I'm no expert,' he says. 'But it seems to me it's a fairly irrevocable step for a young girl like you.'

My quick wit dog-paddles frantically, trying to keep an inch ahead of him. 'On the contrary. Because I have few years behind me, I have many more before me. I may make any number of new starts in my lifetime.'

Silence descends, for perhaps five painful minutes. I don't allow myself to fidget. I resist the urge to jump in with further justifications. I do have time, however, to ungag my internal voice of caution and listen to its slightly hysterical opinion that my sane mind's been sent on a slow boat to China.

'It might work,' he allows finally. 'You certainly seem cold and logical enough.'

I don't mind *logical*. But *cold*? Hardly a compliment. And *he* should talk!

'It would certainly be a further test of that ingenuity you love to exercise,' he adds.

I open my mouth to thank him, then close it again. There's never a chink in his armour, no place on that hard face or body for any softness to land. Besides, he hasn't really committed himself one way or the other.

He stands smoothly, with none of the awkwardness most people experience trying to lift themselves from a lounge chair, and walks over to a small window that looks out on the night.

I remember something then. And wonder if I'm not signing Charley Boule's death warrant with my next words.

'I must tell you, Captain, Charley has asked me to deliver some messages for him. He's at least partially aware of what you're doing. He knows that I gather information for you. I think he knew from the moment Percy recommended me as a piano player.'

'What are his messages about?'

His voice comes unsurprised from the shadows. He doesn't seem even slightly disturbed that Charley might have sniffed out the rudiments of his operation. That fact alone tells me that my intuition is right. French Charley's, as a base for gathering information, is fast outliving its usefulness to Roberts. And if I don't pursue this risky new bet, then so will I.

'I don't know. I've made it clear I've no intention of delivering the notes.'

'Go ahead, do what he asks. Just make a copy of any message he gives you and pass it on. To me, personally, when next I'm in town. Along with anything else you find … significant. Boule is a gnat trying to pierce the hide of an elephant. I'll know if he causes any real trouble. I am, however, interested in any talk of further expeditions to New Guinea.'

'Percy mentioned that. But I haven't picked up on anything. Why would you want Charley to stay away from New Guinea?' There I go again. 'Sorry …'

He walks back into the light and takes his seat again. Apparently the subject isn't especially delicate. His tone is light. 'The French are establishing themselves in the New Hebrides: buying up the best land from natives and Europeans alike. But it's the Germans who want New Guinea. This is a delicate time in European diplomacy. Disraeli's still in office, but word is that his time is over. The Grand Old Man will be prime minister again next year.' He lifts one booted foot and rests it on his knee. 'Gladstone is particularly reluctant to provoke German sensibilities, and England wants no part of New Guinea. But it's clear they'll be forced to intervene if — no, when — the Germans go too far. In the meantime, men like Boule are an accelerant. If they're allowed to collect the kindling and keep feeding the fire, that is.'

'But Charley's French, not German.'

'You must have gleaned something of his character by now.' His mouth twists slightly. 'Boule knows everything there is to know about whoring. Makes his decisions not out of patriotism so much as the proud tradition of selling himself to the highest bidder. The question then becomes: which of two undesirable clients will he lie down with in order to turn the most profit? He figures, quite rightly, that he'll be in a better position to exploit New Guinea if the Germans take control. England wouldn't tolerate his like.'

I digest this. It would explain Roberts's occasional 'pirating'. He is probably a privateer. German expansion into New Guinea would necessitate all sorts of maritime traffic, and the British flag would be unwelcome. A privateer could disrupt those activities without adverse political implication.

He draws a piece of paper from his pocket and holds it out to me. 'Fuller will be on the Lizard most of the time from now on. If something happens that requires our urgent attention, send a telegram to this address with the message: *Your new saddle has just arrived.*'

I take the paper and slip it into the pocket of my skirt.

'Otherwise, I'll see you next time I'm in town,' he says. 'Do you have anything else to tell me?'

'Only more about the French gnat, I'm afraid.'

I tell him about the Chinese junk some weeks back that docked with, so the rumour went, opium charcoal for the goldfields. It was well known that the Chinese diggers handed it out to the blacks to burn on their fires. Once they were addicted and docile, they could be bribed into ambushing European camps. What was new was that Charley had shown an unhealthy interest in the whole illicit venture, and I suspected he was somehow sponsoring the operation.

Roberts sighs deeply. 'Where's Fahey when you need him?'

'Organising another ball?'

He nods. It's a long-running joke in Cooktown, dragged out when Bartley Fahey, now the water police magistrate, pays no attention to what's going on at the docks. The original ball in question, given mainly for the benefit of the upper classes on the hill behind Cooktown, was organised when Fahey held a position as sub-collector of customs. The size and grandeur of the event is still talked about; including the extravagance of shipping in tons of ice from Townsville for the occasion.

'Good enough,' Roberts says. 'You'd best get back to work.' He dismisses me with a curt nod.

There's nothing to do but leave. I think he's forgotten about Lizard Island, the signalling job, but when I'm almost at the door he delivers his last words on the subject.

'It's clear that you understand the further you go in this operation, the more money there is to be made. Have you considered, however, that the deeper your involvement, the more you have to lose?'

10

From the secret diary of Mary Watson

7TH DECEMBER 1879

'You frightened the life out of me!'

The next night, I'm almost home from work, dodging mud puddles, when he steps out of the shadows in oversized boots. I recognise the warm conversation mints on his breath, but the battered old muleskin coat and cabbage-tree hat are unfamiliar. In the dark, the effect is sinister, his face almost hidden by the brim.

'You've put your trust in the wrong man.' His voice is a low growl.

The aftermath of a storm drips warm pencil-lengths from the eaves of the Federal Hotel. Gaslight catches his twitching hands.

'I don't know what you're talking about.'

Fingers close around my wrist. 'You only think he's on your side.' His voice sounds older, more confident. Then I realise the habitual stammer is absent, as if he's drawing power from the anonymity of the dark. It's enough to give me pause.

'Who, Heccy? Who is it I can't trust?'

'He's killed before. He'd kill you now, if he thought he could get away with it.'

'Who?!'

But he doesn't say. Just tips his face forward so it's totally eclipsed by the brim of the hat. For a moment I think he intends to kiss me, or perhaps bite me. Then he jerks back.

'Let me go!' I tell him.

The handcuff-grip unlocks, and a flood of pins and needles rushes in. I rub the skin. Breathe out. Look up, but he's gone. Dissolved back into the alley as if he's never been.

The thunder moves north, shaking the last coins in its collection box.

Three nights later Bob says: 'I'm no good with the airs and graces of courting.'

He kissed me just seconds ago, on the cool sand near the tied-up boats in the harbour. Under a moon like a huge blister pearl with black fingers trawling over it. I'd closed my eyes. Tasted pipe tobacco. The vague seaweed undertow of the ocean. Pretended it was Percy.

'I like the common touch,' I tell him, my lips still smarting from his bristles. 'When I think of your skin fitting, it's not here in Cooktown. But in a more primitive place. Your island, maybe. Or the middle of the ocean.'

I hold up the toy monkey he bought me, lolling on its stick, to the moon's light. Its smile seems leerish, surrounded by apricot cheeks, red jacket and black bow tie. The outfit of some voodoo doll.

We've spent the evening strolling through Chinatown, by the water. Wandering the narrow, covered alleys flaring with lanterns and banners. He led me, two fingers in the small of my back. Past the pyramids of oranges and apples. The counter with its enormous glass jars of fish-shaped sweets.

'I've tried them,' I admitted when he offered me some. 'They taste like sweetened beeswax seals on the backs of important letters.'

Bob asked how long I'd been nibbling on bits of Her Majesty's post.

I said it wasn't much different to licking stamps.

He chuckled, steering me casually away from the opening in the opium tent, where the toothless man with small knives in his eyes handed out pieces of dripping sugarcane.

He bought the toy from the very last stall.

Now, his medicinal balls chatter amongst themselves, considering my comment.

'Aye,' he says. 'The cloth of my skin don't fit right in Cooktown.'

The ocean in the distance keeps opening the same bottle of fizzy water. Pouring out a glass, then putting the stopper back in.

Bob sniffs the air. 'A good fisherman can scent a patch of slugs twenty miles away.'

'What do they smell like?'

He smiles crookedly. 'I never said I was a good fisherman.' He sniffs, and his nostrils flare. 'It's not the slugs themselves, but the fast-running tide that goes with them.'

'I know the ocean smells stronger when there's an onshore breeze, but that's not the same thing, is it?'

'No.' Suddenly earnest, he takes my hands in his. The monkey dangles between us. 'Ye're like a breath of fresh air, Mary. Ye smell like flowers. Not hothouse blooms, but those tough, no-nonsense ones that grow by the roadside, drinking up the sun.'

'Must be my new perfume, Caprice,' I say. I test the aroma of the air myself and decide it's ripe for revelation. 'Have there been other women in your life, Bob?'

He stares out to sea. The edges of the stars are softer than usual. And brighter. Pasted onto the sky with watery cornflour glue. I can almost hear the mainsail in his head creak as it stretches back into the distant past.

'The fairer sex have always wanted something from me,' he says. 'I've been played a fool many times. I've always had a soft spot for a bonny face.'

'I see,' I say, and inwardly yawn. Clearly I haven't been specific enough.

He guides me gently around so that I'm bathed in moonlight. Follows the wings of my eyebrows, then the rest of my features. I endure the scrutiny, teeth clenched.

'Do ye mind me saying? It would soften yer looks no end if ye didn't pull yer hair quite so tight away from yer face.'

'Do you think so?'

'I do find ye bonny, it's just ...' Instead of only his foot, this time he shoves his leg into his mouth, all the way up to the kneecap. 'Anyway, look at the Germans. They don't value beauty in their wives. It's strength, thrift, good nature and obedience that count.'

'You forgot youth.' If my voice were any drier he could strike a match on it.

'I know it's too early to ask. But do ye think we might ... That is, I know full well ye're half my age. But ye seem so different to other girls.'

I hear the strange, excited chatter of Chinamen plying their wares in the distance. The exotic wafts of cooking: onions, shrimp paste. A repeated chipping-metal sound: some bird in an invisible tree. Light and shadow play across Bob's damaged face.

'I've heard some talk, Bob. About a woman you knew on the goldfields. She disappeared a year ago.'

Seconds play out. Water slaps its washing against wharf pylons. The bruised mass of the sky moves its grudge closer.

'That nonsense again. Who says so?'

The wind's winding up. I raise my voice just a little to compensate. 'It doesn't matter who. But why is it nonsense?'

'A case of mistaken identity.' His medicinal balls make an abandoned sound, like the sign outside a deserted inn clanking in the breeze. 'A slug fisherman from Barrow Point had a sable belle for years. She ran away from him. Ended up on the goldfields, then was never seen again. Ye know how stories go. I was on the goldfields for a time. Now I'm a slug fisherman. Seeing most lips that pass loose talk are numb from drink, it's not really surprising they'd think it me.'

The delivery is smooth. Only a trained ear could hear the small squeak of a tight new shoe.

'Why would a native woman who runs away from a white man be noteworthy?' I ask. 'If it were the other way around …'

I'm thinking of the naked, white Normandy woman, the one whom diggers on the goldfields have seen on and off for years. No one's found out how she came to live among the natives. Or why.

'There was some trouble from her tribe. Threats to kill the fellow. I really can't say.'

It could be river water kicked up by the wind that's peppering my arms. Or the dirt flung off Bob's spade as he digs himself a deeper hole.

'Ye must believe me, Mary. I'd never stoop so low.'

He's pensive on the brisk walk back. His medicinal balls have fallen silent. But he does lift a damp frond out of my way and warns me to watch my step as we clamber up the gravelly slope to Charlotte Street. We step onto the nearest verandah just as tumult descends. The nails-on-tin above our heads means we now have to shout.

'I have to go.' Bob pulls his coat up over his head. 'I have to speak with Will Hartley. He's the merchant who handles my slugs. Do ye want to climb Grassy Hill the day after tomorrow?' There's a gleam in his good eye. A definite challenge. 'If ye're up to it.'

'Oh, I'm up to it. You'll find I'm up to almost anything.' Amazing how confident I sound, even to my own ears.

With a last crooked smile and a flick of his forked tongue, he pulls his coat down tighter on his head, leaps off the verandah and runs headlong into the rain.

11

From the secret diary of Mary Watson

11TH DECEMBER 1879

It's not Heccy Landers who stops me on my way home tonight, but another man, lurking behind a tree on the other side of Charlotte Street. He calls my name. I turn. He slips his long body into the nearest shadow. I look behind me to make sure no one is watching, then half-walk, half-skate across the muddy road. The smell is like a handkerchief that's washed a hundred dirty feet being held over my nose.

I follow Percy down a slight slope, through the trees and into a secluded clearing. The moon shimmers in the humid air with the consistency of half-cooked eggwhite. Just enough light through the branches to see that he's distracted. Twitchy. Something joyous in my chest jumps up to meet him.

'I didn't expect you back in town,' I say. 'I thought you would be gone longer.'

'I'm off to the Lizard tomorrow. I'll be grounded there for a while. I've pushed my luck about as far as it will go with Watson.'

His body is tense. He doesn't seem at all happy to see me. A waft of something decaying rises from the river. When he turns, his green eyes are blazing. 'What do you think you're playing at with him?'

'With Bob?' I take a step back and almost fall over the root of a tree. Even in the half-light, I can see a vein prominent on Percy's forehead. That laconic mouth is taut. 'Haven't you talked to Roberts?' I rub my hands up and down my arms, though I'm not cold.

'I've spoken to no one. I've been chasing up the Chinaman, remember?'

'Did you find him?'

I wonder if I imagine something furtive scuttling across his face.

'No. And you're avoiding my question. What are you doing playing up to Watson?'

'Dirty White Neckerchief — I mean, Collins — didn't turn up to receive my message on the dock. He'd had an accident. Roberts himself came into Charley's. I gave him the message that the Chinaman was still nowhere to be found.'

'What's that got to do with Watson?'

'I'm getting to that. It was Charley who introduced me to Bob, with some vain hope that I'd marry him, go to Lizard Island, and then help Charley with his smuggling operations.'

'Did he now?'

Wires under the surface of his face tighten skin over bones. He seems far more concerned with Charley's underhand tactics than me talking to Roberts. But why?

'I told Captain Roberts all of the above,' I go on, 'and then it occurred to me that I could marry Bob and be your signaller on the Lizard. You can't object, surely? Someone has to do it.'

'Damn you to hell! Why can't you stop meddling in things that don't concern you?'

He rakes big fingers through his hair and glares at me. The moonlight has a curious effect on his eyes, emptying them of colour. He hardly looks human any more. I almost reach out, try to break whatever mad spell he's under, but I'm afraid of what he'll do if my fingers come in contact with that coiled-up bundle of nerves.

'I don't understand why you're so angry. You haven't got the Chinaman. You need someone on the Lizard.'

He must realise he's not being rational, because he takes a couple of deep breaths.

'It's dangerous and stupid. And you'll have to bed him. Did you think of that, Mary Oxnam? You with your clever little plans. Your eagerness to make money. You know Watson went around with a black woman? They say he killed her out on the goldfields.'

'He says it was someone else. Not him.'

I shouldn't be upholding Bob's story. I didn't believe it when he told me, and I don't believe it now. But this isn't about Bob's peccadillos. It's about Percy's regard for me.

'Don't tell me you've fallen in love with the old Scottish git!'

'Of course not!'

He rubs a hand roughly over his mouth. Even the familiar woodsy cologne he uses smells perturbed, as though some big animal's giving the trunk of the pine tree a shake.

He pulls his pipe from his pocket. His next words are low and measured. 'It's perilous. And no job for a woman. You'd have to climb that hill to signal at night, and you may have the dubious company of cranky blackfellows from the mainland.' He tamps the bowl and goes to light it. The match flares. His face flashes huge in front of me. He shakes the match out. 'The truth is, I feel … some degree of responsibility. For your welfare. I'm the one who employed you, after all. You don't know what Watson's like. I do. I don't want him getting his dirty hands on you. You are still a vulnerable young girl, despite your bravado.'

The spontaneous joy comes back for an instant. He doesn't want Bob to have me. He wants me for himself! But as quickly as the heady feeling swirls me around, a killjoy hand falls on the whirligig, stopping it dead. The killjoy makes me repeat his words, his tone, in my head. Over and over until I hear the discrepancy. His voice was halting, but not because of some underlying affection. He was making the speech up as he went. Having failed to catch the insect with vinegar, he'd thought, reasonably enough, to try honey. And something else — that unfamiliar accent had crept back into his voice. For some reason, all of a sudden I want to get away from him.

'We'll talk about it again when you've settled down,' I say. 'I must get home now. It's not safe in the dark.' I don't wait around to hear his response.

12

From the secret diary of Mary Watson

12TH DECEMBER 1879

Crunch-crunch go my boots through the wiry grass. *Click-click* goes Bob's pocket as he strides ahead of me. I pull myself from wind-stunted tree to tree. My slippery palms squash opportunistic ants crawling up my arm. 'Whose idea was this anyway?' I try to sound a good sport, but my hat is slipping off. A swamp oozes under my petticoats and in my armpits.

'We're almost there,' he says over his shoulder. 'The view from the top will be worth it.'

'Can we sit on this log, Bob? Just for a minute.'

I collapse in the shade. The air presses in on every side. He seems pleased with the discrepancy in our energy levels. It occurs to me that this climb is his way of denying his age. Showcasing his stamina. A prize bull in the stockyard, leading himself around by the ring in his own nose.

I indulge his self-regard. 'You must be very fit. I'm done in already.'

He's looking at my hair. Remembering his suggestion, I've let a few tendrils fall around my face, albeit resentfully. Now given our exertions, my bun is threatening to come apart altogether.

'Yer new style is bonny,' he says.

I take a lungful of air … and swallow a fly. It buzzes and twitches in my throat. A small bundle of filthy hay inside a vibrating hessian bag. It's too much to politely ignore. I excuse myself; go behind a bush and cough until it comes up.

Bob is suppressing a grin when I get back. 'Breathe through yer nose. It's the fourth rule of the bush.'

'What are the first three?' I wipe my mouth on a handkerchief.

'Carry a hat, a stick and a gun. The hat's for the sun. The stick's for snakes. The gun's for the blacks.'

The breeze catches his words, blows them through the open window of the sky. A cloud flings its net over the sun. The ravaged half of Bob's face falls into a bolthole of shadow.

'Ye asked about my past, lass. What about ye? Any suitors?'

Spoken casually. But I've heard that tone before: some rattlesnake rustling beneath insouciance. Men are always eager to stake their claim.

'Not suitors, exactly.'

'What exactly, then?'

I seize on a safe subject. 'There's a lad who works for Charley in the bar — Heccy Landers.'

'I've seen him mooning.' A pinch of amused spice now. 'A lovestruck calf.'

'I wouldn't go quite so far.'

In the distance, there's a whitish line. A tear where the water catches continually on the sharp rocks beneath.

'Ye're far too modest.' He finds my hand on my lap. Squeezes just a fraction more than he needs to. 'This Heccy Landers, he's the same age as ye. It would be natural if he courted ye.'

'As you've observed, Bob, I'm a bit of an odd one out. Age means nothing to me.'

His fixed smile dries to a crack. 'It must mean something, or ye'd look at a man, not graze his face then look away.'

I hesitate, wondering how to strike the right balance between honesty and girlish reticence. 'It's the scar. Sometimes I don't know which side is in charge.'

'Ye daft donsie, there's only one of me.' But there's no heat in it. He's clearly relieved I don't find him repulsive.

'Yes, I know. Silly, isn't it? On account of my youth, I expect.' Then, because I can't resist the troublemaking imp itching at my tongue, 'Perhaps you'd be better off with someone your own age.' I feel his body stiffen in annoyance beside me.

The cicadas accelerate their clicks, reinforcing their net in every direction until the air reverberates. I see something move near a tree halfway down the hill. Put my hand up to shield the glare. It's probably the pendulum effect of the sun through moving clouds. The light playing high-altitude tricks. Or Heccy, playing unwanted sleuth.

'What is it?' Bob asks. His nose is turning pink in the sun.

'A wallaby?'

The twisting path all the way up was strewn with their spoor, the size of miniature musket balls.

'A man should've brought his rifle. Nothing nicer than wallaby stew if it's done right with carrots and onions and mashed taties.'

'Do you keep livestock on the Lizard?'

'Some goats and ducks. The goannas are partial to poultry, though. We've lost some goats too.'

'Big goannas, to carry off a goat.'

When he doesn't answer, I realise they must be two-legged goannas. The kind that come over from the mainland in canoes and carry spears.

'Onward and upward,' Bob says, and I stand. Reluctantly.

There's the rub of raw flesh on my left ankle, and every time my boot moves over it a heated blade slices more ham off the bone. I hobble the rest of the way. Bob doesn't offer any help. A punishment for my earlier reference to his age?

He's right about the view from the top, though. The ocean spreads out like a sheet of beaten silver, held at just the right angle to blind the sun. It's tucked in at the horizon, and on either side by half-moons of land. On the left, tufty grey trees move upwards to the firm blue mattress of sky. Stuffing pokes out here and there in patches of white.

We find a rock large and smooth enough to sit on. I unlace my boot, wincing. The blister's bled through my hose. I take a handkerchief, pack it wadding-style over the wound and cautiously put the boot back on.

Bob watches the operation in silence. An eagle circles high, sedately looping transparent wool around an invisible pair of widespread hands.

'Ye shouldn't see Heccy Landers,' he says. 'Not if ye're considering me for yer husband.'

'I can't help seeing him. We work together.' I test my foot on the ground: a blunt pain this time. He's jealous. Not a good sign. I told Captain Roberts that, if I marry Bob, he'll likely shrug off my desertion at the end of the operation on Lizard Island. But perhaps that analysis was too hasty.

I search for a distraction. 'Where is the Lizard from here, Bob?'

He points to the left, over the mop-head of vegetation, beyond the long sickle of shoreline. 'More than a hop, step and jump to the north. Too treacherous and far for ye to see.'

Treacherous? Perhaps. Some might look at that vast blue distance and imagine the million blades of reef just under the surface. I look and see a fertile field, sword turned ploughshare and just about to churn the sods of good fortune. On a day like this, my young lungs full of fresh air, anything seems possible. And no obstacle — not Captain Roberts's warning, not Bob's jealousy, not Percy's disapproval — seems a serious enough challenge.

Bob takes off his hat and wipes his brow with the back of his hand. 'It's an isolated place. Ye may not cope with it. Not many women could.'

'I'm stronger than most women,' I tell him without expression. And then, making conversation, 'Did you catch up with Will Hartley the night before last?'

For an instant he seems a startled boy, caught with his hand in the biscuit tin. The scar looks angry in the sunlight. I wonder if it ever itches.

'Oh, aye. I caught up with him eventually.'

'Did he give you a fair price for your slugs?'

His lopsided gaze falls on me. 'That's a curious thing for a girl to fret about.'

I shrug. 'It's the nature of my employment to hear rumours. Word is, Hartley's creative with his share of his clients' profits.'

'Is that so? I'll have to look into it.' His voice says he has no intention of doing so.

My foot throbs. White clouds above us suddenly sport black eyes. It's time for more feminine weakness, not altogether manufactured.

'Any chance of a piggyback down?'

At the bottom of the hill, Bob leaves me with a peck on the cheek and a doff of his hat. I head for the pharmacy to buy some plasters for my heel. I'm almost to the steps when I hear two men arguing loudly in a room upstairs in the Federal Hotel. They mustn't realise the window has been left half-open behind the curtains. I can't see them. And I can't hear what they're saying. But I recognise that French accent wound up several notches. And the other man's spitting fury. Lord knows, I was on the wrong end of it myself not so long ago.

Charley Boule and Percy. How curious.

13

Every profession has its hazards.

From the secret diary of Mary Watson

I know as soon as I walk into French Charley's for my shift that something's wrong. I grab Heccy's arm as he passes with a tray full of glasses. 'What is it?'

He looks down at my hand then up to my face. The glasses tinkle. I see then that his fingers grip the tray so tightly they're almost transparent.

'Nicole. D-d-dead. Down near the river, l-last night.'

I breathe out audibly. Nicole! Who next? I'm not so shocked, however, that I don't notice something amiss about Heccy's reaction. His long face is bright and his eyes glinting, but he's forced the rest of his features into an attitude of stillness. It's a curious contradiction. As though he's a jeweller carefully turning something over this way and that under a light, not wanting to give away the implications of what he sees. But the stammer undermines him.

'S-strangled. That's what you g-get for being a whore of B-B-Babylon.'

'I thought you liked Nicole?'

'She was a s-stain in front of God's eyes.'

Still that intense face. I decide to let his internal saint and awkward grief fight it out inside him.

'Did you follow me when I climbed Grassy Hill this morning?'

'N-no,' he says, but his cheeks turn pinker.

'I can look after myself, Heccy.'

'Y-you just think you c-can.' His jaw tightens. 'Bob Watson is a b-bounder.'

'Is he the one I shouldn't trust, then?'

He doesn't answer. Just gnashes his teeth. I can see them moving, top set over bottom, like a wheat grinder, just under the skin of his cheek. Time to straighten him out once and for all. I soften my voice.

'Any man in my life would be a bounder to you. There is no chance for you and me, Heccy. I'm sorry, but you must get used to it.'

His next words are almost whispered. 'M-maybe you're like Nicole. I know you d-don't really c-care for Watson.'

I feel the heat drain from my face. What's that saying? Out of the mouths of babes? I don't need reminding that I'm leading Bob on. Any reasonable critic could accuse me of something not far away from prostitution.

'M-Mary. I'm sorry. I d-d-didn't mean it.'

'I know you didn't. Where's Charley?'

'In his office. M-Mary?'

'Yes, Heccy, what is it?' I'm impatient to get away from him now.

There's a hectic zeal in his voice. 'I'm glad she's d-dead. She shouldn't have spoken t-to you the way she did.'

The door's open. Charley's at his desk. I catch him just as he hastily places his head in his hands. He must have heard me coming. Anyone who doesn't know him might conclude he's devastated over the loss of a young girl in her prime of life, rather than just overwhelmed by the logistics of replacing her at short notice.

'I'm sorry about Nicole,' I say.

He looks up and nods. Then, as though deciding it's not quite enough of a performance, the pupils of his eyes move skywards and his palm comes to rest over the heavy weight of his heart.

'You despised her, yes? You wished her dead?'

'I didn't know her well enough for that sort of passionate response.'

And neither did you, Charley. So why the theatrics?

He shakes his head. 'What a strange girl you are. Too strange even for Cooktown. Perhaps not too strange for Lizard Island.'

It's my day, apparently, for unflattering commentary on my character. 'Charmed, I'm sure. What have you heard about the Lizard, Charley? I may as well add it to the list of doom stories rattling in my ears.'

'I have warned you against Watson already. But that island — some say it is a special place to the blacks. That tragedy comes to any European living there.'

'Good old Mr Some has an opinion on everything, doesn't he? For instance: Some also say that businessman foiled in nefarious plan will find way to scare rival.'

My Confucius parody doesn't impress him, if the twitch of his nose above the manicured moustachios is anything to go by.

Thunder's wagon-wheel rattles in the sky. We both look to the window.

'I have problems of my own, *chérie*. You will succeed, or you will be fish food. Either way it is of no great interest to Charley Boule. Perhaps you will take that stammering dolt Heccy Landers with you, eh? Wear him at your hip to repel the blacks, the way you repel mosquitos by rubbing that lavender oil all over till you smell like a field in Toulouse. They won't kill and eat a redhead, or so it is said.'

'Who won't? The mosquitos?'

'*Mon Dieu!* The blacks.'

'Why not?'

'How should I know? Perhaps they taste of beets. Perhaps their god has red hair. You think Charley Boule makes a study of such things?'

He's winding himself up to a state of exasperation, which is only mildly entertaining. He seems to have forgotten he was the one who brought up the subject in the first place. He slams both hands on the table and stands. I have to keep the conversation going; my fishing trip isn't complete yet. I need to find out for Captain Roberts if Charley is planning another trip north.

'I'm touched by your concern. But I'll leave Heccy with you, if you don't mind, and take my chances. Will there be an investigation into Nicole's murder?'

He shakes his head slowly. 'That useless sack of bones Fitzgerald is not due back until tomorrow. Brooke, that little deputy of his, struts around like a peacock, asking stupid questions that make him look like a big policeman rather than uncovering the truth.'

As much as I hate to agree with Charley about anything, his *précis* of Jocelyn Brooke is spot on. Thin, nervy, officious and incompetent in equal measure. Unlike Fitzgerald, who is merely incompetent and, on the whole, far less trouble because of it.

I wander over to Charley's shelf of maritime memorabilia and hear him sink his considerable bulk into his flatulent chair again. I pick up an old compass, turn around to hear its history. He twists the wick on the lamp higher to get a better look in the darkening room.

'*Grimenza,* 4th July 1853,' he says. 'Peruvian barque. Wrecked Brampton Reef, six hundred and fifty lives lost.'

I put it down. Pick up a rusted cleat.

'Ah, your namesake: *Mary*; schooner, wrecked 26th May 1821. Driven ashore at Twofold Bay.'

I pick up a torn piece of timber, knowing full well which wreck it's from.

'*Maria,*' he says curtly. 'February 1872. Wrecked east of Bowen. Forty-nine lives lost.'

'*Maria?*' I pretend to ponder the name for a few seconds. 'Wasn't it heading north to New Guinea on a gold expedition?'

He's far too interested in his hobby not to answer. I've set the words down like a trap on the branch a possum habitually scampers over. And here comes the possum.

'Stupid plan,' is all he says. 'What imbecile sets sail in cyclone season?'

I put the wood from the *Maria*'s hull down on the shelf. Say, with my back to him, 'Didn't you fund an expedition to New Guinea, Charley? I'm sure someone said you did. Of course, it would have been a better-planned trip than *Maria*'s. Better chance of success. Earlier this year, wasn't it? Before I came to Cooktown?'

I turn around, a look of interest on my face, to see suspicion pulling a stitch tight at the corner of each dark eye. Too fast! I should have eased into it.

'Why the sudden interest in gold prospecting, *chérie?*'

I shrug. 'I'm not interested. I'd have to be deaf, however, not to hear the rumours that your expedition was similarly flawed. Not by embarking in the wrong season, but by having not enough picks and shovels. Not to mention a crew more interested, when they got to Port Moresby, in the local women and alcohol.'

Royal flush.

'*Quelle absurdité!* I pick the best men. Plenty of equipment. It is not my fault they get sick. Not my fault that ...' His face is as red as a fiery dusk in the lamplight.

'What, Charley? What wasn't your fault?'

'*Rien!*'

'Why don't you try again?' I ask evenly. 'Send another expedition. The gold must still be there. That is, if the Germans haven't dug it all up and sent it home to gild chamber pots for Bismarck.'

'I do not have the means for another trip north.' The words are tight with impatience. 'And I do not talk shipwrecks with you. You know nothing about them. Nor Germans.'

'Yes, Charley.' I'm the epitome of a demure young lady now, having received all the information I need. I've observed Charley's altercations with the miners who have come back into town. They don't have the money he demands of them. An expedition to New Guinea would require serious cash and I'm fairly sure that, for the moment, he hasn't got it.

'Any idea who killed Nicole? Who was she with last night?' I ask.

Charley rubs his forehead. 'After closing, I do not know. As you are aware, she has ...' He pauses to correct himself. '— had a tendency to conduct her business outside. Were you with Watson last night?'

'No. Why?'

'I tell you already and you do not listen. He has a dark side.'

'So dark that he saw fit to murder a prostitute?'

He stands abruptly and paces over to one of the windows that looks out on Charlotte Street. The twilight is the colour of mustard paste. 'Why is it inconceivable to you that Watson could have strangled her?'

'Nothing's inconceivable, I suppose, but what would be his motive?'

Charley sighs as the sky's first sweat-drops fall. 'More sticky rain. How I hate Cooktown.' He whips around. 'What would be any man's motive? Why shoot the horse that you want to ride?'

'To avoid paying the stable owner. Perhaps you should lower your prices. And stop taking your customers for complete fools.'

Charley raises one eyebrow. His look is so patronising it annoys me into being specific.

'Drugging gold-diggers with your alcoholic concoctions, then allowing the girls to go through their pockets while they sleep. That's a recipe for murderous intent.'

Now the mouth twitches upwards at the sides, but not in amusement. 'Speaking of avarice, *chérie*, there is, in addition to the inconvenience of being one girl short tonight, five pounds missing from my drawer.'

'When did you notice it was gone?' I ask calmly, knowing that the money is not part of the business as such, and so is not counted regularly. In addition, his illicit cargo is delivered no more frequently than once a month. That's why I took the money. I felt confident he wouldn't bother checking until the next time he had to make a payment. And by then, many other people would have been in his office.

'Not for some weeks,' he admits, looking disgruntled that I don't confess. 'I do not understand. I always lock the drawer.'

'Are you sure? I've seen you get your cigar pinch out of there. Do you sometimes forget to secure it again?'

'Charley Boule does not forget something of such importance!'

'Well, I'm sure I have no idea. If you haven't left the drawer unlocked, how could money be missing? Perhaps you miscounted in the first place.' I touch his desk lightly. 'I could deposit your cash for you tomorrow, if you wish. Or do you mistrust me as much as you mistrust the Bank of Queensland?'

'*Au contraire.* I mistrust you more than every bank in the colony stood end on end.'

But it's all wind and red pepper. He waves me away abruptly. Outside, the rain is winding up to what will be a prolonged crescendo.

14

No blackfellow too wild! No pretence too flimsy!
Thank God for the protection of a worthy constabulary.

From the secret diary of Mary Watson

14TH DECEMBER 1879

Bob's gone fishing. To give us both time to think, he says. And thinking is all that I've been doing. With a dollop of worry thrown in for good measure.

My palms itch madly. The most tormented of the two gets the attention of fingernails. I've scratched so much the skin looks like I've been dragged behind a wagon. What's their problem? Hanging on the ends of my arms like two malcontents, complaining that they can't catch everything that's been thrown at them since that fateful afternoon in Brisbane. If I've coped, why haven't they?

Haven't you heard the one about itchy palms meaning money soon to come? I tell them, but they refuse to answer. Just glare at me like two handfuls of scarlet fever.

I hear the footfalls of horses first. Shortly afterwards, Fitzgerald's posse gallops out of a shimmering steam-pot to the south.

From the boarding-house verandah's wicker chair, I watch the native troopers dismount. First their legs, iron-windmill thin, in tight black trousers. Then their torsos in dusty green shirts. The horses' pelts shine like polished timber as they're led to the trough where they bend their heads in unison. A dozen hinged and bristly coconut halves open and close, scooping water.

It's barely past noon. Two black cockatoos shriek in the melaleuca, ripping out beak-sized bandages of bark. Butter's melting in the icebox. No one's got rid of the cat that crawled under the boarding house and died; the aroma of maggoty flesh rises up in sick, sweet waves.

Through the shimmer of heat, I see Fitzgerald climb onto a box that's materialised from nowhere. He's readying himself to address a handful of wilting spectators on the subject of his latest foray into cannibal country. He takes off his hat to reveal a tideline of dirt.

'We've accounted for the Merkins responsible for the wounded digger on the Deighton. Sadly, at that same camp we found further evidence of outrage.'

His dentures seem to be holding today. Only a small gap between gum and prosthetic betrays him when he attempts clipped consonants. He reaches into a reed-woven dillybag and pulls out first a length of blonde hair, then a pair of lady's cotton drawers. He acknowledges the rising tide of gasps with a few serious nods. Adjusts his teeth with a hand on his cheek.

'We caught one of the young girls of the tribe. After questioning, she confessed that this hair and these undergarments belong to the lady of the missing family shipwrecked near Cape Melville last month. You need only imagine what those poor wretches went through at the hands of such savages. Needless to say, we'll leave no stone unturned.'

Another waft of dead cat reaches my nose. It goes well with Fitzgerald's speech. Questioning, I know, is a euphemism for torture. The natives would confess to anything if it meant a shorter gruelling. The leafy branch in my hand picks up its fly-swishing pace. The wicker chair squeaks in response. My palms throb.

The crowd is mesmerised. I can tell by the vigorous head-jerking that Fitzgerald's words, plus the heat, have softened the arithmetic in their heads. There were four Europeans in that family shipwrecked at Cape Melville: a husband, wife and two sons. Yet Fitzgerald will come back in a week or so with a report of two dozen blacks killed in response and no one will think to question it.

'Inspector.'

I catch up with Fitzgerald half an hour later, outside the Commercial Hotel. It's too early for drinkers. The limp rugs of a few stray dogs drape over the wooden boards. An old Chinaman with a hunchback and broken sandals sweeps the doorway with a moulting broom. Fitzgerald's talking to the water police magistrate, Bartley Fahey. At a guess, I'd say acquiring sanction for his next punitive expedition into the bush.

Fahey has a moustache in the American style so popular in the cities. It sticks out horizontally either side of his upper lip like a bundle of kindling. He's dressed in soft serge trousers, vicuna vest, calf-leather leggings and a camel-coloured linen hat. He apparently never sweats. Is never caught in a downpour. Never attracts splashes of mud ... moral or otherwise.

I wish they'd hurry up. I want to ask Fitzgerald if he knows when Captain Roberts will next be in Cooktown. Through some bizarre principle I can't understand, the inspector's apathy attracts information. He seems to hear a lot about what white-skinned citizens are up to and when and where, but he neither cares nor bothers to put the information to any useful purpose.

He turns his head in my direction. 'Young Mary.'

He hasn't had a chance to clean up yet. There are dark stains that look like old blood on his britches. A long purple scratch down one cheek. He's rubbed the skin at the brim line of his hat, but it hasn't improved matters. The lines across his forehead are filled with a murky slurry.

'Miss Oxnam.' Bartley Fahey nods in my direction perfunctorily, as befits his estimation of my position: equidistant between lady and prostitute. Then proceeds to ignore me while he has his final words with Fitzgerald.

'So, Harvey, don't forget we're expecting you and Clara for the boating picnic on New Year's Eve.'

'No, indeed.' Fitzgerald straightens his hair. Dusts off his dirty trousers. 'And about the blacks, sir?'

'Dreadful business.' Fahey looks into the middle distance, then back at Fitzgerald. 'But don't overdo things.'

His voice is weighted with distaste for the good inspector's professional misconduct in the past: flogging an elderly black woman with a stockwhip at the Burdekin River crossing, for instance, for no reason other than that she didn't move fast enough out of his way.

'Wonderful fellow,' Fitzgerald says as Fahey strides away in the rippling sun. 'He understands the frontier problem so well, and yet manages to keep himself above it all somehow.'

'I imagine living on the Hill helps,' I say tonelessly. 'Inspector, I need to ask you something.'

'Let me guess. About Watson and that mess twelve months ago?'

The bush telegraph is working overtime. How long has Fitzgerald been back in town? An hour?

I trot out my old, tired defence. 'He says it wasn't him, but another fisherman from Barrow Point.'

'Well, he would, wouldn't he?' Fitzgerald smiles with fatherly concern. 'How could he hope to snare a decent girl otherwise?'

He lifts a hand to the driver of a bullock team as it passes. I step back to avoid the worst of the mud the hoofs throw up. The wagon is only carrying half a load: a modest supply of food, drink and ammunition; and probably a small sack of mail for the few foolhardy diggers left scratching for gold on the Palmer. It sounds like there's a mouse under each pressure point of the tie-ropes — every time the wagon hits a depression in the road, there's a corresponding squeak.

Fitzgerald's in the mood for reminiscing. 'You know, back in the rush, four times as many teams went out to the fields. Charlotte Street was just one long coming and going.'

'We must all accept change, Inspector. Better still if we leap before we're pushed.'

His eyes, overbright in his dirty face, give the impression he's thinking carefully on the matter. But it seems he's just trying to remember what we were talking about before.

'Watson just wants to impress you, that's all. It's every man's right to try, and every woman's prerogative to pass judgement.'

'I'm flattered, Inspector, but hardly illuminated. It's vexing not to know what one's prospective husband is capable of.'

'Men are capable of anything, particularly away from the public eye.'

I look carefully at his face, and he looks back, guileless, saddened by the fatal flaw afflicting all males. Except him.

'And keep in mind,' he adds, 'with the blacks, it's not killing. More like self-defence, or bad luck. That should set your mind at rest.'

'Well, I can't say it does.'

Through the trees, just past the shoreline, terns drop like miniature folded umbrellas on a patch of baitfish. The breeze has the bite of hot, white teeth in it. I hear a snuffling rustle and look up to where a puff of air harries the curtain of an open window.

'Look at it this way,' Fitzgerald says. 'If she'd made it back to her tribe, they would have killed her themselves. The smell of civilisation was on her, you see.' He blinks. Even his eyelids are dirty. 'To tell the truth, most men in Cooktown are partial to a cup of black coffee every now and then. Even those upstairs on the Hill. They're usually just a little more discreet about it.'

'Is that a confession, Inspector?'

He shakes his head. 'Haven't the stomach for it myself. Now, a nice cup of white tea ...'

When I just stare at him, he has enough good grace to look abashed.

'On an entirely different note,' I say, 'the owner of *Blackbird*, Captain Roberts, has left something valuable in French Charley's. I picked it up under one of the tables. Would you know when he's next due in port? I should like to return it to him in person.'

'I could take it for you.'

'I'm sure. But you're so busy. Didn't I read in the *Herald* about some illegal Kanakas escaping from the *Stanley* when she was wrecked in that cyclone? And what about that dreadful business with Nicole, Charley's girl? I daresay you'll be applying some intense policework to the murder investigation.'

My sarcasm passes over his head and floats gently out to sea. He straightens his shoulders, managerially.

'All I need, really. Women of the night going off with the wrong man. Blacks on the rampage. And as if that isn't enough, ten Tanna Island Kanakas on the loose. Though I suspect by now they've all succumbed to the fever. Or snakebite. Or the Myalls.'

My attention hooks on the only interesting piece of information in his litany of complaint. 'Do you know who killed Nicole?'

He taps his nose conspiratorially. 'Not quite yet.'

'Sub-Inspector Brooke must have thoroughly briefed you, then?'

I do my best to sound impressed, even a little dazed, at how the wheels of justice can turn so swiftly. But he shakes his head, unwilling to give Jocelyn Brooke any credit.

'The bare bones only,' he says. 'No, it wasn't Brooke's detective work, but evidence found on the body. Don't press me for further information, young Mary. It's an ongoing police investigation and therefore hush-hush. Let's just say we're pursuing a strong lead.'

As though either of them could catch up with a strong lead even if it dawdled. If he'd just tell me what evidence they have, I could probably figure it out myself in my spare time. Distractedly, I push the hair back from my sweaty forehead.

'What's the matter with your hand?' he asks.

'Just a rash.' I close the angry palm and look up at him expectantly. He seems slow in his responses and a little unsteady on his feet. I wonder if he doesn't have a touch of sun fever. 'Captain Roberts, Inspector?'

'Oh, yes. *Blackbird*'s in Townsville for repainting. I don't think he'll be putting out until well into the new year. But I imagine he could enlist some other vessel passing through to pick up the missing item.'

'Yes, I expect so,' I say lightly. But it's not what I wanted to hear.

I know better than to send a telegram to Roberts. He made it clear that would be only for emergencies. But even so ... well into the new year! By then Bob will have almost certainly asked me to marry him. I need a lucky card, and I need it now. If Roberts decides on someone else for his signaller after I've said yes to Bob, I could finish my life as a sea-slug fisherman's wife, stuck on a vile little island with no prospects at all. And no way to move on.

But ... I do have a chance. I've told Roberts I can do it. He's all but said he'll trust me with the job. All *but* said ...

I need solid confirmation. And soon.

My palms are raging again. Nothing to do but scratch.

15

There comes a time in any girl's life
when she needs a woman-to-woman talk.

From the secret diary of Mary Watson

16TH DECEMBER 1879

It's nine at night. I'm not lying in wait for Laura; I've just slipped out the back door on my break to get some fresh air. I'm standing in the shadows when I see her tottering back into the light, having visited the privy. On the spur of the moment, I decide it's as good a time as any to ask her about Bob. She's as bright as a Christmas decoration, humming some carol to herself. She doesn't see me in my brown dress, lost in the garish colour of her own world. I wait until she reaches the halo of kerosene light near the door, then reach out for the sleeve on her low-cut red blouse. She jumps.

'Jesus Christ in a yak cart! Why yer sneakin' round like a murderer?' She pulls away.

I wrinkle my nose a little at her acrid perfume. 'I want to talk, Laura.'

'Well, I don't wanna talk, Mary Oxnam.'

She straightens herself. Readjusts her bosom. She wears a pretty pink ribbon around her neck; rouge, like two fat coins, painted on her cheeks. Her hair curls fetchingly around the contours of her face. A pretty face, I must admit. The same shape as mine, but finer-boned, so that the overall effect is one of fragile strength rather than belligerence. I can see why Bob would be drawn to her.

'Be careful out here in the dark,' I say. 'Take someone with you when you go to the privy. You don't want to end up like Nicole.'

'What kinda bastard …' Her painted eyes spring a leak. 'I'm gunna blubber now and muck up me face.'

I offer her my handkerchief.

'She didn' do nuthin' to nobody, that girl. Sweet as the day is long.' She blows her nose noisily, then tries to hand the handkerchief back.

'Keep it.'

She nods once, gives a rough sniff, and pokes the crumpled material between her breasts. Then she remembers who she's talking to. 'What d'ya want from me, Mary Oxnam?'

'I want to ask you about Bob Watson.'

Fruit bats start up an ear-scraping click-screech in the dark trees above us.

'I ain't see'd him fer a year.'

'Yes, I know. Charley told me. But it's what happened when you did see him that interests me.'

She brings a finger up to her painted lips, taps the small indentation under her nose. 'Ya wanna know if he'll rough ya up, do ya? Well, what goes on between the sheets is between me client and me. Charley says not to tell or half the hoi polloi from up the Hill would be a laughin' stock.'

'This is different. Bob and I might be getting married.'

Inside, someone plays a piano accordion. The sound wheezes in and out. A man laughs, huge as the moon. The high tinkle of broken glass.

She smoothes down her hair, touches the ribbon around her neck. 'I can see yer stuck, ya silly bitch. In one way I feel sorry for ya, and in another I wish it was me in ycr place. Go on, piss yerself. It's a big joke, ain't it? Me and Bob. But he told me he loved me. Not many of 'em say that.'

'I daresay they don't.'

Now there's singing, drunken and off pitch, picking up the rough, pleated squeeze of the music. She searches for the slightest hint of a smirk on my face, then relaxes, seemingly satisfied it's not there.

'I guess he didn't mean it, though,' she continues. 'He didn't come back, did he? He woulda come back, wouldn't he? If it were true what he said?'

'Yes.'

'They're bastards, ain't they, men? Or don't ya know that yet, Mary Oxnam?'

'Some of them are,' I say, thinking about Papa.

She shrugs, and the frills at her shoulders jiggle. 'You think you're all grown up, don'cha? But yer not. You don't understand why I'd let meself get hurt like that. When yer pa is handy with the switch, ya just get used to it.'

I can't let this pass. 'Why wouldn't you want to get your own back now you're older? Use the switch yourself?'

'That's what you'd do, ain't it?' Her eyes narrow. 'The difference twixt you and me is, I'm a proper woman. Nice and soft like.'

'Like what, Laura? A punching bag?' I can feel blood's slow pump in my head. This conversation is getting a bit too close for comfort.

The roll of her eyes is pitying. 'Ya gotta do what they want. The sooner ya get that idea in yer plain little head, the better.'

There's a long glance from my hair down to my boots, but she's not quite as caustic about the task as Nicole was. There's something else playing around her mouth. Not envy, surely?

'I gotta get on,' she says. 'Don't ya worry 'bout Bob. That's what us workin' girls is for — to get the rough stuff outta their system. I daresay he'll be different with you. You being untouched — like. A wife takes over where a mother leaves off. And a man wouldn't beat his old ma, now would he? If you're a good wife, you'll be all right.'

I don't mean to speak my next thought out loud, but the itching of my palms distracts me into mumbling, 'What if I'm not a good wife?'

There's a rustle in the bushes, probably a rat. We both move a little closer to the light near the open door.

She snorts, then shakes her head. 'Well then, ya silly cow, you'll deserve whatever comes to ya. I can't stay here yabbin' all night, I gotta go to work. I ain't one of them bleedin' telephonists makin' me money standin' up.'

The next day I'm almost past the butcher's on my morning walk when I see Heccy. He's headed for French Charley's, trotting briskly with a crate of empty bottles. He glances at me, and I know by the look on his face that there's been another murder.

'Wait up, Heccy! Who is it? Not Laura?'

A hot wind tousles his red hair. His eyes are watery. Over his shoulder, the bay seethes with miniature white cockscombs.

'M-M-Marjorie,' he says.

Marjorie? I try to bring her face to mind. A chatty girl. Plump, agreeable. She had a blackened tooth in front that she touched up with Chinese white paint. She'd fan it dry, then spend the evening in a difficult juggling act: keeping her moist top lip in the snarl position away from it without appearing as though she would bite any man who came near her. She couldn't have been more than seventeen.

'She's been d-dead a week. They only j-just found her, in some reeds in the m-m-mangroves.'

'A week! Didn't Charley notice she was missing?'

'He thought she'd gone with one of the m-miners.'

That would make sense. Occasionally, for a price, Charley would allow a digger to take one of the girls to a prospectors' camp for a week. Provided she was returned in one piece.

'I suppose you're happy to hear it, are you?' I ask. 'One less sinner.'

A Chinaman carrying two buckets of coal on either side of a long pole shuffles his hips side to side as he passes. His conical hat, held on by a string around his neck, has been blown off his head by the wind. It sits on his back like a pointed hunch.

'It's not m-my fault she was a whore.' Heccy's face is pale, his freckles stark in the sun. 'It's the L-Lord having the last word.'

I look down at his hands holding the crate. Big, powerful hands he hasn't yet grown into. Charley's told me something of his background. How he comes from a strict Methodist family. How his mother and father were killed in a house fire on the property they were caretaking at Ingham and, orphaned, Heccy's search for work brought him to Cooktown. French Charley's was the only employment on offer. I wonder how he copes with the constant assault on his morals, night in, night out. I remember the night he stopped me in the alley. How he seemed so much more powerful; the cabbage-tree hat pulled low over his face, the long coat. The remarkable absence of his stammer.

'You wouldn't have hurt those girls, would you, Heccy?'

'M-me? No!' His shock seems genuine enough.

'Was Marjorie strangled like Nicole?'

He nods, tightly. 'With that r-ribbon round her n-neck.'

My focus sharpens. All of Charley's girls wear satin ribbons in different colours.

'Is that what Nicole was strangled with too? Her ribbon?'

He nods again.

Carefully now. 'How would you know a thing like that?'

'Sub-Inspector B-Brooke's telling the story all over t-town.' He mumbles something else, which I can't hear clearly.

A shadow falls over us. It's a relief to have the sun gone. But there's a grey, sinewy centre in the cloud overhead; a muscle of rain cramping, getting ready to release its load.

'Where's Fitzgerald?' I ask. 'Does he know that Brooke is sabotaging the investigation?'

Heccy shifts the weight of the crate from one arm to the other. The bottles clatter and ping. 'He's g-gone bush again. After the b-b-blacks that killed that family.'

16

An accident by any other name would smell as fishy.

From the secret diary of Mary Watson

19TH DECEMBER 1879

The afternoon sun boils a seafood stench off Ah Ping's fish stall on the wharf. I still come here occasionally. It seems less suspicious than an abrupt absence after my regular assignations with Dirty White Neckerchief. Today, a man in stained tan trousers held up by a frayed leather belt approaches me.

'Miss Oxnam?'

I turn briefly. The sun's in my face and I can't make out his features clearly. Just a dark, man-shaped shadow cut out of feverish sky.

'Yes,' I say. 'Would you excuse me just one minute?' I turn back to the Chinaman in his blue pyjamas and skullcap. The air from the stall is weighted with stagnant water, grease and incense. 'How much, Ah Ping? And don't say a shilling. I won't pay it for a couple of snapper.' I point at the glistening silver pile in his basket, each fish with pink-red gills like the underside of poisonous mushrooms.

'I sell for very good price, missy. One shilling, two fish.' His head is shaved in front, his face a shiny, blank slate.

'I'll catch my own for a shilling,' I say. 'Five pence, two fish.'

He shakes his head. The waist-long queue of hair at his back twitches like a horse's tail swatting a fly.

'Keep them then.'

I begin to turn away and he relents, his voice burdened with a century's sorrow.

'All right, missy. Five pence, two fish.'

I hand over the money. He drops the snapper into my basket. I turn slightly to give the man my full attention. Step back from Ah Ping's stall to put the sun behind him. I want a clear look at his face. It's then I notice the lugger tied up behind Ah Ping and his baskets, not ten feet away. Actually there are two luggers — there's another twenty yards down the pier. I hadn't noticed either, too concerned with my bartering. I look down to the man's stained pants again and make the connection.

'Is one of those Bob's? Has something happened?'

His brown eyes smile as he takes off his battered canvas hat. He looks to be around Bob's age, perhaps younger. It's hard to tell — sea spray has eroded the cliffs of his face. He's certainly a good deal taller than Bob. And so thin his trousers would fall off if not for the extra holes in the belt, raggedly fashioned, by the look, with a bait knife.

'Porter Green,' he says and holds my eyes for a minute. 'I work for Bob and Percy Fuller over on the Lizard.'

He holds out a hand as beaten up as his hat. The pinky and ring fingers are missing. I shake it briefly. The sensation is odd — like palming a cocked gun made of skin and muscle.

A coolie pushing a barrow full of melons almost runs into us. 'Look out! Sorry, sorry.'

'You look out,' Mr Green snarls. 'Or I'll stamp your backside with my boot.'

The 'sorries' continue all the way down the dock, the hat bent so low over the barrow it's in danger of overbalancing the body beneath it. In few words, Mr Green informs me that the nearer lugger is Bob's *Isabella*. And that Bob's had a small accident.

'Is he all right?' I ask.

'A bit knocked about. A few days' rest will set him well. He's not bad enough for the hospital. We took him to John Adam's dispensary.'

'What happened?'

Porter Green's long, thin face shows a faint web of wrinkles when the light hits it a certain way. A kind face, actually. He waits, as though I could answer my own question if only I wanted to. Something's not quite right here. The silence stretches. The sun's out again, and reflections off the water dance up through the beams at our feet.

'It's a long story,' he says finally. '*Petrel* couldn't go out because she split her mast. That's Percy Fuller's boat. Bob's partner.' He gestures over his shoulder to the lugger furthest away from us. 'That's why she's in Cooktown, you see? I limped her over from the Lizard. Had to brace the mast with timber and rope. The carpenters from Victoria Stores have been shaping a new mast all morning.'

Porter Green reminds me a little of Riley Robinson: never taking the short cut in conversation if there happens to be a more scenic route.

'I see. About Bob's accident?'

'Percy was on *Isabella* with Bob when it happened. I'll let Bob tell the story.' He lifts his hat. 'Must get aboard and hurry the work along. I want to leave this afternoon. I'll take *Petrel* back to the Lizard when the new mast's up. Percy has errands in town. He and Bob can come home on *Isabella* when they're ready.'

I look down the dock to *Petrel*. It's not a particularly impressive sight. The mast is out, and it looks unbalanced compared to *Isabella*, right in front of me. Two Chinamen, in the usual outfit of pale blue drawstring trousers and buttoned tops, lean with their backs to me on the port rail. They're waiting for something. The one on the left holds a bandaged foot out in front of him, and a walking stick. He puts one hand on the rail and leans heavily on it.

My eyes widen. I've seen that hand before. It's unmistakable, even at a distance. Ugly as a chicken's foot, with two long curved nails curled around the railing and three others broken off. It's the hand I saw on the wanted poster. The hand of the runaway Chinaman. The one Percy said he hadn't found.

My head buzzes with heat and confusion. What does it mean?

'Mr Green, just before you go. Those two Chinamen ... on *Petrel* ...?'

He turns, and squints. A sudden hot gust of wind pushes my skirt against my legs.

'New coolies to work on the Lizard. I'm taking them back with me. Bob signed off the old ones a while back, but we can't manage on our own. There's the farm needs tending for our fresh vegetables, and someone to cook and clean up at the house.' He shakes his head. 'I have to wonder where Percy's head is, to come up with a crippled John Pigtail. I suppose it's not up to the hired help to ask questions.'

I close my eyes briefly and try to think it through. Then open them again on what might be an important point.

'Who chose the other Chinaman?'

'Bob, for better or worse.' He rubs his chin. 'He's a bit long in the tooth, but he seems wiry enough.'

I glance back to the second coolie. There seems nothing remarkable about him. I wonder if I'm not giving in to paranoia, speculating that he too might be somehow sanctioned by Percy, and, by extension, Samuel Roberts.

'Are you on a contract too then, Mr Green?'

He nods. 'I'll be signed off eventually, just like the black boys, the Kanakas and the Chows.'

'I'm sure Bob and Mr Fuller regard you as a member of the team,' I say. And then, because I want to know if he knows what the fugitive Chinaman's done. 'You don't get to Cooktown much, I guess?'

He shakes his head. 'Hardly ever. There could be a war on and I'd have to wait till someone came back to the Lizard to tell me about it.'

So he's unlikely to have heard about the murdered shopkeeper, to have seen the wanted poster.

'Mr Fuller's Chinaman,' I say casually, 'what happened to his foot?'

'Lost some toes a few days ago. I don't know the details. He can hobble, I suppose. But with Chows a dime a dozen ...'

'Yes, indeed.'

I chew the inside of my cheek. If the Chinaman mends quickly ... Percy's made his preference plain about who should handle the signals from Lizard Island. A headache rumbles behind my eyes.

Porter Green is clearly oblivious to the real business to be done on the island. Interrogating him won't get me anywhere.

'Nice to make your acquaintance, Mr Green,' I say. 'I must get on and see Bob.'

'Please call me Porter, Miss Oxnam. And I don't think it's the last time we'll meet.'

'Perhaps not,' I say, with a smile. 'Time will tell. And it's Mary.'

'Mary, then.'

His smile is surprisingly soft: a creature breaking out of a cocoon, the wings of innocence still wet. Oh, for some of that innocence right now! A simple world of sea and slugs and sun, instead of all this complication.

Petrel seems to bob more vigorously in the water as he approaches, as though recognising him and wagging its tail. He leaps the yard-wide gap onto the deck. Brown arms. Straight back, as though a rod is attached to his spine. The two Chinamen stand a little straighter when he's aboard. Their wait in the marinating sun is over. Green mutters instructions and they turn to. Ugly Hands moves with alacrity despite his injured foot and walking stick. He's using the cover of his large hat well: it's pulled low over his eyes so that no one on the dock can get a decent look at his face. Doubtless he knows it's in his best interests to get out of Cooktown as soon as possible.

I put the fish into the icebox at the boarding house, wash my hands, then make my way to John Adam's pharmacy. I need time to think, but, as usual, don't have it.

The hollow tink of a rusty, crumpled bell above the door announces my entrance. John Adam stands erect behind the counter, a picture of eloquence in white: beard, pith helmet and suit. He looks ready to be presented to the Viceroy of Delhi, and I tell him so.

He responds with a salute of Empiric proportions and tells me he's off for a rehearsal of the Harbourmaster's Parade next

Sunday. I'd seen the crowd gathering at the end of Charlotte Street, including the chubby little mayor, melting in his robes. This is the other side of Cooktown, held apart from debauchery and squalor; province of the three-decker businessmen from the Hill, so-called because they're allowed three votes apiece in local elections.

'How's the patient?' I ask.

'Irritable,' Adam says. 'He wants to get out of bed. Truth is, he probably can — this afternoon. I've organised a room for him at the Sea Wah Hotel. He should rest up for a day or two. He'll need Allcock Plasters for back pain. A blood cleanser for his scrapes. Probably some quinine wine, as he seems a little low in spirits. Oh, and some clean bandages and a walking stick for that leg. I've got the essentials together.' He produces a bulging crate from under the counter. 'Unfortunately, Bob didn't have any money on him when he came in.' He grins like the slot in a piggy bank.

I sigh and open my purse. After the money's safely stored in the till, Adam becomes more expansive.

'Though normally I'm immune to idle talk, something compelling has reached my ears, Miss Oxnam.'

I watch a leech slide damply up the glass inside the big jar on the counter. A dozen others on the bottom knot and unknot, oozing over each other in a nauseating pile.

'This idle talk, is it compelling in substance? Or in the desire to pass it on, Mr Adam?'

He brushes his forehead and eyes with his hand. 'This something concerns you, Miss Oxnam.'

'Really? I would have thought myself far too ordinary to attract gossip.'

'Well, I'll rephrase. Not you in particular. Rather, any white woman who marries Bob Watson.'

'I see. Well, then. You'd better inform me.'

He licks his lips. 'As you must know by now, the wild blacks go over to the Lizard regularly in their canoes. But why, Miss Oxnam? Perhaps ... because Bob was involved with one of their own kind a year ago.'

'I'm tired of this story and variants thereof. Unless you have something of vital interest to add to it. What's done is done.'

'Maybe it is done, if you believe Watson's side of the affair.' He looks around as though Bob might have lurched from his sickbed to listen at the door, then beckons me with a chapped finger.

I move a little nearer. Up close, his teeth are yellow. There's no mistaking the smell of opium-laced cough mixture on his breath.

'Talk is, Watson disposed of her.' He puts a hand to his neck, performs a mock strangling. 'And, if you marry him, you'll be the one to pay the price. Those blacks are her tribe. They want revenge. What better revenge than to kill a European woman?'

A fly crawls slowly across the counter. Adam picks up a swatter and flattens it. We both stare at the mess.

I pull back so I don't have to breathe in his acrid-cherry exhalations. I'm nonplussed. The whole breathless revelation has the whiff of a play being badly acted out. I am, however, interested in who put him up to it.

'I'm surprised I haven't heard this before, Mr Adam. It makes me think that someone is trying to deliver the information to me directly. But who, I wonder? And why have they, and you, seen fit at this particular moment to show an interest in my long-term health?'

The mouth thins. The brow lowers, chastisingly. 'You shouldn't be so dispirited about human nature, Miss Oxnam. There are some who, through simple Christian charity, would want to do everything in their power to avoid a tragedy.'

'I'm sure you're right.' My purse is still in my hand, and I touch the clasp lightly. His eyes follow my fingers. 'Nevertheless, I would be greatly indebted to know who gave you this timely warning. I should like to thank them personally for their care.'

I open the clasp and extract my last pound note. Well, technically, Charley's pound note. But I'm sure he wouldn't mind donating it to Bob's rehabilitation fund.

I look to the shelf behind Adam, then hold out my hands, palms up. 'I have a nervous itch. Perhaps some cream?'

He clucks his tongue. 'Oh, my word, yes. And you must wear gloves to bed at night to prevent doing further damage to yourself.' He turns and pulls a tube of ointment from the shelf. 'That will be nine shillings.'

I place the pound on the counter. He reaches to take it. I lightly place my finger over one corner.

'Are you sure you can't remember, Mr Adam, who gave you the information regarding my dangerous situation?'

He licks his lips. Bears down on the counter with both hands. Finally the name squirms out, triumphant, from under a rock of amnesia.

'I believe it might have been Percy Fuller. Watson's partner. I hear so much, you see. And I'm not good with names and faces.' He raps the side of his helmet with his knuckles, as though checking the level of brain fluid therein.

I smile and lift my hand. 'The life of a shopkeeper is hectic, isn't it?'

'Pharmacist, Miss Oxnam.' The smile's still locked in place. He takes the note delicately.

'Of course. Pharmacist. Keep the change, won't you? Now, I must go and see Bob.'

17

Killer whales always go for the tongue.

From the secret diary of Mary Watson

I hear the medicinal balls first. Bob's hidden behind boxes of bandages and a crate of Madame Kurtz's Reliable Female Pills, lying low on a cot. His leg lies in a wooden splint held up by a canvas loop tied to a ceiling beam. The good side of his face is grazed plum-red from temple to cheekbone. The scowl suggests his mood's similarly raw. I doubt the quinine wine will help much. The air's dusty with discontent and the smell of cooped-up male.

'I see you've been in a skirmish. Is there a window somewhere I can open?'

Gazing around, I find only a small square hole, just large enough to let the flies and mosquitos in. It looks out onto a tiny patch of simmering yard.

'Did Porter tell ye? It happened on *Isabella*.'

I set my crate of medicines down.

'What's all that?' He attempts to sit up straighter and look.

'Supplies for your recuperation.'

The scowl deepens. 'Enough to run a bedlam house. How much did he charge ye?'

I tell him — minus the pound that greased the skids of Adam's tongue.

'I would punch the thieving bastard. I'll fix ye up for it.'

'Porter said you'd tell me about the accident.'

His cheekbone tightens under the scar. The ugly graze on the good side almost balances out his face. The medicinal balls argue in his pocket.

'Ye ever see killer whales attack a humpback?' His eyes pull away from me, falling overboard into his own mind. 'It's the worst thing. Birds shrieking. The ocean churns then boils blood-red. Killers work as a pack: worry at the humpback. It dives. But they chase it down. And when it rises back up to breathe, no matter what way it turns, they're at it again.'

'Why are you telling me this story? Did you get attacked by a killer whale?'

I'm not sure if it's his compulsive tone or the stuffy room, but I feel a sudden wave of dizziness. There's an empty crate in the corner. I drag it to his bedside and sit. Now, we're almost at eye level.

'They go for the tongue. That's all they want. They rip out the tongue and let the rest of the poor beast sink to the ocean floor to die a slow death.'

'How can you stand it in here?' I pull at my collar. 'This heat is smothering.'

He shifts his weight a little. Winces. Moves his sore leg with two hands.

'We saw the attack out on the reef. It happened just feet from *Isabella*. A five-ton lugger can capsize or end up with a hole in its hull if a whale throws itself sideways.'

I look through the small cut-out in the wall. There's a threadbare goat tied to a post in the yard. It chews a mouthful of dead grass, then wails piteously, the sound dragged over the bumpy washboard in its throat.

'Fuller shoved the tiller to starboard. The deck bucked under me. I would have fallen overboard and into one of those killers' mouths if it wasn't for the deck rope that caught around my ankle.'

'It sounds as though Mr Fuller thought quickly,' I say.

'He didn't have to yank the tiller so hard.'

'Perhaps he panicked. I certainly would have.'

'Fuller never panics.'

He doesn't have time to elaborate before another voice is behind me in the room.

'I thought I felt my ears burning.'

I put my hand on the crate to swivel around. As though my palms didn't hurt enough already, the movement pushes a splinter sideways into the plump pad of skin under my thumb. I look at its sting for a second: a miniature log in a hectic-pink sea. Another corrugated bleat from the goat. Another turn on the hawser of tension already in the room.

'Mary Oxnam, meet Percy Fuller, my partner.'

'Miss Oxnam.' Percy takes off his hat. Plays the part of a complete stranger with consummate ease.

Now, if only I can do so well.

I offer my undamaged hand. 'Mr Fuller,' I say, trying to ignore my rollicking heart. 'Bob tells me your quick action saved *Isabella*.'

Today he's dressed casually in biscuit-brown trousers and a green shirt. It picks up the green in his eyes. When he bows his head forward I see a cowlick sending the otherwise neat part into a frenzy.

One eyebrow twitches. 'Please, call me Percy. And that wasn't what he said at the time. In fact, the conversation doesn't bear repeating. Not in front of a lady.' That ghost of a smile I'm so often haunted by lifts the right side of his mouth.

He pulls out his pipe and a plug. Begins the ritual of teasing out the tobacco. The smell of fruity splinters and old moss fills the confined space.

'Would you mind not?' I ask. 'I feel I can't breathe in here.'

He shrugs. That phantom smile again. His green eyes are a hailstorm hovering over me. He transfers his attention to Bob. 'I've come to break you out, Watson. Take you to the Sea Wah. You can rest up, perhaps hobble down to the gambling table tonight. Risk all your marital savings on the roll of the dice, eh? Cook up some more smelly books with Will Hartley.'

'Shut yer mouth or I'll shut it for ye.'

My eyes are on Bob's face, curious both at Percy's words and Bob's violent reaction to them.

Percy turns his attention to me. 'Did your fiancé tell you, Miss Oxnam? About his confusion over slug types? You see, there is a sliding scale of value in different slugs that we collect. Red pricklys are the most prized and fetch the most money. Watson and our friendly local merchant Will Hartley have been playing hide the lolly fish — a lesser variety — with Chinese epicures in Shanghai. Trouble is, if you boil up lolly fish in a copper boiler so that they look like red pricklys and sell them as such, you run the risk of killing off the epicures with verdigris, eh, Watson?'

'Is that true, Bob?' I ask.

'I said shut yer fecking mouth!'

'Hearty words for a man on his back.' Percy's tone is blithely indifferent.

I search for something to say that will break the dangerous mood in the room.

'I'll take Bob to the Sea Wah. I have to see Bill Smith at the Steam Packet next door, anyway.'

I bank on Smith's name distracting Bob from Percy's taunting. Bill Smith of the Steam Packet Hotel is one of the players in Charley and Bob's game of pass the small parcel in the South Pacific.

'What business could ye have there?' Bob turns a suspicious eye on me. The medicinal balls clank like the toll of an angry bell.

I touch my waist lightly, feel the outline under my sash of the envelope Charley gave me last night; the first of the notes Captain Roberts said it was all right to deliver for my crooked boss.

'Something fell out of his pocket in one of the rooms,' I say, clear-eyed. 'I'm just returning it.'

It's an alibi the bawdy house is always useful for, considering every man in town ends up upstairs at French Charley's at least once a week, sans trousers and shirt.

Percy and I stand on Adam's verandah, waiting for Bob to get dressed. I look at my watch: ten to three. At three, Adam will put up his closed sign, pick up his parade sceptre and, feeding his fantasies of Bwanahood, stride down to the gathering crowd at the end of Charlotte Street.

Percy could be a wild cat from the same imaginary jungle. He leans on the verandah rail, facing me. I even think I see a tail in his eyes, swishing back and forth, deadly, playful. Then I realise it's only shadows cast by the sunlight shining through cracks in the tin above our heads. His hair, which was dark blond indoors, is now peppered with gold.

'Permission to smoke now, Miss Oxnam?' he drawls, and reaches into his pocket to bring out the pipe and tobacco.

'I wouldn't presume to tell you what to do. And if I call you Percy, you must call me Mary.'

I speak at a conversational volume for the benefit of passers-by. Customers come and go through the pharmacy door, each counted by the coin-click of the bell above. When the coast is temporarily clear, I lean towards him and lower my voice for a more private interaction.

'I thought you couldn't find your runaway Chinaman. What do you mean by sending him to the Lizard?' I hadn't intended to sound viperous, but there's no mistaking the hiss in the words.

His eyes narrow. The crow's-feet splay on the skin around them. 'My, aren't we cultivating a sense of our own importance?'

The tightness in my throat won't go away with swallowing. Two young boys in short pants run shouting along Charlotte Street, trailing a blown-up pig's bladder floating on the end of a piece of string. The sun shines through it, illuminating the red veins until it looks like a travelling globe of the world, all the trade routes marked out in crimson rivers. He's right, of course, about my tenuous position. Even now I feel a scratchy noose around my neck. Although that doesn't mean he has the right to kick the box from under me.

But anger will get me nowhere. Instinct's telling me to match his cool tone with my own. Only minutes ago I saw him throw a spark casually into the tinder of Bob's temper, then step back with amused interest to watch him burn. He'll do the same to me, if I let him.

I attempt to sound more reasonable. 'You knew that I'd planned to position myself on the Lizard so I could do the signalling job. Why bribe John Adam to scare me off marrying Bob? How far would you go to keep me away?'

An old woman comes out of the pharmacy. Percy waits until she sways away on the stilts of rheumatism. 'How far would I go? Not so far as your vanity might imagine.'

He inspects his pipe thoughtfully. Then, when he decides the pile of tobacco is stacked just right, puts the stem to the corner of his mouth. A small flare. A pellet-gun's pop as he draws in. He drops his match into the dirt over the railing. His next words seem almost an aside to himself. 'I counted on Adam having a big mouth, but not quite so big.' He rests one leg over the other. Squints slightly through the smoke. Dark stubble covers the field of his chin. 'I don't think it's a good idea you marrying Watson. And I've told you why. But you're a grown woman ...'

This backflip catches me off guard. I look over his shoulder for a few seconds to muster my thoughts.

'Let me get this straight. You've suddenly given up on dissuading me from the signalling job? After you've gone to all the trouble of priming Adam. And right at the point when you've found your Chinaman?'

'A man's entitled to reconsider.'

'Or have his mind changed for him by circumstance. Could it be you didn't know the Chinaman had an injury when you figured out where he was? He can't do the signalling job anyway with his busted foot, can he? How high is that hill on the Lizard? Eleven, twelve hundred feet? A bit much to hop up. And it's a little late to line anyone else up for the job.'

His jaw tightens and I realise I've won. This hand, at least.

'You don't miss a thing, do you? Been down to the docks, I take it.'

I look around once more to make sure no one is listening. 'Why is he still going to the Lizard, then?'

Percy picks at a loose splinter on the railing. 'Something may go wrong. No one is invincible, not even you, Mary Oxnam.'

'And if something does go wrong? Exactly where does your murderous friend come into it?'

He stares at me blandly. 'Ah Leung is very good at cleaning up messes.'

'What does that mean?'

One of Charley's girls, Gloria, sashays up the steps and giggles when she sees Percy. Her strawberry-blonde curls jiggle. She purses her ruby lips.

He dips his hat in mock gallantry. 'Mademoiselle Gloria, if I'm not mistaken.'

She fiddles with the mauve ribbon around her neck and then opens her mouth, torturing the air with her *faux* French accent. 'May wee, Missyer Fuller.'

The flirting irritates me. 'Hurry along and fetch your syphilis medicine, Gloria.'

She fixes me with a glare of disdain. 'For your hinformation, Miss Hoxnam, I hain't got siffless.' She gives me a look there must be a name for in some infectious-diseases dictionary. 'If ya must know, hit's me bunions.'

She disappears inside.

'I wonder if she'll be next.' Percy draws a slow finger across his throat.

'Why would you say that?'

'Jocelyn Brooke's been shooting his mouth off. Apparently Nicole's body had a note left on it. So did Marjorie's. Seemed to imply there'll be more murders to come if Boule doesn't close down the salon.'

So that's Fitzgerald's so-called 'strong lead'. He must have told Charley. And, knowing Charley, he's probably decided he'd rather let his girls die than go voluntarily out of business. But I can't dwell on that now. Bob will be out in a minute.

'Did you deliberately wrench the tiller too hard on *Isabella*?' I ask Percy. 'Did you want Bob to have a convenient accident?'

'He's quite clumsy enough to organise his own demise. He doesn't need any help from me.'

'I wonder,' I say slowly. 'If Bob dies before he marries, your partnership contract probably stipulates you inherit his half of the business. Is that right?'

He draws on his pipe and squints through the smoke. 'I'm not interested in his stinking slugs.'

'No. But you'd be interested in having the island all to yourself, wouldn't you? Are you responsible for that scar on his face?'

Seconds stretch. 'Can't claim that one. One of his Kanakas, a Lifou man, came at him with a tomahawk.' He looks up briefly at the roof, the sinews of his throat visible. 'When you cut the rice ration in half, you have to expect the natives to get tetchy. Still, turnabout's fair play. The Kanaka fell overboard shortly afterwards. Now *that* was a nasty accident. With so many reef sharks about.'

The sky turns darker behind his shoulder, the air dragging over Cooktown like wet wool. My eye is drawn into the glowering distance. Small thorns of white prick the steely ocean.

'Was any of it true? That propaganda you told Adam about the blacks wanting revenge on Bob?'

'I stand by it as a theory. Let's just say you'll have more to worry about on the Lizard than the smooth unfolding of the operation.'

The verandah slats vibrate just a little. Thunder, too low to be heard, but not to be felt. I look into Percy's green eyes. The tail's still swishing, but slower now, like a metronome.

Gloria's back, a paper packet in hand, swinging the pendulum of her hips. At the bottom step, she looks over her shoulder. 'Why don'cha come and visit me sometime, Missyer Fuller?'

'I might just do that.' But he's looking at me when he says it.

Gloria wanders away. Percy pushes off the railing with one hand. He winks at me and I feel small pulses of blood at my temples.

'Merry Christmas, Mary. I hope we both get what we want.'

And then he's gone, leaving only the smell of tobacco, and the rack of my own discipline tightening behind my forehead.

18

*It's not auspicious to stir a cranky Scot
at Christmas time.*

From the secret diary of Mary Watson

Bob uses the stick to half-sway, half-hobble to the Sea Wah. It's only a hundred yards from the pharmacy, but it takes us a good ten minutes. As we arrive, the first fat dollops of rain break open on the ground. Inside is stuffy and dark. Mrs Sea Wah, the Chinese owner's wife, is waiting in the foyer. She hands Bob the key in a dainty swish of brocade gown and oriental perfume.

'You need peace and quiet, Mista Watson?'

'Peace and quiet would be lovely, Mrs Sea Wah,' I answer for him. 'Have you given Mr Watson a room a bit out of the way?'

A butterfly pin in her coiffed hair almost takes flight as she nods. 'Number fourteen.' Each stair's a frayed mountain to climb. Bob won't let me help him.

On the landing, I step ahead of him and open the door. The room's spartan. Single bed. Chest of drawers. A window, closed now against the unpredictable weather. The air inside is stale and wet. Mould spots the walls. Dead flies are scattered on the floor under the sill. The snuff of dust motes makes me sneeze.

'This is a vast improvement on the dispensary,' I say, but his mood hasn't lifted.

I'm just about to leave him to soak in it when he hobbles to the bed, collapses onto it and pulls something from his shirt pocket. It's a wad of cash held together with a clip.

'I've just been paid for the slugs. I'll give ye some money to go back to yer family in Rockhampton. Get away from Cooktown for a while. Tell them about me. If ye come back, well and good. If ye don't, I won't blame ye.'

I ignore his outstretched hand. Neither side of his face seems even remotely approachable.

'If you want to be rid of me, Bob, you need only say so.'

'It's not that.'

'Well, what is it then? You're injured. You need me.'

'I don't need ye.' And then, more gently, 'A man must look after himself.'

I stare for a few seconds at his bandaged leg. 'I'll go and find Percy then, shall I? He can come and minister to you.'

'I don't need anyone!' he says, louder, and pushes the notes towards me.

'My family will try to talk me out of marriage with you.'

'Aye.' He nods, apparently having thought about it and become resigned to the possibility.

'I don't need Papa's permission, Bob. I'm of age.'

'Still, ye must do it.' That stubborn, unyielding glare.

I try to process this new development. If I refuse to go, it will look like I'm hiding something. But what could be the reason Bob wants to send me away? He's found out something about me and/or the operation and he wants to know more? He thinks it will be easier to find out my real intentions if I'm not in Cooktown? Who could give me away? Charley, perhaps? Heccy? Not Percy now, surely? It's apparent his Chinaman is not up to the task of signalling, and time is pressing on all of us …

Bob's still holding his hand out with the money in it. There's no excuse I could come up with that would seem reasonable. And the trip could have its own rewards. The last person I want to see is Papa. But Townsville is a port of call on the way to Rockhampton; the steamer would load coal there. And I definitely need to see Captain Roberts. It's a risk, but if I could locate him in that few hours' stopover, if I could talk to him frankly … I'd know whether or not to marry Bob.

The pound notes in his fist are starting to bend from the force with which he's squeezing them.

'Why are ye just standing there? I've not asked ye to dig yer way to China with a soup spoon.'

I reach for the money. 'All right,' I say, 'I'll go. But not until we've spent Christmas and New Year together. Think of it. A whole decade turning over its new leaf. What a wonderful omen for our … for the future.'

He adjusts his wounded leg, then leans back against the pillow with a grunt. I take the cash without looking down at it to ascertain the amount. The last thing I need him to think is that I'm money hungry. He gazes at me intently now, unsmiling. I tell myself it's just the way light sways through the window that suggests suspicion in his gaze. His next words sound more like a business proposal than a heartfelt entreaty.

'Be clear, I've asked ye to be my wife. I expect an answer when ye get back.'

Townsville

Summer, 1880

19

From the secret diary of Mary Watson

5TH FEBRUARY 1880

The sky's same moody stare. The same abrasive sun, rubbing a hole in the clouds. But the wharves at Townsville are different to Cooktown's. Less mud and more activity. A termites' nest of Chinese scurrying to load or unload cargo and passengers. Out on Ross Creek, a penny ferry pulls a seam tight in the water behind it. A wide flat-bottomed lighter loaded with wool bales is steered by four men with long oars — two slides forward, one slip back — out towards Cleveland Bay.

I've been locked in a waltz with a swaying deck for days. It takes a few minutes to adjust to the stillness of the dock. There's a smell in the air I'm familiar with: the grisly mix of hot tallow, bone and blood. Smoke from a chimney well south of the docks confirms a boiling-down works.

'Are you going into town too, Miss Oxnam, while they take on coal? Would you like to take a stroll along Flinders Street? There's a marvellous milliner here, they tell me. And my word, I do need a new hat.'

A boorish woman built like a bank-front gestures ruefully at what resembles a small marsupial curled up on her head and tied under her neck by its tail. She's battered my ears with her drivel for two days.

'A sunhat might be more appropriate here in the tropics,' I venture.

'Oh yes, but not on a shopping outing, dear. Only for on board.' Her tone suggests I'm lucky she's around to correct me before I make a serious *faux pas* in public. 'I've seen a darling one I'd just die for. And I mean *die*. Just like the ladies are wearing to the races in London. Black crinoline it is, with a band of natty red velvet and a cluster of cerise roses.' She clasps her hands together in an attitude of prayer to the deity of artificial flowers. 'Twenty-seven and six, which is scandalous really, but these days you do have to pay for quality. As I was saying to —'

The entire three-hour stopover could be taken up with her finishing her sentence. 'I'm afraid I'll have to leave you to shop on your own, Mrs Buxton. I must meet someone.'

I'm saved when she gets a whiff of the boiling-down works. 'Oh! What a stench!'

While she digs around in her bag for a handkerchief to hold over her nose, I make my escape.

After questioning a few sweaty dockhands, I learn that Samuel Roberts is in his favourite spot on the upstairs balcony of the Exchange Hotel.

He sees me cross Flinders Street and lifts his hat a fraction of an inch. How did he know I was here? One of his spies must have seen me aboard the steamer, or else disembarking. I did ask his whereabouts on the dock. Had he already gleaned that I was headed south? Was I naïve to imagine, even for a second, that my life is my own any more?

I wave back and, in the process, neglect to see a buggy turn the corner at speed. Just in time, I overbalance backwards in the dirt. I see a rolling horse's eye. A spoked wheel finishes inches from my face as the driver pulls violently on the reins. After some 'sorries' and 'totally my faults' and an admonishing 'you should look where you're going', I'm pulled roughly to my feet by the captain himself. I wonder, dazedly, how he got himself down the stairs of the hotel so fast.

'Are you hurt?' he asks.

'Only my pride.'

I dust off my brown skirt. His bearded figure looms over me, blocking out the sun. In my peripheral vision I see the buggy turn the next corner with considerably less horsepower.

'You have me at a disadvantage now,' I say. Then, even more inanely, 'And doubly, because I've told you so.'

His eyes are charcoal, but the gap in his beard where I guess his mouth to be seems to lift, implying amusement. As if there has ever been a time when I have not been at a disadvantage in conversation with him.

'I'm sorry. I'm babbling. I think I've just had my wits knocked out of me.'

'I doubt it. You're here to talk business, I assume?'

When I nod and straighten the waist of my skirt, he offers his arm to lead me the rest of the way across the road. The muscle beneath the long black sleeve, like the rest of him, is as unyielding as a rifle barrel.

Still babbling: 'You don't seem surprised to see me.'

'No.'

'Is there any time since I've been in Cooktown that you haven't known exactly where I was and what I was doing?'

He thinks about this, searching his mind for the odd lost moment. 'No.'

He gestures up the stairs to the verandah. The view from up there is pleasant, the light breeze refreshing, but he steers me by the elbow to a door. 'Come inside. I have a drawing room out the back.'

He leads me into a dark room with a lamp blazing on a desk in the corner. Deep-red velvet curtains cover the windows. Black leather smoking chairs circle like wagons around a small occasional table. He walks over to a makeshift bar in the corner.

'This is very plush,' I observe, unsure whether to sit or stand.

'I rent it for two shillings a week. It's private. And no one disturbs me. Would you like a drink?'

'No, thank you.'

'Sure? It might put some colour back into your cheeks.'

'All right, then.'

I watch him pour whisky into two glasses and add lumps of ice from a bucket. He looks up and catches me examining my hand.

'Only a graze,' I say, and hold my hand out, palm up, to prove it.

He glances at the injury, hands me my drink, and gives his prognosis. 'You'll live. A bit of salve and a pair of tweezers for the tiny stones. What's the underlying rash?'

'I can't seem to get rid of it. Perhaps it's a Cornish prognostication. They've a superstition to fit every ailment.'

'Perhaps it means the owner of the hand is about to pick up more than she can carry,' he ventures dryly.

I take a sip of my drink. I've never been so close to him before. His clean skin has a particular smell, undisguised by cologne. Not unpleasant, just unsettling. Something restless under the surface, pacing the perimeters of self-imposed bars.

'Sit down.' He indicates a chair facing him, and I perch on the edge of it. 'I don't flatter myself you came all this way just to see me.'

The ice makes small cracking sounds as it surrenders to the potent liquid. I take another tentative sip. It's strong, like swallowing bull ants in liquid form.

I tell him I'm on my way to Rockhampton to see my family.

He guesses the reason immediately, or maybe he already knows why. 'So Watson's asked you to marry him? Congratulations.' He lifts his glass in a mock toast.

'I won't give him my answer until I know if I can have the signalling job on the Lizard.'

'Haven't you spoken to Fuller?' He clearly can't be bothered with the trivial detail of hiring and firing.

Another sip. The alcohol stiffens my tongue. 'It's not just a job to me, Captain. It's my life on the line.'

'Indeed it is.'

'And, as it is my life, I'm not about to beat around the bush. Is that Chinaman of Percy's on the Lizard to pounce on me if things don't go to plan?'

'It's a little late to get cold feet.'

'Cold feet I can cope with. It's the rest of me I have a sentimental attachment to keeping warm.'

A flicker in those black eyes. 'A healthy survival instinct is good. It will keep you on your toes. What news of Boule?'

Oh, just for once to get a straight answer, and not be left dangling over a pool of crocodiles!

I tell him quickly how, to the best of my knowledge, Charley's not heading north to New Guinea anytime soon. I reach into my bag for copies of two notes the Frenchman gave me. 'They seem to be grids of letters. I can't make sense of them.'

Roberts takes them and walks to the light on the desk. He holds the notes under it, first one then the other. His face and arms throw long shadows on the wood.

'Mmm. Playfair cyphers, at a guess. Just one step up from a substitution scheme. Pairs of letters are encrypted instead of singles. It will take me a while, but it won't be too hard to crack.' He straightens up. 'Who are these intended for?'

'I've delivered the first to Bill Smith at the Steam Packet Hotel in Cooktown. The second is for a bookshop owner, Monroe, in Rockhampton. Charley gave it to me when I told him I was sailing south.'

'So Boule knows you are going to Rockhampton and exactly how long you'll be gone?'

'I had to tell him I wouldn't be available to play piano. Why? Should I have been more vague?'

'It's not critical what you did or didn't tell him. It just means, without you in Cooktown for a specified period of time, a situation there will need an even closer eye kept on it.'

'What situation?'

But he's turned his attention back to the notes. 'If these are dates and times for drops or pick-ups in the passage, I'll have to make sure they don't correspond with ours.'

'I don't understand why you let Charley get in your way so often,' I say, thinking of the fate of others foolish enough to try.

Roberts looks up, his dark eyes cold enough to burn. 'Correct. You don't understand. It's not your business.'

I swallow the nervous saliva in my mouth. His next words take me by surprise, even though they are what I came to hear.

'So. I take it you are prepared to assume the responsibilities of signaller on Lizard Island?'

There's something I can't identify in his tone. It couldn't be satisfaction. Surely not?

'Yes, Captain. Yes, of course.'

I sink back in the chair. Where's the relief? The jubilation? The self-applause at my own cleverness? Could it be the cunning little rat feels herself quietly manoeuvred into a trap. With a big black tomcat standing over it.

'I've a shipment of rifles for the Transvaal in July,' he says.

'The Transvaal? I thought the Zulus had been defeated.' My glass is sweating long tears. I take another drink.

He strokes his beard, still studying the cyphers. 'It's the Boers. There's trouble brewing over annexation. And now they've discovered gold at Witwatersrand ... Fuller will explain the signalling procedure once you're on the Lizard. There will be four changeovers altogether, but it's only the swap in the passage that need concern you. My part is over after the drop in the Fijis.'

'I see.' Politics is not really my area of expertise. But I can't afford to be indifferent when it's politics that will be paying my wages.

'Why would Britain choose such a convoluted route to move its armaments? I thought the idea of the Suez Canal was to make sea journeys more straightforward.'

He takes another drink and gazes into an empty fireplace. 'After a while, you'll lose your curiosity about such things. Thirty years I've been at it. I started off back in the fifties working for the

Chinese government in its war against the China Sea pirates. I learned early on not to ask questions.'

There's silence for a few seconds, broken only by the far-off sounds of the street. I notice the smell of dirt from the back of my skirt, like stale brown yeast. The buckshot of stone in my palm still stings. I notice the painting on the wall for the first time. It's a copy of Brueghel's *Two Monkeys*. They're chained together. One gazes out a round window at the wider world of a harbour. The other looks inwards towards the prison of a room.

Roberts's next words are in a more contemplative tone. 'At a guess, I'd say it's an issue of detection by the French. Disraeli's bought Ismail's sharehold in the canal. But until the British can fully occupy Egypt, Grevy's henchmen will be out with their spyglasses, baguettes and little pots of stinky cheese monitoring every dockside cargo. That's why Britain will send a decoy ship carrying a few guns through the Suez at the same time.'

'While the other vessel goes its merry way in the South Pacific with the bulk of the armaments. I take it the French want Africa too?'

A real smile now, and the long beard is made half an inch shorter. 'Does a frog leap when you poke it with a stick? And they're not the only ones. Germany, Portugal, Belgium, Spain, Italy. The only ones to miss out on a piece of Africa will be the Africans.' He downs the last swallow of whisky, then looks at the empty glass as though more might spontaneously appear. 'I'll contact you and Fuller with encrypted notes while you're on the island. It's not unusual for passing boats to anchor in the harbour and visit the homestead. Neither is it irregular for passing vessels to deliver mail. Fuller visits Cooktown regularly enough if further contact becomes necessary.'

So that's it then. I'm being dismissed.

I stand. 'Will I see you again in person?'

'Not unless there is a compelling reason.' He meets my eyes, briefly. 'Good luck.'

I look back at the picture. Which monkey is it worse to be, I wonder. The one that dreams of freedom? Or the one that accepts its fate?

If I survive my time on Lizard Island, I'll leave with enough money to build a new future.

If.

He has one more thing to say before I leave. 'Keep fast to your duties, Mary Oxnam. But mistrust everyone but yourself.'

I turn to face him. He's standing in the shadows. 'Even you, Captain?'

There's a long pause. 'Yes. Even me.'

Rockhampton

Autumn, 1880

20

Why is it every plain girl ends up with a pretty sister?

From the secret diary of Mary Watson

2ND MARCH 1880

Twelve-year-old Carrie and I stroll the waterfront towards Monroe's bookshop. It's the first time I've felt able to breathe since my arrival. The atmosphere in the family home is, to put it charitably, poisonous.

I'd sent a telegram from Cooktown to let Mama and Papa know I was coming. I'd phrased it as though I'd thought to see them before marrying. I'd tried, unsuccessfully perhaps, to make it read as a kind of peace offering. Of course, I had no way to know if it worked. I didn't expect a telegram in response, and couldn't wait for one in any case. So, when the ship docked in Rockhampton, my stomach churned. A sick headache pounded behind my eyes. The rash on my hands flared and I found myself compulsively running my palms up and down the sides of my dress to relieve the burning itch.

But there was no getting out of it.

I scanned the crowd for their faces: saw Mama's, careworn, under her blue bonnet. And, standing next to her, Papa. His waistcoat askew. His face with a glazed, fixed stare I knew only too well. It took all my courage not to run.

Up close, the stink of rum. He couldn't have shaved for the occasion, no. He lunged for me. Planted a wet, sadistic kiss on my cheek while his hands held my arms in a vice. I swallowed, every inch of me cringing.

'Well, well. It's my darling daughter. She just couldn't keep away ...'

I wrenched back with a shudder and turned to Mama. I knew what she must see in my eyes: that stupid, weak child pleading for protection. But some things never change. Her mouth, as always, was a painted rim, edging the dish where she washed her hands of everything.

'Hello, Mary. Lovely to see you, dear. Good trip?'

But I've managed for nearly three weeks. Only a few more days, then the steamer will head north again, with me on it. Only a few more days to keep holding my new-found independence up in front of me like a shield.

What can he do to me in just a few days?

Out on the water, a slow-moving cutter makes its way sedately up the river. The heat is calmer, drier, here in Rockhampton. When I ran my brush through the requisite hundred times this morning, hair clung to the bristles. Ground and air seem to have a different relationship. In Cooktown, the pressure always pushes down from above. Here, the sky is only lightly tethered to the ground.

If only my heart were so buoyant.

Carrie's chattering away. My ears have only been half-listening. I realise why when I give her my full attention. She's luminously pretty in her white dress with the pink sash, and transparently boring as she shares the mechanics of creating the kiss curls that hang over each of her ears. Apparently, sugar-paste works better than gum at keeping them in place, but there's the issue of attracting bees and hornets while outdoors. This last comment intrigues me. It gives a whole new meaning to a head abuzz with thought.

A boy in short pants rides past on his penny farthing. He almost overbalances in his attempt to get a better look at Carrie; the penny wheel totters like loose change, the much smaller farthing wheel at the back skitters to one side.

He veers around the corner, and I turn to her. 'Another admirer?'

'Oh, that's just Thomas Rielond. He's such a child. Only sixteen.'

'If he's a child, what does that make you?'

She gives me a condescending look. 'I'm a woman now, Mary. It happened when you first went to Brisbane.'

'Physical changes don't make a woman.' A bitter tablet's dissolving in my throat. This isn't news I wanted to hear. My next words are weighted. 'How are things at home?'

'Awful.' She wrings her hands. 'Poor Papa started drinking again, and it's all the bank manager's fault for refusing to extend his line of credit. If only someone would give him a chance!'

I realise then how busy he's been, working on her mind since I've been gone. I'm starting to feel nauseous again.

'He's had chances all his life, Carrie. And he's bungled them.'

My voice sounds faint to my ears, as if I already know she won't listen to me. And why should she? I'll be leaving again soon, and she can't let me dismantle her ways of coping. Once the blinkers are removed, her life will become intolerable. As mine did.

A barge passes us, ironing the water flat. I lift my face a little to a sudden gust of breeze. But Papa opens his puppet's mouth again.

'Why are you so hard on him, Mary? Is it because he didn't marry Mama before you were born? Or the late christening?'

'First illegitimate, and then left to the Devil, that's me,' I say with a flippancy I don't feel. 'Do you know, the old biddies back in Cornwall think Hades is in the north? The day Papa finally got around to the baptism, they moved the font to the north door. That way I could toddle out and straight into Satan's arms. After eighteen months, I was already damned, you see. No sprinkle of holy water was going to make a difference.'

A single slate-grey cloud hangs above us. Otherwise, the day is clear and, unlike life, defined with a sure pencil around its edges.

Carrie's face pales. 'Oh dear.'

'Silly girl. Don't believe any of that nonsense. If God would blame a child for something that wasn't her fault, then I'd rather cosy up to the other side anyway.'

The cloud pulls its dirty pillow slip over the sun. Carrie looks up, her voice a whisper. 'Look. He heard you. You shouldn't be so blasphemous.'

I shrug. 'He's never listened before. Why would He start now?'

The breeze coming off the water smells … not stagnant, exactly, but lifeless. With mossy undertones, as though the river's been breathed in and out through eroded banks too many times. My palms itch again. Damn John Adam and his useless, expensive cream.

'Try not to be alone with him,' I say.

'Why?'

Her voice is almost convincingly perplexed. It's as though she's trained herself to move carefully around an unthinkable idea without running into its sharp edges.

I stop her with a hand on her arm. 'Listen, Carrie. I mean it. Whatever he says to you, however he tries to justify his actions ...'

The flesh beneath the white leg-o-mutton sleeve goes taut. Her mouth trembles at the corners.

'I have no idea what you're talking about. You deserted the family. You have no right to an opinion.'

She looks away before I can see her expression. I have to guess what I might see when she turns back. Divided loyalty? Fear? Uncertainty?

'Papa's right about you,' she says finally, and shakes me off. Angrily, now. Her head flicks to the front, her features as blank and regimented as a soldier on parade. 'There's no worse punishment for a parent than an ungrateful child.'

I open my mouth to defend myself but my emotions are jumping over each other, paralysing speech. The unuttered words have only one direction to go — inside and down, past the lump in my throat, past the pain in my chest, to settle in a deep uneasy hollow where they release their toxin.

The distraction inside the shop is a relief. That safe story smell of silverfish and ink. Ideas trapped between thin pages, where they can do no harm.

A middle-aged man appears. I assume it's Mr Monroe. Whoever he is, he looks like my mental picture of Augustus Snodgrass, the friendly poet from *The Pickwick Papers*.

Carrie whispers, as though she's in church, that she'll wait outside. A brief splash of sunlight falls on the floor as she leaves. The door tinkles in reverse, a duller sound than on entering, the bell's tongue clucking with disappointment at another lost customer.

'May I help you?' I expect him to hook two thumbs into the small pockets of his waistcoat, but he doesn't. 'Your young companion, she's not well?'

A ruffle-wristed hand points in Carrie's direction. She's sitting on the courtesy bench outside, cooling herself with a white paper fan.

'My sister doesn't enjoy books as I do. Unless they are about what the fashionable ladies on the Continent are wearing.'

He nods conspiratorially. 'I have observed that the more decorative a woman, the less her interest in serious reading.'

If he realises he's just insulted me, there's no sign of it. I let my eyes wander over the shelves, hoping he takes the hint.

'Is there anything in particular? Or are you just browsing?'

'The latter,' I say.

As I wander the aisles, I can just hear Carrie humming a tune. Slightly off-key, like a disoriented bee in the background. Past Shakespeare, past Trollope. I don't mind the cobwebs, or the layer of dust over everything. It has been so long since I've had a decent book to read. Bob's given me a generous amount of money. More than I need for my return trip. I'm sure, given the isolation of the Lizard, he wouldn't begrudge me some hours whiled away in words.

I pick up a compendium of novelettes by Charles Dickens, drawn by the titles of the stories: 'Hunted Down' and 'The Detective Police'. I also reach for Edmund Hodgson Yates's *Running the Gauntlet*.

I take them to the counter, then wait while Augustus Snodgrass wraps each book in brown paper and string. Increasing the world's load of banality, he ventures, 'You'll have reading matter for some time.'

'I'm to live on an island after my marriage,' I tell him. 'I expect I'll get through them quickly and be looking for more.'

'An island! My word. *Robinson Crusoe* would be just the thing.'

'Yes, it would. If I hadn't read it already.'

'I see a definite trend in the titles you have chosen. A young lady for intrigue and adventure?'

You don't know the half of it, Augustus!

'I love taxing my mind with a good mystery. Oh, and speaking of mysteries ... Mr Monroe, is it?'

He nods, curious.

'I have a delivery for you.'

'For me?' One hand finds his chest in exaggerated surprise. 'From whom?'

I reach into the interior band of my hat, remove the note and pass it across the counter. 'Charley Boule of Cooktown.'

'Ah, Monsieur Boule, my old companion.' In a sleight-of-hand motion he scoops the prize off the counter and under it, to where I presume there's a shelf.

'How much for the books, Mr Monroe?'

'For a friend of Charles Boule, two shillings.'

'And for everyone else, one shilling?'

'Yes. Quite. How amusing.' He smiles with forced politeness, but something else stirs in his eyes. 'You didn't say which island you were moving to, Miss ... uh, I'm sorry I didn't catch your name.'

'You're quite observant. I didn't say which island. And you didn't catch my name, as I didn't pitch it. Good day, Mr Monroe. Calm waters in your pursuits.'

Carrie grumbles non-stop on the walk back. 'Smelly old books. Why would you bother?' She stops to remove a small stone lodged in her boot.

'Dreadful weakness, isn't it?' I sigh deeply and look into the far distance. 'If only I were like you, Carrie dear, and could see stretching the mind for the waste of precious grooming time it is.'

She stands, sticks out her tongue at me and flounces off four steps ahead, the hem of her white dress dragging in the dirt. She looks so small and vulnerable, it makes my heart hurt.

21

As if the world needed another shabby taxidermist.

From the secret diary of Mary Watson

4TH MARCH 1880

Nine in the morning and he's already drinking. I take the necessary inventory: hollow cheeks, jerky limbs. There's a twitch near his left eye I've not noticed before. His clothes hang loose on his frame. A bad sign if he's forgoing food in favour of rum.

I glance over my shoulder to check that the back door is open. Half-hearted rain continues outside. The sky's steel bucket is full of dribbling holes.

He lifts his glass. The ice has long melted. 'Why'd you come back? To tell me you're deserting us? Too late. When you went to Brisbane ...' He stands unsteadily at the mantelpiece, talking to the window. A wet thread of droplets tries to pass through an even wetter needle-eye on the pane. When the window doesn't answer, he turns to face me.

'With the bilge pump underwater and a ten-degree list, Papa, who could blame me for deserting ship?'

'Like a rodent? And, like a rodent, you're back now to scavenge what you can from the wreck?'

I look around the room. 'Slim pickings, by the look.'

'You always were an ungrateful bitch.'

The words escape in a spray of spittle. His free hand tenses into a fist. The chair I'd thought an adequate distance away seems suddenly too close.

He makes a movement and I jump. But he's not headed towards me. He shambles stiffly over to the table for another drink. His body's all at sea, rocking from side to side, the skin unsteady over its deck of bones.

Mama has cleaned up after him, as usual. Called a stonemason in to repair the mantel where he took to it with a mallet. The curtains have been mended from his tailoring efforts with a broken bottle. Thank God he doesn't own a gun. But how would I know any more what he does or doesn't own, could or couldn't do?

The shabby furniture, too, is marked by his temper, and by its age. The fabric on the tweed armchairs worn as thin as Bob's hair. The fake French armoire has pigeon-toed feet. And there is a new addition.

Papa follows the direction of my gaze. A fishhook inside his mouth lifts the right cheek, then lowers it. I wonder if he's developed some kind of palsy.

'What do you think?' he asks.

In the glass cabinet are three wax-and-dye gumtree branches. A stuffed kookaburra, a magpie and a crow each have a perch. The crow's unblinking eyes gleam like polished onyx in the gaslight.

'It suits you perfectly, Papa. I think it's hideous.'

'Hideous,' he throws back sarcastically. 'Come now, I hear you've become a collector of sorts yourself. Let's see. A job, and now a fiancé. What say you as an expert? Are the new birds as worthy as the old ones?'

There is some sort of mirrored glass at the back of the cabinet, so that his face seems trapped inside. I think of the dozen exotic parrots, bristling with carpet fleas, back in Cornwall. Nailed to their dead branches. They went off to auction like everything else. Carried out the door by the bailiffs.

I turn my attention to the armrest beneath my elbow. Pick at a loose thread. 'Do your customers at the Red Lion know you're drunk when you serve them? It can't be good for business.'

I don't know why I'm provoking him. The anger rising in me seems determined to shout over the top of the fear.

He moves quicker than I thought he could. Pins me against the chair by grabbing a handful of my hair and wrenching it backwards. His eyes are bloodshot, a maze of red threads. His mouth two inches away from my chin. My stomach turns to water.

'Does your husband-to-be know the concepts of love, honour and obedience mean nothing to you? If you've failed at being a daughter, why do you imagine you'll succeed at being a wife?'

He lets my head go abruptly. I feel a sting at the root of each strand. He doesn't move away from the chair. Pins me into it with his arm. But then, a miracle. An avaricious thought flashes a shapely leg at the pugilist in his mind.

'Does he have any money, this man of yours?'

He pulls a handkerchief from his pocket. Wipes a smear of drool from his chin. I've pressed my body so far back in the chair, I can almost feel the wall behind. When I don't answer, he moves his head even closer. I can see the open pores on his nose. Almost taste his breath.

'Answer me!'

'No!'

But I have money, Papa. And I'm soon going to have lots, lots more. And you're not getting a penny of it. Not one single farthing.

Something in my face pierces his fug. He staggers away towards the bottle glinting in the half-light of the window.

When I can breathe again, I wonder about the reprieve. Oddly, I remember Fitzgerald's comment that Bob's sable belle could never return to her tribe because the smell of civilisation was on her. Perhaps the smell of the larger world was on me now, and it gave Papa just enough pause to leave me with the advantage. Too slight to make me feel protected, though. I'll wedge a chair under the doorknob of my bedroom tonight.

Papa's still counting Bob's imaginary coins in his head. 'He must have *some* means. What does he do for a crust?'

'He's a sea-slug fisherman.'

'Slugs!' He swings around. 'You always were a girl with limited charms, but still … sea-slugs!'

I ignore my itching hands. 'He's a Catholic and a Scot.'

'A popish Mac! This gets better and better. You'll be bowing your head to female idols soon enough.'

'He's also your age.' I can't seem to stop myself.

He looks me up and down. Insects crawl under my skin wherever his gaze touches.

'The only man you could get, eh? I suppose a fellow doesn't stare at the mantelpiece while he's stoking the fire. And those slug fishermen aren't too fussy. Naked gins on board to do their bidding every time they turn around.' Something else occurs to him. 'Are you in the family way? Is that why he's marrying you?'

'Why would a man feel the need to do that? You didn't bother when Mama was pregnant with me.'

He comes at me again. But I'm ready for him this time. I'm at the doorway before he can change direction. The drink has done its work.

He stops. Shrugs. Laughs. His fingers twitch. He tosses off the last of what's in his glass. Glances once more at his precious stuffed birds in their cabinet with a slow smile. I barely have time to dread what's coming.

'Go to your slug fisherman. I couldn't care less. I still have Carrie.'

22

I've always thought it a ridiculous homily:
Mother Knows Best.

From the secret diary of Mary Watson

5TH MARCH 1880

'Your passage is booked then?'

I'm sitting at the table peeling carrots. Mama has a skinned rabbit on the board. She swings the cleaver and deftly severs the head, a leg, a leg ... I dodge a droplet of moist flesh that flies off the cleaver's blade. Dripping spits in a pan on the wood stove.

'Yes. In two days' time, I'll be gone.'

She rolls the rabbit pieces in seasoned flour. The prickle of pepper tugs the hairs inside my nose.

'Are you going to tell me what this is really about? I'm your mother, Mary. I know you better than anybody.'

'You don't know me at all, as a matter of fact.'

I slice the carrot into circles and pop an orange coin in my mouth to quell my irritation. I watch her working. The meat has bled a little into the flour. The red glue sticks to the board as she carries pieces over to the stove, lays them one by sizzling one in the pan. A wild, hot smell fills the room.

With her back to me, she asks, 'What kind of a man is he, this slug fisherman? A reprobate?'

'Of course not. And even if he were, I'm of age. I don't need your permission.'

Under a worn housedress, her shoulderblades shuffle from side to side as she shifts the meat. She's looking old, I think. Developing a permanent slump. The hair over her ears has turned decidedly grey. And the curves of her body have melted into a single pile of flesh at her middle.

She turns around abruptly, wooden spoon in hand. 'Will you take Carrie with you?'

'No.'

'Just for a little while. It's Papa, he's been ... unwell. I'm worried ...' Her voice trails off. She can't, or won't, meet my eye.

'You weren't worried when I was at home.' The rasp in my voice surprises, embarrasses, me.

'I did fret about you. I still do.'

'You've no need to, now I'm away from Papa.'

'He's not well,' she repeats, as though it's some magical chant that excuses everything.

'Why don't you and Carrie just pack up and leave?'

I stare out the window at the buddleia bush. The sun has broken through the clouds, highlighting its lavender torches pricked with small flowers.

'Where would we go? To one of those homes for abandoned wives? They make you eat mouldy bread. You sleep with no blankets in winter. We'd be worse off than the blacks. And, anyway, he'd come looking for us.' Her mouth works as though to say more, but no words emerge. Eventually, she sits, carefully placing the spoon on the table. 'I've tried my best.' She puts floury hands to her head, then rubs her temples. White dust runs across her face. 'I'm getting one of my headaches.'

I look at the candlesticks on the hearth that need silvering: remnants salvaged from the jaws of the bailiffs. The milk jug next to them with its tracery of hairline cracks. Next to that, the brown salt pig with its corner broken off. The dilapidated sadnesses of her life laid out in a neat line of self-pity.

I take the carrots over to the pan. Red pinpricks of rabbit blood dot the dimpled skin. I tip the vegetables in and put the lid on. 'Does this need water?'

'A few splashes,' she whispers.

From now on, she'll play some fragile saint, every angry word a nail driven into her wrists. I lift the lid again and add water from the kettle on the stove.

'I'm having a cup of tea. Would you like one?' My voice is deliberately robust.

'All right.' Wanly. 'But I doubt I'll be able to drink it.'

I bring the teapot over and turn it around three times. That's the way it's done. Not twice or four times. I've never thought to question why three is the critical number.

She puts her hand over mine. 'I just want you to be settled. But you've always been so restless. Full of secrets. You're more like Papa than you think. A sparrow flew into the house the other day. You know what that means?'

'You left the door open?'

'Bad luck of the worst kind is coming.'

'You don't need a bird to predict that. Just look into the face of your husband for once instead of staring at the floor. And by the way, I'm nothing like Papa. If I thought I were, I'd have slit my wrists long ago.'

She puts a shocked hand to her mouth. 'You mustn't say such wicked things!'

I pour a liverish river of tea into her cup. The leaves are coarse. And rabbit is the cheapest meat at the butcher's. I wonder if Papa intends to ask for a loan before I leave. A few brown logs float to the surface of my cup. I retrieve them with a finger.

'This Lizard Island. What will you do there?'

'Help Bob with his business, I suppose.'

She gives me a queer look through the steam of her tea. 'You know I can't come to the wedding. Papa won't allow it.'

'I know.'

'Please, Mary. Take her with you? Just for a while, until I secure a place for her at a school in Brisbane. I've been slipping some coins out of the till in the pub when Papa's not looking. In a few months I'll have enough.'

I think of my own slippery fingers in Charley's drawer.

'Lizard Island is no place for a twelve-year-old girl. Particularly a dressed-up doll like Carrie. She'd be bored witless. And you can't make her go, even if you could convince me to take her.'

And I have plans, Mama. I can't imagine Carrie in any of them. Not without disaster following her every prancing-pony step.

'She'll do what I say. And if Lizard Island is no place for her, then it's surely no place for you either.'

I stare down at the cleaver on the table with its glittering metal, its no-nonsense handle. How easy life would be if the pieces that didn't fit could be neatly severed from the whole.

Mama sips her tea with convalescent's hands, lifts her headache bravely over the rim of the cup. 'You're a good girl at heart, Mary. I know you'll do this.'

When I open my mouth to say no again, she throws the bait in. And, like all the best snares, the mechanism comes down before I have time to jump backwards.

'You'll never forgive yourself if you leave her here and something bad happens.'

Lizard Island

Winter, 1880

23

*When all at sea, there's nothing to do
but keep an eye firmly on the horizon.*

From the secret diary of Mary Watson

3RD JUNE 1880

Logic has deserted me. My body won't be talked out of seasickness. *Isabella* shuffles under my feet. The burned sun sheds orange flakes on the surface of the water. The ocean's a rocking sheet of oriental silk pulled tight beneath the hull — until a fish jumps, pushing like a needle through the surface.

Carrie's screech pecks a hole in the precarious equilibrium of my inner ear. 'I can smell manure!'

Unfortunately, her voice is not carried away by the breeze. She's at the bow, her pretty tip-tilted nose turned up under her tip-tilted hat. 'Why did you have to bring this ... this ...'

'Menagerie?' I offer. 'It is a big word, isn't it?'

My eyes take sickly inventory. *Isabella*'s laden with supplies for the island: food, seeds, Carrie, Bob and me. Twenty hens, a dozen ducks, two pigs. And, because I couldn't resist, one of Virgin Mary's puppies.

'I know what it means!' Carrie whines. 'You think I'm dumb. Well, I'd rather be dumb than homely.'

With perfect timing, the pig in the pen nearest her grunts, then squirts out a large green bowel motion.

'Ooo. How perfectly revolting.'

She holds a handkerchief over her nose and drapes herself decorously over the rail to find a pocket of fresh air. One quick hoist of those shapely calves and she'd be overboard, I think. I wonder if Bob, being Scottish, has some experience of caber-tossing.

I catch his eye as he sits at the stern, relaxed, his hand resting lightly on the tiller. His good mood is apparently Carrie-proof. What's left of his hair licks the edges of his battered face. His scar in the saffron light of afternoon is a smile turned sideways. He gives me a newly married wink. The soreness between my legs flares.

I can't say I've been overwhelmed with the joys of intimacy. I've had more stimulating rides in a horse and buggy. But I smile back, the dutiful wife, giving hearty thanks for the industrial quantity of French contraceptive sponges in the bottom of my bag, purchased from the catalogue of Mrs B Smyth.

Whatever Bob's reason for sending me away to Rockhampton, he was clearly happy to see me when I returned. And delighted with my acceptance of his marriage proposal. Even the thought of accommodating Carrie on the Lizard brought nothing more than a minute's rueful grimace and a shrug. With so many other things to think about, I've decided to let the sleeping dog of his then-puzzling behaviour, lie.

'How's the slops bucket in yer belly, Mrs Noah?' Bob asks. 'Yer wee sister doesn't seem to be suffering.' He glances at Carrie, who smirks with malicious pleasure.

'Neither am I,' I say briskly. My voice clearly doesn't match my face.

'Look to the horizon.' He eases the rudder slightly to port. 'Just till ye find yer sea legs.'

The mainsail whipcracks, gathering an extra handful of breeze. I do as I'm told and lift my gaze. To the east, the ocean turns over under its pale blue blanket. To the west, the craggy edges of Cape Bedford. It does help, a little.

When we left Cooktown this morning, I looked back only once. We glided past the steamer wharf, the shopfronts and their verandahs receding to a row of teeth along dusty Charlotte Street. The final image struck me with its aptness: one stray dog humping another on the sand near the pier.

I look down to the woven gold ring on my finger. Bob had it made specially by an artisan in Chinatown. Already there's an irritation beneath it to match the rash on my palms. So this is marriage? Yet another reason, should I need one, to be forward thinking. To keep my eyes firmly locked on the horizon.

Coming on dark, the sun's a wheel of red-vein cheese slipping off the edge of a breadboard. The sea turns leaden, smoothes the shore of the horseshoe-shaped beach ahead. We approach the Lizard on its western side. My first impression is of a reclining, muscular back bedded down; the rest of the body turned away in rejection. Encroaching shadows. Hills of grey granite, stinting shrubs. A burned red smell washes up my nose.

'Something on fire, Bob?'

He steers *Isabella* closer to shore. Wavelets lick the hull. He points to a small hut, perhaps fifty yards inland and barely visible, from which smoke twists upwards like rope.

'Mangrove wood burning in the smokehouse.'

'For the slugs?' Something in the begrudging air makes me want conversation.

'Aye. We boil them in the tank for a wee while. Twenty minutes give or take. Then we gut them, leave them to dry in the sun. Next, they smoke for a day till they shrivel, ready for packing. Come keep the tiller steady, while I pull down the mains'l.'

I move aft. The tiller feels warm from his palm. It tugs to port. I pull slightly to starboard to correct it.

Bob goes to the boom, unwinds the lanyard from the cleat. With a series of shrieking arm-over-arm pulls, the canvas descends in a grey puddle. He drops anchor over port side. The water is shallow.

The ocean elbows the hull a few more times. Carrie sits next to me and rubs her arms, then suddenly slaps a spot on the back of her hand. 'There's mosquitos, Mary.' Her voice is thinner than it was in daylight.

'Where's the tank you boil the slugs in, Bob?' she asks.

Bob points to an even dimmer shape on our left, about halfway to the smoking hut, thirty yards up from the shoreline: a ship's water tank, cut in half. It sits on iron bars over a cold firepit, well above the high-tide mark.

'It looks like one of those pots for boiling missionaries. In the newspaper cartoons.' Carrie shivers a little, pulls her shawl tighter.

'I was thinking of "The Owl and the Pussycat",' I say.

She cocks her head. 'They went to sea in a beautiful pea-green boat, didn't they?'

Bob laughs. 'Well, the tank's not lovely, nor green.'

Carrie puts an arm around my waist, her earlier posturing swallowed up by the darkness. 'I don't like it here, Mary,' she whispers.

I squeeze her shoulder absently. Even the animals are quiet. 'Things will be different tomorrow.'

There's a hill in the far distance, behind the shape of what must be the house. From somewhere near the base of its swelling, I think I discern a thinner twirl of grey smoke in the darkness. A blacks' fire?

I don't draw Carrie's attention to it.

The boat drifts, with a small jolt, onto a cushion of treacly sand. Bob rolls up his trousers, then lights the kerosene lamp. I hear the rusty swing of its handle as he jumps overboard into a soft, wet explosion. Night noises drift from further inland. A bird's call I've never heard before. A series of squeaks, as though someone's scraping chips off a shiny surface. The small amount of water under the hull has gravel in its throat. It's as if the island is trying to push us away with little shoves, send us back to sea where we came from.

'Ye both wait here.'

I follow Bob's dipping light as it moves towards shore. Several moths the size of saucers circle around it. The air has a chill that cuts through the material of my dress.

Carrie slaps a few more times at her arms and neck. 'I'm frightened.'

'What of, silly girl?' But I already know.

She moves closer. I feel her thigh against my own. 'I get feelings sometimes. In my stomach ...' Her voice trails away.

'Biliousness?' Even in the dark I can feel her scorn. 'Well, then, perhaps you're touched, Carrie, like every inbred Cornish woman.'

But she doesn't rise to the bait. 'I'm not inbred, and you aren't either. You must feel it too.' She taps her finger in the middle of her forehead. 'What's the word? Something like haunted ... but not quite. I just know we shouldn't be here.' She puts her arm on the railing, turns her head away. 'I wish I knew more words. What is it?'

Possessed is what she's looking for. As in: belonging to someone else. Already occupied. Full up. No vacancy. Trespassers will be dealt with in a timely fashion. Yes, Carrie, I feel it.

'I'm sure I don't know what you mean,' I say.

'You pretend you don't. I haven't forgotten that time back in Truro. The morning you woke up, looked at the snow falling outside, and told me that Grandfather was dead.'

'He was, dear.'

'I know that. But Mama hadn't been into his room to call him down for breakfast. He hadn't yet been found dead when you said it.'

'You misremember. Mama had already been in to tell me.'

'I recall it perfectly. I was six. Six year olds remember things.'

I bite my tongue. Six year olds also forget things when they're sharing a room with an elder sister. When those things are to do with your father.

'It doesn't matter,' I say. 'You're just tired. And it's dark.'

Bob is back and planting three tall stools in two feet of water. He stands next to the lugger, one arm outstretched, the other holding the lamp that flares and flattens under its glass, in danger of going out in the breeze. His face is lit from beneath, a battered skull, both ancient and wise.

'A man's pride tells him to carry ye both to shore. His bad back tells him to mind his own business.'

'I think your plan is very chivalrous, Bob. Come on, Carrie, you first.'

'But I can't swim!'

'You don't need to.' I give her a gentle push. 'Bob's made a bridge in the water.'

He coaxes her over the side, taking her weight under one arm. I hear her yelp of surprise, then a groan as her shoes take on water. A short time later, Bob's back and enticing me over.

'I won't drop my new bride.'

I wonder if I imagine the hint of play in his voice.

'Come on, Mary.' I can hear the anxiety in Carrie's. She doesn't want to be left on the beach alone.

Bob lifts me over the side. 'Oops.' He pretends he's losing his grip on me and I slip towards the water.

'Bob!'

He gathers me up tighter and I punch him on the back with my free hand.

He's still chuckling when I feel the cold, clammy water in my hose. Then my shoes fill up. My foot finds the stool. Bob guides me by my elbow.

I have to trust the steps are as long as he says they are, that something solid will be where he says he has put it. A few long, dark steps of faith to the shore.

There's no turning back now. Not even from a place that clearly doesn't want us there.

24

*A house can seem more a strategic outpost
than a home.*

From the secret diary of Mary Watson

The first thing I hear are the three tethered dogs barking somewhere to our right in the darkness. Bob's already told me they are here to warn the homestead if any blacks approach. After the sand, there is coarse gravel underfoot. Then the house, sixty yards up from the beach on a grassy knoll. Squat, no-nonsense. Made of limestone blocks, like a neat little cell. Bob opens the heavy door, lights a match. The scar on his face strikes out like a shiny copper blade. Rough benches loaded with old newspapers. Fish traps. Packets of hooks. There's moonlight coming through the far wall. Sharp leaves of light pierce cracks in the mortar, like the ivy-patterned, pressed-metal ceiling back in Cornwall. A slop of playing cards spilled over the surface of a trunk. A tobacco tin's upturned lid, filled with coins. Last year's flyspotted calendar discarded on the floor. A ball of twine with a large needle sticking out of it sits atop the collapsed lung of a sail in the corner. The house reeks of locked-up earth and shellfish. It wouldn't have hurt him to clean up a bit.

I take a deep breath.

'It's a mess, all right.' Bob rubs his mouth.

Carrie's voice comes out of the shadows. 'But it's so small. And where will we sleep?'

'There's a wash bucket behind ye.' Bob's turning to leave. 'I'll unload the beasts. The rest can wait till daylight.' And then he's gone.

'Mary?'

'Shh, Carrie. What's that noise?'

'It's the ocean sloshing in my boots.' She looks at me flatly. The lamplight catches her cheekbones, hollowing the flesh beneath.

'No, something else. Like singing.'

The sounds of the dark outside are mostly muted. There's the fizz and swell of sea in the background. The breeze, lisping to the closed window shutters. Something with 'S' in it. Solitude? Isolation? I hear one of the pigs give a clotted snort in the distance. Virgin Mary's pup howls for its mother. The dogs onshore respond with barking.

'Smelly old island,' Carrie says. 'What about our valises? They're still on the boat.'

I shake my head to clear it, ignoring her melodramatic shivers.

'You heard Bob. Only the animals are coming off tonight. Until then we make do.'

The wash bucket he had pointed to has only a few inches of water in it. Another, next to it, holds dirty shirts fermenting in what smells like a mixture of swamp water and molasses.

Some noise makes me turn to the open doorway. Percy's Chinaman lurches inside. Those ugly, chicken-feet hands hold a tray in front of him. He's discarded the cane, but his foot is still bandaged. He drags the leg stiffly along beside him, flinging it out in a half-circle, then putting his weight down on the ball of the damaged foot when he needs to. A grim reaper with a skin-and-bone scythe.

I hold my breath for a few seconds. We stare at each other. A port-wine birthmark around his left eye is the colour of old blood in the kerosene light. It wasn't visible on the poster, but then his face had been in profile. His skin, apart from the eyepatch of discolouration, is smooth and alabaster, darkening slightly at his forehead where the hair's been shaved back to line up with the edge of a skullcap. There's that all-too-familiar enigmatic expression of every Chinaman I've encountered. But in these calm waters, a few fins circle lazily.

I look down to the food. A brownish mess of vegetables with fried eggs on top. I wonder if it's poisoned, but decide it's not. That wouldn't be his style. He'd rather lie in wait for me. Slit my throat when I'm not looking. He's had practice with the Chinese shopkeeper, after all.

Bob comes back in. 'Mary. This is Ah Leung. Ah Leung looks after the garden. Ah Sam, the house.'

'Where is Ah Sam, then?'

I don't take my eyes off Ah Leung. I hope my tone makes it clear that I don't want him here.

'He will be at hand soon. He's helping unload.'

'Ah Leung.' I acknowledge the Chinaman coolly.

The head lifts briefly, but he doesn't speak.

Bob claps his hands a few times and Ah Leung backs out of the doorway, head bowed more in insolence than deference. But Bob doesn't seem to notice.

I find some enamel plates, share out the food, and hand Bob a plate and a fork from the box on the table. The stools are still wet so we sit on upturned crates.

'Could you fetch the canvas cot for Carrie?' I ask.

Bob frowns, then speaks around a mouthful of cabbage. 'I told ye, no more's coming off tonight.'

I look at the stained mattress on the floor.

Carrie's eyes widen. 'Mary, we can't all sleep together!'

I'm too exhausted to argue. 'Apparently, we can. You'll be one side of me, Bob on the other.'

He makes a grunting noise as if even this is too pretentious for his liking.

The eggs are congealed, the vegetables cold, but we eat anyway. I spear a vegetable I can't identify. Some sort of spinach, but stringier. Everything's doused in soy sauce.

'Do you know much about Ah Leung?'

Bob looks up, a smear of yolk on his chin. 'John Pigtails are all the same to me. Why do ye ask?'

I chew a piece of egg. 'No reason.'

So he knows nothing about Ah Leung's past. I wonder, should I tell him what the Chinaman has done? I'll bide my time, I decide. Ponder first which way the information might be turned to my advantage.

Bob locks us in for the night with a thick, horizontal plank of wood that fits neatly across the middle of the door. There's a round hole at eye height.

'To keep us in or something out?' I question him.

I already know the answer. The opening is the perfect size and shape for a rifle barrel.

'It doesn't hurt to be ready.' He doesn't say ready for what.

There is a banging noise outside. A metallic clang and a cry. An angry exchange in the seesaw intonations of Mandarin.

While I wash up the dishes in an inch of clean water, Bob rigs up a curtain so that, when Carrie does get her cot, she'll have a makeshift bedroom. She peels off her boots and hose, then perches on the edge of the mattress. Exhaustion's visible in two smudges under her eyes and the slope of her shoulders.

'Are you all right, Carrie?'

'I'm tired. I want to lie down.'

The fight's gone out of her. I see an old woollen coat hanging by a hook near the door and fetch it. When I come back, she's on her part of the mattress. Bob lifts an eyebrow as I wrap the coat around her, tucking her in on both sides. She looks up at me mutely.

'Better?' I ask.

'Can you help me unhook my petticoats? I'll use them as a pillow.'

I reach discreetly under her skirt and loosen a tie at her waist. 'Wriggle a bit. There.'

The calico's still warm from her body, smells like violets and talc. She scrunches and then positions the material under her head.

'I haven't combed out my hair.' Her eyes are closing.

'It doesn't matter, dear. We'll do it in the morning.'

I push a strand away from her forehead, then stand and walk over to where Bob's rolling his medicinal balls slowly around in his left palm.

I keep my voice low. 'You could have told me we wouldn't be getting anything from the boat. We might have grabbed our nightgowns and valises at least.'

'Ye must get used to roughing it. There's no bobby-pin shops out here.' He lifts his head in Carrie's direction.

I turn away, mutter under my breath.

'What did ye say?' He pulls me roughly around.

'Shh. Let me go.' I shake him off.

His eyes narrow to slits. 'It's my roof. I'll yell it off if I've a mind, ye got that? And watch yer mouth. No mumbling behind a man's back.'

I'm not in the mood for his hair-trigger pomposity. I can hear that distant, thin, nasal vein of singing under the obviousness of our voices. 'Are there blacks on the island?'

He shakes his head then glares at me, unwilling to abandon his rancour.

'But I can hear them.' I cock my head a little more.

'I would know if they were.'

He sounds so sure. Maybe he's right and it's all in my head. Is it possible to have a third ear as well as a third eye?

Bob picks up his pipe, the scarred side of his face the colour of liver. 'First chance I get, I'll teach ye how to shoot. Meanwhile don't tell me to be quiet in my own house!'

25

Loyalties are not always straightforward.
They can be as ragged as an eagle's wing.

From the secret diary of Mary Watson

4TH JUNE 1880

I can hear the breeze sweeping sand from the doorstep when I open my eyes. Carrie has inched halfway down the mattress, and Bob's gone altogether. I'm staring at an impressive spiderweb in the corner, large as a ship's wheel, when Percy steps into the house unannounced.

I motion with a finger on my lips for him not to wake Carrie, then slip out of bed still wearing yesterday's clothes. I follow him outside and we face each other on the packed earth that serves as a verandah. He has a bruise the size of a fist turning sallow on his left cheek.

'What happened to you?' I ask.

Isabella is small in the distance. The ant-sized man on board must be Bob, passing a box over the side to a pair of black palms. He's using three Kanakas in the same way he used the stools last night. Each item drifts hand to hand above the water, in the bright sun, until the last man on shore stacks it with the other cargo above the high-tide line.

Percy looks over my shoulder to Carrie. 'Three in a bed, eh, Mrs Watson? That's a bit adventurous, even for these parts. What do the Frogs call two strumpets and a businessman? *Ménage à trois?*' His pronunciation of the French words is impressively authentic.

'There was scarcely a choice,' I say tightly. The salty air's spinning my loose hair. I tuck a lock behind one ear. 'Once Bob gets Carrie's canvas cot set up, I'll find a way to give us all some privacy. What about you? Did we kick you out into the cold?'

It's clear that more than one man has been living in the house. All three of them probably: Bob, Percy and Porter Green. The spoor of male habitation is everywhere.

'There's a wooden shed further up the beach that suits me well enough.' He points to the right. 'You must visit sometime. I'll attempt to provide a cup of tea. Green's done the same, only further away still.'

'Where is Porter?'

'On the south side of the island, floating logs of red mangrove around for the smokehouse.' In the crisp morning light, his eyes are the colour of old linen embroidered with emerald thread. I look again at the bruise souring around the edges.

'Did you and Bob get into a fight?'

'Over you, Mrs Watson? No.'

'I wish you wouldn't call me that.'

'What should I call you?'

'Mary.'

'Well then, Mary. And you must call me the man who restrained himself on your behalf. You'll have noticed your husband came to your marriage bed in one piece, or as close as he's ever passed for it.'

'Should I be grateful? You had little choice in the matter, I imagine. You might not think much of me, but I'm a better bet at the moment than a crippled Chinaman.'

'*Touché*. I can see that flattery will get me nowhere.'

'It might. If I sensed you meant it.'

I look down to the water again, past the lugger. The Pacific unfolds like a blue cloth, pleated in white further out. The air, to my Cooktown lungs, has the strength of smelling salts. I rub my arms. It's cool this morning. Ah Leung lurches past with a bucket in both hands. It's painful to watch that Quasimodo gait, his conical hat bobbing above him. He doesn't acknowledge me. I wait until he's around the side of the house and out of hearing range.

'Where's he going?'

'There's a pandanus swamp and the farm about a quarter of a mile away. He's gone to fill the bucket for our tea from the freshwater spring. I hope you're not too thirsty — with his injury, it takes him a while to manage it.'

'What happened to his foot?'

'Gangrene. If you think Cooktown is a cesspit in the wet season, try being on the Palmer. Dry creeks turn into torrents. They throw the diggers who die of typhoid and dysentery into the flood, and the bodies float downstream, contaminating the water. You know the Chows only wear those ridiculous slippers? Ah Leung cut his foot and it got infected. When he smelled the putrid flesh, and saw his toes had turned black, he cut them off with a cleaver.'

I shudder. 'That's where you caught up with him, the Palmer?'

'That's right.' Said a touch too carefully. 'I tracked him down to a deserted blacks' camp near Big Oaky Creek. He'd made himself a bark humpy and was living off Palmer River soup.'

'What's that?'

'Weeds boiled up in muddy water.'

Something's not quite adding up in my mind, despite Percy's dramatic re-enactment.

'All along you've been so keen to find him, which suggests he's worked for you in the past. Why didn't he try to contact you so that you could hide him somewhere, or bring him to the Lizard even earlier? Who knows ... maybe you commissioned him to kill that shopkeeper. In which case, the least you could have done was provide cover for him.'

'You have a vivid imagination.' Again, that too-controlled response. He's no intention, it seems, of explaining himself.

'At any rate, keep him away from me. I want nothing to do with him.'

At last, Percy looks me in the eye. 'Don't tell me you've had a run-in with the staff already.'

He lights his pipe. The smoke rises in a thin taper past his squinting eyes. Then he, too, stares out to where the *Isabella* is a bobbing speck in the far distance. The sky above is a smoky blue: like the tip of a kerosene flame. The white dots of a couple of seagulls float inside it.

'I haven't exchanged more than a single word with him,' I say. 'I just don't want him hovering over me like a crippled vulture.'

Percy sucks on his pipe. Then pulls it out to inspect the tobacco. He taps his front teeth lightly with the bowl.

'You've become quite peremptory since your promotion. Or is it marriage that's given you this extra pluck? You can't go running behind my back to Roberts out here.'

Now there's an unpleasant hardness in his gaze.

'I've never gone running to him — unless you were nowhere to be found.' I challenge him to argue the point.

His bottom lip twitches. 'You'll have to deal with Ah Leung, whether you like it or not. He's in charge of the garden. If you want him to bring you vegetables, you'll have to engage with him in at least a semi-pleasant manner.'

'I'll fetch my own vegetables,' I say.

'Really? And watch while he cuts off a head of cabbage with his big glittering cane knife? The farm's a long way from the house. No one would hear you scream.'

'Your attempts to scare me are so obvious as to be ridiculous.'

Carrie has wandered to the doorway and stands blinking slowly in the light. Her hair looks like small mice have made a nest in it. She yawns.

'Percy Fuller, my sister, Carrie.'

'Charmed, I'm sure.' He's looking her up and down.

She takes a step out the door to stand behind me. 'Mr Fuller. I'm not at my best.'

'You look fine to me.' So fine, it seems, he doesn't bother breaking his gaze to address me. 'About that oriental issue, Mary. A woman has nothing to worry about if she just does her job properly. But I'll keep an eye on the matter.'

'You'll have to detach it from my sister first.'

His head makes a measured turn towards me. 'Pretty things should be looked at, not hidden away.'

He turns and walks towards the beach, then calls over his shoulder. 'You and your sister should explore a bit. Wander over to the farm, maybe up to Cook's Look. That's where the good captain surveyed his passage through the reef.' He points to the hill almost directly behind the house. 'It's only half a mile or so. You can see from here to tomorrow on a good day.'

'We'll take it on advisement.'

When he's shrunk to just a kink in the shimmer, Carrie stretches her arms up. She turns a couple of times and lifts her face to the sky. 'What was that about an oriental issue?'

'Oh, just a general discussion about Chinese women on the mainland doing piecework for half the wages that European ladies can manage.'

'Percy's a nice man. Handsome, too.'

'Handsome is as handsome does.' I sound sour to my own ears, like a crotchety old spinster with lemon juice squirted in the milk of my voice.

'It's so lonely here.' She's looking out over the patches of shrubby bush, the grey granite stones.

Lonely? Well, isolated, at least.

'Look, an eagle!' Carrie says.

A huge bird is above us, surrounded by zigzag tips of light. The shadowy wingspan must be four feet across and barely tilting as an updraught holds the muscular ballast of its body steady. A small snake wriggles in its beak. Cruel hooks curl beneath.

As it floats slowly over the house, heading for Cook's Look, I consult the list of superstitions in my head, but draw almost a blank. Something from *The Iliad*? Didn't Zeus send the bad luck of an eagle with a serpent in its beak to the Trojans?

Whatever the message, good or bad, it's further away now. A ragged hole heading straight for the sun.

26

Everyone keeps a box of secrets.

From the secret diary of Mary Watson

I find the camphorwood box in the corner behind some fishhooks as I'm cleaning up. The rusty chain attached to the lid rustles its links, then pulls taut as I open it. A set of worn rosary beads on top. An old pipe chewed down by the white ants of Bob's teeth. The naphthalene of mothballs. A yellow, water-stained letter, kept instead of sent, dated a year ago.

Dearest sister ... My eyes scan down and grab a paragraph: *Marry? Never. I would sooner blow my brains out than do so and struggle more than before. Of course, things would have been different if Mother was a normal woman* ...

I hear a crash thump: something irreplaceable, ruined. My jaw aches from grinding my teeth. But I know better than to go out and speak my mind. I'm learning fast about Bob's temperament. He's agreeable when soothed, maliciously stubborn when crossed. If I want any of our things to be salvaged, I'll have to hold my tongue.

I put the letter down, close the lid and slip the box back where I found it.

Outside, it's worse than I thought. Everything is upended. My trousseau on its lid. Carrie's port sprung open, on its side, dresses lying in the dirt. I put things to rights as best I can, then go back into the shadowy house. I don't want to unpack until the place is clean.

By eleven o'clock, I've swept the hardened earth floor. Coughed on clouds of fine sand and dust. Shooed geckos and millipedes from the thatched ceiling with the broom. When I look up, Percy's filling the doorway again. My hand goes to the scarf I've tied over my hair and under my chin.

'New broom through the old house, eh?'

'Hardly new,' I say, looking at its moulting, worn-down head. 'I wish I'd thought to bring one over.'

'We'll buy another next time we're in Cooktown. In the meantime, Porter and I will knock you up a couple of walls for privacy. And make a bedframe.' His eyes flit to the corner where I've leaned the mattress Carrie, Bob and I slept on last night. 'But I'll get started on the pigsty and fowlhouse first. Reinforce the wire. Goannas like nothing better than eggs for an appetiser, followed by chickens.'

'Where's this elusive Ah Sam who's supposed to be helping me with the housework?'

He grins. 'If you're of a mind to get your head bitten off by your dear husband, go and ask him.'

'No, thanks.' I grimace. 'Don't you and Bob have to go fishing?'

I look to the pieces of sky his head and shoulders haven't eclipsed. The clear blue's only gathered up a few white spun-sugar puffs.

'We'll get you settled in first. The weather's been unpredictable, anyway. It looks fine now, but could blow up later.'

He turns away to sneeze from the cloud of dust I've stirred up, then leans on the doorframe.

'I thought the dry season was when you got most of your fishing done.'

'It is. But bad weather sometimes surprises us this time of year. May and June ... fine weather can turn foul in a heartbeat. A sailor needs to be on his toes.'

'When exactly does cyclone season start?'

He has a match propped in the side of his mouth, manoeuvring it with his teeth so that it levers up and down. 'It's obvious you're not a born-and-bred Queensland girl, or you'd know. About the beginning of November, give or take. It's all over, or should be, by the end of April.'

'That's a long time to be landlocked.'

'Worried we'll all get sick of each other, Mrs Watson?'

'Not exactly.'

'I guess you're wondering how your old man is going to support you until the wet season?'

'Not particularly. I can support myself, remember?'

But he's determined to be provocative about my marriage of convenience. 'You should be worried.' He pulls his pipe out of the pocket of his dark trousers. From the other pocket, a plug of tobacco. He spits the match on the ground then parks the pipe in his mouth to get it out of the way. His next words are spoken around the stem. 'We collect about half a ton a month of slugs when the weather's good. Let's see. Slugs were worth about a hundred pounds a ton last month, give or take. Of course, as Watson and I are partners, we each get half. Half of what's left, that is, after the blacks, Kanakas and Chows have been paid. And then there's supplies, repairs, the odd bribe ...'

He's not finished. But I've finished listening. I turn my back on him and drag an empty crate over to the corner, trying to imagine how to divide the large room up into smaller ones. I've decided what's essential. A bedroom with a door for Bob and me. For Carrie, the curtained alcove with enough room for the cot and a washstand.

'Sea-slug fishermen are the lowest of the low, you should know that. Bottom feeders, just like the slugs they catch. Of course, Watson *is* a charmer.'

I hear Bob's swearing brogue outside the door, accompanied by a thump. Another tinkle of breakage.

Percy raises an eyebrow and lifts a hand in sarcastic farewell.

Bob lumbers in, my treadle machine in his arms. I look up warily. His face, already a patchwork of bad needlework, is sewn up even further with annoyance.

'Next time I've a mind to drown a Kanaka, I'll tether this to his ankle.' He dumps it roughly on the floor, then pulls a dirty handkerchief from his back pocket and wipes his palms on it.

'I'm sure you'll think it's useful after I've mended your clothes,' I say. 'That's unless you've just broken it in your bad temper, in which case it will just be an expensive doorstop.'

He puts a hand to the small of his back and shoots me a filthy glare.

'Have you come across that box of soap yet?' I ask sweetly.

'The soap, the bath. The whole kit 'n' caboodle of the bathhouse waiting for nothing but assembly.'

'So this is marital bliss. No wonder I've remained a single man.' Now it's Porter Green's thin figure blocking a column-length piece of the sun.

Bob gives him a sideways glance, ignoring me. 'Seems a husband's nothing but a packhorse. Just as well you've stayed away ...'

'Mary.' Porter dips his hat, then looks around. 'Where's your sister?'

'She's gone for a walk.'

'Oh? Which way?'

'Along the beach.' I point south, to my left. 'Why, what's the problem?' I turn sharply to Bob. 'You said it would be all right.'

Bob shakes his head. 'It *is* all right!'

Again the hand goes to a spot halfway up his back, as though he's supporting a paling that's about to come loose. He wanders out the door, mumbling curses.

'Don't worry about him,' Porter says. 'He's always riled when his back's bad. And he's not used to having a woman around.' A slight breeze clacks morse code on the shutters.

Not a white one who's not a prostitute, at least. I bend over to try to heft the treadle machine onto the crate I've just dusted.

'Here, let me do that.'

He's stronger than he looks, his thin arms like high-tensile wire. But my heart plummets as he lifts and I hear the tinkle of something dislodged inside.

'Forget it,' I say. 'It looks like I'll be sewing by hand.'

My eyes sting with frustration as I pick up some soiled cloths and head out to the washhouse. Porter's in the way and I tell him so, with a tight smile. His own face is full of sympathy. I can smell wine gums on his breath as I pass.

'I'll have a look at it,' he says hesitantly. 'Though we might need a new part or two when we next go to the mainland.'

'Please don't worry yourself. If anyone fixes it, it should be Bob.' I look down to the cloths, filthy with the dirt of many months' neglect. 'It's about time he learned to clean up his own messes.'

In the dark, mildewy lean-to, I dump the cloths in the stone trough that passes for a sink. I eye the copper in the corner over its cold hearth. It eyes me back, I swear, its big belly gloating. All of those fish-stinking clothes I'll soon have to boil up. Hopefully, sooner or later, the nowhere-to-be-seen Ah Sam will arrive to help.

Porter's followed me, and now is loitering outside the washhouse door.

'I was married once,' he says and scuffs his boot. 'She died of childbed fever.'

'I'm sorry to hear it. And the baby?'

'Shortly after.'

'And you've never thought of marrying again?'

'Oh, I've thought of it. But it hasn't thought of me.' He seems to realise, then, that he's holding me captive while I've still so much to do. 'Apologies. It's just a long time since I've had a woman to talk to.'

'I hear you might build me some walls today?'

I hear banging in the distance, which I assume is Percy starting work on permanent pens for the animals.

'Yes, of course.' He fingers his belt with the ragged holes. 'Mary?'

'Yes, Porter.'

His eyes have a caution in them. 'Tell your sister not to wander too far from the house on her own.'

I could have told him the scream wasn't sustained enough to signal real danger. I've heard Carrie's whole repertoire. There's the whine that can escalate to a full-blown gale when she doesn't get her way. The glass-breaking soprano of genuine fright. Then this particular high-C squeal with a yelp at the end, for surprise.

But Porter is already running towards the beach.

I follow, slowly, after untying my dirty apron, hanging it from a peg on the washhouse wall and picking up my sunhat. The peach slant of winter air shines through its wicker.

Down at the beach, there's a large gathering: Percy, Porter, Bob, a Chinaman I haven't met who must be Ah Sam, and two Aboriginal boys. Carrie has her nose buried in Bob's chest. He's patting her awkwardly on the back.

'What's all this nonsense?' I ask.

She straightens up, rearranges herself.

'She had a wee fright,' Bob says. He has the same guilty look on his face as when I quizzed him about Will Hartley, his slug agent in Cooktown.

'So I see.'

'I was picking up shells when I saw this monster in the corner of my eye!' Carrie adds.

'Just an old goanna.' Bob's tone suggests he's already told her this. 'They won't hurt ye if ye run away. Just don't stand still, or they'll run up ye as if ye were a tree.'

Carrie shivers delicately.

Percy snorts, mallet in hand, *Women!* written across his face. He strides back up the beach.

'But it was huge!' Carrie spreads her arms to their widest expanse. A hanky dangles from one hand like a limp flag. 'And ugly. I can't bear ugly things.'

I wait for her to look my way, but she doesn't. The two Aboriginal boys are staring at her, transfixed. Despite their wide travels and bush knowledge, she's clearly a species of shrieking creature they've never encountered before.

The ocean's throwing packages of foam on shore, then pulling back, leaving ribbons of white bubbles behind. Bob looks out over the water, then adjusts his hat. His scar's turning pink in the sun. 'If the fuss is over, I've fishing nets to mend.'

'Aren't you going to introduce me, Bob?' I tilt my head in the direction of the men I've not yet met.

'Ah Sam,' Bob says, 'this is the new missy.'

Ah Sam smiles modestly, bare feet shifting in the sand.

Bob turns to me. 'Ah Sam is all yours. Except for when there's slugs to be boiled.'

'Nice to meet you, Ah Sam.'

No response. Then he bends his head a little.

'Ah Sam!' Bob tries to coax him into speech.

'It's all right, Bob. He's just shy.'

The smile is grateful this time. He's older than Ah Leung by five or ten years, which might make him forty-five or fifty. But he looks strong, which is the main consideration as far as I'm concerned. He mumbles something I can't decipher, then steps backwards for five paces before swivelling on his heel and heading in the direction of the pandanus swamp.

I turn to one of the Aboriginal boys. He wears only a small loincloth around his hips, and he's so thin that his ribs stand out beneath the ritual scarring. Bob's already told me that his boys were recruited from Cape Direction, far to the north-northwest of the Lizard. That they have no connection with the blacks that came over from the mainland in their canoes.

'This is Darby,' Bob says.

The boy's head drops. He inspects his suddenly fascinating toenails.

'How old are you, Darby?' I ask.

He consults Bob with a quick flick of his long lashes.

'About sixteen, would that be right, Darby?'

Darby looks up. 'Me seventeen, missis.' He has a surprisingly low voice, as though a toad's squatting at the base of his vocal cords.

'Seventeen. My word. You're tall for your age.'

He straightens up, pleased, showing me that he's taller still than I imagined.

'And this is Charley Sandwich.' Bob waves a hand in the direction of the other boy.

'Me eighteen,' Charley says, a gleam of one-upmanship in his eye.

'Why do they call you Charley Sandwich?' Carrie's found her voice and the colour is back in her cheeks.

'Yer a guts, eh, Charley?' Bob says. 'And not just for sandwiches.'

Charley nods seriously, as if this were a condition to baffle the finest medical minds in the country. His hair clings to his head with tight, black-sheep curls.

'Got hollow legs, eh, boss?'

By way of proof, he holds them out one at a time and shakes them. Carrie giggles.

I pretend to listen. 'I must say, they do sound empty, Charley.'

Another considered nod. 'Breakfast already fall through.'

Something catches my peripheral vision: another fuzzy head disappearing behind a clump of pandanus palm that divides the beach from the flat land in front of the house. One of the Kanakas?

Bob follows the line of my eyes. 'The four Malo men stick with each other. Ye bide them from a distance.'

'Shouldn't I introduce myself?'

'I wouldn't bother.'

'Can't they understand English? Not even pidgin?'

It seems an innocent enough comment, but it incurs a scowl.

'I said not to bother.'

I pull my hat down over my eyes. 'Come along, Carrie. We've a lot of unpacking yet to do.' I turn and walk purposefully back to the house.

'What's the matter with Bob?' Her words are little pants following me.

'A bad back, apparently.'

'Is that all? Is it because I slept in your bed last night?'

'If so,' I say, and feel my jaw tense again, 'he'll be in a better mood tomorrow, I'm sure.'

27

From the secret diary of Mary Watson

8TH JUNE 1880

'Think ye can make it?'

Bob's sitting on a stump, pulling on his boots in the sunlight. The new day's skipping saucily across his eyes. High, arrowing clouds chase each other across the blue slate above us. He smiles and the reins of his scar pull tight. One eye compresses as though to wink, the other doesn't. He *is* in a better mood. As he should be, considering he's taken advantage of every night since Carrie's been in her own bed behind the curtain.

'You asked me a similar thing, remember? Before we climbed Grassy Hill.'

I'm standing with the washing basket, about to head to the two 'Y's of timber strung with rope that make up the clothesline, about ten yards away. I've not yet had a formal washing day with the copper and mangle. Just scrubbed a few things of Bob's, Carrie's and mine with soap and water and wrung them out by hand. There's a whistle across the plain, carrying the faint sting of sand.

'Aye, but Grassy Hill's only five hundred feet. A wee dribble to Cook's Look at eleven hundred. Ye may not make it to the top, considering ye swatted and puffed like an adder on the lesser climb.'

He's counting on friction to spark my competitiveness. But he doesn't need to bother. I have, after all, a particular interest in learning how to pace myself up Cook's Look.

'I was hot,' I correct him. 'And had a blister on my heel.'

The thin hair over his ears flaps with the wind. He didn't wear his hat when he was unloading the boat a few days ago. Even though it's winter, there's a pinkish tinge to his face and a reddish scarf painted around his neck. He puts both hands on his knees and stands, adjusts his trousers at the waist and, using one hand as a shade, stares out to sea at the white caps. 'Some kelpies out there, all right.'

'Kelpies?'

'Ghosts that look like horses. They promise a bonny ride. Then, when a daft man climbs on their back, they dive, drowning his poor lost soul.'

And I thought the Cornish were superstitious.

'Just let me peg the clothes out,' I say. 'They'll dry in no time with this wind.'

'Where's Carrie?' he asks.

I look over to where she's sheltering in a break of trees. They sway and bend around her, but she's calm in the centre of them, sitting on a stool with her sketchbook and pencils.

He follows the line of my eyes. 'Keep her close to the house,' he says. 'I've seen the smoke of a blacks' camp over near South

Island.' He points to his left, somewhere beyond the swamp and the farm.

'Surely they're no threat to us unless they land on the Lizard?' I reply. 'You told me there were no canoes here.'

'The islands are a short paddle from each other. Just precaution. No danger.'

I remember old Riley Robinson's words about the Lizard. How the blacks are drawn to it like a fingernail to a scab. I shift the basket a little under my arm.

'Tomorrow or the day after, we go down to the beach.' Bob's pointing to his right. 'I'll teach ye how to shoot.'

The grass smells of sun and insects, sprinkled with sea. I wonder how that eagle we spied the first morning on the island would view our progress: Bob and me moving upwards, into the vault of a cobalt sky. Grey granite rocks everywhere. When I use them as handholds, they graze my palms.

There's a cairn of rock and a signal flag at the summit, just as I knew there would be. Bob points out a waterproof box anchored to the rock with a metal pin.

'While I'm out fishing, ye can run up a flag if there is need. I'll teach ye their meanings before we go back to sea.'

The view is dizzying. At altitude, the wind reminds me of two charwomen either side of a vast bed, whipcracking a brand new sheet over us. The climb is forgotten: the balding patches of dry ground, the mangy hummocks of grass, hordes of vicious meat ants beneath them.

Bob points east to where sunlight glasses the water, tells me the story of Captain Cook climbing this very summit to try to plan a safe passage through the reef. His words are too harsh for the moment's solemnity. I just want the whistle of the wind to pass through me. His breath is hot and unpleasant in my ear.

'See green out there? That is middling deep. Light green, shallow. Yellow-green, more shallow still. Straw is sandbanks. Jet-black patches, reefs.'

'So he puzzled it out by colour?'

He steers me by my shoulders to where he wants me to look. 'Aye. He followed that dark blue line.'

And there it is. A royal snake twisting through the ocean; a velvet-deep passageway to safety. Beyond it, something white leaps into the sky.

Bob notices where my gaze is hooked. 'Foam and spray. From rollers striking the reef. At night, if ye listen, ye'll hear God grinding his teeth under the sea. Or maybe the Devil.'

I take a deep breath of that sapphire air.

'There's the house, look.' He's twisted me around to face the west again.

I give a perfunctory glance to my new home, snug as a key in the palm of the lowland. There, a moving speck that might be Carrie heading for the door. From up here, it's clear just how dry and bristly the Lizard is. Patches of grey. Bald earth. The creek, a urine trickle heading for the sea. But the magnificent restlessness of the ocean is something else again. All the land's mediocrity is forgiven.

'What do ye think, then?' Bob asks. There's a proprietary pride in his voice that annoys me.

'It's beautiful,' I say. 'Stupendous even.' A white cloud, like the steam from a kettle, pauses above our heads before drifting on.

My next words don't really seem my own.

'Who could blame the blacks for wanting it back?'

28

Why would a woman need a husband
when she has a rifle?

From the secret diary of Mary Watson

10TH JUNE 1880

A sharp in-breath as I wake, bile on my tongue. It's the same dream I've had every night since we arrived.

Somehow, I'm in Bob's head as he lands *Isabella* on the sandy tongue of the Lizard. It's been a long time since he's lived here. Under a full moon with its cataract of cloud, his boots chew dark gravel to the house. There's that island noise he finds so reassuring: the corkscrew screek of pandanus leaves opening the ocean's bottle of wine.

The heavy door to the house breathes open and he slumps with relief, seeing how a fire has been lit and is making those satisfying cleaver-meets-marrowbone cracks. Nothing wrong. Nothing wrong ... except his pipe has been moved from where it usually sits on the mantel. Dark streaks of blood stain the wall, and a woman (is it me?) and her child look up from the light, their skulls aglow ...

Dawn light seeps through cracks in the limestone wall. A seabird's call in the distance. As always, that high-tide backwash of waves. Bob is asleep next to me; a series of whale breaches as he snorts through his nose, then dives again into the comparative silence of a mucousy gurgle, ready for the next surge.

Nothing wrong, I tell myself. Nobody's died. It's just a dream. But if I am the woman, then who is the child? And why is there nothing left of either of us but skulls?

When my heart slows, I grab my robe in the half-dark, stumble out to the door, opening it on the new day's shivery air.

Ah Sam is boiling water for tea in the cookhouse. He looks up with a nod and a smile. Dry crinkles of heat rise from the pan he's heating for pancakes. A crisp, biscuit smell. I pull the robe tighter around me. It's a bit too early in the morning for philosophical conversation, but I still haven't quite shaken off the small hand of sleep.

'Missy?'

'Ah Sam. Do you believe that dreams can predict the future? I had a dream, set on this island at night. I think I was dead. There was a baby.'

He pales. 'You don't say that.'

Clearly time to change the subject. 'You think the men will go fishing today?'

He relaxes a little. 'Maybe. But maybe squall coming.'

I look over the flat-as-a-postage-stamp sea. The sunrise is only just reaching this side of the island. The water's still plush dark, though shot through with cracks of simmering grey. The horizon's a newly lit wick — its flames gain confidence, spread sideways over the ocean.

'It doesn't look like bad weather,' I say.

Ah Sam shifts his bare feet on the earthen floor. Picks up a rag to lift the kettle from the fire. His face is flushed with heat.

'Small cloud in sou-east, light wind from west.'

He hands me a pannikin full of tea and I blow on its surface to cool it. The brew smells of woodheaps and tannin. 'Well, you'd know more than I would.'

Ah Leung hobbles around the corner like a misty troll, barefoot apart from a filthy bandage, hoe in hand. Percy's right: I'll have to interact with him to a certain extent. But the exchanges won't work unless I let him know who's boss.

'Ah Leung. I'd like a cabbage for dinner. And are there any melons?'

He looks up briskly, his face a plaster cast. I know he's capable of relaxing. When I go to empty the vegetable peelings into the chicken coop after dinner, I hear him laughing as he talks to Ah Sam in their hut.

'Melon not very good.' He turns. 'Pineapple only.'

'Well, pineapple, then. I want onions too,' I tell his retreating back.

His shoulders lift then fall in resignation. I shuffle back to the house nursing my tea.

Bob comes, yawning, out of the open door. He lurches past me without looking up. I hear him exchange a few words with Ah Sam in the cookhouse. He emerges with tea. What's left of his hair sticks up, as though he's had a cartoonish fright. The light on the water has a reddish core, with orange corrugations. Sure enough, now the darkness has lifted somewhat, small clouds are visible in the southeast, just as Ah Sam predicted.

'Ah Sam says there might be a squall today. Will you go fishing?'

'Hmm.' He rubs his eyes, looks out over the ocean, then up to the sky: consulting the runes. 'Hard to say.' Sips his tea. 'Want to be rid of me, do ye?'

'No,' I say evenly. 'But surely you must go out fishing soon.'

He doesn't answer. Just scratches himself, then hawks a gob of spit onto the ground.

Carrie's awake. I can hear her moving around inside.

'What's for breakfast?' she calls out to no one in particular. 'I'm starving.'

'Get dressed,' Bob says to me. 'After we eat, I'll give ye that shooting lesson.'

There's nothing soft about beach sand when it's blowing in your face. I'm prone in the hard grass on the lowland, facing the sea. The bristles itch all along my torso. Bob stands next to me, giving instructions.

'Hold the butt up against yer shoulder. Firm, mind.'

'Won't it hurt when I fire?'

'It might, if ye hold the stock away from yer shoulder and the recoil slams it back to bone ...' He leaves the sentence unfinished.

I pull the rifle more tightly against my shoulder.

'Now rest yer cheek on the butt. Drop yer head down a wee bit so ye can line up the target through the backsight. Now what did I say? As distance increases, ye move yer right hand up the barrel. Just a whisper, mind. Or else lower yer shoulder. And when the target's beyond twenty paces away, aim above the point ye want to hit. All right?'

Sun streams off the water, a blinding foil of light striking the already-holed billy lid he's propped up on a broken crate on the beach. I line it up in the backsight. Fire. A sizeable pony kicks me in the shoulder. A puff of sand erupts in front of the target.

I wince and lay the gun down. 'I thought you said this would lessen the recoil!'

'If ye don't believe it's worse the other way, try it.'

He's irritated. Again. I can hear his medicinal balls clinking away in his pocket.

'Well, what did I do wrong then? Why didn't I hit it?'

'Ye didn't aim above the target. It's more than twenty paces away.'

He's not right, I'm sure of it. Ten paces, fifteen at the outside. I grit my teeth and end up chewing sand.

'Well, I'll load another cartridge. Try again.'

'Yer sure yer poor wee shoulder can take it?'

'Quite sure,' I say with caustic calm.

I close my eyes against the flying sand. Then open them again. I talk myself slowly through the process, unwilling to ask him for help. I shut down the flap of the backsight. Grip the breechblock firmly. Draw it back as far as possible with a jerk, raise the muzzle of the rifle while I'm doing so. It takes me a good minute to get the old cartridge case out and put the new one in. Bob delights in pointing out how slow I am. How the blacks could have speared me a dozen times and held a corroboree by the time I'm done.

I put the butt up to my sore shoulder. Line up the sight, move the barrel half an inch higher, and fire. I hear a satisfying tink and the billy lid skitters across the sand. It almost makes the extra pain worthwhile.

I'm not allowed to bask in the glory of my achievement. Bob's already got the revolver out.

'Now, with the revolver, ye must learn a whole different way for loading and unloading. It's only accurate when yer target is close — ten paces at most. The rifle's for when the blacks are halfway over from the swamp. The revolver's for when they're knocking on the door. Ye shouldn't have to kill. Just fire into the air and they'll run away. Let them know ye mean it.'

In another hour, the billy lid is more holes than metal. I've proved to Bob's satisfaction that I know enough to defend the homestead.

I've also reassured myself that if I have to defend myself against Ah Leung — or anyone else who threatens me or Carrie — then I can.

29

From the secret diary of Mary Watson

Ah Sam was right about the squall. Three o'clock and a stiff breeze blows that locked-up horse-stall smell of dried seaweed up from the beach. Bob's mending the wire racks in the smokehouse. Carrie's peeling potatoes, and I'm stringing beans from the garden for dinner. The wind's a sou-westerly and getting on our nerves, bashing the washhouse's spindly door against the frame.

The sound has slapped my ears for half an hour and I can bear it no longer. I plough my face, exposed wrists and ankles through the grinding air outside to hook the latch. I take one quick look at the ocean. Through the blown mist, the water's a series of galloping white manes. Bob's sea kelpies. I close the door against the weather, but still those cloven hoofs kick at the roof. Nostrils snort at the shutters. Rubber lips whinny at the shotgun hole in the door, calling me out to play.

Just above the washing-up bench, the shutters on the south

wall shudder. I walk over and adjust the lever on the window frame enough to peek out. The leaves of the pandanus rustle like a nest of vipers. Even the small, horizontal bands of wind I've let in play havoc with my bun and I reluctantly close up the gaps again.

I hold bobby pins in my mouth, twist the hair behind me into a snail, then fasten it back in place at the nape of my neck. It's claustrophobic in the house. A closed box. No light. No fresh air. The conversation is similarly stifling.

Carrie's been niggling me ever since I came back from shooting practice this morning.

'Papa says I should take up a position as a governess in Maryborough where I can be nice and close to him and Mama.' Somehow I have to impress on her that she can't stay near Papa.

'Don't take a job in Maryborough. Apply for Brisbane, or anywhere he can't easily get his claws into you.'

'Papa said you'd try to turn me against him.'

I've suddenly no time for the gaps in her memory, the blind spots of her allegiance. Her supercilious ignorance. 'Go on, spit it out.' I slam the bowl of topped-and-tailed beans on the bench, throw the dishcloth on top of it.

'All right, I will.' She tips a bald potato head back into the water bucket. The brown tide splashes onto her dress. 'Papa said you made up stories to disgrace the family. Hideous, hateful, unforgivable lies.'

'Why would I do that, Carrie? Exactly what would I have to gain by lying?'

She looks at me coldly. Picks up another potato. Begins her useless, wasteful little chipping away at it. 'It's always gain with you, isn't it? But some things you can't get. Like beauty. Like love.

You're not Papa's favourite any more, it's as simple as that. What you lack has driven you mad.'

I take off my apron carefully, hang it on a hook on the wall. 'Maybe I should have just left you there.'

I wrench the door open, afraid my head will explode with all the angry wasps vibrating away inside it.

'Where are you going? It's blowing a gale outside!'

I look back at her. Her blue dress disappears into the house's shadows. Only her teeth and eyes sparkle. Like a Cheshire cat.

'The mad always walk around in tempests, don't they?'

'Why exactly did you marry Bob?' she calls out after me. 'You don't love him. Are you going to break his heart the way you've broken Papa's?'

I don't have to bang the door shut. The wind does the job for me.

The air swirls like eggwhite in Chinese soup. Gulls beat uselessly with their wings, going nowhere. I move forward, mindless, battered and pushed, until I find myself at the edge of the mangrove swamp.

Inside, it's quieter. The gusts fade to a wet blanket flapping in the distance. My feet slog through puddles of stinking mud. It's an old, old smell. A graveyard of dead men's fingers poke up. The ground pocks and slithers with secretive crabs.

I can hear something under the sea, behind the deep cannon booms on the reef to the east. A low, atonal tune, held, then amplified. That same singing I heard on my first night on the Lizard. Almost certainly a trick of acoustics. But thinking so is one thing; my nerve's creep, quite another.

It's a relief to break free of the squelching mud, tread the bank of the stream, where the roots of the swamp oaks remind me of those whalebone hoops in petticoats, their curved arcs diving into the water.

Something moves on the far bank. A rustle in the tight-packed trees. I should have brought the gun. What's the use of knowing how to fire it if it's resting against the wall in the house?

A bird explodes and flaps in a low trajectory along the creek. Something moves in the dark place behind it. I backtrack into the shadows. A sudden injection between my eyes. Pinpricks around the collar of my blouse, on my ankles, my hands. Mosquitos. I'm not even aware that I'm stumbling, one eye still on the far bank, when I back into something solid and my chest seizes.

'What the hell are you doing?'

'I have to get out of here!' I push past him, maddened, dozens of erratic sewing needles piercing my exposed skin.

I've never been so glad to see the blurry, windblown eye of the sun burst through the fast clouds and glint on the grey granite rock. The wind has suddenly dropped to the point where just a few high branches quiver. The air's ears are still ringing, though. A high, almost-inaudible screech, more felt than heard, now moving out to sea.

I tell Percy what I heard, what I thought I saw.

He's unimpressed. 'Probably a goanna. They get pretty big. Or a snake.'

'I thought maybe the blacks.'

My fear sounds ridiculous now that the sun has returned. Broad daylight. Humid yellow poured over everything.

'There's none on the island as far as I know. And if you're so worried about them, why did you take off on your own, without a gun?'

Why, indeed.

We walk back towards the house. Already, the bites itch intensely. I know if I don't cover myself in the mix from the bottle on the shelf — lavender oil and citronella — I'll have infected sores all over me in a few days. Bits of palm leaves and other vegetation — detritus of the squall — crunch under our feet.

'How did you know I was here?' I ask.

'I went to the house. Your sister told me. She watched which way you went from the door.'

As though she cared what might happen to me.

'I could strangle her sometimes.' Relief's loosened my tongue. I look up at his profile. He turns, and counters my stare.

'Why did you bring her here if she annoys you? It's no place for a young girl, especially an attractive one like your sister.'

I reach out and stop him with my hand. 'What's that supposed to mean?'

But he has no intention of answering. At least, not yet. His hands dig deep in his pockets. He stares straight ahead.

'Have you heard from Roberts?' I ask.

'No.' He pulls his pipe out, looks at it. 'But the shipment's not until next month. Have you been up to Cook's Look?'

'Yes. Bob's shown me the flag box.'

'Well, then. It must be time for me to show you the lantern, and how to signal with it. As soon as Watson takes himself off somewhere.'

Something catches my eye down on the waterline. Two young Kanakas, dressed only in loincloths, drag their legs awkwardly through the shallow water. I can't make out what they're doing. Dancing? Some slow waltz that requires no partner?

Percy follows my gaze. 'There's a piece of fish stuck between their toes,' he says. 'When a sandworm sticks its head out, they grab it between two fingers and pull it out of the sand. They use the worms for bait.'

'Clever.'

'It's all about enticement,' he says. 'Sandworms to the fish. Fish to the sandworms later on, when they're dangling on a hook. And, finally, a man's mouth to the fish.'

I have a feeling this isn't a nature lesson. 'What are you trying to say?'

'Your husband has a weakness, Mrs Watson. A soft spot for pretty young girls. By bringing your sister here, you're dangling something irresistible between your toes.'

'I don't believe you.'

His voice is calm and cold. 'I don't care if you believe me or not. It's no saddle off my horse what happens to her. She's your sister.'

30

Every stumpy has a story.

From the secret diary of Mary Watson

17TH JUNE 1880

It's been another week of sulky weather. A blustery wind from the east, rippling the skin of the waves as it tries to push them back to sea.

Every time I look at Bob, I see him through Percy's eyes. Every time Bob looks at Carrie, I feel sick.

Coming on dusk. Sky coloured like the flesh of an orange, with white streaks of pith. The axe blade lifts, falls, splinters the chunks of mangrove wood. Backlit, Bob's silhouette has found the hard core of air and is cutting it into stringy pieces. The resin's molasses-pepper tang all around us.

I've deliberately positioned myself on a crate near the house, a few feet away from the chopping block. For want of something to say, I mention that I've noticed one of the Kanakas is missing his arm below the elbow.

Bob looks up, sweat on his tortoise-shell forehead. 'Aye. A slug boat's often got a stumpy. Tomahawks go astray.'

'Is that what happened to Porter's fingers? A loose tomahawk?'

'Aye, but not on *Isabella*; a boat he used to work on.'

The axe falls again. A piece of sap-bleeding wood ends up six inches from my feet.

'Watch it.'

I'm kneading bread dough in the bowl between my legs. It's been oppressive in the gaps between the wind's tantrums. Strange for the season. The air's yeast has been rising all afternoon. I punch down the swelling stomach in the bowl. Hear the broken air pockets collapse with a satisfying burp.

Bob picks up another piece of wood and sits it carefully on the block.

'How do they keep working, these stumpies?' I ask.

The axe descends. He straightens, just stiffly enough so I know his back is still bothering him. 'Hands are easy to replace with hooks. Now, an ear or a nose ... like Nosy Ned, sliced right off ... Ye can't build a new honker out of spit and bailing wire.'

I roll the worms of dough still clinging to my fingers downwards into the bowl, wipe my hands on my apron and stand. 'How could you accidentally chop off your own nose, no matter how drunk or stupid you were?'

His head turns briefly towards me. 'I didn't say they were by mistake. And I didn't say they did it themselves.' The axe comes down on the neck of the wood. 'We'll go fishing tomorrow,' he adds. 'Come hell or high water.'

'Who will go with you? Percy? Porter?'

He looks sideways, mistaking my curiosity for anxiety at being left alone. 'Aye. Porter's always with me on *Isabella*. Fuller will be taking *Petrel*. Ye'll be all right. Ah Sam and Ah Leung will be here.'

Dinner's over. Carrie's writing a letter home under a lamp in the corner, her tongue peeking from the side of her mouth. Percy's playing solitaire at the table. Porter's sewing up a sail, forcing a large needle through a leather brace and into the canvas. Bob's spent half an hour teaching me the meaning of each flag in the box on Cook's Look.

'Now tell me once more,' he says.

I look over his shoulder and into the dark corner. 'Red diagonal cross, white background: I'm in trouble; need help. Yellow background, solid black circle: will you be back before nightfall?'

'How would I answer affirmative?'

'Blue, red and white stripes.'

'Negative?'

'Blue and white checks.'

'What if we're on a good patch and are going to stay overnight?'

'You'll hoist the blue background with white diagonal cross.'

'Good.' Bob pushes back his chair. It scrapes a little cloud of dust from the dirt floor.

Porter glances up from his labours. 'You've got yourself an attentive pupil there, Bob.'

Percy's hand stills on the cards for a second, then he continues his slow unpeeling.

Carrie dips her fountain pen in the bottle of ink. 'You won't have to run up a flag though, will you, Mary?'

'I hope not.' I stand up and gather the last of the dinner dishes.

The island outside is unremarkable: a furled flag in its dark box.

The next day, I hear him whistling at first light. Looping the thin filament of sound from one end of the still-dark house to the other. Casting out his net. Finally, I give in to the inevitable and swing my feet over the bed that Percy's made for Bob and me out of mangrove wood. It's utilitarian: four posts, and rough slats to rest the mattress on. But it's better than sleeping on the floor.

I pull myself groggily into routine. Ah Sam's in the cookhouse, the tea already steaming in pannikins. I yawn as I wander out to take one, and notice the liver spots on the back of his hand. I decide he's older than I thought initially. Perhaps sixty, but strong and agile nevertheless.

Outside, salt vapour in my nose. A few yellow-breasted sunbirds land to peck with their black beaks the crumbs of damper I threw out for them last night. Bob's already striding down to the beach. The sun on the water in front of him like a fuzzy layered pearl with a crimson shell around it.

I blink and run fingers through my hair. The sea air has made it coarse and wiry, like the saltbush that grows all over the island. If it weren't for Carrie — a constant reminder of the beauty I lack — I could abandon vanity altogether in a place like this.

'No squall today, Ah Sam?' I ask as he steps out to empty the tea slops.

'No squall today,' he says with some authority.

Close to shore, *Isabella* and *Petrel* dip like dancers bowing to each other across the water. The Malo Island Kanakas wade through the shallow swell, carrying out hessian bags to store the slugs. The one-armed man has a tangled lump of shark hooks on the ends of pieces of weighted lines to drag the filled bags of slugs to the surface. I'd thought, somehow, that these Islanders were mute, not having heard them utter a word. But now they're talking to each other in their own tongue. Even from sixty yards away, the sound carries. Deep, dry voices, like wagon wheels on a hard-packed road.

Bob's pushing his legs through the water, heading for *Isabella*. I hear him yell something to Percy who's walking down towards the beach. The high-pitched squeal of some adjustment on one of the luggers, like a squeaky shoe pulled onto a hard foot. Everywhere, day's early dazzle throws down its broken pieces of mirror.

Carrie moves up beside me. She looks at the pecking birds half a yard from where we're standing. 'We'll be all alone when they go.'

'Yes. Just you and your mad sister.'

She hugs herself in her nightdress, her face still crushed with sleep. 'I'm sorry I said that. Mary?'

'Hmm.'

'Did Mama ask you to bring me here?'

I look her in the eye, but briefly. 'Yes.'

I sip my tea, and taste the metallic edge of overbrewing.

31

From the secret diary of Mary Watson

18TH JUNE 1880

When I go to collect the eggs, the coop's a frenzy of feathers; a churned-up smell of acrid manure and panic.

I call for Ah Sam as he's passing on his way to dig another nightsoil pit. There's not much room in the pen; even less when he follows me in, shovel in hand. His body odour mixes with the poultry smells — joss sticks, dried fish. There's a whiff of human excrement still clinging to the spade. I'm reminded of Bob's theory that you need an overdeveloped sense of humour and an underdeveloped sense of smell to appreciate the Chinese. As if a slug fisherman is as aromatic as a rose.

I put my head in the nesting box.

'Careful, maybe snake,' Ah Sam says.

Not oriental smells now, just stale wet straw and blood. A dead chicken slumped in the corner; one of the ducks next to it, mauled and lying on its side. Its chest rises and falls erratically under blood-damp feathers.

'Put it out of its misery,' I say.

I step back out and let Ah Sam take my place. A single dull thud of the shovel. When he emerges, there's blood mingling with the other messes on the blade.

'Lizard?' The muscles in my arms are quivering.

He nods, then points to a spot in the corner where the wire's been torn apart. So much for Percy's reinforcement. My still-irritated palms are sweaty. A hot tide of rage surges in my head.

'Why didn't it eat them? Why leave them like that?'

A furrow between Ah Sam's eyes. 'You disturb them. Maybe another hole at back. They are hungry for egg first, then meat.'

'What they'll get is my new-found rifle skills,' I say. 'Check for more holes and throw the carcasses in the nightsoil pit. Oh God, it stinks in here!'

I step under and out of the wire door to take a lungful of fresh air. Now, I can think a little more clearly.

'They can obviously get through the wire. What's the best way to stop them, Ah Sam?'

'They have big claw.' His hand describes a huge-hooked talon in the air.

I look down at the shovel. 'Wood. They can't claw through wood, surely? What about some of those logs Porter floated around from the other side of the island?'

'They for slug, missy. And they climb up.'

I presume he means the lizards and not the slugs.

'We'll tie them together, one on top of the other log-cabin fashion, on the inside of the fence. With the chicken wire on the outside, so that the lizards can't climb.'

He looks dubious, but the plan makes perfect sense to me. He puts on his hat and his eyes disappear in its shadow. He knows we kill the odd chicken and duck for the table ourselves, and probably wonders what all the fuss is about.

'It's my poultry, Ah Sam. I decide when it lives and dies. Not some lizard.'

He nods again, this time with a tad too much tolerance for my liking, as if I'm half-witted and in need of sympathy. 'Boss not like it, missy.'

He's right. Bob won't like it. He'll do a Scottish reel when he sees his precious smoking logs shoring up my chook pen.

'I'll deal with the boss. Well … don't just stand there like a tin shilling. The new pit can wait. This can't. Chop, chop. Tell Ah Leung to help you.'

He puts down the shovel with care. Breathes out deeply. When I put my hands belligerently on my hips, he shakes his head, turns, and makes his small, deliberate steps towards the beach.

The sun's at about four o'clock when Ah Sam yells and I hurry outside. I can't identify the luggers at this distance, but one tacks towards the island, dark as a kernel against the apricot flesh of sky surrounding it. The mainsail's paler: bulging with air. *Isabella*.

I grab the apron from the cookhouse. Ah Sam, in the distance, runs towards the boiling tank and kneels to light the wood fire under it. Ah Leung empties a bucket of sea water into it, then hobbles back for more. A rope of seagulls swoop and circle, tying themselves in knots in the air above.

By the time *Isabella* is anchored in shallow water, I'm in the midst of the action. Fire laps the sides of the blackened tank, sending out its tongues of sear.

Three Kanakas, one after the other, jump overboard. Each of them carries a hessian bag of wriggling slugs. They dump them unceremoniously at the water's edge. Ah Sam drags one over to the tank. Ah Leung pulls a knife from the waistband of his trousers and slits open the loose string stitching at the top of a bag. Then they lift it from the bottom, Ah Sam taking most of the weight, and pour the wriggling contents into the tank.

The smell is the first thing that hits me. Oily sea and hot muscle. The sight is worse: the tortured movements of those fat, bloated bodies. I tell myself that they are simple creatures, that they can't feel pain. But I don't quite believe it. Some of them have ejected their internal organs in a mess that floats on the surface in a lumpy white scum. A sour taste rises in my throat. Ah Sam hands me the stirring paddle with a sympathetic look. The heat up close feels like it's lifting the surface of my skin.

A witch with her cauldron, I stir the horrible porridge. Flame like acid on my ankles. Some of the slugs are three inches long, some almost a foot. Some dark, some mottled. Still others armoured with what look like spines. All of them are hideous.

More bags reach shore. Ah Leung and Ah Sam pour in more live creatures to mix with the dead. A Hieronymus Bosch painting come to life. Now the sky's awash with screaming birds and sticky flies. The fire breathes in and out. I would swear it's far longer than twenty minutes before Bob finally yells at the Aboriginal boys to douse the flames.

The slugs cool in their filthy stew. I leave off stirring, rub the back of my hand across my sweaty forehead. There's an angled pain between my shoulderblades. A film of filthy ointment coats my skin.

Bob dips a wide, flat strainer into the tank, lifting the cooked *bêches-de-mer* from the water. I watch dully from a distance, sitting on the sand, weighed down with tiredness. All I want is a bath.

Percy's not yet back with *Petrel* and I'm dreading the sight of his sail. The whole process will have to be repeated.

I catch Porter's eye as he gathers the discarded hessian bags on the beach, using the fingers remaining on his right hand like pincers. He's exhausted too. As he bends over, his shoulders seem to fold in on themselves. Wrinkles stack up under his eyes.

'What happens now?' I call.

He shuffles slowly over. His shadow blocks the bright flood of colours on the sunset water. 'They're gutted and pegged out to dry for a few days. Then they're taken to racks in the smokehouse and cured.' He rocks back and forth on his heels as though to unkink a cramp.

'I know that. I mean, do we have to wait for Percy?'

'Percy's onto a good patch over near Eagle Island,' Porter says. 'He's staying out overnight. Should be back about lunchtime tomorrow.'

I move my shoulders around, trying to loosen the tight belt inside them. 'Thank heavens for that.'

Bob empties another still-steaming scoopful of slugs onto the sand and then runs his knife longitudinally down the bodies. The guts not already ejected in the water are flicked away on the end of his knife, into a flurry of seagull wings and beaks. I watch his surgical strikes. No movement wasted.

The smaller slugs are turned inside out on the sand, held open by a hinge of skin. Charley Sandwich holds down the bigger ones that would tend to curl inwards, while Bob hammers wooden pegs through them to keep them flat. The whole perimeter around the staked slugs will be covered with old sailcloth to keep the birds away.

Already the sky has darkened to blue ink. The trees behind us have put on black overcoats.

'Why don't you go and put some dinner on?' Porter says gently.

Bob looks up from his butchery. 'Aye, go on. All the men must be fed.'

'Ah Sam?'

'I need him and Ah Leung here.' Bob's words are curt and brook no argument.

Well, that's that, then. Not a word of thanks. And how anyone could eat with the stench of slugs all over them is beyond me.

I look at the ocean longingly. Toy with the idea of walking in fully clothed just to feel the cleansing wash of the waves. But in the end, I just stand at the moving white lace on the edge, rubbing sandy palmfuls of cold water up and down my arms.

The sun's almost gone to bed when Bob and Porter finally come to sit under the rustling pandanus near the house. They shovel in the stew I made from pickled pork, a cabbage and some gnarled carrots Ah Leung dumped on the doorstep a few days ago.

Ah Sam, Ah Leung, the black boys and the Kanakas have already been fed. They lined up earlier for a heaped plate and a torn edge of damper. Carrie took her dinner and scuttled inside, frightened by the big Malo men with their bottomless silence and almost luminescent mahogany skin. I wasn't scared of them, but fascinated. Handing them the food was the closest I had been. But not close enough, it seemed, to crack their code. Each of them took a plate gently enough, but with no expression. Not so much as a twitch of mouth or eyebrow. Unlike the Chinese, who use their features as a device of concealment, these Islanders, to my eye, seem able to remove themselves altogether from their circumstances. A poker player would love to own such a face.

While Bob and Porter eat, I watch the Kanakas wander away to their bark humpies down along the beach. The few times I've had to brave the outdoor privy at night, ten feet from the house, I've seen their fires fifty feet to the north. At first my heart stalled, mistaking them for mainland blacks, until their size gave them away. I'd stood transfixed then. The flames seemed to rise to their chins, the huge halos of their heads floating above.

Bob's and Porter's plates are empty and on the ground next to them. They're having a smoke and swatting mosquitos.

'Very nice, thank you, Mary.' Porter sits on the ground with his back to a tree, ankles crossed, relaxed. Almost asleep judging by the hooded droop of his lids.

Bob says nothing, but his medicinal balls talk slowly to each other. He's brought out the flagon of rum from the house and is drinking straight from the neck, his dirty-nailed thumb in the opening of the handle.

'Will you kill me a goat, Bob?' I ask.

I know he's let loose some goats on one of the small offshore islands. I can't face the thought of half-rotten salt pork for one more meal.

He puts the flagon down and wipes his mouth with the back of his sleeve. 'I'll give some thought to it,' he says. 'When I've nothing else to do.'

The exposed yellow belly of the black snake on the horizon finally rolls over into night. A few high birds in the distance seem motionless.

Porter uncrosses his ankles. Bob offers him the flagon. He takes it, hitches up his belt. 'I could do it, Bob.' He lifts the bottle by his two-fingered hand, supporting it with an open palm and his thumb on the underside, lifts it to his mouth. Swallows. Puts it down again, then wipes his mouth with a none-too-clean handkerchief. 'The goat, that is.'

'Compliments on her cooking. Aiming to please. Ye wouldn't have taken a shine to my wife, would ye?'

I can't tell if he's joking or not.

Porter's face colours to deep plum.

I answer for him. 'Don't be a fool.'

Bob catches up with me near the house, half an hour later. I'm emptying the slops bucket. His fingers bite into my shoulder and his scarred face is an inch from mine. Saliva bubbles at the corner of his mouth.

'Don't ever call me a fool in front of another man.'

He stinks of slugs and rum, and some red pepper of arousal that makes me want to get as far away from him as I can.

'I've stirred your stinking catch, now leave me in peace.'

'I'm tellin ye, don't flirt with him or ye'll be sorry.'

The scar is in stark relief; a pale fault line in the landscape of his face.

'Will you beat me up? That sort of sorry?'

His smile is like the knife blade he used on the slugs. 'Keep pushing and ye'll find out.'

Carrie wanders into the doorway, backlit by the lamp in the house. 'What's going on?'

Bob looks at her for a long, sickening minute. 'Ye're a bonny filly. Useless as a kingshood hanging on a mare, but bonny. How did ye end up with such a nag for a sister?'

'Leave Mary alone.' Carrie's voice is surprisingly firm. Her face is pink, her eyes blazing.

I stand between the two of them. Hold her back with one arm. 'Go away, Bob,' I say quietly. 'Before you do damage that can't be mended.'

'I'll second that.' Porter steps out of the darkness.

Despite his slight build and the fact that he, too, has been drinking, he's still sober. I see it.

So does Bob. The odds of winning or losing flit across his eyes, apparently falling in Porter's favour. He glares at me, then staggers drunkenly into the night. The medicinal balls clank unevenly.

I let go of the breath I've been holding.

32

Stain-removal tips
can come from the most unlikely places.

From the secret diary of Mary Watson

19TH JUNE 1880

It's a prank. It must be. I hold my nose with one hand, use the slug-stirring paddle with the other to rotate the dirty clothes through the putrid water left after boiling the catch. The flies are in plague proportions today, as if word passed around after yesterday's gorging. Remembering how I'd swallowed one on Grassy Hill a lifetime ago, I keep my mouth shut and breathe through my nose. Unfortunately, that makes the smell worse.

Percy came back with *Petrel* at eleven. Another fifty pounds worth of slugs to boil. Another steaming extraction of bodies. Another series of longitudinal disembowellings with a fishing knife.

'Don't tip it out,' Percy told me when I was about to call for Ah Sam to empty the tank slops into the sand.

'Makes good soup, does it?'

'It's the best stain remover there is.' He squinted into a

winter sun made of shimmering gauze. 'Soak the dirty clothes in it, you'll see what I mean. It's also good for polishing brass and copper, though I don't think the idea will catch on in cultured society.'

So here I am, red-eyed and straw-haired, stirring up the laundry.

Percy walks past on his way to the smokehouse. 'Eye of newt and hair of Bob,' he chuckles.

I glance at him. 'Tell the truth. This is a joke at my expense, isn't it?'

'Yes, I'm sorry. I couldn't resist. I'm afraid the clothes are ruined. There's a kind of acid in the water. It'll weaken all the fabric until it falls apart. Maybe if you rinse them fast in sea water, the acid won't have a chance to do so much damage.' He wanders away, whistling.

I yell curses at his back, which he ignores.

'Ah Sam!' My voice is edged with hysteria. 'Come and help me!'

I drag one of Bob's shirts out of the water with the paddle, dump it on the sand, then a pair of trousers. Frantic, I drop stinking garments onto the beach until every piece of my folly is removed. I'm covered in sweat and my arms quiver with the effort.

It takes a few seconds of blinking down at the clothes to realise that the fabric is as solid as it ever was. And that all of the stains are gone.

Six days later, I'm taking in the washing in the cool dusk when I see the two empty buckets parked outside the Chinamen's sleeping hut. Ah Leung was supposed to fill them with fresh water before dark and bring them to the house. He moves quicker and with less of a crooked gait than when I first came to the island. He has no excuse to not do his chores.

I've never seen inside his and Ah Sam's inner sanctum and have no intention of stickybeaking now. I'll just call at the door. Make sure we have fresh water for dinner, and for tea in the morning.

The cloying incense of sandalwood knots in my throat as I draw close. I can hear a low voice chanting something incomprehensible over and over. The door is open a crack. And, of course, the curious heroine with her washing basket under one arm peers through. How else could the story go?

There are two cots, one pushed against the wall on my left, one on the right. In the centre of the small room, equidistant between them, a dozen candles burn around a small altar. In the centre of it sits the ugliest red clay figure I've ever seen. It's squat, with a toad's face, a bulging stomach. Oversized feet. Large hands. It has a pound note stuck in its mouth, and a piece of green ribbon — from my sewing box, if I'm not mistaken — tied around its neck.

Ah Leung's back is to the door as he kneels in front of the joss. He leans forward and lights another candle with a smouldering taper. Then he stretches out fully on the floor so that I see the cracked and dirty soles of his feet. He's taken the bandage off his damaged foot. It's the big and second toes that are missing, replaced by the closed-oyster-shell texture of scar tissue. The remaining three digits seem as small and pale as newborn mice.

I back away, afraid to keep watching, afraid the fumes of incense will make me cough. Already my throat tickles.

I sneak just one more glance before I go. Ah Leung's head turns sideways for a moment. Through the fog of smoke, his face is waxen, deadly serious. The birthmark glows deep claret, swelling like a blood blister in the strange light-play of the room.

I keep retreating until I feel I can safely turn and walk towards the house.

Ah Sam is inside the cookhouse. A few moths waltz back and forth in the shine of the doorway. I look out and over the water. Dusk tonight is like a confectioner's kitchen. The red-apple sun dips into a crackled-candy horizon.

'Ah Leung didn't get the water for tomorrow,' I say. 'You'd better see to it.'

He casts a quick, apprehensive look towards the swamp, where it's as good as midnight already.

'Well then, go and fetch Ah Leung to do it,' I say. 'Maybe if he gets a fright, he'll be more inclined to do his chores in daylight.'

I'm scraping green mould off the pickled pork with a knife, Ah Sam's favourite proverb in my ears: Eye no see, heart no grieve. I reach for the tin of curry powder. It's a trick he's taught me to cover up the taint of the crypt. Still, I won't let him cook anything other than breakfast, having seen him stone the raisins for the bread with his teeth. Spit in the bowl if the mix is too dry. Take the yeasted dough to bed, tucked under his smelly armpit, to make it rise.

Porter has promised me fresh goat soon, but until then we must make do. Ah Sam bustles around in the kitchen with a handful of beans. These, too, I've seen him top and tail with his incisors.

I reach out my hand. 'Give me those. You go and boil water for the potatoes.'

'One day you trust me, missy.'

'I do trust you, Ah Sam.' It's not altogether true, but it sets the tone for my next words. 'It's Ah Leung I wouldn't turn my back on.'

It's a punt I don't expect to pay off; the Chinese are almost always loyal to their own kind. But, surprisingly, he responds.

'Ah Leung stupid man. Very bad temper. I know him from Cooktown when he run that salon.'

There are three kinds of Chinese salons in Cooktown: gambling parlours, opium dens and brothels.

'Did Ah Leung have a betting shop?'

He shakes his head.

'An opium den?'

No, again. 'Fuckee shop,' he says mildly. 'Down on waterfront.'

I think of the surly cripple with a cabbage in one hand, a hoe in the other and bile instead of blood in his veins. I've never seen a more unlikely pimp.

'I had no idea.' I go back to peeling the potatoes.

'His girl go with white man, no come back. He very angry with white man now.'

'He's angry with white women, too,' I say, turning to him. 'I saw the joss in your hut, Ah Sam. It has one of my ribbons around its neck. Is he putting a hoodoo on me? Do you pray in front of it?'

'You should not look at that, missy.' He's genuinely shocked. His thin shoulders lift and fall under the pyjama coat. 'Joss for good fortune. Ah Leung use it so he not be found out —' He realises suddenly that he's said too much.

'About the shopkeeper? You know about that, do you? Is that why the money is in the joss's mouth?'

He nods once, reluctantly.

I carry the pan of peeled potatoes over to him. He takes it, but doesn't set it on the fire.

'But what about the ribbon? If it's not to put a hex on me ...'

'I don't know, missy.' He won't meet my eyes.

I attempt to think it through. Ah Leung is making propitiation to the gods so that he won't suffer punishment for his murder of the shopkeeper ... The next thought makes my eyes widen. Should I have believed that Percy found Ah Leung on the goldfields? It seemed serendipitous at the time.

'Did Ah Leung kill those prostitutes in Cooktown, hoping to put French Charley's out of business?'

The pan jiggles in Ah Sam's hands. He shakes his head rapidly, his queue bouncing from side to side. 'I don't know. You say nothing, missy.'

His voice is all I need to convince me. Another hornets' nest of possibilities is given a good shake in my head. Percy, probably acting for Roberts, must have wanted the Chinese shopkeeper to disappear. So he called on his factotum, Ah Leung, to do the deed. But what about Charley's girls? What would Percy — or Roberts, for that matter — have to gain by their murders? It doesn't make sense. Ah Leung must have acted on his own, fired by revenge for his failing waterfront brothel. The next question must logically be: does Percy know just how volatile, and therefore dangerous, Ah Leung really is? He clearly thinks he has the Chinaman under control. But does he?

I wish I'd never seen the joss. The night seems suddenly much larger; the mainland that much further away.

33

As any good tactician knows,
one should never negotiate
from a position of fear.

From the secret diary of Mary Watson

2ND JULY 1880

Five o'clock, and balmy for July. We're sitting outside on upturned fruit crates. Bob with his pipe, me with my cross-stitch. From here I can see the birds landing on the piece of wood I've nailed to a branch as a feeder. Terns and doves, black noddies with their white caps like wimples, all arguing over the damper I've soaked in honey then placed up there on the end of a stick. Only now is the breeze creeping in: shivering off the overbite of the reef. Down at the shoreline, wavelets pick over shellgrit, as though looking for something valuable. I stitch a little bit more into the darkening sky.

Ah Leung slinks into view with some onions. His hands are smudged with soil, dirt caked beneath those ugly fingernails. I look directly into his face and tell him to put the vegetables down next to me. He starts to back away. I decide the time has come for a bit of provocation, with Bob around as insurance.

'Haven't I seen your face before, Ah Leung? Away from the island, that is? I'm sure I have.'

He pales slightly and tenses. But he has no need to worry just yet. I'm only testing him. 'I could be wrong, of course. I have a terrible memory at times.' I look down to my stitches, pull the cotton through.

'Where did ye work before Fuller took ye on?' Bob asks the Chinaman, only marginally interested.

'Cooktown.'

'Doing what?'

'This and that.'

'I'll come over to the farm tomorrow, Ah Leung, shall I?' I say. 'You can show me all of the things you are growing and what you will grow in the future. I daresay crops take some careful planning if one is to harvest anything worthwhile.'

My fingers go professionally about their business. Nothing for a few heartbeats. Only the far-off waves. The squabbling birds.

'All right,' he says finally.

I've laid the bait. The question is, what do I do with the beast when he takes it?

After he's gone, Bob stands to go into the house. I tell him I'll enjoy what's left of the sun just a little longer, until all that's left on the horizon is a thin purple ribbon. Just like the ribbons Charley's girls wear around their necks. Just like the ribbon Ah Leung stole from my sewing basket.

Bob looks down at me. 'Why would ye think ye'd seen Ah Leung before? How could ye tell one John Pigtail from another.' He thinks a bit further on the matter. 'He does have that birthmark, I'll grant ye.'

A small beetle with an orange stripe down its back crawls out of the pile of onions. I watch its slow progress.

'Probably I didn't recognise him,' I say, sounding suitably vague. 'Don't you wonder why Percy chose a crippled coolie to come to the island?'

He shrugs. Looks out to sea. 'Fuller told me he could work with his gimp ... and it's not as easy as ye might think, getting Chows out here on the Lizard. Lots are frightened to come.'

'Why? Because of the mainland blacks paddling over?'

'Aye. They fancy — quite rightly mind — they'll be first eaten. Wild blacks prefer their flesh, ye see.'

I've heard this before and think it nonsense. Though the Chinese might be less dismissive of the rumour.

'What about Ah Sam? Where did you find him?'

'He was working at the Sea Wah. He asked could he come to the Lizard having heard our old Chows had been signed off.'

'He wasn't worried about the blacks?'

Bob looks sideways at me. 'Some Johns just want to get away from the mainland. A gambling debt. Or trouble otherwise. So long as they work, I don't care what skeletons jangle about in their closets.'

The farm's a quarter of a mile from the house. The next day it's an easy stroll in the afternoon's buttermilk sun. At the edge of the cultivated land, cabbage moths flit. A vine climbs on a chicken-wire frame, drooping with its weight of pencil-length beans. A peaceful place: I can feel it straightaway. Rimmed with coconut and banana palms, pawpaw and sugarcane. The spiky heads of pineapples on the left, rockmelons trailing hairy stems over bare soil on the right.

The romance of nature's burgeoning aside, it doesn't pay to think too much about the process. I've been told that Ah Leung fertilises the vegetables from the nightsoil pits. He's cleverly dug the garden beds exactly the right width so that he can deposit human waste efficiently: by hobbling between the rows, two holey buckets at either end of a bamboo pole across his shoulders. Another good reason for thoroughly scrubbing everything that comes from here before eating it.

But he's not fertilising today. His conical hat bobs over near the sweetcorn. The papery husks rustle in the faint breeze like the material they use to make Chinese parasols. He looks up briefly. Blinks coldly.

'Is any of that corn ready?'

Tight-lipped. 'How much?' He stands and rubs his knees. The material's stained with soil.

Their washing — his and Ah Sam's — never finds its way to the communal pile. I've seen each of them, at different times, down near the sea's edge with a bucket of fresh water, rubbing the material of their pyjamas with lye soap, hats bobbing in time with the movement. I've also noticed the branches near their shack decorated with dripping clothes.

'Ten cobs,' I say, and hear a series of squeaks as he tears the corn silks from the husks.

I walk over the rows, careful not to tread on any seedlings, then form my apron into a hammock. He tosses them in.

'I've seen you before, Ah Leung,' I say. 'You robbed and murdered a shopkeeper. I saw your "Wanted" poster.'

I've decided that boldness is the only approach. If I lay my cards on the table and force his own hand, then the air might clear somewhat between us.

A goanna lumbers between two nearby coconut palms. I'm not frightened of them. Still, with their mottled skin, long muscular necks and flicking tongues, I can't help but read them as inauspicious omens. I watch its body shift side to side, as though at the centre of an invisible tug-of-war. It's taking its time in moving away, unbothered by our presence.

'You should be careful.' Ah Leung holds his head very still, staring at the lizard. 'Lots of things that hurt on this island.'

'You should be careful too, Ah Leung,' I say calmly. 'I know that you probably wanted the signalling job, but it's hardly my fault that you hurt your foot. We are both on the same side, you know. We must work together.'

No response.

I tell him that I'll also have a cabbage. He picks up a cane knife. It swishes downwards as he severs the head from the plant. He throws it into my apron.

'I know what happens to criminals over in Shanghai,' I say. 'Decapitations in the village square. Your knife just reminded me. Of course, if the Chinese in Cooktown knew where to find you ...'

His fist tightens on the handle. The curved blade glints in the sun. Do I just imagine the slight shake in the hand that holds it? He's waiting for what I'll say next. I can hear my heart in my ears. Let him think what he will: that I know only about the shopkeeper; that I've figured out he killed Charley's girls. If he's unsure how much I know, it might work in my favour. So long as he's aware that, if he gets rid of me, it won't be the end of his problems. Just the beginning.

'I've told several others in Cooktown what I know about you, Ah Leung. They are under instruction to make your crimes public if anything happens to me.' I look down at the cane knife, then up to his throat, smiling slightly. 'It's a barbaric practice, but I'm sure there are more than a few people who would line up to dip their money in the blood from your severed neck.'

There's a sound behind me and I turn. Charley Sandwich strides across the clearing, kicking up the dirt with his bare feet.

I see a silver glint of movement in my peripheral vision, swing back around, but the cane knife hasn't moved. Gratifyingly, Ah Leung's face looks paler than usual.

'What is it, Charley?' My throat is tight from tension, and my voice sounds too high and squeaky.

'Boss s'posem you come back.'

Charley stares suspiciously at Ah Leung. Ah Leung drops the cane knife with one last, unreadable look.

'Which boss?' I ask.

'Mister Green boss. He kill goat.' He holds his arms wide to show me just how big the goat is.

'Fresh meat at last!' I say.

Charley licks his lips and nods enthusiastically.

'How about you help me with the goat, Charley? Maybe you and Darby can have some.'

'Yes, missis.' He rubs his stomach. 'Fill belly up.'

'Well, I don't know if we can quite manage that. Pleasant chatting with you, Ah Leung,' I say casually, over my shoulder.

He hasn't moved.

Charley and I walk towards the house together. I pull the sling of my apron tighter around the corn and cabbage.

'Charley, what do you think of Ah Leung?' I tilt my head backwards towards the farm.

'Him sour bloke. I like other one more better.'

'I like Ah Sam better too.' I think of something else I've been meaning to ask our black boys. 'Are you worried about the mainland natives coming over in their canoes?'

This hits a rawer nerve. 'They spear Darby and me.'

'Not just you two, probably. We'll just have to make sure that they don't come too close.'

He doesn't look reassured. We reach the beach, and he points southwest. 'Wild black that way. Not far.'

It looks like he's pointing to the southern tip of Lizard Island. Or something beyond it.

'Now?'

Charley nods.

'But Bob said there's no blacks on the island.'

He doesn't want to contradict the boss, but his mouth is set.

'What do they want, do you know? Why do they come to the Lizard?'

But he either doesn't understand me, or won't say.

34

All men in the far north carry a knife.
The trick is knowing how to use it.

From the secret diary of Mary Watson

3RD JULY 1880

An afternoon in Gehenna. Stripped, hacked and portioned. A hot red smell in my nose. Grease under my fingernails.

The blade flashes in Porter's hand as he bends over the dead goat, holding one of its horns. He flenses the skin from the body in economical tearing motions, aided by the wedge of the knife, until there is just a ribbed bag of shadowy organs, rivers of crimson veins just under the surface.

The intestines stream into the dirt when he runs the blade up from pelvis to rib, the muscle in his thin arm flexing like a ball squeezed then released. The black boys know the routine in a way that I don't. They run to grab as much as they can of the slippery mess and then stand back waiting for the rest.

Porter turns the carcass over, makes an incision to expose the kidneys, cuts the ties that hold them like coin purses to a belt, then flicks them towards Charley and Darby. I step back to avoid a splash of blood, and hold my nose.

'Thanks, boss.' Charley's still expectant.

'Shoo now,' Porter says.

The boys move to a spot three feet away and look hungry there, instead.

The Kanakas have slipped silently into the background.

Porter glances up at me, his forehead shining. His fingers are dripping. There's a strange, almost indifferent lust in his eyes.

'You have to give them all some,' he tells me. 'It's good policy to keep the workers happy.'

I motion with my head to the Islander men. They move closer. Porter portions the meat and I hand out the pieces, each with its garnish of flies. Charley leers at the collapsed purple pouches of lungs in the cavity.

'All right, take them, you little guts,' Porter says with a grin, deftly cutting the organs free and tossing them over. 'One day I swear you'll eat so much you'll explode.'

Back in the cookhouse, Ah Sam and I begin our preparations. Even in winter, fresh meat won't last longer than two days. From under the tub, he drags out a small tin safe with a flyproof insert of wire netting. We work as a team. I cut slits into the surface of each portion. He massages salt thickly into each cut, then places the pieces on a wooden slatted rack. He sets a dish beneath it so the brine can drain away.

'What now?' I ask, washing my hands in a few inches of brackish water.

He points to the salt pig. 'Tomorrow more salt.' He straightens up. Presses a fist into the base of his spine. 'Next day, more salt. Three days altogether. Then store in tub.'

He helps me chop up some of the fresh meat that's left for stew. The corn and cabbage I collected from Ah Leung go into the pot. Soon, a savoury steam rises up. Ah Sam asks if I want potato. I tell him the ones in the house have sprouted and are green all the way through when cut. I'll give them back to Ah Leung for planting.

'Just boil some more water for rice,' I say.

He raises an eyebrow, but obeys.

I wonder what's so controversial about rice. It's not long before I find out.

The sun's gone down, bloody as the goat. It's dinnertime. Bob greets his plate of food with a scowl and that old argumentative glint in his tight eye. He pokes the rice with his fork.

'I'm not going to eat that muck. I've not sunk so low.'

Porter's watchful, his eyes moving from Bob to me. He forks in a mouthful of stew and chews slowly. Percy looks up with a spark in his gaze, as though sensing the night's entertainment's about to unfold.

I count to ten in my head, then another ten.

I listen to the bristles of wind outside, painting the sky in wide brush strokes. I try to conjure up some oriental calm.

'The potatoes are green,' I say. 'And rice is the only dry food the insects leave alone. Would you rather have a mouthful of creepy-crawlies?'

Bob raises the eyebrow on the sinister side of his face. 'Aye.' He takes a swallow of rum from his pannikin. 'So long as they're not Chinese creepy-crawlies.'

'You could always cook your own dinner, Watson,' Percy says pleasantly.

'And ye could mind the shit coming out of yer gob.'

A knot in my stomach tightens. Porter puts a hand on Bob's arm. Bob shakes him off.

Carrie's already put down her fork, her eyes small, like a wary animal's.

Percy takes a mouthful of rice, exaggerates his pleasure in its chewing. 'Delicious, Mary. I always think rice adds an indefinable something to any meal.'

And then the whole sorry carnival cranks up its routine.

'Come outside and fight like a man. Or don't ye have the mettle to back up the mouth.'

'I'm a lover, not a fighter, Watson. Unlike you with those trollops at Charley's.'

Bob lunges over the table. Plates, food and cups go flying. Percy lands a punch.

I've had enough. I upend the table and, while I'm at it, kick over the scraps bucket. Drag my arm along one of the shelves so that fishing gear, bottles of buttons, canisters of food go flying. I doubt they even notice.

'Kill each other. See if I care. I'm not staying around to watch this. Come on, Carrie.'

The door bangs against its frame. I have no firm plan but to head for the moon in the distance. I can hear Porter calling my name from the doorway, but I don't turn. Behind us, there are fading expletives and the fleshy whack of knuckles.

'Where are we going?' Carrie asks. 'I'm cold. I haven't got my shawl.'

I slow down enough for her to catch up and put my arm around her. 'We'll sit on the beach for a while until they cool off.'

'But it's so dark. It's not safe.'

The molten-rush to my head has subsided. The moon's a great, new-minted sovereign in the black silk money-bag of the sky. Its light is eerie, a cold, colourless pall, but it does make everything from here to the swamp visible.

'Nothing can sneak up on us,' I say.

We sit on the sand with our skirts folded beneath us. The ocean whispers. That same moon that can seem so anaemic and out of place on land is in its element over the water: a silver gown laid over a rumpled bed.

'I'm sorry, Carrie. It's a rough life for a young girl.'

'You're a young girl too,' she says.

I turn to see a deep-yellow light bobbing towards us from the direction of the house. It could be any of the men. I watch, but don't stand.

Porter's face, underlit by the lantern, looks old, sagging over its support of bones.

'Are you coming back?' he asks.

Neither of us moves, so he sits down next to Carrie and stares out to sea. White foam creeps up the damp sand, then leaves ribbon trails as it retreats over the pock of pipis, the small quiver of gleaming stones.

'Have you noticed how the ocean smells salty blue by day? But at night it's more a weedy indigo?' I don't know why I've said it.

'Colours don't smell.' He smiles in the dark. 'But I somehow know what you mean. Are you coming back?' Again, that patient tone.

'Is the fight over?'

'Yes,' he says. 'You mustn't get upset about those two. They've been at each other from the beginning: like bucks sparring.'

'They're not young bucks and they should know better.'

'Yes, they should.'

We sit in silence for a bit longer. Carrie rests her head on my shoulder. I absently stroke her hair.

'Have you always been the peacemaker, Porter?'

He shrugs, a bit tightly, as though I've accused him of being boring.

'You're a kind man. This business, this island … it doesn't seem the place for you.'

He hesitates before speaking. 'Trouble is, I don't know anything else but slug fishing. And the longer a man does work like this, the more time he spends alone, the more he's set in his ways. But … it gets pretty lonely after a while.' He rubs his mouth. 'I suppose a man, even if he managed to get a girl, wouldn't quite know how to act.'

'Like Bob?' Carrie says. I've almost forgotten she's there. 'He's not very good with Mary, is he?'

'No, not very.'

The words are spoken easily enough, but I sense resentment there too. Not fresh, but old. A burned-on crust. What would he envy Bob for? His business? His ability to find a wife? Something that happened a long time ago that I have no knowledge of?

'She doesn't love him, you know,' Carrie says. 'Maybe that's why Bob is so angry all the time.'

'Carrie. Hush.'

'Tell you that, did she?' Porter pulls his knees a little closer up to his chest.

'No … I just know.'

'Carrie a romantic,' I say dryly.

'There are worse things to be.'

Carrie finishes the conversation off for all of us. 'It's only fair, though. Bob doesn't love her either.'

By ten o'clock, the two men, at least temporarily, have settled their differences. Carrie's asleep. Porter and Percy have gone to their huts for the night. It's just Bob and me. It's a shock to hear him say in an ordinary voice, 'Today would have been my poor mother's birthday.' He gingerly reaches for what will soon be a black eye.

I pull a sock over a smooth knucklebone. Pick up a darning needle. 'Oh?' I draw the needle through, readjust the material. After half an hour's cleaning up the mess in the house, I'm not sympathetic.

He's sitting in a partial patch of darkness, outside the civilised circle of lantern light. I can hear the wet-fish suck on his pipe, the slow click as the medicinal balls roll into the past. His movements look like shadow puppets on a wall.

'Aye, she was a wonderful mother,' he says. 'But addled in the head.'

I think back to the letter I found in his box: *Things would have been different if Mother was a normal woman.*

'She killed my father, did ye know?'

I count a slow six seconds. Listen to the insomniac sea turning over in its bed. Another suck on the pipe. Another brooding silence. The shift of stones close to the house. A lizard?

The balls rotate a half-click. Bob's fingers in the dark work away like industrious worms, independent of his mind, or so he thinks. Truth is, I'm starting to read his moods by their rhythm. They tell me now it's safe to ask a question.

'Killed him? How?'

'Rat poison. She served it up one night on his beef.'

'Did she mistake it for mustard?'

But he's not interested in discussing the details. 'Just so ye know: I'm not addled in the head like her.'

I bring the cotton thread up to my teeth and bite through it. 'Of all the things I think you are, Bob, mad is not one of them.'

It occurs to me I should say something more. He's holding out an olive branch of sorts. And it does make my life easier when he's in a reasonable mood.

'You know, I think it might be Australia that leaves the lid off the rat poison.'

He looks up, head cocked quizzically. 'What nonsense is that?'

'Well, it's so big, isn't it? So empty. So full of that lonely blue light, with dry green beneath it.' As I speak, I feel a sudden pang for Truro. For everything writ small and delicate. The peach-pink hollyhocks that line the lanes, turning their faces like rapturous parishioners towards the church on the hill. 'It's a wonder more of us don't lose our minds.'

He looks at me flatly. 'One problem with that. My mother, the rat poison — it happened in Aberdeen.'

35

While the cat's away . . .

From the secret diary of Mary Watson

6TH JULY 1880

It's ten in the morning. Bob was off at dawn to take the slugs to Cooktown in *Isabella*. He's promised to be back in a few days, or even tomorrow, with a new broom, newspapers, mail and fresh oranges. Carrie's collecting shells down on the beach. Porter has gone line-fishing on the north side of the bay. Percy and I are discussing the merits of a certain brass lamp he has set up on the small table between us. The door is open so that I can see or hear anyone approach.

He holds the lamp up by its handle for me to peer through the overlapping triangles of glass.

'It's a simple set-up. The fewer moving parts the better with these things. Basically, what you have here is a kerosene-lit candle in a protective case. You control the flame with this wheel.'

His long fingers turn the gauge one way and then the other. The flame obediently flares and subsides.

'But surely that's not enough light? And how do I direct it?'

The comma of his smile twitches. 'Meet the latest in nautical gadgetry: the polygon reflector.' He tips what I thought was a fixed glass case up and down and then sideways. It makes the flame a distorted smear. 'You can only really see how it works at night. It's the same principle as a lighthouse. The panels concentrate the light according to which way they're turned, like a segmented eye.'

'How do I stop the candle going out in the wind?'

He lifts a dark upturned box off the floor. 'It's shielded. The flame won't blow out. Still, don't remove this until you're in position or there's a danger dear husband will see the light. Neither do you want another boat caught in its crosslight. The beauty of the reflector is that you can direct the light with accuracy. Look here,' he touches a strip of metal atop the lamp with his index finger, 'this is the sight, just like on a rifle. You wait for the signal from your contact, and aim at it like you're about to shoot. You'll need to keep it very steady. The feet,' he points to four threaded bars in the wooden base, 'are adjustable. You should be able to make it stable on any fairly hard surface, even a rough one. Any questions?'

'Only a few that might make me sound stupid.'

'It's better to sound stupid now than to *be* stupid on top of that hill,' he says.

I look at the signalling lantern again. 'I wonder why the process needs to be so complicated. I understand that the purpose of the signalling is to make sure the coast is clear of French boats so that Roberts's handover of guns can proceed.'

'Yes.'

'So the first boat will flash a message to me on Cook's Look, and then I will relay it to you when you're out fishing. Then you'll signal another boat further up the coast.'

'You don't sound stupid yet.'

'Why is the triangle necessary? Why can't the signalling boat send his message directly to you?'

'You don't come from a nautical background, do you?'

I shake my head. His eyes pass over the things on the table between us. He picks up a ball of twine and holds it up.

'The world is round. So is the ocean.' He positions one finger either side of centre of the ball so that there is a swelling between them. 'Imagine my fingers are two boats and this twine is the ocean. See the bulge that prevents them seeing each other? The distance vessels can signal at sea is limited by the ocean's curve. The higher you are, of course, the further you can see. From Cook's Look you can signal to both of us.'

'I see. And the boat you intend to signal further up the coast is close enough not to need another high point like Cook's Look.'

'Correct. Any more questions?'

'No,' I tell him. 'Not yet, anyway.'

'Fine.' He reaches into his trouser pocket and pulls out a narrow bundle wrapped in a rag. He unwinds it, revealing a silver-plated compass — brand new by the looks — three pencils, a folded sheet of paper and a box of matches. 'The ship you'll be signalling to will have no trouble finding Cook's Look, but you won't know where to look for her. I'll give you the correct direction to search beforehand; that's what the compass is for. The pencils and paper are for recording your messages. Keep them here.' He rewraps the bundle and slips it under a metal clamp screwed to the lamp's wooden base.

He pushes a spring-loaded lever on the side of the lamp several times; it raises and lowers a black metal square over the glass front. 'This is the shutter. Push it down and you're signalling. Let it go and the beam is cut off.'

He illustrates the effect by shining the light on the palm of his hand. It gives off a much brighter glow than I'd imagined.

Percy continues on about how to exchange passwords with the contact, and with him when he's positioned at his co-ordinates. How each message will need to be repeated; how to ask for a message to be repeated if there's any confusion about what was sent; how to confirm that a message has been received. It's complicated but it all makes sense. When he asks me to repeat what I've been told, I do so without hesitation.

When he's finally satisfied that I understand, Percy reduces the flame until it disappears. The lamp is still warm; he lowers the wooden cover over it and snaps shut the catches.

'That's all there is to it. Your contact will signal for ten seconds once every thirty seconds to help you keep sighted on his position. Get some practice covering and uncovering the light smoothly. Don't make a mistake or we'll both be sunk.'

'I can't keep it in the house,' I say.

'Of course not. It'll be in my hut, under a pile of clothes in the southeast corner. On my shelf you'll find a bottle of kerosene, more matches in a waterproof box, extra pencils and paper. Use them as you need them.'

We both hear Carrie whistling, crunching over the gravel towards the door. Percy calmly sweeps the lantern and case under the table, covering it with a stack of hessian bags. By the time she walks in, he has his pack of cards out of his pocket and is introducing me to the finer points of whist.

She puts her hat down on a box in the corner.

'Find any shells?' Percy's getting to his feet.

'No. But there's a schooner dropped anchor in the bay. I saw three men in a rowboat heading for shore.' She claps her hands. 'Company for a change, instead of lizards and rancid old slugs.'

'I'd better get a welcoming party together then.' Percy picks up the bundle of hessian bags and steps towards the door. 'I'm glad you like the design of the new brooding cage for the chickens,' he says to me. 'Carrie, why don't you find Ah Sam: get him to put the water on and make tea for our visitors?'

'But my hair! I need to do something with it. And I have my oldest dress on.' She grabs her hat again, but not before peering in the mirror on the shelf for half a minute first.

Percy winks at me on the way out.

'The lady of the island, Mrs Watson. Her sister, Carrie.'

Percy's performing the introductions. There seems far too little space in the poky house for the three visitors: Captain Laymond, goutish, middle-aged, with a chiselled goatee; and two of his crewmen, short, slight, caps in hand. Carrie looks supremely disappointed in what the sea has washed up. The darker-skinned of the two crewmen, on the other hand, is staring at her as if a mermaid has materialised.

Carrie murmurs something about going for a walk, leaving the four men and myself. Ah Sam busies in, dumps the teapot on the table and just as quickly leaves. I doubt we'll see anything of Ah Leung. These are strangers who might very well have seen the "Wanted" poster.

'Please, Captain, take a seat. I apologise for our rustic circumstances.'

What I'd thought serviceable furniture — crates for seats, a rickety table with saucers of water under the legs to keep ants from the food — all of a sudden seems embarrassingly primitive.

'This is a palace compared to life on board, Mrs Watson.'

He smiles vacantly, then turns to Percy to discuss business. He's headed for New Guinea, it seems, delivering medicine and shovels to the new goldfields. Sunlight shines through the narrow shutters in prison bars, dazzling the dust motes into somersaults and falling in fingerlengths on the table. The crewmen guzzle my tea and cake. The swarthy one keeps glancing out the open door, obviously hoping for another glimpse of Carrie.

'More gingerbread?'

I play the dutiful hostess towards Laymond, smile fixed in place, wondering if he carries a note from Captain Roberts. I even open my mouth to ask at one point, but Percy, reading my mind, looks across the table and says 'no' with his eyes. All three men take an extra piece of cake. No one seems to notice the extra crunch of weevils.

Twenty minutes later, the teapot is empty, the last gingerbread crumbs have been fingered up, the weather and shipping news has petered out. Carrie returns just as they stand to leave.

The captain's drained of small talk. 'I'm sorry I missed your good husband, Mrs Watson. Oh, I almost forgot. I've a note from a ladyfriend of yours, passed to Captain Roberts out of Townsville and subsequently to me when he found I was travelling north.' He reaches into his trouser pocket and offers me an envelope which once was white.

Carrie's eyes brighten. 'Who is it, Mary? And why didn't she just send it to Cooktown?'

She tries to intercept it with her busy fingers, but I get there first.

'It's probably one of my chums from Brisbane who knows that Captain Roberts and I were acquainted during my time in Cooktown. She may have seen him and taken the opportunity to pass a letter on.' I fold it neatly and I place it in the pocket of my apron. 'A special treat for after dinner.'

'Nothing for me, Captain Laymond?' Carrie asks hopefully.

'Alas no, miss.'

The crewman who is so transfixed by her makes a small noise in his throat, as though he would happily give her no end of things and a letter would be the least of them.

Porter wanders in with his fishing rod and a clanking bucket full of bream. The scaly-silver smell fills the small space. He wipes his hand on his trousers and Percy goes through the introductions again. I wonder if I'm the only one in the room to pick up on Percy's impatience.

By the time a second round of niceties has been observed, the afternoon has worn on. If we don't get rid of them soon, they'll expect to stay for dinner and drink Bob's rum. Percy decides the time's come as well.

'I would extend our hospitality, Captain, to yourself and your crew on board. We should, of course, be delighted to have you all spend the rest of the day and evening with us. But with Captain Watson gone ... and the ladies ...' He wears a slight look of discomfort and sends an additional quick tilt of his head towards the amorous crewman.

Laymond nods twice, reluctantly, and rubs his nose with the back of his hand. Either he's encountered Bob's temper before, or else he appreciates the awkwardness. 'Say no more.' Nevertheless, he glances longingly at the flagons lined up on the shelf in the corner.

We all walk down to the beach to see them off. Carrie skips ahead. The cool scent of clean bone wafts up from the sand. Small wavelets jostle each other near the shore.

The oars of their rowboat lift and fall wetly as they head towards the schooner.

When Carrie wanders up to the house again, out of eye and ear shot, I pass the note to Percy. 'Take this. She'll search until she finds it, otherwise.'

He pockets it in one smooth movement. I lift my hand to the men rowing back to the schooner. None of the three respond.

It's almost dark when I notice white steam from the stack of another ship, anchored far out in the harbour. I fetch the looking glass from the house and hold it up to my eye. Hard to make out, as the ship's backlit by a glowing sunset, but it looks as though a French flag's flying at its stern. There are two masts made of steel with the smokestack equidistant between them; big guns silhouetted on deck at bow and stern. An odd, scooped hull makes the ship sit low in the water. It's a French man-o'-war. I call out to Percy, who has just come back from chopping wood in the mangrove swamp.

He takes the glass from me and snorts when he holds it up to his eye. 'What now? Bloody Frogs. That's all we need.'

He hands the glass back in annoyance. I take another peek. They've lowered a small boat over the side. Four spider-like figures climb down a rope ladder, balance themselves, then sit, taking up the oars. The ship behind them is now a bulky shadow on the flushed ocean.

'There's four of them headed for shore,' I tell Percy.

'Damn it. I don't want them on the island.' He runs a rough

hand through his hair. 'Though it's probably just a courtesy call. Smiles on the surface and daggers underneath.'

'I suppose it would look suspicious if we don't act welcoming.'

Percy sighs deeply. 'I suppose so. Look, I'll go down to the beach and meet them. Maybe go back to the ship with them and make small talk for a while. That should be enough to appease them into keeping their noses out of our business. Here, give me that glass again.'

I hand it over. The blond hairs on his forearm as he holds it aloft turn golden in the fading light.

'Wouldn't they find it strange that we don't want them on the island?' I ask. Then a grim scenario occurs to me. 'What if they've found out about the drop and they've come to take care of us?'

'You've read too many murder mysteries. They're not armed.' He moves his head forward slightly as though looking closer. 'One of them's even raising his hand in greeting.'

'Of course they're not armed. If you go back with them, they'll torture you until you've told them everything you know. Then they'll kill you.'

But I don't really believe it. I can see the men's outlines with my naked eye now. Their bodies are relaxed, not combative.

Percy hands me back the looking glass. He walks leisurely towards the water. 'I'll tell them there's someone in the house with a fever,' he says over his shoulder. 'The last thing they'll want is a dose of our foreign germs.' Something about his voice gets my attention.

I notice again that careful intonation that I'd puzzled over back in Brisbane. Percy's told me nothing about his life. Perhaps he originally had a Cockney accent, and has carefully coached himself out of its twang and into the more gentlemanly style of the Queen's English. Everyone wants a fresh start in the colony. And Percy is more ambitious than most …

I stand there, braving the mosquitos and the rapidly cooling air, watching as the boat lands. Percy gestures up towards the house, then towards the man-o'-war. After a few minutes, he climbs in. Two uniformed crewmen leap over the gunwale and push the boat back to sea.

Percy comes back while Carrie and I are eating dinner. He tells me the French ship has anchored in the bay for some minor repairs and will be gone by morning. The captain told him they're on their way to New Caledonia and that they wish our patient well.

'Patient?' Carrie's ears prick up.

He doesn't blink. 'Did I say patient? I meant operation. Our slug operation. Both vaguely medical, I suppose. I suspect I'm getting my murds wixed because I'm overtired. Ladies.' He stands abruptly, picks up his hat and disappears into the darkness.

'I'm surprised you didn't show an interest in the new visitors,' I say to Carrie.

'I saw the ship. A weird-looking thing. But then I decided to go on an expedition over to the other side of the island.'

'You've been told countless times not to wander too far.'

'What can happen in the daytime? If I see a lizard now, I just glare at it until it goes away.'

'I'm not worried about the lizards. Charley Sandwich thinks there are blacks on the island.'

'Bob said there aren't any and why would he lie?' she counters. 'I've seen no signs of them.'

After dinner, she starts a whole new line of enquiry.

'What did your friend say in the note? And which friend was it? Can I read it?'

I bend over the kitchen bench in my apron, scrubbing at a pan. The caked-on residue has defeated both Ah Sam and me. It's a relic from Bob's bachelor days, when cleaning cooking utensils apparently just diluted the flavour of the next meal. In a last, futile attempt, I put some elbow grease into it and almost knock over the kerosene lamp that is sitting on the bench.

'The letter was from Hope. You wouldn't know her. A nice girl I met in Brisbane. And it was just the usual gossip. Nothing of interest to you.'

She picks up her embroidery. 'Hope. That's a pretty name.'

And an even prettier sentiment, dear Carrie.

It isn't really a lie. The note was full of trivia. I barely had time to glance at it, before I passed it over to Percy, but I saw enough to know it contained bland pleasantries about the weather and social goings-on in Brisbane. My eye was drawn to the items of most interest to us: the prices of overstrap shoes and ladies' light-tweed coats for spring. When the template, with its cut-out holes, is laid over the note, the prices will miraculously become dates, co-ordinates and times for light signals.

It's just after nine when the tied-up dogs growl, the sound like sacks of rocks rolled back and forth over sets of rusty pipes in their throats. They are rarely allowed off their tethers as they harass the chickens and put them off laying.

'What's wrong with them?' Carrie peers through the slush of cold cream smothered on her face.

'I don't know. Probably a lizard at the fowl pen. I should go out.'

As I say the words, the barking starts: a warning sound, with teeth in it. My eyes drift to the rifle propped against the wall near the door.

'No! Don't.' In the shadows, with her white nightdress and face cream, Carrie's a luminescent ghost.

There's a shuffle of pebbles just outside the door. Hard to discern under the dogs' high-pitched cacophony, but there. More like an extra texture than a sound.

Carrie's heard it too.

'Goanna,' I say. 'You know how they come close looking for meat scraps.'

I go over to the shutters, thinking to open them just enough to look out.

'No, don't,' she says again. 'They'll spear us dead.' She worries at the neck of her nightdress with little picking fingers.

'You've changed your tune. I thought you were sure there were no natives on the island.' I'm trying to make light of it. But I feel nervous myself. 'I'll just have a look around.'

'No! You can't leave me here!'

I'm stymied. Left wondering what would greet me if I did open the door and step outside. Perhaps in the distance, the sea covered in its white-veined caul of moonlight. To the east, the distant boom of the reef. Maybe a lizard near the house, lumbering side to side like a chain-mailed wagon. Its eyes like the devil's beaming out at me just before it runs away.

There's a bang on the door. I jump. Carrie screams.

'It's just me. Porter. Let me in.'

I lift the wooden bar. He's dishevelled, as though woken from a deep sleep. The dark-streaked moon peers over his shoulder. There's something in his hands. A small, pale thing. A lady's woollen hand-warmer, with paws. Virgin Mary's pup. Its neck's been wrung. The head's a limp ball, hanging much too far over the side of Porter's hand.

'Oh, no.'

Porter steps inside.

'What happened?' Carrie chews on her fist, her eyes glossy pennies.

Porter says something to her in a low but firm voice. She drifts like a little cloud behind the curtain. A small squeak as she sits on her bed.

I put a finger out to stroke the fur on the puppy's back. Still warm. I take the little body into my hands.

'Who did this? Where's Percy?'

'He's taken the rifle and is scouting around with Ah Sam.'

I immediately think of Ah Leung. I'm almost positive that this is my punishment for our talk over at the farm. But I can't tell Porter that. Not without having to reveal the whole story.

'The other dogs?'

'They're all right.'

I hand the pup back, gently. 'Will you tell Ah Sam to bury him? Somewhere deep. Where the lizards won't dig him up.'

His eyes reach out to me. I know what I'll see in them: caring, comfort. But I can't be weak. I turn away before I change my mind. 'I must go to Carrie.'

36

Sometimes poker requires a prophecy
of what will happen three hands ahead.

From the secret diary of Mary Watson

7TH JULY 1880

Four in the afternoon. The wind stiff and sou-easterly across an ashen, dismal sky. I'm standing near the bird-feeder, about to fling some stale bread, when I see *Isabella* anchored in the harbour. Behind her, a dry storm flashes its ivory teeth. The man-o'-war is gone.

I hear Ah Sam's footsteps and say, 'Better put the water on for tea. *Isabella*'s back.'

'Maybe I'll have a bath first,' Percy says, 'if I smell that much like a Chinaman.'

There's a catch in my chest as I turn. 'Have you had a chance to decode the note yet?'

He's looking out to the lugger, where Bob's yelling at one of the black boys. Any minute I expect the first splash of water, someone wading ashore. Percy's eyes are two small seas, churning. His blond hair leaps against small tethers on his scalp.

'No. Not with all the excitement in the afternoon. And last night I was worn out. Tramping around in the dark looking for mischievous blacks didn't help.'

'Perhaps you should have searched a little closer to home,' I say, my voice thin in the breeze.

He looks sideways, noticing some sign of strain that must be visible on my face. 'What does that mean?'

'I wouldn't mind betting it was Ah Leung who strangled the pup.'

'Why would you jump to that conclusion?'

He's all of a sudden attentive in a way he wasn't before. I open my mouth to tell him about my suspicions about Ah Leung and Charley's prostitutes. How I'm starting to think the Chinaman isn't just a hired assassin. How I wonder if he has a taste for murder for its own sake. But the stillness of Percy's head freezes my tongue. He seems not so much curious as carefully focused. My sixth sense tells me to change tack.

'He's openly insolent. He obviously wanted the signalling job. Now, he's trying to scare me away.'

'Why would he? He might be getting more agile on his bashed-up foot, but even if you did conveniently disappear, he can't yet climb the hill.'

Percy sticks his hands deep into his pockets. I don't know how to answer without showing all my cards.

'Just tell him to leave my animals alone,' I say finally. 'He's no better than one himself.'

Whatever I've said, or haven't, seems to work. The intensity drains from Percy's gaze.

'Now dear hubby's back, it will be harder for us to talk. Come with me and you can decode the note now. I'll keep watch at the door.'

'What about Carrie?'

'I saw her with her sketchbook over near the pandanus patch. She won't bother us.'

'All right.'

I throw the rest of the bread down on the ground for the birds. Halfway back to the house, I ask a question that's been preying on my mind.

'Do you really believe there are blacks here?'

'It wouldn't surprise me. The Lizard's only two miles across but there are plenty of places to hide if you don't want to be noticed. I've seen still-smouldering wood on campfires around the south side of the island. The natives have uncanny hearing. They probably jump in their canoes and paddle around into one of the coves when they hear any of us coming.'

'I'll have to tackle Cook's Look at night soon. What should I do?'

'Take a gun. You know how to shoot.' He makes it sound so easy.

Carrie hurries over, holding her hat on her head with one hand, her sketchbook under the other arm. She looks very pretty: winter roses in her cheeks. Only the coal smudges under her eyes give away last night's strain.

'Mail, Mary! And fresh fruit!'

'Yes, I know. You go down to the beach. I'll be there in a minute.'

We hurry back to the house. Percy follows me in the main door and then through the makeshift bedroom doorway he and Porter cut out of one of the new walls. The house is much more of a home now. The once large communal space divided into eating area, Bob's and my bedroom, and an alcove just outside our door that's curtained off for Carrie's cot, a small washstand and a packing-case cupboard.

Percy hands me the note. I retrieve the grille from the pages of Wilkie Collins's *Hide and Seek*. Despite the overcast sky, there's enough light to read without the lantern. I flatten the paper on the crate that I use as a bedside table then place the grille over it. Our eyes meet, briefly.

'I thought you were going to stand guard at the door.' My voice has an unwelcome thickness to it.

'Try not to worry too much about the blacks. We fired a few shots into the air last night. Hopefully they'll get the message and hightail it back to the mainland.'

I hear voices down at the tideline: Carrie's, Bob's. The muffled bang of something thrown on the ground. That endless background whooshing of the sea.

'We must hurry,' I say. 'Look.'

As I suspected, the high prices of fashion magically transform under the tunnel vision of the grille to a date and time.

'Midnight. Twenty-fifth of July,' Percy says. 'That's only a few weeks away.'

'We'll get caught if we don't stop now.' I refold the note and hand it back to him. 'I don't want Bob or Carrie to find it. Get the co-ordinates and tell me later. You have your own grille?'

'Mm.' Still he doesn't move. He looks briefly at the rough-hewn bedframe. 'How's the old four-poster handling its marital responsibilities?'

A heated flush pours into my cheeks.

'Just go.' My throat is constricted now. 'Bob will kill you if he finds you in here.'

Carrie's found the oranges. Citrus oil stings the air around where she sits, cross-legged, on the sand. Her fingernails dive into the dimpled skin. She would have tumbled headfirst into the mail sack as well, except it's tied with a piece of tightly knotted cord. Bob's told her it won't be opened until later, when we're in the house. There are newspapers, I've been informed: the *Queenslander* and the *Cooktown Herald*. Christmas in July!

I knew that Bob was to sign off two of his Kanakas in Cooktown. Sure enough, two different dark-skinned men are hauling crates ashore.

Bob, his trouser legs rolled, walks towards me. He seems relaxed, in a good mood, and when he's close enough I smell the reason. A familiar scent, faint under the sea spray, but insidious. The cheap perfume that Charley's girls wear.

I paste on a welcoming smile. Tell him about the pup, the visit from the schooner and the brief anchorage of the man-o'-war. He blinks in the cloud-silvered light. Even the scarred side of his face seems to have been on a holiday. But what's that saying about being lulled into a false sense of security?

'Do ye think a man's got money to burn? Why did ye put double postage on the letters ye gave me?'

I open my mouth to defend my heinous crime, but Percy appears before I can speak. The two men exchange a few words about last night.

Bob's reaction is predictably defensive. 'It's a fecking dog, that's all.' And *my* dog, no less. No wonder he doesn't care.

I leave them to it: Bob asking blunt questions; Percy reorganising the tobacco in his pipe with the end of a match. I grab an orange from the box on my way and put my nose to its pitted skin. Then I breathe in deeply.

I know Bob won't quickly forget his grievance about the extra stamps. It will save him feeling guilty about his trip to the bawdy house.

It's three days later and I realise Percy's right. It's difficult for us to be alone with Bob on the island. The smokehouse seems the only spot where he doesn't often go.

A nauseating soupy steam of fish and red mangrove hits the back of my throat. The men have been fishing again since the trip to Cooktown. The wire racks from floor to ceiling on either side radiate heat from fires that have just been lit beneath them. The hut's rapidly filling with smoke that will soon make breathing impossible. Dozens of slugs are laid out on the racks. When they've finished curing, they'll be the size of dried sausages. They'll rattle like walnuts.

Percy tells me the co-ordinates for the light signal. Sweat streams from his nose, his chin. 'Don't write them down anywhere. Keep them in your head.'

My head? It's about to explode. 'I have to get out of here.'

I push the door open and stand, woolly-brained, for a second, breathing deeply the clean sea air.

A minute after I've started towards the house, I hear the door creak open again. Percy, leaving. I glance back. He's heading in the opposite direction, north, down along the beach. Carrie's at the shoreline, dangling her toes in the water, one hand holding up her dress. Percy lifts an arm towards her. She waves back.

Bob's rummaging through a box of fishhooks in the corner when I walk into the dark house. He straightens up. Sniffs the air. 'Have ye been in the smokehouse? Ye stink of wood smoke.'

The bruise on his forehead from the most recent fist fight with Percy has faded to faint yellow. His eyes glitter in the shadows.

'I wanted to see inside. You've never shown me.'

He crosses the room in three big steps. 'Leave out of it. The heat drops ten degrees when the door's ajar.' Then his mood abruptly changes. I can smell arousal on him, just as surely as he can smell mangrove smoke on me. 'Mind ye, if it's hot slugs ye're curious about …' He rubs himself against me. The medicinal balls in his pocket clink.

Carrie appears in the doorway, unannounced.

Bob steps back, exhaling loudly. I straighten my apron.

His eyes are on Carrie's breasts as she stretches to place her hat on the high hook.

Come evening, I hand him a plate of stew. Without rice. Let him dine on the weevils in his damper instead. He doesn't acknowledge the food, just picks up his fork and starts mindlessly eating.

Across the table, Percy is reading the *Cooktown Herald*. He's taken a dip in the sea; everything, including his hair, is washed free of the smokehouse.

Bob wipes the rough bread around his plate. He watches Carrie across the table, soft in the lamplight. Watches her mouth as she chews. Watches the food travelling down her soft throat as she swallows.

I put down my fork, feeling sick. I know what he'll want from me tonight. And straight from the brothel, his body will have a punishing edge to it.

The rum on his breath is cloying as he pulls me towards him in the bed. I offer no resistance when he unbuttons his trousers. I open my legs, not willing to give him the pleasure of forcing them apart. I look over his shoulder, eyes open, as he grunts in my ear. I move only once, when his full weight is on my lungs and I can't breathe.

'Can't ye wriggle a bit?' The words are ground out of him in short, sharp bursts.

'Like Charley's girls do? Would you like me to wave my legs in the air as well? I know you've been whoring. The smell was all over you when you got back.'

His thrusts become more painful and I bite down on my bottom lip. I feel something tear inside me. Please God, let it be my own flesh and not the contraceptive sponge.

After an age, he rolls off me and turns away. Over his shoulder, he mutters, 'Who wouldn't need a live woman after pounding a corpse.'

37

Old fishermen have their stubborn lore.

From the secret diary of Mary Watson

23RD JULY 1880

Two days before the drop. Somehow, Bob has to be off the island on the night of the twenty-fifth. Percy told me to leave it with him. But there's constant acid in my stomach.

After dinner, I sit in the corner, sewing up a pair of Bob's long johns. He, Percy and Porter are playing poker. The bad side of Bob's face, with the lamplight shining on it, reminds me of a mine collapse. Porter's his usual calm self: deep cheeks, watchful eyes. And Percy, when he turns so I can see his features, is cool. Too cool. The flame in the middle of the table flaps side to side like a bright fish, beached and dying. Porter adjusts the wick and it settles into a single, glowing pear. They're talking weather. My needle dips in and out, pulling the fraying threads together as best I can.

'Mackerel sky at sunset,' Bob says. 'I won't go out tomorrow.'

Percy puts three cards on the table, face down. Bob, as dealer, unfurls three more to replace them.

'We'll have to fish the day after that, unless you want to go native: eat grubs and goannas,' Percy says.

'No point fishing in bad weather. Ding *Petrel* and you'll pay to fix it.'

'Come on, man. When did you get so scared of a few clouds? It's not cyclone season.'

'Don't call me a coward, or I'll spoil yer face.'

Percy is hardly moved to trembling by the threat. The tip of his tongue probes the top row of his teeth for an errant shred of meat. He inspects his cards, then rearranges them in his hand.

'We should stay overnight and pick the bones clean: clear the patches around the Lizard before we have to move on, find another station. Unless you'd rather leave them to grow fat for the next fisherman who tries his luck on your old patch.'

'What makes ye think I'd want to keep a lazy bastard as a partner next time?'

The lamplight deepens the furrows on Bob's forehead. His scar's a dark fissure. His left hand finds his pocket and he grunts. The medicinal balls are more articulate, beyond his bluff and bluster. He's thinking over Percy's suggestion.

Porter intervenes, ever the voice of reason. 'What about the blacks? If we go out overnight, they'll know Mary and Carrie are here on their own.'

'Ah Sam and Ah Leung will be with me,' I say. 'And I know how to shoot.'

Percy's lopsided smile twists like a finch gliding on one wing. 'True. I've seen Mary hit a shilling halfway down the beach from the sandhills.'

Bob's impatient. 'It's yet to be proved the blacks are even around.'

Porter's still frowning.

'You mustn't worry,' I tell him. 'I'm used to looking after myself.'

'Ah, so a man's not good enough to look after ye?'

Belligerence has crept back into Bob's voice. But I won't antagonise him, no matter how much he might desire it.

'Not at all,' I say evenly. 'I'm just not helpless.'

I put down the material and walk over to the basin. It still holds a few inches of liver-coloured water. I've no particular passion for washing up, and I could leave the dinner dishes for Ah Sam in the morning, but it's an opportunity to legitimately turn my back on Bob and stare at the much more interesting view of the closed shutters.

A few seconds' silence in which the wind could change in half a dozen different ways, few of them good. The three go back to talking business. I'll have to leave it to Percy. Nothing I say to Bob makes any difference.

I look down to the basin. In the half-light, my hands seem luminous. Attached to them ten white baitworms dive beneath the surface, then come up again for air. I slowly wash the plates with a piece of rag, thinking … sink or swim. With the extra ballast of my wedding ring, it could go either way.

One of the dogs growls in the distance. The pigs start up their clotted snorting. I look over my shoulder. Porter looks at Bob. Bob looks back down to his cards. Carrie's having a nightmare behind the curtain, a series of small yelps.

'I'll just go out and check,' Porter says. He picks up a spare lantern and a rifle from the corner behind the door.

'There's no fecking blacks on the island, I tell ye.'

I wait for one of the others to offer to go with him. When they don't, I wipe my hands on a dry cloth. 'Be careful, Porter,' I say.

He's back in half an hour. With a shrug, he rests the rifle in its usual spot, places the lantern on the bench, and then comes to sit at the table so the game can resume.

'Nothing, so far as I can see,' he says.

Bob grunts and picks up the deck even though he dealt the last hand. He starts to distribute the cards with supercilious flourishes of his wrist. Porter opens his mouth, probably to call him on his error, then closes it again.

'Next time, ye might listen to what a man says.'

Porter doesn't reply.

I, for one, have had enough of listening to Bob. I stand and head for the bedroom.

'Goodnight all.'

'Goodnight, Mary,' Porter's smile is gentle. The other two don't even look up.

The next morning Bob's sitting on a stump outside the house, hammering the soles back onto a pair of reef boots. The thin strands of what's left of his hair wave slightly in the breeze. The rest of his balding head is pink in the sun. Lizard-mating weather: that's what he calls these days when a dry storm shines pale and watery as an old man's eye on the horizon and the wind shuffles down the iron slab of the sky.

Just be pleasant to him a bit longer, I tell myself, as I pick up the egg basket. Carrie's collecting shells. Ah Sam's clearing around a stand of palms near the privy. Ah Leung's at the farm. The black boys are chopping wood.

I feel his eyes on me as I pass. And pass I must. There's no other way to get to the poultry pen. Instead of meeting his gaze, my glance flits over his fishing pants with the hole at the knee. Then his faded shirt. 'Playing cobbler, are we?'

I turn away, as though the churned-up ocean's suddenly caught my attention. It's foaming in spots, like soap's been added to the usual mix of water and weed. This morning, when I took an early stroll, jellyfish like peg bags full of Reckitt's Blue strings dotted the waterline.

'Aye, if we're going out overnight, we'll want the gear first class.'

'Yes, of course.'

I move away, thinking I've got off lightly. But he catches my skirt with his hand.

'How about a wee kiss?'

I bend down and kiss him on the cheek.

'That's a grudging peck ye might give an old aunty.'

Just keep the peace. I kiss him, full on the mouth this time, tasting tobacco.

'Need some mending done?' He winks with his good eye.

I think of the lizards I've seen mating over near the pandanus patch. The flattened female under a wrinkly monster jabbing and jabbing. His rotten-meat breath in her ear. Filthy claws digging into her sides.

'Maybe,' I say, my heart heavy. 'If you clean your teeth and scrub that muck from under your fingernails.'

'I'll catch up with ye later then, when there's no one else around.'

My fate impending I smile thinly and indicate, by lifting the egg basket, that there's work to do before he has his fun.

The tone of my day is sealed when I find what's left of two dead ducks in the fowl pen: a trail of blood and feathers and all the eggs gone. There's a hole torn in the wire above my improvised barrier of logs. I stalk back towards the house, the hot sting of tears in my eyes, something on fire in my head. By the time I reach the flat ground near the homestead, my blood lust has cooled a little, but my frustration hasn't.

Bob and Darby stand behind the house underneath the outstretched wing of a sail draped over a makeshift wooden frame. They're looking for small tears in the material by inspecting places where the sun shines through. I put down the scraps dish and egg basket, and look up at another eagle flying overhead. Against a brilliant sky, it's just a moving patch of shade with serrated edges. I've decided there must be an eyrie in one of the rock overhangs on the far side of Cook's Look.

Bob apparently sees what he's looking for in the canvas. 'Get me the sail needle and thread. Quick fella.'

'Yes, boss.'

Darby scurries out from under the sail and runs towards the house. Bob slips out and into the sun, his palm still under the offending tear. He concertinas the sail against his chest while he waits.

'We've lost two more ducks to goannas,' I tell him, trying to control myself. 'I don't know how to keep them out of the pens.'

'I have enough to worry about without yer blasted poultry. Daft idea using my good mangrove logs. I could have told ye it would never work.'

My hands clench into fists.

Darby's back, panting. He hands the needle and thread to Bob, who pulls the patch over his knee. Darby bends double to get his breath back. From above, his hair is a forest of curls.

I pick up the scraps. 'Thanks for the help. I'll just figure it out for myself, shall I?'

Bob looks up coldly, all trace of his earlier amorous mood gone. 'I thought ye were clever enough to work anything out. Ye certainly knew how to manoeuvre a man into marriage.'

My heart stops for a few beats. He can't know, surely. It's just his self-regard talking.

'Exactly why would I do that, Bob? Why would my life's ambition be to live on a God forsaken island with a cranky Scot who is never grateful for anything I do?'

He shrugs. 'Maybe ye saw a chance to better yerself. Sea-slugs might not be to yer taste, but I'm sure ye don't mind the money they bring in.'

I feel something taut inside me let go. He doesn't know.

'Since we've been married you haven't tossed me so much as a single pound.'

He reaches into his pocket with his free hand, extracts a couple of notes and throws them on the ground at my feet. Darby's eyes are as big as saucers, looking from one to the other of us and then at the money that the breeze is already flirting with and will soon blow away.

I turn my back on Bob and his insult and walk. I see Ah Leung near the bird-feeder and I want to talk to him. After that I'll consult Ah Sam about the hole in the coop.

'Darby, you'd better pick up the boss's precious cash and give it back to him,' I call over my shoulder. 'We all know how much it means to him.'

Bob swears and I hear him spit on the ground, but he has nothing more to say.

Already, yellow-bellied sunbirds, brown honeyeaters and skipping banded finches with their dark-trimmed hoods are watching me from the trees. Waiting for their honey bread. Because of Ah Leung's limp, water splashes over the sides of the water buckets he's carrying. His pyjamas are wet and cling to his legs at the thigh. I've never realised how knobbly his ankles are beneath the hem of his pants. Almost as ugly as his hands.

'Stay, Ah Leung. I want to talk to you.'

I reach up with the nailed pole to place the bread on the plank of wood in the branch. I wonder if I imagine the tingle of a red-hot curse between my shoulderblades. When I turn, his face is as bland as ever. He puts down his buckets and stands imperiously still.

'If you strangled my pup then you're not as smart as I think you are.'

I watch his face carefully. There's a small hiss of air as he breathes out. A slight lift of his lips.

'I no touch your dog.'

'Well, then,' I say, 'that must mean it was the mainland blacks. In which case, you'd be more than a little concerned right now about your own skin. Is it true what Bob tells me? That they're particularly partial to oriental flesh?'

I see his lips straighten. I have his attention.

'I hear that you had an interesting job on the waterfront in Cooktown, Ah Leung. A salon, in fact. You must have been concerned about competition from French Charley's. I heard that some of your girls deserted you altogether, preferring European clients ...'

A few beads of perspiration appear above his eyebrows.

'Who knows what lengths a man might go to if his livelihood is seriously challenged.'

'What you want?' The words have no inflection.

'I told you. I want you to let me get on with my business without interference.'

'I do nothing to that dog.'

We stare at each other for a few long seconds.

'I need vegetables for dinner,' I say.

'You want corn?' Each word is like a tooth being pulled.

'Whatever you think is ready,' I say. 'I trust you to make sensible decisions.'

He nods once. Picks up the buckets and moves away. I watch his awkward gait head for the farm.

My palms itch, letting me know — as if I didn't already — that the conversation hasn't tied up the loose threads of worry the way I'd hoped it would. If Ah Leung didn't strangle the pup, that leaves only the mainland blacks as possible culprits. These same blacks Bob insists are not on the island. And Percy, Porter and Charley Sandwich think are here. But why would they do it? Not for food, as they didn't take the corpse. It could only be to try to scare us. What do they want?

I look out to sea, barely processing the swells and valleys of shifting blue water. I suppose now there's certainty where there had been doubt. The natives are here and, for whatever reason, trying to impose themselves on us. Tomorrow night, I have to climb Cook's Look. It's not only Ah Leung I'll need to watch out for.

The crunch of twigs behind me makes me spin around. But it's only a goanna, glaring at me with its black, egg-eating eyes.

38

The sounds of one night on an island
could fill a whole diary.

From the secret diary of Mary Watson

24TH JULY 1880

One more night before I brave the darkness with my signal light.

The men are playing cards around the table again. Percy's not doing very well, but he's playing two games. He raises the stakes with his final chips.

'There's a good patch over near Eagle Island,' he says. 'We could take the luggers out tomorrow and stay overnight. I'll work the south side, you the east.' He's counting on Bob's cantankerous nature to surface and he's not disappointed.

'I take the south,' Bob says. He puts his cards on the table face up. 'Three tens. My trick.'

Percy shakes his head slowly. '*Isabella*'s not as stout as *Petrel*. There's less chance of broken gear if I take her south. Or don't you remember what the undercurrents are like over there?'

'I forgot more than ye'll ever know. *Isabella* won't break up. She's got a good captain.' There's a thimbleful of goading in each of Bob's eyes.

Percy taps his finger impatiently on the table. 'Well, take your bloody south, then. It's not worth fighting over.'

'Oh aye, I will.' Bob's smug hand sweeps all the pennies in the middle of the table towards him.

From where I'm sitting, I can see Percy's cards. He lays his three aces on the table, face down.

I return to my needlework, listening to the night outside. The ocean's particularly noisy, as though it has a sore throat and is gargling cod-liver oil. What else? Pandanus leaves rustle outside the shutters. A loose piece of tin on the smokehouse roof. Every now and then, the wind opens its creaky tweezers under it, then closes them again.

But the dogs aren't barking. At least, not yet. No sound of stealthy claws on gravel. No screech and scatter of feathers from the fowlhouse. No low-pitched singing to snake into my brain.

I could almost feel safe.

The signalling date has finally arrived. The men left at first light. I waved them off with only a slight quickening in my chest.

As the day wore on, my nerves wound tighter. By dusk, they were ready to snap and sting.

Now, at ten thirty at night, the wind's dropped. A calm fatalism has descended on me. The reef's thunder is reduced to a grumble. Pickpocket fingers of white foam advance and retreat on the swell, creep back and forth over the shining sand. There's a smell of some dead thing wafting up on the breeze.

Above my head, there are small fishing nets full of stars. Under my arm, the rifle.

The moon's so low its light is a web strung between the dark trees.

Carrie's so used to Ah Sam's bitter tea, she didn't notice the sleeping powder I slipped into it. I checked on her before I left. In the faint lantern light, the shadows of her pale eyelashes fell like soft palm fronds on her cheek. Her breathing shallow but even. The catalogue of dresses she'd been looking through on her chest, still bookmarked with two slender fingers.

The door of Percy's hut grates open when I push it gently. Ah Sam hasn't got around to cleaning the glass on the lantern I'm holding. It's dirty with soot, but there's still light enough to see. A bedroll. A small wooden box on the ground next to it. Dirty clothes piled in the corner. And, under the clothes, the signalling lamp in its dark case. I pick it up and am about to leave, but can't resist a quick look around first.

I hold up the house lantern to a small shelf nailed to the wall. On it is a spare pipe, a comb, a revolver and a box of bullets. Next to those, a bottle of Rangoon oil for lubricating his rifle, which he must have taken with him on *Petrel*. A brown-paper package of rifle cartridges. A few folded newspapers dating from the last trip to Cooktown. A single book: Rouvière's *Les Saints* in a deep blue leather binding. I open it to a random page and hold the sooty lantern closer. Not a translation but the original French. Odd. Perhaps it came from the captain on the man-o'-war? Why, though? Percy could hardly entertain himself reading it. Perhaps he thinks Charley Boule might be willing to pay a few shillings for it when next he goes to Cooktown?

I give up my half-hearted detective work. It's time to leave. I snuff the lantern flame and set it just inside the doorway. I close the door and place the outside hook in its eye. Bob won't miss the lantern. Percy often takes one then returns it a few days later.

This time, this climb, I've thought to bring gloves. They're protection against the abrasive granite rocks, but also to avoid being burned when I handle the signal lamp.

I feel safe enough in the clearing. I have the gun and a 360-degree view, aided by thin streaks of moonlight. But when I start climbing, I realise that I can't watch my back and concentrate on the terrain at the same time. The higher I go, the lower the moon hangs in its sling, the cooler and fresher the air, the stronger the sense I'm being watched.

It's not so much the sight of the blacks I fear, but their calls. I've read and heard enough to know that the screech of the black cockatoo — that haunting, extended whoop — is often the last thing Europeans know before they feel the heat of the spear.

Everything twitches around me, as though impatient in the night's light breeze. Shrubs and stunted trees rustle gently. Behind me, looking west, the ocean's hair's being combed: a white flash of swirl here and there, marking submerged rocks near shore.

By the time I reach the summit, my breathing's so heavy in my own ears, I'm afraid it will interfere with other sounds I should be listening for. The climb was hard. My legs are trembling with the effort. But I know that waiting here, on top of the mountain, will be worse. I'm offering a still target to whatever might be lurking in the night. There's only one route to escape, and that's the crooked rocky path that any threat will come from.

I sit. The boulder feels cold and hard beneath me. I stare northwest, in the direction I know the signal will appear. Nothing yet. But I'm a little early. I light the lantern with a match, then cover it with the wooden hood. There's a wide, flat-topped rock two yards away, fairly level, from which I can send my signals when the time comes. Cool, indifferent moonlight falls in patches around me. The sea, from this distance, is a velvet animal turning over in its sleep.

I could have imagined the first crack of a twig behind me, but not the second. Not a lizard, not this high.

I turn. Slowly. Raise the rifle to my shoulder.

'Don't shoot.'

A figure materialises against the backdrop of moonlight and shadow. It steps towards me. The small flame inside the lamp the figure's holding flares wildly in the breeze.

My intestines cramp into something solid again. 'Ah Sam! Go back.'

'Why you here? Very dark.'

His face, underlit by the lantern's weak light, glows at his chin and forehead.

I draw my skirt over the black box that covers the lantern. 'I felt like a walk.'

He shifts his weight from one foot to the other, grunts with disbelief.

'Ah Sam, listen to me. You mustn't tell Bob about me coming up here.'

His eyes narrow to coin slits. 'Why? You signalling a boat?'

The lantern box is surprisingly hot against my leg. I'll have to move soon or my calf will burn.

'When you come down?' he asks, shaking his head. His queue swings from side to side like a dark snake wriggling on a hook.

Cold fingers of logic count the bones at the back of my neck. I'll have to shoot him. There's nothing else for it. I mentally go through it in my mind: lift the barrel, take aim, fire.

'Please, Ah Sam.'

He knows what I'm thinking. 'Kill me, then.' He looks at the gun, my finger already on the trigger.

I catch the glint of metal at his waist. He has a dagger tucked into his pyjamas. He's followed me all this way, with only a dagger to protect himself. I'm beyond exasperation.

'You are the most stubborn Chinaman I've ever met. Here, take this.' I turn the rifle around and hold it out towards him, butt first. 'Keep watch for me.'

He nods. 'Do what you do, then we go down.'

He turns his back to me, sets the little lantern by his feet and stares down the path into the dark.

At first I think the signal might be a natives' fire on one of the nearby islands. But it's from the exact direction Percy told me to expect. I count the seconds between flashes; it's my contact, without a doubt.

I set the signal lantern on the flat rock. Remove the cover and aim it, using the sight like Percy told me to. The whole apparatus is so hot it's only bearable with my gloves on. It's hard to maintain my aim, and it takes longer to adjust the lantern's feet than it did when I practised down in the house. When finally I have it aligned, I press the shutter and count slowly to ten. The shutter lever is devilishly hot. It's burning through the glove, but I dare not move my fingers. I feel the sear of blisters forming. There's a five-second pause in the first password — not quite enough to relieve the pressure points. The ensuing five-second flash is agony.

Eventually I get it right, though now I'm using my thumb on the shutter. It's a slow process, but the exchange of passwords is successful. The message is long. My fingers throb as I write it down in pencil. Then the repeat to make sure I've got it.

What's left is to re-align the lamp and exchange passwords, then send the message to Percy. The rough ground has bored holes in my knees. My calves, worn out by the long climb, are cramping. The moon, though low, is thankfully still bright enough for me to read the paper on which I recorded the message. Next time it might not be; I'll have to be better prepared.

By the time I acknowledge Percy's signal that the message has been received, I'm exhausted. It must be one o'clock in the morning. My dress is soaked with nervous sweat, even though the air's cool. Every joint aches. My two burned fingers feel as though they're soaking in a dish full of molten metal. I put out the lamp and repack everything. It takes several minutes for me to stand, longer before I can turn around and walk a few steps.

Ah Sam is still at attention, the rifle held at present-arms, staring into the gloom. He doesn't speak, and doesn't turn to look at me. Calmly, he picks up his kerosene lantern and leads the way home.

39

From the secret diary of Mary Watson

26TH JULY 1880

The morning sky is wrapped in a straitjacket the colour of tobacco. Ah Sam hands me my breakfast tea. I wince as the heat hits my burned fingers. There's a different smell about him today. Mixed with the usual oriental miasma is the splintery-yellow sandalwood of the candles in front of Ah Leung's joss.

'I want you to clean out the fowl pen later,' I tell him.

'All right.'

He doesn't look up. Goes back to the groats he's been stirring with a flat spoon. The heat from the fire blisters then bursts the mixture on the surface, as if in sympathy with my injury. A not unpleasant smell of wallpaper paste wafts up from the pot.

Carrie steps, yawning, into the doorway. 'I slept like the dead last night.'

'Must be the sea air.' I don't meet her eyes in case she reads the guilt in mine.

Ah Sam spoons groats into two bowls on the bench. He has a cut on the back of his wrist, like a thin, reddish worm. And his arm seems stiff as he moves it. Was it something that happened as he climbed the hill last night?

I pick up the bowl with its wooden spoon, blow on the contents. Carrie takes hers outside.

'Are you hurt?' I ask him.

Sweat runs down his creased neck from the warmth of the fire. He looks at me again, tit-for-withholding-tat in his eyes. 'Men come back soon,' is all he says.

'Is Ah Leung ready to help you heat the tank water?'

'Ah Leung sick today.'

The Chinese are barely ever sick.

'What's the matter with him?' I look down at his hand again. 'Did you two have a scrap this morning?'

He shrugs.

'Is he too sick to help with the slugs?'

He nods.

'Well, it's just you and me then.'

He wraps his palm in a rag to lift the pot from the fire and sets it on the ground outside the door to cool. Later, he'll tip the dregs into the chicken pen before scrubbing the bottom clean with sand.

I take my bowl out into the overcast day. The sun breaks through for a moment, shining on half of Ah Sam's face as he turns to pick up his conical hat. I lower my voice so that Carrie can't hear.

'Ah Sam, you won't tell Bob, will you?'

He stares at me, expressionless. I wait for a minuscule nod, or even a shake of his head. But nothing. Just that flat stare.

I've suddenly lost my appetite for breakfast. So this is what it comes down to.

I wonder how I would be feeling now if I could have brought myself to pull that trigger last night when I had the chance.

A southeast chop on the water. The sea full of needles. I abandon my hat when it keeps blowing off. Pin it in place on the sand with a large rock. The brim flaps like a tethered bird.

Like a couple of convalescents — me with my burned fingers, Ah Sam with his sore arm — we've stacked wood next to the boiling tank. We've ferried splashing bucketfuls of sea water across the beach until the tank's filled twelve inches from the brim. My back, legs and shoulders ache, partially from last night's exertions and partially from today's. To pile insult on top of injury, the blister on one finger has burst.

I leave Ah Sam to keep a lookout for the luggers while I go to feed the poultry and collect eggs.

I'm in the pen, flinging handfuls of vegetable scraps to the sea of pecking around me, when I hear the creak and groan of boat timbers, the bird-screech of a sail coming down.

Ah Sam is at the crumbling border where sand meets earth. 'Hold this.' I pass him the battered dish and head down towards the water.

Something's wrong. I can tell by the way Bob wades in long, angry strides towards the shore. I hold my breath. What if something went awry with the signalling? What if Bob saw the light? But he's not looking at me as he stalks in wet pants towards the house. I exhale in one long stream of relief.

'What's the matter?' I have to almost trot to keep up with him.

His expression is grim. Closed down. The two sides of his face under lock and key.

'We lost a Kanaka, and a day's fishing.'

'Lost? How? Bob!'

'Shark,' he barks over his shoulder.

Porter's level with me now, his trousers rolled up but still wet at the cuffs. The stubbled shadow of his face turns away. A whiff of unwashed male.

'What happened?' I ask him. 'Bob said a shark.'

The battered hat he wears night and day is missing. He looks naked without it. A two-toned forehead: pink above and brown below. He brings the hand that's missing two fingers up to his forehead, rakes back his brown hair. Stares at Bob's retreating back, blinks twice, but still doesn't look at me.

'He came at Bob with a tomahawk. So Bob threw him overboard. Just leave him alone for a while.' He looks down to the water's edge where Ah Sam is supervising the remaining Kanakas as they heft the hessian bags of slugs ashore. 'Where's the other Chow?'

'Sick, apparently.'

'I'll go and check. If he's on the verge of death, I'll let him off the hook. Otherwise, he helps.'

Carrie wanders down to where I'm standing. 'Not more revolting slugs.'

'Go and get an apron,' I tell her. 'I need your help.'

'No, thank you.'

'It wasn't a request. It's about time you pulled your weight around here.'

Almost noon, and we've just finished boiling Bob's slugs when *Petrel* appears, heading for the shallow water near the beach.

Waves fan out under its bow, grinding the already wind-broken glass of the water. Small dark figures move across the deck, preparing to drop anchor. The sky has cleared, as clean and fresh now as it was murky this morning.

My eyes are stinging from boiling-pot smoke. Carrie lasted ten minutes before declaring she was going to vomit from the stench. Now she's sitting, a small sulking figure in a dirty pink dress, under a pandanus palm.

Bob's up near the dunes, pegging the larger slugs open with wooden pins to dry. He stands up, shields his eyes to look out to *Petrel*. Impossible to tell what he's thinking from this distance.

The wind's changed direction, and gains vigour as the new catch is carried ashore. Ah Sam's thin whistle and a few words of Mandarin blow up from the shoreline. A pale Ah Leung is stacking wood for the new fire under the tank. He has a bruise the size of a duck egg on his forehead and seems to be favouring his left side, as though his ribs are tender. Ah Sam has emptied the putrid slug water onto the sand and has Bob's Kanakas filling the tank with fresh bucketfuls from the ocean. The two Chinamen glare at each other every time their gazes cross. I'm sure they've been fighting. But over what?

Percy walks calmly up through the clear blue material of the day, as though a hole has been hacked out for him to pass through. The water's whipped into eggwhite peaks now. His hat tears off his head and cartwheels down the beach. Even his retrieval of it is measured. No hurry. No anxiety. His mood seems the antithesis of Bob's. He closes the space between us in slow strides. He's whistling to himself.

My hair has come loose and whips into my mouth. The sand grinds down the skin on my face.

'Profitable trip, Percy?'

'Very.'

I close my eyes, briefly.

'You did a good job,' he adds.

'What job would that be now?' Bob's voice. Because of the wind, we hadn't heard his medicinal balls approaching.

Percy points to the drying *bêches-de-mer*. 'Boiling the slugs. She's a natural.'

'A well-trained monkey could do it.'

I shrug tightly and my shoulders ache anew. 'You'd have to pay it more bananas than you pay me.'

Percy, at least, sees the tiredness in my face. 'I'll boil this lot. Go and have a lie-down. You've earned it. I'm sure you wouldn't begrudge your wife a rest, Watson?'

At first I think Bob will argue, but it seems the day's taken its toll on him as well. He grunts and walks away.

'Is it really all right?' I ask, when he's gone. A salt crust has gathered on my lips. But I know better than to lick them. It will just make them sting even more.

The lines on Percy's face have deepened with exposure to the weather, but his cat's eyes are clear, sailing through calm waters.

'Yes,' Percy says and smiles. 'Couldn't have been better. Roberts will have some cash for us both. He'll leave it with his agent. I'll pick it up when I'm next in Cooktown.'

'How did you explain the light signals to your crew?'

He winks. 'They were asleep by nine, completely buggered. But even if they weren't, none of the Kanakas or black boys have a particular interest in anything other than their wages. If one of them did see, I'd slip him a bribe to keep him happy.' He rubs his chin. He needs a shave. 'Now Porter would be a different prospect.

He sees far too much. I never take him out on *Petrel*.' He thinks of something else. 'Oh, and by the way ...'

'Yes?'

'A schooner captain out of Townsville passed on a note while we were out fishing. There is no firm date for the next drop. Some delay at the far end of the operation. We'll have to put up with each other for a bit longer yet, it seems.' He lifts a hand and absently touches my hair. 'I never thought I'd say it, Mrs Watson, but you and I don't make a half-bad team.'

40

Why is it, wherever there are fowls,
there's always foul play?

From the secret diary of Mary Watson

23RD AUGUST 1880

Nearly a month has passed since the drop. And the latest update from the fowlyard reads like an itinerary of the dead. Three chickens. Five chicks. Two Muscovy ducks found over near the smokehouse. The clouds build like suds in the west. Carrie's stomping on the sea grapes that line the shore, while a coal wagon of dry thunder in the distance heads north.

Ah Leung is digging two new privies: one for us; one for himself and Ah Sam. He'll fill in the old holes, but not before pilfering some of the contents to fertilise the farm. He'll then just place the flimsy walls and roof of the old structures over the new holes.

Ah Sam and I are washing the clothes. Scrubbing off the muck, then lowering them on a pole into the big copper full of boiling water and a bag of Reckitt's Blue. When they've been boiled, we'll pass them, with strenuous turns, through the cumbersome wooden box mangle. I wipe my brow with my apron. In the closeness of the tiny washhouse I can smell the vague aroma that clings to his clothes: dried sweat, joss stick, fish.

He looks up from the copper. His face is serious, the colour of clarified butter. So drawn that the skull is almost visible under the skin.

'Thank you,' I start cautiously, 'for not telling Bob.'

Inside the seed pods of his eye sockets, some swift calculation stirs. 'One day you trust me, missy.'

He's said this to me before. It's as though the words have some special import.

He goes back to his stirring. The ink smell of the blue bag rises to my nose. His thin shoulders lift and fall under the pyjama jacket as he lifts a pole's worth of clothes from the water. I direct them with another pole over to the mangle. Hot water splashes on the floor and into the fire. A hiss of annoyance. Wood smoke and steam rise up.

Carrie appears in the doorway. 'Bob says you'd better come.' Her bottom lip is trembling. 'One of his dogs is dead.'

'From what?' But my pulse already knows.

'Spear.' She's washing her hands with invisible soap, staring straight ahead. 'It's the blacks. Bob was so angry he tried to shoot the three he saw, but they got away in their canoes. They'll be back. And we'll be next. Do spears hurt, Mary?'

Ah Sam flinches beside me as though the hot water has splashed him.

There's a porcelain glaze in Carrie's eyes. I wipe my wet hands on my apron and walk over to her.

'Listen. They've seen what rifles can do. They'll be too scared to come back.'

Her eyes clear just a little.

'Ah Sam, leave this and come with me,' I say. 'Bring the shovel.'

Neeps, a mixed-breed cur, was already on the island when Carrie and I came. Now he's lying patiently on his side, in no particular rush to be buried. The wind on his tan hide gives the illusion he's still breathing. The shadow of palm fronds play over him. He looks peaceful — until the eye is drawn to the fixed stare, the blood drying on his grey muzzle and the ragged hole where Bob dragged the spear out. Flies gather at the wound.

Ah Sam is carving out a plot just up from the beach, where the soil is loose.

Carrie's pale and quiet. Bob's pacing up and down, wearing a goat track into the dirt.

'Black bastards,' he spits. 'They'll not get away with it, I swear.'

'You didn't care so much when my pup was killed,' I say.

I should know better than to stir him when he's already angry. But I know enough not to taunt him over his mistaken belief that there are no blacks on the island.

'It's only to scare us, Bob.'

He shoots me a wild look. 'Ye think I'm a fool and don't know that, woman!'

'Why are they trying to scare us?' Carrie's voice is high and thin. 'What do they want?'

Porter comes up behind us and looks down at the dog. 'I think they just want us off the island. They want us to go away.'

Bob swings his head around, glaring. 'They'll not make me run like a frightened rabbit.'

Porter chews the inside of one cheek. 'Maybe it's time to call in some help from the mainland. Jocelyn Brooke. Or Harvey Fitzgerald.'

I feel a flash of disquiet at this. Police, albeit incompetent ones, would call the wrong sort of attention to the Lizard. Roberts would be unhappy. And it would certainly compromise my position.

'What would we tell them?' I ask, trying to sound reasonable. 'That two dogs have been killed and we've seen fires over the hill? It sounds like an average night outside the Steam Packet.'

'Aye,' Bob says, rubbing his nose roughly. 'We have to take care of this mess ourselves.'

Porter frowns. The wrinkles running from mouth to chin deepen. 'You read that last lot of papers from Cooktown. Other fishermen have seen blacks' fires at South Direction, Eagle and Barrow. What if it's a concerted effort and not just hit-and-miss scare tactics? Maybe they want to claim all the islands in the area.'

I look up. 'Can they really organise themselves to that extent?'

Percy's opinion that the blacks come to the Lizard because of a personal vendetta against Bob is still in the back of my mind.

'It depends how badly they want something,' Porter says to me, then turns to Bob. 'Come on, man. No use wearing a trench in the sand. We'll think on it. Meanwhile, those cleats on *Isabella* won't replace themselves.'

I'm left alone with Ah Sam, Carrie and the dead Neeps. Ah Sam has the hole already three-quarters dug, and not in the amateurish fashion that I would have accomplished it. Neat, vertical incisions of the spade. Symmetrical. No movement wasted.

'You look like you've done that job before,' I comment.

He looks up briefly. 'I dig many graves, Thursday Island ... missy.'

'You were a gravedigger?'

It occurs to me how little I know about him. About any of the Chinese here in Australia. In some ways, they're as mysterious as the blacks. Springing from nowhere, and returning to nowhere when their work is done.

'You must have wished for lots of people to die,' I say.

A smile plays around his lips. The shovel digs in again, the dirt parts like pumpernickel under a bread knife. He tells me that the Catholics were most stubborn, refusing to keel over and make work for him. But the Anglicans and Chinese made up for it. Sometimes they even obliged by kicking off on a Sunday, which meant an extra bob.

Half an hour later, the job is done. The hole filled in. We walk back through the already sinking afternoon. For no particular reason, I decide that Ah Sam won't betray me.

41

From the secret diary of Mary Watson

10TH SEPTEMBER 1880

The men went fishing again this morning. Both luggers expected back by dark. But, come seven o'clock, when the reddish sun's already going down in the bishop's-purple sky, there's no sign of the boats. No flag when I scan the water with the looking glass.

There's some comfort in habit. Particularly on a night that stretches endlessly ahead. We've eaten our dinner of fresh-caught reef fish and boiled potatoes. I'm emptying the dirty inch of washing-up water on the ground outside the door.

Ah Sam comes up beside me. He doesn't speak, but shifts his weight from one foot to the other, as uneasy as I am.

'They said they'd be back. Why would they stay out? Could something have happened?'

He shakes his head. 'No flag.'

We both look across the ocean again. No flag. No emergency. Just a good patch of slugs both boats are unwilling to relinquish.

Nice to know how little my and Carrie's safety counts for. Only Porter would be pacing the deck, trying to cajole Bob into hastening home.

Ah Sam walks towards his hut. I turn to the house. Carrie's sorting through a jar of old buttons for a match to one she's lost off a blouse. I pick up my mending and sit in the rocking chair Bob usually claims as his own, with a lamp at my elbow.

At nine o'clock, I step back outside. The ocean's wrapped in the cobweb of the moon. Stars wink like light shone through pinpricks in a dark cloth. But there's no whip crack of pale sail tacking towards the island.

I hear the commonplace bark of one of the two remaining dogs. The usual feathery jostle of the chickens.

'Mary, where are the corn plasters? I won't be able to get my boot on tomorrow if I don't do something.' Carrie stands barefoot in the doorway, wearing her nightdress.

'In the first-aid box, on the shelf.'

I turn to go back into the yellow light, glancing sideways into the washhouse as I pass. The fire under the cooking pot has burned down to embers. I can hear their bony clicks and pops.

'I can't find them.' She's rummaging around where the pans are.

'Wrong shelf. Oh, for heaven's sake, let me look before you make a mess.'

I sit up suddenly in the dark, not sure what's woken me. There's an extra thickness in the air around the bed to my right. A solid shape blocks the stripy dawn light through the coral blocks. A small snap, like a branch splitting. The sound of heavy breathing. Movement. A glint of tooth.

'Who's there?'

No answer.

'How did you get in?'

I drag air into the closed squeezebox of my lungs. I can see the whites of eyes now, with a stale-yellow tinge. I fumble to light the lamp.

It's Darby, swaying on the balls of his feet. The shadows cast under his cheekbones are gouged holes in a cliff face. His forehead has a snake-skin shine. He shakes his head suddenly and shivers. The last corner of some blanket pulls away from his eyes. Sleepwalking.

With the distraction of Carrie and her plaster, I must have forgotten to barricade the door.

A few bird sounds from outside. The thumping of my heart. I wonder if he's woken Carrie.

'You've been walking in your sleep, Darby.'

I swing my feet over the side of the bed, pick up my boots to check in each for spiders, and, without making any sudden movements, slip my feet into them.

'Debil, debil, missis.'

'What does that mean?' I keep my voice even and reach for my robe.

'Debil, debil.' He's shivering more violently now. 'You leave this place, too right.'

I feel a creeping on the skin of my arms. 'I'll leave soon enough, Darby.'

He shakes his head violently. 'You leave plenty soon.'

And then he's gone, the breeze creaking at the open door.

Later that afternoon, Bob attempts to calm me.

'So ye had a fright? Darby's not a wild black. Ye said yerself ye left the door open.'

'So it's my fault, is it?'

The men came back at ten this morning. Eight bags of slugs have been boiled and staked on the sand to dry.

I can smell the dark sugars of burned bread. I pick up a cloth and go out to the cookhouse. With a long-handled paddle, I scoop the loaf from the open oven, carry it back to the house and dump it with more force than necessary onto the table. Hot yeast, steam and the flaky pitch of charcoal wafts through the room. The sides are black and the bottom is worse.

'Just as well a man's already ate!' Bob's looking at the charred offering with amazement.

I wipe my forehead with my apron. 'Why didn't you run up a flag yesterday afternoon? To let me know you were staying out.'

'Ye would not have seen it. We were the other side of South Direction. Ye've not struck me before as a nervous woman.'

I throw the paddle down on the table to join the bread. 'Two dogs dead. Natives hell-bent on scaring us off the island. I think I've a right to be upset when I wake with one of them standing right next to the bed! Luckily Carrie slept through the whole thing. She'd be out of her head by now, otherwise.'

'I told ye, he's not a wild black.' He utters each word with infuriating slowness, as though I were a simpleton.

I go to stand near the open door, lift my cheeks to the breeze. Take a deep breath. Chant the word 'calm' in my head a few times.

'What if your tame boys are in league with them?'

He sits on a chair near the table, plants his dirty, booted feet two inches from the bread. Pulls a sheath knife from his belt and starts picking his teeth with it. 'Ye don't know how it works. Darby and Charley would be first to go. Then John Pigtail. We'll be last. Not enough salt in our flesh ye see.'

Percy looms in the doorway, blocking the light. 'Ah, fresh bread.' His nose twitches uncertainly. 'It might be all right in the middle.'

'Ye always were a greedy bastard,' Bob says.

'Better than being a dirty one. Get your feet off the table. Burned or not, I'd rather have syrup than toe jam on my slice.'

Bob jostles his medicinal balls carelessly. After a minute, just long enough for Percy to know he's not being obeyed, he puts his feet on the ground.

Percy pokes at the bread with a finger. 'Next thing you know, the goat milk will sour. You need to look after your wife better, Watson.'

Bob reaches for his knife again, but Percy gets there first. 'Thanks.' He wipes the blade on his trousers, then carves a rough wedge from the loaf. A rush of yeast steam belches out. 'See?' He holds up a slice. 'The middle's all right.'

'Give my fecking knife back.'

Percy shrugs, puts it down on the table. He's almost out the door when Bob throws it. The blade hits home in the doorframe.

I snap. 'You're mad. You're as mad as your mother.'

He reaches me in three strides. Grabs my hair and pulls my head back. 'Say that again, I'll knock ye senseless.'

I turn my head away from the spittle spraying from his mouth.

'Let her go.' Percy pulls the knife from the wood and steps back into the room. 'Only a worm of a man bullies a woman.' There's a layer of ice in his eyes.

Bob opens his fingers and I step back, rubbing my head.

'Want her for yerself, do ye? Ye can have her. Just don't expect too much, unless ye like hammering a nail in a plank of wood.'

The next few seconds pass in slow motion.

Percy moves towards Bob, knife in hand. Bob lifts a forearm to deflect the blade. Percy hits him so hard in the face with his other fist that Bob crumples to his knees. He doesn't move for what seems a long time. Then he stands groggily, one hand supporting himself on the table. He gingerly readjusts his jaw, then staggers out of the house.

'Where's your sister?' Percy's breathing harshly.

'On the beach.'

'I'll go and get her, bring her back here. Then you barricade the door and don't let him in until he cools down.'

'What have you done? We can't go on like this.'

'Yes, we can. For a while longer, at least. Just one more drop. The operation will be finished then.'

'He'll be impossible to live with.'

'No, he won't. He's a bully. Once bullies are bested, they pull their horns in. He'll go off for a while then come back as though nothing's happened.'

I'm not convinced.

Bob slinks back at dinnertime. He doesn't speak. Just heads for a flagon in the corner, and a pannikin. He sits in the rocking chair in the shadows.

I set the table. My body feels like a coiled spring. Even the soft clink of cutlery seems too loud.

Percy must have spoken to Porter. Both men come in for dinner, hats in hand, their movements excruciatingly ordinary. Ah Sam hurries in with the stew. I spoon some food onto Bob's plate, take it over with a fork. He ignores me. Keeps rocking without looking up. His medicinal balls clatter and clank unsteadily in his pocket. The flagon is already half-empty.

I take the plate back and put it on the table.

Porter watches me push the same piece of potato around with a fork. 'You're not hungry, Mary?'

Bob gets up, his centre of gravity unsteady. Bangs into the corner of the door as he wanders outside. I hear a long stream of pissing. A few unintelligible words. I look down at the table, not wanting to meet the other men's eyes. I sneak a look at Bob as he staggers back towards the rocking chair still buttoning his pants up. There are wet spots on his crotch, down the left leg. Old memories of Papa flood back with a vengeance.

I look over to Carrie. She looks at me. I wonder if we're both thinking the same thing.

How could I be so stupid as to put us both back where we started from?

Porter breaks the silence first. 'Are we going out tomorrow, Bob?'

I hear the tinkle of rum splashing into an empty pannikin. The rocker squeaks a few more times. 'Aye.' Nothing more.

My head throbs. It's the child locked in the cupboard behind my forehead, banging her fists on the door to get out.

42

From the secret diary of Mary Watson

11TH SEPTEMBER 1880

At eight o'clock, Bob sinks sideways in the chair. By eight thirty, he's almost slithered to the floor. At nine, Porter and Percy half-carry, half-drag him to bed. I hear him fall with a solid thump onto the mattress.

Porter smiles wanly when they come back. 'You're better off with him this way, rather than argumentative.'

'He might wake up later. I'm not off the hook yet.'

He goes over to the flagon, picks it up and shakes it. 'No, he won't stir this side of sunrise. He's swallowed enough to put an elephant in a trance.'

'Poker?' Percy suggests. He's already cleared the plates. He shuffles the battered deck, then cuts and flicks them together.

'Sorry, old boy. I think I'll call it a night. My teeth are playing up.' Porter yawns, exposing two rotten molars at the back of his mouth. I've noticed him from time to time rubbing clove oil gingerly on his gums.

'What about you, Mrs Watson?' Percy asks. 'You want to turn in with hubby, or can you spare the time for a quick game?'

I glance at the bedroom doorway. 'Just one game. Then I think I'll sleep in the rocking chair.'

Porter waves from the doorway and disappears with a lantern into the inky night.

'Just let me check on Carrie,' I say.

Behind the curtain, her back is to me and she's breathing deeply. The sea is calm tonight, rocking itself to sleep.

Percy looks up and smiles. 'Out like a snuffed gaslight?'

'Yes. I'm sending her home as soon as I can. This is no place for her. It's the kind of atmosphere I was trying to get her away from.'

When I don't elaborate, he cocks his head towards the corner. 'Would you like a drink?'

I shudder.

'Oh, come on. You won't turn into a boozer with just a few nips. And you need to relax. You're like fence wire pulled too tight.'

He fetches two pannikins and pours an inch in each. The first swallow stings my throat. The sensation, not the flavour, reminds me of the drink I had in Captain Roberts's room at the back of the pub in Townsville.

Percy laughs at my expression. 'Now the area's numb, try again.'

'I've experimented with that strategy before. It doesn't work.'

But I take another sip regardless. With hardly any food in my stomach, it's enough to make my head feel like a kite in an updraught. I flinch at a rough-sawn snore from the bedroom.

'Why did you bring Carrie here?' Percy asks. 'You knew she'd be one more complication.'

I run my tongue along my bottom lip. 'I told you in Brisbane why I left home. When I went back to Rockhampton just before I married Bob, I learned my father had started drinking again. I was afraid for her.'

'So you brought her here, to live with another drunk?'

'I know how it sounds. I didn't know what he was like. I thought I could handle Bob.'

I push my mug across the table for more rum.

'Now, now, Mrs Watson, not too much or you might accuse me of taking advantage of the situation. I have my principles. You *are* another man's wife.'

My mouth twists. 'In name only. *Are* you going to take advantage of the situation?'

My words come out less crisply and dispassionately than I would have them. I blink slowly as I study Percy's face in the lamplight. The green of his eyes would be indistinguishable at night but for the sparkling gold flecks.

He pulls out his pipe and a plug. When he lifts a hand to tamp the tobacco, the light picks up the sinews at his wrist. 'Is that an invitation?' he asks, looking into my eyes.

The taste of rum is drying to a bitter paste on my tongue.

A sudden gust of wind under the door wobbles the lantern flame for an instant.

Then, somehow, he's behind me. I feel him against my back. He's undoing the buttons of my dress one by one. His mouth is on the side of my neck. The dizziness in my head turns into heat that moves down my backbone.

'Come with me. Back to my hut. Away from him.'

I close my eyes. The room still spins. 'What about Carrie?'

'He won't wake. She won't wake,' he murmurs into my neck. 'I promise.'

'All right.'

My voice is thick, my nose filled with the sharp aroma of his smouldering pipe, an inch from my face.

Outside, the night rustles its silks. The moon hangs suspended in a gelatinous sac.

His door creaks open. He sits the lantern on the floor. Hastily sweeps away the newspapers on the bed. He seems so much larger in the small space. The lantern paints him in shadow as a hunchbacked monster gliding across the ceiling.

I turn to face him, and he finishes pulling off my dress. The material falls at my feet. I kick it out of the way. The camisole and petticoat are next. Then I sit on the bed while he unlaces my boots.

'Look at your poor toes.'

I glance down at them. They almost all have hardened calluses. A combination of neglect and the filing-down effect the sand seems to have on everything.

He eases me back on the bed and kneels over me, undoing his trousers. 'There's a storm coming, hear it? The wet season will be on us soon.'

As he speaks, I hear a low rumbling in the distance. And then he's on top of me, whispering something I can make nothing of. His muscular thigh between my legs. I open my mouth on the small, sweaty hollow of his shoulder, where a single cord pulls tight, releases, pulls, releases.

Now the lantern on the floor paints our movements on the wall next to his bed. The hunchback's gone. He's a silkworm. One long hitch-and-slide after another, moving forward and back, forward and back, trying to shake off a cocoon.

But my legs wrap tight around him. They'll have none of his attempts to escape.

43

The care of a good man always brings solace.

From the secret diary of Mary Watson

2ND OCTOBER 1880

Percy's been ignoring me for three weeks. Coolly, politely. Firmly.

I've no appetite. My dresses are loose. My wedding ring slipped off at some stage of the morning last Wednesday. I found it again in the bread box at dinnertime.

I've caught Porter watching me, frowning. Sometimes his gaze falls on my reddened fingers with their chewed nails. Sometimes he stares at the slight hitch I can feel at the corner of my mouth.

'I've brought you something,' he says now.

I'm kneading bread dough at the table: earthy spores of yeast up my nose, the peach light falling in segments through the shutters and onto the dirt floor. He pulls a hand from behind his back. It's a cream-smooth nautilus shell with tiger-striped markings.

He's apologetic. 'Not as big as some of them can get. Up in the Strait, they can grow to a foot.'

'It's beautiful.'

The shell is cool and slick. I peer into the open cavity and up an endlessly twisting staircase.

'The animal grows outwards from the shell, sealing each chamber behind it. The last fully open chamber is the living one.'

'So it just closes all the old doors behind it?'

His glance grazes my face. 'Yes. Wouldn't it be marvellous if we could do that?'

I'm caught by surprise, distracted by his hands gathering up both of my own; the mausoleum-cool shell in the centre of our four warm palms. His eyes have a patient question at their centre.

'What is it that you want, Mary?'

'Right now?'

He nods.

Want, as opposed to need? I fix on a specific, tangible target. Something that's not so big as to yawn like a cavern when I approach it.

'I want Carrie off the island, away from here.'

'Is that all?' He lets my hands drop.

I don't know what else to say that won't betray me. He looks at me for a long moment then nods once, slowly.

'I'll go over with Bob when he next takes the slugs to Cooktown and see what I can do about getting passage home for your sister.'

And then he's gone and I'm alone with the creaking house, the shell and the dough.

A week later and I'm staring at the shell again. So long, this time, that its stripes shimmer in the afternoon sun, orange into cream, until the surface looks like the mandarin dainties Grandfather Oxnam used to bring back in brown-paper packets on his weekly trips in the buggy to Truro. The taste of a miniature boiled-sweet sun is on my tongue. Saliva squirts into my mouth.

When Carrie comes in, I ask her if she remembers them, or was she too young?

'I remember.' Without being asked she ties the spare apron around her waist, fetches the bucket and the potatoes and brings them over to the table. She sits on the stool and starts peeling with the knife. 'We used to eat them under the monkey-puzzle tree,' she says. 'I'd lie on my back looking up at the bits of sky. It was like lying at the bottom of a wolf trap, with all the crossed branches above.'

'Funny, I always pretended the branches were the thatched roof of my own secret house, where only the people I invited could stay,' I tell her.

'Except you never invited anyone. You preferred to be alone.'

Today's bread dough is shiny and smooth now. I set it aside in its dish, drape a cloth over it. Then fetch the beans Ah Leung dumped at the door this morning, and begin topping-and-tailing them.

'Do you remember the fig tree in St Newlyn's churchyard? The one with a curse on it?' Carrie asks, looking up.

The corners of my mouth feel heavy, nevertheless I can't stop a smile when I think of the old schoolyard chant. 'Who plucks a leaf will need a hearse,' I recall.

'It's not a laughing matter,' she says, with a seriousness that doesn't suit her face. 'Didn't you hear the story of the church warden who took his shears to it when the branches blocked the gutters? He fell off his horse shortly afterwards and died.'

'Lots of men in the country have falls from their horses, Carrie.'

The ocean's particularly calm today. We hear a swishing sound, accompanied by low, anti-tonal singing. Ah Leung with his scythe is clearing the long grass around the clothesline.

'Well, then,' she continues, 'remember the Archdeacon of Cornwall? He made a visit to the church in sixty-four. He tore off a few leaves to prove that the power of Christ was stronger than the power of the Devil. And guess what?'

'He had a heart attack and went to his maker. I know the stories, Carrie. He was ten years older than God himself. It was about time he kicked off from something.'

'Well,' she's digging around in the salt pig with the wooden spoon, mounting her arguments, 'what about the blacks?'

'I didn't know they'd been to Cornwall.'

She gives me a flat look. 'That bone that they point at their enemies. It's a human bone. And it doesn't matter if you know you've had it pointed at you or not. It doesn't matter if you believe it's nonsense. You waste away and die. Just like that.'

'We all waste away and die,' I say, 'eventually. Who's to say it wouldn't have happened anyway?'

She shakes her head. 'You're so stubborn! Even to the point of being wrong.'

I feel a small shiver in my chest. 'That's possibly the most accurate thing you've ever said about me.'

I take Porter's nautilus shell over to the sill by the shutters so that when the light shines through, it will fall on its smooth surface.

'Mary, you didn't ever … you know … the fig tree?'

'Pick a leaf? Of course I did. Who could resist a challenge like that?'

'How could you be so reckless!'

'I'm not dead, am I?'

Ah Leung's still carving up the grassy air outside. The evening birds chatter at the feeder.

'Do you remember much about Grandfather, Carrie? Apart from the sweets?'

I'm thinking of Porter. Somehow I've conjoined the two men in my head. It seems somehow right, even perceptive of me, this balmy afternoon.

'He had neckerchiefs in different colours. And a walking stick with an eagle's head.'

'Clever girl. That's right.'

She's encouraged by my praise. 'He used to write letters with special paper. I remember the box. It had solid triangle shapes on it and palm trees. I asked Mama what the triangles were and she said they were pyramids.'

I nod. 'Charta Egypta. From the land of the Pharaohs. I memorised all of the writing on the box before I knew what the words meant.'

'Why?'

'Well, you know how, before you learn to read, when it's the shapes of words and letters you fall in love with?'

'Not really.'

I've lost her. But, we continue our work in a companionable silence.

Later, after the vegetables are done and the light has turned bruised-orange, she says, 'I was jealous of you and Grandfather. You always went on walks with him. You used to come back knowing all the names of the trees and plants. He never took me. You were his favourite.'

I don't deny it. 'I wish he'd been my father.'

I look down to the backs of my hands. They're blotchy with work. I've lost so much weight lately, the veins look like purple worms under a thin, writing-paper surface.

'I've asked Porter to get you passage on a steamer out of Cooktown,' I say.

She pales a little. 'I thought you didn't want me to go back to Papa.'

'I don't. By the time you go, I'll have some money you can take.'

Percy hasn't yet been to Cooktown, but there are at least three dozen bags of slugs ready for transportation to the mainland. He will come back with the money that's owed me.

'But where will I go?' she asks.

'If Mama hasn't managed to save enough for the boarding school, there's a landlady I know, Mrs Menzies, who runs a house in Brisbane. She's an old harridan, but, if you pay your board, she can help you to find a job. You might have to lie about your age. Promise me you'll do it. You're not too young for domestic or governessing work. And you'll get all meals free, a bed and a small allowance.' Mr Wilson's fleshy face swims into my vision for a few seconds. 'Just stay away from drunks and lechers, no matter how attractive their propositions sound.'

I steel myself for her defence of Papa. Her accusations of paranoia. But they don't come. 'But what about Mama?'

I look across to the nautilus shell. It glows faintly in the last light. 'What about her? She's like me. She's made her bed, and now must lie in it.'

Her eyes are full of a new idea. 'But *why* must you lie in it? Come with me! We can have a place together. We can change our names so that Bob can't find you.'

'I can't leave the island just now, Carrie. Not yet. But when I can, I'll come for you. I swear it.'

44

*Sometimes the weather
can suit a mood perfectly.*

From the secret diary of Mary Watson

3RD NOVEMBER 1880

A bleak day. Wet and dirty. Percy and Bob came back from Cooktown a week ago. Percy had a wad of pound notes from Roberts, for me, hidden in a rolled-up copy of the *Brisbane Courier*. Less welcome was his news that there's still no word on the new drop date.

Carrie walks up behind me as I stand outside the door to the house, rubbing my palms up and down my skirt and swaying slightly in the nor-easterly bluster.

'I can't believe the men are going out in this.' Her skirt moulds her legs at the back and she holds her hat on with one hand. Her lips have small hairline cracks from the wind. 'Someone will fall overboard for sure.'

A quick, let-it-be-Bob look passes between us.

'Only the good die young,' I say dryly.

She looks down at my hands, clucking her tongue. 'You should have asked him to get you some cream for that rash when he was in Cooktown.'

'I've tried it before,' I say, remembering John Adam's rancid-smelling ointment. 'It doesn't work. And I ...'

The rest of the sentence is left hanging but understood: *wouldn't ask him to get me anything.* We exchange another glance.

Carrie's bed is separated from ours by only a thin wall. She is well aware of how things stand.

Bob returned from Cooktown with a disappointing profit for his slugs, a lingering scent of the brothel on his skin and a violent glint in his eye. He's taken me roughly every night since. Slapped me twice: once on the cheek, a short, sharp sting; once across the ear, leaving a background noise in my head. Not ringing exactly; more like a hissing crackle — the sea's feet, in riding boots, treading on discarded bark. I hardly notice the bruise on my cheekbone, until the wind strikes its nerves in a certain way that makes the teeth behind it ache.

I find myself thinking a lot about Laura from French Charley's these days. How far did Bob go with her? How much violence had she put up with? A few bruises? A broken bone or two?

The only thing that comforts me is the fat pile of notes now hidden in my locked box under the bed. The money that will enable Carrie to leave.

I hear Bob's medicinal balls approaching. He's been in the house, looking for the bottle of ammonia used on the luggers for the long-spined sea-urchin stings. I see it dangling from his hand as I turn to speak to him, having to raise my voice a little to ride over the whistle of the wind.

'Are you coming back tonight?'

His eyes are steely with a mix of indifference and something else I can't quite pin down. The scarred side of his face is a pitted silver landscape in the light.

'Ye'll miss me, will ye?'

His fingers move towards my face, carefully, snake-charming. The rough tips barely touch my skin, pass lightly over the bruise, darker, I'm sure, against the cream of my complexion. He knows I won't flinch. Not with Carrie next to me.

'Ye look like something the moggy dragged in,' he says.

I can't fathom what he's thinking these days, and it makes me anxious. Does he know what happened between Percy and me? How could he? More likely, he's finally noticed that our marriage is a sham. But if so, what was the tipping point? What made him sure? How did my charade go wrong?

He looks to the ocean, as though tired of my features. 'We may stay out.' Then: 'We could have made it work, ye know.'

'What did you say?'

I stare at his face, but his attention is fixed on the sea. The click of the medicinal balls in his pocket slows. Wind tousles his sparse, greasy hair. He turns, something watery and naked in his eyes, before he hastily dresses them in the low-grade contempt I've become used to.

'I said we'll work the slugs overnight if we get on to a good patch.'

He strides off towards the luggers. A wave of the nausea I've battled on and off for days rises to my throat. I lower myself casually to the ground, as though I've just thought to sit and watch the preparations for a while. I draw my knees up to my chest.

Carrie sits next to me, the bottom of her skirt wrapped around her boots. 'Are you ill?' she asks. 'You're very pale.'

I close my eyes briefly and swallow. 'I'm all right. Something I ate disagreed with me, I expect.'

We watch in silence as the wind churns clouds to grey butter and the crews make ready to weigh anchor. One of the Kanakas pushes through an agitated swirl of ocean, a thick stack of hessian bags balanced on his head. The sky's bearing down with its sackful of wriggling rain.

Percy's walking across the beach, a coil of rope over one arm. The wind has pasted his shirt to his back. He bends at the water's edge, rolls up his trousers, starts a little at the first cool infusion of sea. The material darkens as he wades through the weedy chop towards *Petrel*. Gulls dip overhead. Somehow, in their small brains, they've made the connection between the men and the slugs. They're obviously smarter than I am at calculating cause and effect.

'Stop it, Mary!'

I shake my head, come back from the bleak place behind my eyes, and turn towards Carrie. 'Stop what?'

She's looking at my hands. There's red under my fingernails. My absent-minded scratching has made my palms bleed again.

Bob's prediction was wrong. The men aren't out all night, after all. *Isabella* came back at one in the afternoon. Now, at three, with Bob's slugs boiled and pinned onto the sand to dry, *Petrel* anchors in the shallow water. It's still swelteringly hot. The horizon's bright scarf shimmers around the sunburned neck of the world, and the sun's glaring like a feverish eye. The wind's died, leaving only high, striated clouds and a fug of humidity. As usual, the seabirds have gathered. The sky above *Petrel* is a piece of tin with the small, metal hooks of their cries scraping down it.

Ah Sam takes off his hat to wipe the sweat from his brow, then puts it back on. His bare feet are filthy, the nails black, the corns covered in sand mixed with grey ash.

He's just set fire to a new load of wood under the boiling tank. He and Ah Leung have filled it with water. The flames leap like dragon's breath. I stand to the right, upwind of its torture, until it subsides to a useable heat.

I'd managed to stir Bob's slugs earlier without too much trouble. But Percy's are another matter. It's all I can do to approach the tank. The tipped-in creatures fume, hiss and stink: squirming in their greasy stew. The nausea is back in force. My eyes sting, as though each eyeball has been pulled out, polished with a rag made of fish scales, then sat back into its socket. No amount of blinking takes the irritation away.

In the middle of my misery, Percy wanders up the beach, almost a mirage in the rippling heat. His trousers rolled up and his slouch hat on sideways.

'All right, Mrs Watson?'

I don't answer his question. Just keep stirring. Try not to vomit.

His chin is unshaven. He pokes his pipe through an opening in the undergrowth and pulls a box of matches from his pocket. Seeing that they're damp, he grabs a piece of driftwood from the sand and holds it to the fire until it catches alight before bringing it to the tobacco in the bowl. The flare makes his eyes sparkle for an instant. The skin beneath them looks raw from the salt air.

'I notice there were only four bags from *Petrel*,' I say. 'Bad trip?'

'Weather was against us. How many bags did your husband get?'

'Eight.'

'He'll have cause to think he's a better man than me, then. For today, at least.'

He hooks my eye, and I should feel elated after so much evasion on his part. But it's too little, too late.

He blows smoke through his nose in a long, slow stream. 'You look like death on toast.'

I think about Bob's earlier comment. 'Is that better than something the moggy dragged in? I think I'm pregnant.'

His jaw tightens like a hawser on its scaffold of bone, then lets go. 'If you are, then you'd better get rid of it quick smart, or your work for Roberts is over. Just as well Ah Leung's foot is mending nicely.' He tilts his head on the side. 'Funny, I thought you were smarter than that. My mistake for trusting a woman, I suppose.' He turns to leave.

Not this time. I grab a handful of his shirt and jerk him around so that he faces me. In my peripheral vision I can see Bob further along the beach with the Kanakas, rearranging the net over his drying slugs. He's watching us. I don't care.

'It might be yours.'

'And how exactly did you draw that conclusion? Don't you make enough hogmagandie with your husband to do the job? No wonder he's such a surly bastard.'

His face is hectic and creased, the smarmy arrogance replaced with something not really under control. My hand falls away, but I don't take my eyes from his.

'I've been using something with Bob.'

'But you didn't with me? What a calculating bitch you are.'

There's a taste in my mouth like an old attic smells: shredded paper, mouse droppings.

'Get yer hands off her, Fuller.'

Percy lifts both arms in mock surrender. 'I think you'll find the good lady is exercising her claws on me, Watson. Seems she thinks I'm not pulling my weight. Just because I only managed to bring in a paltry catch.' He looks regretfully down to the beach where his now-empty hessian bags are lined up on the damp sand. 'A fair little cost accountant, your better half. Still, you must be in the good books with your haul.'

Bob looks between us in narrow-eyed suspicion. He says something to Percy in a long distortion of words. Their bodies shimmer, flip like fish in a hot white net. Nothing is exactly where it should be. Even the sky is tilting sideways.

Carrie dips a flannel in the enamel dish of water she's brought to the bedside and wipes my brow without first squeezing the cloth out. Trickles run down my cheeks and neck. The coolness tickles.

'I'm fine,' I say, and still her hand with mine. Try to get my bearings. 'What time is it?' The light through the open doorway is burned umber; the rest of the room, darkening. Then I smell the savoury layers of stew. 'Dinnertime.'

I start to rise, but she stops me with a hand on my chest. 'I've made it. The men are eating.'

I blink. There's a twinge in my back. I must have fallen awkwardly. It's a miracle I didn't tumble headfirst into the boiling tank.

I can hear low voices from the other room.

'What happened between Bob and Percy?'

'They're prowling around each other like old tomcats — as usual.'

'Neither of them are that old,' I say.

She shifts her weight on the bed. 'Well, Bob's not too ancient to get you pregnant. You are, you know. Fainting is one of the symptoms.'

'When did you acquire a medical degree?' My mouth is dry. I'd love a drink of water.

'I've browsed your Dr Foote's *Medical Common Sense.*' When I look doubtful, she becomes defensive. 'Well, I haven't got anything else to read, have I?'

'What would Dr Foote know? He's a podiatrist.'

'A what?'

'A foot doctor. It's a joke. Dr Foote — a podiatrist.'

'Ha, ha.' She won't be distracted. 'Dr Foote says you shouldn't wear your stays now that you're in the family way. It constricts the blood flow to the baby and that's what makes a woman faint.'

'Even if the baby's smaller than a grain of rice?'

'The blood supply to the womb increases three hundred per cent in the first three months,' she quotes.

'And doesn't continue exponentially, I hope, or the mother-to-be would end up exploding.'

'What's exponentially?'

'It doesn't matter. Carrie, I can't get up if you don't get off the bed.'

'You shouldn't get up. Dr Foote says —'

'Enough!' I give her a gentle push and she stands.

She took off my boots and hose when she put me into bed, but didn't clean off my soles, so the sheets are gritty with sand. I stand, put my feet into slippers.

'Help me off with the sheet. I don't want to lie on a beach all night.'

'Yes, all right.'

Together, we pull the skin off the bed.

Her eyes fill with tears. 'I don't want to leave you on the island with all these men. It's not right. Porter's booked me a berth on the *Wotonga* out of Cooktown on the fourth of December. He's paid for it himself and won't hear of being reimbursed. But of course I'm not going now.'

'Yes, you are. Nothing's changed.'

'But how will you have a baby on your own on the Lizard?' She lowers her voice. 'And to that horrible ...' She tilts her head in the direction of the voices.

'If I don't miscarry, then I daresay I'll go to Cooktown for the confinement. Bob will hire a nurse and rent me a place to stay. If he won't, then I'll throw myself on the mercy of Charley Boule. Let everyone in town know what a rum show of a husband I've ended up with.'

'You sound so cool and sensible about it.'

'Would it help to be heated and hysterical?'

She puts her small hand over mine. 'Shall I bring you some dinner?'

'No, you shall not. I'm not an invalid.'

I walk out into the communal space. Four sets of male eyes look up.

'Feeling better, Mary?' Porter puts both hands on the table to stand, but I motion him with my free palm to stay sitting.

Ah Sam places a damper on the wooden board. I hand him the sheet. 'Will you shake this out, Ah Sam?'

When he's gone, I turn to the one man in the trio I now have any time for. 'Sorry about the fuss, Porter. I'm just a bit under the weather.'

I wonder which one of them carried me to bed and decide it must have been him. Neither Bob nor Percy would care enough to do so.

'Carrie's told me you've organised her trip home,' I go on. 'Thank you.'

'It took a while to confirm. But yes, I've had word from the mainland that there is a berth.'

Bob lifts his head, his brows damp in the steam from the stew, and pins Porter with his eyes. 'When?'

'Fourth of December. On *Wotonga*.' Porter lifts his plate to the rim of the pot, spoons out a second helping of stew.

I see that Carrie's cut the carrot pieces too big. They'll be hard in the middle, whilst the potato, cut too small, has turned to mush. I glance at her. She's seen me looking at her handiwork and is waiting for admonishment. I smile at her gratefully.

Bob helps himself and looks across the table at Percy. 'Fuller, didn't ye say ye'd booked passage on the *Egmont* on the eleventh?'

Percy nods curtly, his face a mask. 'Family in Melbourne I have to catch up with. Before they return home to London. It's almost cyclone season anyway, Watson. I'll take any catch we accumulate between now and then to Cooktown when I go.'

He sounds defensive and I wonder why. He must be lying about his reasons for leaving. He'll probably take the opportunity to tell Captain Roberts that I'm pregnant and no longer able to do my job here on the island. How lucky, as he said, that Ah Leung is healing. Well, Ah Leung may yet have a fight on his hands. I need the money from this next drop if I'm to bring a baby up on my own.

For a few seconds, the world stops spinning. I realise what a monumental decision I've just made in the blink of an eye. Whatever else happens, I will not get rid of my child.

Bob taps his front teeth with his fork. 'We'll all go over before the fourth. Mary, to see Carrie off; me, to sell the slugs. We could come back to the Lizard — Porter, Mary and me — on the eleventh, or a wee while earlier. We could all do with a break.'

He bends to his food again, shovels another mouthful in. It's obvious what's behind his sudden desire for us all to have a holiday in Cooktown. He doesn't want Percy taking the slugs. Or, more specifically, dealing with Will Hartley, the slug agent.

'Sounds fine to me,' I say briskly. I pick up a plate and help myself to some stew.

Percy's worried — I can tell by the small line the size of a matchstick between his eyes. He must know that I suspect he'll run to Roberts with my news. And, quite rightly, he's concerned I'll say something, do something, to compromise him in response. But he gives himself too much credit. There's a hard kernel of survival in me now. What plant might grow out of it will be anybody's guess. But I'm not about to throw away my only chance of a future because of some spite I might feel towards Percy. I've no intention of sabotaging the operation.

In bed, later, Bob turns me over roughly, but I'm having none of it.

'If you want me to lose this child I'm carrying, then go right ahead.'

I hear a sharp in-breath. He flops on his back. After a few stunned minutes, I hear the slow click of his medicinal balls.

'I've filled yer womb?'

By his tone, no man in history has ever performed such a feat. I don't comment, just keep my back turned, my eyes wide open in the dark.

'A wee bairn. Well now, that changes everything.'

45

From the secret diary of Mary Watson

6TH NOVEMBER 1880

Percy's been talking to Ah Leung. The Chinaman has had a decided spring in his lopsided step these last few days. The damaged foot still drags slightly behind the other, but he's agile enough to climb Cook's Look. He knows it, and so do I.

All I have to rely on now are my wits.

Ah Leung eyes me speculatively as I walk towards the washing line. The salt-butter smell of an early island summer is everywhere. He's been clearing the overgrown grass around the homestead with his cane knife. At this time of year, venomous snakes lurk in any vegetation allowed to grow beyond ankle height. The stunted bushes behind him clatter with cicadas. The heat is soporific, but I can't give in to its seductive ennui.

'Lovely day, isn't it?' I call.

The sun glints off the cane knife's steel as he stabs it in the dirt. He looks to see if anyone else is around. No time to waste on preliminaries, it seems.

'You leave here soon if you know what's good for you.'

His voice gloats from the shadows under the pandanus. Moving patches of light and darkness stripe his face.

'And why is that, Ah Leung?'

The enamel of my careful politeness has worn thin. I pick two wooden pegs from the canvas bag that hangs on the clothesline. Dust off a film of dirt. Pinch one peg to the collar of my blouse while I haul a pair of Bob's long johns to the line with the other hand. The task would have had me wincing a week ago. But Porter's given me some whale oil in a tiny bottle. Rubbing it on my inflamed palms has brought some relief. I notice Ah Leung staring at my stomach. Bile rises in my throat.

'You know, it's a mistake to accept gossip as truth. Didn't your mother ever tell you that?'

'I kill you now, maybe.'

His voice is so matter-of-fact that I wonder for a few seconds if I haven't misheard. Above the trotting pulse in my ears, I rehearse his own tone and offer it back to him.

'Oh, no, I don't think so. To do that would almost certainly guarantee you'd be drawn and quartered. You forget one important fact. That I've told others what you've done.'

It's all bluff, of course. I've told no one in Cooktown about him. I should have. I plan to rectify that oversight as soon as I set foot on the mainland. I might start with Charley Boule. What better way to set the bullock team of gossip in motion?

I pull a damp apron out of the basket, fetch another pair of pegs from the bag.

'You think you work it all ... out.'

The taunt in his voice makes the hairs on the back of my neck prickle to attention.

'What haven't I worked out, Ah Leung? I'm sure you'll be happy to tell me.'

He scratches his cheek with one of those long, dirty claws, just below the birthmark. 'I tell you one thing you don't know.'

'That's magnanimous of you. What is it?'

'You don't leave here soon, you die. And all because you trust the wrong people.' He shakes his head slowly in mock sympathy.

'You're a fine one to talk about trust. You're a murderer and a thief.'

His sudden laugh is full of phlegmy bullets. What's amused him? My naïvety? My intuition tells me that he's not sophisticated enough to bluff.

But what is it that I haven't taken into account? Who have I trusted that I shouldn't have?

What have I left untended that might jump out and bite me?

Cooktown

Summer, 1880

46

*Some towns never lose their talent
for lowering the spirits.*

From the secret diary of Mary Watson

4TH DECEMBER 1880

Back to a muddy street with shops nudging each other along its mournful length. Back to sagging verandahs and stray dogs. Back to a heavy waterbag of air hanging under a sky as bristly as a horse's underbelly.

'Mary …' Carrie bites her bottom lip. There's nothing more to say.

Her trunk is already on board. All of the money Percy gave me for the last drop is in a pouch stashed in her deepest pocket. She's about to walk the small gangway from shore to steamer. Nothing to do but stare at her for a long few seconds, then wrap my arms around her.

'I'll miss you,' I say. 'Be careful. Remember what I told you about Brisbane. Merry Christmas, Carrie.'

I watch her walk onto the gently swaying boat. She turns to stand at the railing.

'Write to me,' she yells. 'Let me know about the baby. Remember what you said. I love you, Mary.'

'Be careful, Carrie.' I say again, then mouth an 'I love you' back at her. I wave my handkerchief until my arm aches and the steamer is a tiny, puffing speck in the distance. Her smell still hangs on my blouse, mixed with my own sweat.

I make it halfway back up Charlotte Street, then, suddenly, outside the National Bank, I stop and take a deep breath. Something's clogging my throat.

'Mary?' It's Porter. He's been shopping in Walsh's Emporium and has tobacco and a new pipe clasped in the money clip of his three-fingered hand.

I fumble in my sleeve for my handkerchief. Wipe my face. 'Carrie's gone.'

He lifts his arm — to console me, perhaps — then decides I haven't invited his sympathy and lowers it again. He's looking clean and polished after a trip to the barber for a haircut and shave. And he's bought himself a pair of new Blucher boots from Madden's down near the wharf. There's also a bright red-checked kerchief around his throat.

'Are you off courting, then?' I look him up and down, smiling now, and he blushes in a slow tide from the neck upwards.

'No, not really. Who'd want an old sea dog like me?'

There's a flash of lightning over the water. It scatters a noisy flock of white cockatoos from the paperbarks. The sky's turning the dull colour and texture of cob cottages back in Cornwall: straw, bound with glutinous grey clay. For a second, I fancy I can smell the seaweed and waste pilchards used to fertilise the turnip fields. And almost see, in the distance of my mind's eye, the ever-shrinking patches of fertility separated by swathes of balding land, poisoned by arsenic from the silver mine.

Porter counts the seconds until the copper full of rocks tilts its thunderous load into the sky above us. 'Four miles off. I reckon it'll be a pelterer.'

The wind's picked up and I hold my fluttering hat down on my head. 'We'd better get inside. Where's Bob?'

'Nursing a tot in the Sea Wah.' His tone suggests it's more likely a pot than a tot. 'How are your hands now?'

'Healing. Thanks to you.'

I hold my free palm out to show him. He runs a finger lightly across its scarred surface, as though preparing to read my fortune. He looks up and into my face. His bottom lip twitches with something important to say. But when he breaks eye contact, it's clear he's thought better of it.

'Where are you off to?' he asks.

Another flash. The air vibrates. I pull my hand back, a little disturbed by his gentle touch.

'I thought I might make a call on my old friend Charley Boule.'

Charley ushers me into his stuffy office. I'm reminded of the last time I was in this room, just after Nicole's death. Porter's 'pelterer' arrives in an instant, carried by a huge wind flapping the wing of the awning outside. Horizontal rain peppers the window.

Charley sinks into his noisy leather chair and lights a cigar. 'How is the Lizard, *chérie*?' It's hard to hear him over the rain.

'Scaly and cold-blooded,' I reply, thinking of Bob, Percy and Ah Leung. 'I'm having a child.'

He lights the lamp on his desk. It accentuates the shine on his forehead and nose. *'Incroyable!'* An amused grin. A flash of white teeth.

'I can assure you, even a plain woman's reproductive capacities can be quite serviceable.'

'You misunderstand me. It is not that …'

He doesn't elaborate and, not particularly caring for his opinion on my pregnancy, I don't pursue it.

'How much do you know about that Chinese servant on the Lizard, Ah Leung?' I ask instead.

A small jerk of surprise? It's hard to tell with the lamp's flickering. But his smile has definitely gone. He leans back. The chair emits a slippery squeak. He blows a mouthful of smoke towards the ceiling.

'He once had a salon on the waterfront, *non?*' He picks up an onyx paperweight and rolls it in his palm, his thumb stroking its surface.

'I suspect it was he who strangled your girls,' I say.

'I think not.'

'How so? The murders stopped after he left, didn't they?'

'And also after you, Watson, Green and Fuller left. Not to mention that stupid boy Heccy Landers, who went back to Brisbane at the same time.'

'Ah Leung robbed and killed a Chinese shopkeeper. Did you know?'

'I did not,' he says smoothly. 'But what matter? The sooner they all kill each other, the sooner business in town will revert to the Europeans.'

I feel my frustration rising. 'I didn't suspect you would be interested in justice for the girls themselves, but I had imagined the idea of revenge would heat your French blood somewhat.'

'*Touché*. I am ready to combust at any moment. But where is your proof?'

I tell him about Ah Leung's joss with the ribbon around its neck.

'Pah. That is all you have?'

I pull in a quick breath. I felt so sure he would show an interest. Now I'm flummoxed as to where to take the conversation.

Charley saves me the trouble of responding. 'I am tired of this salon, anyway,' he says. 'Charley Boule is not much longer for this town.'

If in doubt, fall back on sarcasm.

'Perhaps you should return to Paris, Charley. A man of your ambition and patriotism needs a large canvas to work on.'

He looks up. '*Sans importance*. A true Frenchman, he carries his country with him.'

I look out the window. The rain is still torrential, but vertical now. The wind's died. Charlotte Street is a muddy series of runnels that won't dry out completely for months. Someone's once white glove floats by in a mini river.

'Why did Heccy leave?' I ask.

'A family crisis I believe.'

'I saw Laura scrubbing floors at the Federal Hotel. Isn't she working here any more?'

'*Non*.'

His curt response brooks no further questioning. Which doesn't stop me.

'Why?'

He gives me a long look that I can't decipher. Then he shrugs. His eyes flit away.

Something occurs to me. Some way I might pierce his armour of indifference. I think of the afternoon I heard him arguing with Percy.

'How well do you know Percy Fuller, Charley?'

He doesn't miss a beat. 'About as well as you think *you* do, *chérie.*'

'What's that supposed to mean?'

But he's giving me that blank look that tells me our grand reunion is over.

'If you will kindly excuse me. I am a busy man. Give my regards to the blacks on the Lizard.'

47

The eleventh hour creeps up
on not-so-little feet.

From the secret diary of Mary Watson

11TH DECEMBER 1880

Bob has spent the week since Carrie left soaking up alcohol and the mercurial charms of the gambling table. As for me? I've kept to myself, lonely, but unwilling to seek out the kind of company that Cooktown keeps. At least on the Lizard, isolation is left to its own devices. Not crammed to bursting with false bonhomie.

Ten thirty at night. I've kicked my boots off, and sit on the lumpy bed with my back against the headboard. To rest, but not to sleep. Our tiny room at the Sea Wah Hotel is suitable for slumber only during the day, when the drunks and gamblers are recovering from the previous night's binge. Bob's down there somewhere, spending up big at the bar. He got a good price from Will Hartley for his slugs, enough that he doesn't seem worried about donating a substantial portion of his earnings to his new best mates, all better poker players than he is. Shouts, curses and the sound of breaking glass rise through the floor.

I bend my knee, bring one foot closer to my chest. It's swollen, either with the heat or pregnancy. The five toes poke out like little piggies on their way to market. I push deeply on the instep. All day I've been on my feet, trying to catch up with Percy. He disappeared soon after Carrie left, as soon as Bob handed him his share of the profits. No sign of him all week. I spent the whole morning on the dock while the packet steamer for Melbourne took on supplies and passengers. Either Percy was already aboard and in no mood to talk to me, or he left Cooktown earlier in the week, having lied about his plans. Regardless, Captain Roberts will soon know I'm pregnant — if he doesn't already.

I start the same treatment on the other foot, relieving the pressure. Bob's planning to take us back to the Lizard the day after tomorrow, weather permitting. Ah Leung will no doubt be waiting on shore, ugly and painful as a stonefish when he realises I'm on board.

I chew on my bottom lip. For the tenth time, I think: perhaps I should telegraph Roberts. But what would I say to explain myself? I can't think of anything that would shift his mind if it's already made up. Truth is, I'm stuck. At an impasse. My thoughts like anxious mice running around a closed wheel in my head.

It's still too hot to sleep, even if, by some miracle, the noise from downstairs abated. But I feel myself drifting away in a sort of semiconscious dream. I'm back home on the Lizard. In the rocking chair. The ocean growls and the wind is up. Heavy gusts disturb the kerosene lantern's flame, rattle the barred door. The rattling grows louder. Louder, and more regular. As if someone is tapping with a stick.

I open my eyes, back in the Sea Wah. Someone's knocking.

I sit up straighter, the pain in my feet forgotten. It can't be Bob. It's far too early, and in any case he'd be thumping and bellowing, not tapping sedately.

'Who is it?' I call out.

No answer. But whoever's outside pushes something white halfway under the door.

I turn up the lamp with an unsteady hand and go to retrieve the paper. As soon as I draw it inside, I hear heavy footsteps walk steadily down the hall to the stairs.

The note is written in strong, cursive strokes. With a fountain pen. *Half an hour. Upstairs, Federal Hotel.*

No signature. It doesn't matter. My pulse races. I know who it is.

Roberts. In Cooktown! And Percy must have known. Must have spoken to him before he left for Melbourne, or wherever else he's gone. Told him with gleeful malice about my changed circumstances.

I sit down on the bed. My feet protest as I shove them back into my boots. Why didn't Roberts pass on his decision through Percy? Why would he wait for Percy to leave and then speak to me personally? He doesn't usually do his own dirty work. I take the kerosene lamp over to the cold fireplace, crumple the note. I hold one corner to the flame, then throw the paper into the ash pit, watching it burn.

Too late to run, and nowhere to hide if I do. I wipe my hair down on both sides, compulsively. And then do the same to the front of my dress. For the first time in weeks, since I took Porter's whale-oil cure, my palms itch painfully. I open the door.

If I were in any doubt about the nature of the summons, the tall man waiting for me at the end of the alleyway alongside the Federal Hotel dispels it. I recognise him from that earlier meeting … a year ago now. Six foot tall, with dull ginger hair, coarse features and eyes full of implacable purpose. He turns and walks quietly down the dark, damp passage. I follow, a lamb to the slaughter, counting steps to calm myself. Too soon, the alley opens up into the shabby courtyard near the back entrance. Three empty wooden rum barrels line up against the wall. A rusty birdcage hangs askew from a gum tree's branch, picking up the moonlight. I hear a possum's leafy scamper somewhere to my left, an off-key tune sung from the bar inside.

The stairs smell of stale beer and the ground-in dirt of gold-diggers' boots. By the time we reach the open door on the landing, my palms are wet.

'Come in.'

Roberts has taken the same cracked leather chair that he had before. As before, the door is left open. I take both as good omens, and caution myself to hold my tongue. Not sink my own ship before I hear the cannon boom. The ginger-haired guard dog stands watch in the hallway. The captain's face is impassive. Nothing to be learned there. I sit, reciting the words in my head so that I'll get the tone exactly right.

'Percy's been to see you?'

'Yes.'

'I assume, then, you know my situation.' I clasp my damp hands together on my lap so that he won't see them shake.

He leans back in his chair, puts one ankle over its opposite knee. If anything, his beard is even longer than when I last saw him. Jet black, reaching down to his lap. He strokes it lightly, just below his mouth. Stares at me, unblinking.

'Yes. I know your situation.'

I'd forgotten just how weighty his absence of small talk can be.

'I bet he told you I'm incapable of doing the next signalling. That Ah Leung is ready to step into the breach.'

'No bet. We're both poker players, remember?' The left side of his mouth twitches.

The saliva in the back of my throat is thick as I swallow. 'I'm not incapable, Captain. It's no easy climb up Cook's Look, but I can do it.'

He stares at me for a few more seconds. Then glances over to the disused fireplace. There's a chip in the corner of the surround. He fixes his gaze on it.

'The drop is now scheduled for September.'

'Next September! But I'll have my baby by then. I'll be more than able —'

He stares at me evenly, hammering my sudden relief back into silence.

'To fight another day?' He finishes the sentence for me, his voice a monotone.

'Something like that.'

My words sound faint to my own ears. Something's wrong. The conversation is so full of holes there's nowhere to step without falling through. What did he say to Percy? What did Percy say to him? Why hasn't he said an outright 'no' to my request to continue?

'Ah Leung —' I start.

'Will be controlled.'

The words he doesn't add — *for now* — hang heavy in the air between us.

I've always thought of Roberts as being emotionless. But I realise it's not quite true. In the flicker of the lamp, his dark eyes are full of knives under a deceptively smooth surface. Like the reef just off the Lizard. And trying to find the safe passage through what he doesn't say is a challenge equal to Cook finding his dark blue line through all of that peril. A challenge I realise I'm not up to at the moment. I search around for something on the surface to help me set my course.

'Why so long until the next drop?'

He makes a gesture I remember: steepling his long fingers, as though completing some circuit necessary to contemplation. I imagine his thoughts passing back and forth through his fingertips.

'It's complicated. An invasion of Egypt is in the offing. It would be to our advantage if a couple of French spies were compromised in the process. One must always be prepared to act.' He looks me in the eye. 'But one must not act until one's opponent is completely committed, and has reached the point of maximum vulnerability. I now judge we will reach that point in September. The thirtieth, to be exact. Subject to developments, of course. Though I'm confident of my calculations.'

'I see.'

No use trying to work out his political cloak-and-dagger code. What I do know is that September is a long way from now … a lifetime.

'The operation requires only one more night of signalling. One more crucial night. Are you sure you're up to the task?'

'Yes, I'm sure,' I say, then wonder if it's true. 'But Captain … what then?'

The foot he has rested on his knee wags side to side like a dog's slow tail.

'Do you intend to stay with your husband on Lizard Island when this is all over?'

'No.'

'Then you would take the child with you, presumably. How will you secure passage without raising suspicion?'

I haven't thought clearly about anything so far ahead, but dare not say so. Reluctantly, I offer the first practical scenario that comes to mind. 'I'll offer Percy money to hide me and the baby on *Petrel*. He could take us south.' Never mind that Percy and I are barely on speaking terms.

He makes a noise at the back of his throat but doesn't comment. Then he stands. His guard dog, alert to the faintest signal, moves into the doorway. I stand as well.

'Wait here ten minutes,' he says over his shoulder. 'Then put out the light and go back to your hotel.'

'Yes, Captain.'

I watch his dark bulk fill the doorway then disappear. I collapse back in the chair and listen to the faraway shrills of a good-time town. They seem even more artificial to me now than they did when I lived here. I've grown used to the different noises on the Lizard. The real sounds of the night.

I can't seem to summon the energy to move, even when the required ten minutes has passed. What pins me to the chair? Nervous tension released? Loss of will? Lethargy? My obstacles are just as real. The outcome just as uncertain. But every now and then, in between anxious moments, I feel calm sneak in. My hands rest on my belly. Over my baby.

In these last weeks, since I realised I'm carrying an extra passenger, I've imagined myself as a mother. Imagined my life after the final drop. The baby will be delivered safely, somewhere away from all this strife. I will have the money to care for it. Our future will be secured.

But things have changed and I must change my thoughts with them. I must keep up. Must keep one step ahead. I've played my cards well enough so far — well enough to escape Papa's hopeless, downward spiral, and help Carrie do the same — but now there's far more at stake than just my own skin. My child will most likely be born here in Cooktown. I will be forced to take a vulnerable infant back to the Lizard. Ah Sam will have to care for it while I climb that dangerous hill again.

Something cold sneaks in. A possible explanation for why Roberts would want me to make this one last climb of Cook's Look. Perhaps he knows that the blacks have become more volatile. Perhaps he's decided I'm not as valuable an asset as Ah Leung is and could easily be sacrificed. His only gamble? That I manage to complete the signalling before I'm brought down with a spear.

Does it make sense? I don't know any more. My emotions seem heightened with pregnancy. What I do know is that fate will force me to ante up my most precious possession. Roberts, Ah Leung, Percy, Bob, the blacks, the signalling job ... all risks, an endless string of dangerous wagers. But how will I ever forgive myself if this last bet puts my baby in harm's way?

I begin to stretch my arms up to yawn, but stop myself. Ridiculous Cornish superstitions about pregnancy twist and turn in my head. *Don't raise your hands above your shoulders or you'll strangle the baby. Don't write in a diary, or the Devil will see the words and come for the child.*

Lizard Island

Winter, 1881

48

From the secret diary of Mary Watson

15TH JULY 1881

Screams ricochet off the limestone walls. Ferrier's face is the colour of boiled beetroot. I've fed him and changed him. What else is there to do? I'm rocking the cradle with just a little more force than necessary when Ah Sam slips into the house.

'What, what, baby?'

He lifts Ferrier in his nightdress. Hangs him over one shoulder like a small sack of slugs, rubs his lower back while simultaneously jigging him up and down. It looks like punishment, but Ferrier's howling subsides to a few hiccoughs. Two minutes later, he's asleep, his head tucked into the Chinaman's grimy neck.

My ears are finally, blissfully, empty.

Ah Sam puts a stained finger vertically over his lips and lowers the baby back into the cradle.

Wretch. His eyes are closed. The dark lashes on his now-pale skin twitch slightly. His mouth's a plump bud, drawing in teaspoonfuls of air, and pushing them out again. He's angelic ... when he's asleep. Daily I marvel at how I could have delivered such a beautiful child. He looks nothing like Percy. Neither does he look like Bob. Which didn't stop Bob converting him to a perfect little Pope-loving son. Heathen that I am, I was forced to wait outside the Catholic Church in Cooktown while the christening ceremony proceeded. I wasn't allowed within snuffing distance of the candles.

But none of that is Ferrier's fault. I look down at his tiny, sleeping face. He doesn't care for Latin and holy water. Already he's devoted to two gods: one on the right, one on the left. And both inside my blouse.

I motion Ah Sam outside and we stand on the gravel in the cool morning breeze off the water.

'You said you might have something for wind?'

He pulls a small bottle from the waistband of his pyjamas. 'Two drop under tongue.'

'What is it?' I open the lid and sniff suspiciously. A sweet, syrupy undertone. 'Does it have opium in it?' He gives me such a look of cultivated innocence that I laugh. 'Well, we'll see how desperate I get.'

Whatever is in the mix, I know Ah Sam wouldn't hurt the baby. Ferrier loves him, gurgles and waves his arms around, trying to swim towards that bland moon-face every time it rises over his cradle. Ah Sam is endlessly patient with him. Tickling his belly to keep him happy while I'm peeling the vegetables. Singing to him, sometimes, in his peculiar, jerky intonations.

I put the bottle into the pocket of my apron and look down towards the water. The Kanakas and the Aboriginal boys have managed to drag *Isabella* pretty much out of the water and onto the beach. The lugger looks like a crusty whale propped up on port side by a few heavy logs. Small waves lick at the stern. The Kanakas, two to a side, wield long, wooden-handled iron scrapers on the hull. Barnacles, weed and black muck fly off with each heavy push. Gulls crowd around the growing ring of dark detritus on the sand. It's hard work: a chiselled wooden screech, followed by the deep-throated language of big men, then another screech. They've been at it since yesterday noon, and don't look likely to finish before late tomorrow.

'Where's Bob?' I ask.

Ah Sam shrugs. If he knows, he's not saying. Bob's mood has been black for a month. Until Ferrier was born, he was as close to happy as I've ever seen him. He stared at my belly in the evenings with a paternal gleam in his eye, even smiled occasionally, and his foul temper was largely reserved for *Isabella*'s crew. He still treats his son as one would any valuable possession. But it's as though I've served my purpose now that I've produced his heir. Beyond the convenience of a live-in babysitter, my position seems largely irrelevant.

'Well, where's Percy then?'

Another shrug. A half-apologetic smile.

Bob and Percy have hardly been out fishing since the baby was born, and their partnership has been more strained than ever since Percy came back from Melbourne. When they do make the effort to harvest slugs, the catch is disappointing. I've been so focused on Ferrier that I haven't troubled to find out what the problem is. But maybe it's time I got to the bottom of it.

Isabella's hull should be clean by tomorrow. Do you think the men will put out soon?'

Ah Sam shakes his head.

'Why not? The weather's fine.'

'No slug, missy.'

'But it's the dry season. Shouldn't there be plenty of slugs now?'

'Fishing bad ... Slugs go.'

I look down to Ah Sam's bare feet, knobbly in the dirt. He mutters something else under his breath. But when I ask what it was he said, he just grabs the basket near the door and trots away to check for eggs.

I step inside to make sure Ferrier is still sleeping, then shuffle out to the cookhouse to light the fire. The bread dough that I've rested in a warm corner has risen. I punch it down, then reach up to the shelf for my baking pans. My hand touches the second shell, a spider, that Porter gave me just before he left six months ago. I lift it down. Finger each of its seven calcified tentacles. I hold the striped pattern up so that it catches the light: stewed apricots streaked with cream.

'The animal inside this one doesn't feel the need to hide,' he told me, 'even though it's vulnerable. You often see them in the shallows.'

He was looking at my hair when he said it. The one thing pregnancy had done for my looks was to make my hair both softer and more curly. He pulled a piece of paper from the shell's cavity and handed it to me. It was an address, nothing more.

'For my sister and brother-in-law, in Umina,' he said. 'If you need me, contact them. They'll know where to find me.'

'Can't you stay?'

We were in the house, saying our goodbyes. Sadness welling up in me. Bob's voice booming up from the beach. It was time for Porter to go.

'My contract's finished,' he said simply, then picked up his swag and turned to face me at the door. 'I don't care what you've done, Mary. Or what you intend to do. Remember, if you need me ...'

And then the doorway gaped without him.

I caution myself to stop daydreaming, and put the shell back, but not before I rub the surface so that it might pick up some warmth from my hand. I put it up to my ear. Porter's still gone. The shell's still ice-box cold. But I can hear the sea calling.

And the address he gave me is tucked away safely in my locked box under the bed.

49

Busy hands are like opium to a nervous housewife.

From the secret diary of Mary Watson

15TH AUGUST 1881

After dinner, in the rocking chair, the rhythm of my fingers orchestrating needles and wool soothes me. The gentle push of my foot on the base of the cradle keeps time. Like a slower, smoother version of working the piano pedals at Charley's.

Bob's sitting on a box, re-sewing the frame onto a landing net with twine and a large needle. He misses and jabs his finger. 'Feck it to hell!' He throws the net in his temper. It lands in a puddle in the middle of the floor.

'You'll wake the baby.'

'I'll wake the bairn if I've a mind to. Ye would forget who gave him to ye?'

Oh, I'm not forgetting, Bob. Not for an instant.

'Well, carry on then. You can put him to sleep again, after he wakes.' I finish the row I'm working on. 'What will you do now the slugs have dried up. Will you try some other ground?"

He runs a splayed hand through his thinning hair. 'Aye.'

He stands, wanders over to the shelf and looks straight through it. His hand finds his pocket. The clinking doesn't seem to bother Ferrier. He's asleep on his back, a white wrap tucked in tightly around him, under the mosquito net. A bird shrieks outside. I can hear palm fronds tickle the darkening sky.

'We must start a new station.' He turns around with a pepper shaker in hand. 'Night Island's about two hundred miles north. We have to sail up and see if it's suitable.'

My mind is jarred into action. If Bob is far away at the time of the drop next month, well and good. But if Percy is going with him ...

'Who is we?' I ask.

'I can't work both boats. I'll take all the men.'

'When are you going?'

'Fuller thinks the end of August, start of September.'

He doesn't normally listen to Percy.

'Why September?' I keep my voice light, concentrate on my knitting.

'We will have taken all the slugs we can get by then. Ye and the wee bairn will come with us. Or ye could go to Cooktown till we get back.'

My palms feel sweaty on the wool. Oh, how careless I've been, even negligent these last months. I should have seen this coming but I was distracted by the baby. I can't go to Cooktown in September and I can't go north with the men. I won't allow Percy even the hint of an excuse to use Ah Leung to signal the next drop. This is unexpected, and it shouldn't be. The signs were there and I ignored them.

I bite my bottom lip, juggling possibilities. If there's one thing I've learned about Bob's stubbornness, it's that I must sound deferential or else I won't have the faintest hope of getting my way.

'It's your decision of course,' I say. 'And you know best. But don't you think it would be better if Ferrier and I stayed here on the Lizard? It's only an exploratory trip. How awkward would it be caring for an infant on *Isabella*? In all weathers? And you know how seasick I get.'

He looks scornful. 'Ye'd be alone for six weeks, maybe eight.'

'If we have enough supplies, and you leave the Chinamen, we should be all right. In fact, why don't you take Ah Leung with you? Ah Sam and I can manage quite well. You know how good he is with the baby.'

I cross my mental fingers, hoping he will agree to take the malevolent nuisance away. But he's shaking his head.

'John Pigtail on a lugger's as useless as tits on a boar.' He thinks a bit longer, rubs his chin. 'All right, ye'll not come with us. But ye have to go to Cooktown.'

I count to five before I speak.

'It's an idea. But, Bob, those last papers you brought back … there's an influenza epidemic. And diggers returning from New Guinea with suspected typhoid. He's so small, your son. So vulnerable to illness. I'll defer to your judgement, but we're safer here, I'm sure. Perhaps you can leave us some kind of rowboat, just in case there's trouble with the blacks?'

'What would ye do? Paddle to the mainland? Ye wouldn't make it past the first sharp edge of reef. Ye know almost nothing of shoal and deep, tide and counter-current. Ye can't even swim!'

'True.' I hesitate. 'It's a problem, isn't it? We don't have to make the decision right away.'

There's no point continuing. That antagonistic edge will just creep into his voice. It's enough to plant a thought in his head. Hope it germinates. I go quietly back to my knitting and rocking. Let his medicinal balls think it over.

Five days later at three o'clock. High clouds skitter like furtive thoughts inside the hard blue skull of the sky, though there's no wind on the ground. Not yet. Now, finally, it's *Petrel*'s turn to be scrubbed clean and repainted. The men have been busy doing repairs on board her, these last few weeks. Percy's bent under the stern with a brush and a small tin of tar, applying it in long, slow strokes.

It's cold in the lugger's shade. The sour reek makes me think I've stepped under a bridge to visit an ogre. Which is not too far from the truth.

He doesn't see me approaching, and startles when he notices me only a few yards away. He wears a dark smear on his left cheek. His light hair is dirty in the shadows. Only the green eyes stir in acknowledgement.

'Where's your husband, Mrs Watson? I wouldn't want him to think anything's going on between us.'

'Bob's fixing a hole in the fowlhouse fence. I haven't time to play games with you. You must convince him to leave me and Ferrier here when you sail for Night Island.'

'Yes. I'll get around him. I always do.'

I wasn't expecting him to agree so easily. I'm paying very close attention now. And I won't let his quick acquiescence soften my formal tone.

'How will you receive the signal if you're two hundred miles away?'

He straightens, shakes his wrist back and forth as though it's seized up in the painting position. 'I'll think up some excuse.

Tell Watson I want to investigate a good patch of slugs a bit further south. Get here in time to take the signal, then hightail it north again before he smells a rat. I'll be in position, don't you worry.'

This is going way too smoothly. I'm not sure what he's up to, but I charge on.

'Before you return to Night Island, I want you to ferry the baby, Ah Sam and me down the coast. I'll pay for the trip out of my share from the drop.'

'And exactly how do you think I'll explain so long an absence to your old man?'

I feel my mouth twist. 'You'll think up some excuse. Bob's used to your walkabout ways. He'll be angry. But I doubt you'll worry about *that* after Roberts has paid us out.'

He turns to gaze over the water. The wind's picking up. It tinks one piece of metal against another somewhere on *Petrel*'s deck tilting above us. Blows his words back to me.

'People will see you. They'll know you've done a runner. Watson will come after you. He'll accuse you of stealing his darling baby boy. And what makes you think you can trust Ah Sam not to blab?'

My voice is firm. 'Obviously, I won't be travelling as Mary Watson. And if I don't keep Ah Sam quiet, we'll both face the consequences. Taking him with me is better than leaving him on the Lizard to tell Bob what's happened when he gets back. As for Ah Leung, he's your pet, not mine. If he doesn't keep his mouth shut, you'll have more explaining to do than just my disappearance. I wouldn't leave him at a loose end if I were you. But I tell you one thing, he's not coming with me.'

There's a far-off look in Percy's eyes. 'Oh ... he won't be idle.'

Something tightens in my chest then lets go. I stare at him. He widens his own eyes then covers his tracks.

'I presume you'll have to eat while we're gone. Ah Leung will tend the farm, as usual. That should keep him out of trouble.'

'Never at a loss, are you, Percy?' I shake my head in amazement.

'Not knowingly, Mrs Watson.'

I can't think about what he's hiding now. I have to finish what I set out to say.

'I'm not fussy about where you set us down. We'll find passage on a bullock train south. I thought you might know somewhere appropriate to make landfall for that purpose.'

'I know plenty of places,' he answers noncommittally. 'And so do the blacks.'

But his tone suggests the idea's not untenable. He must have made his own plans for afterwards. Roberts will want us all to evaporate when his business concludes, and Percy would have already considered how that might be achieved.

'I'll have to think on it,' he says, dismissing the debate, and me. It's as though he's bored — or more worryingly — that the whole conversation about my escape from the island has run the limit of an only mildly entertaining supposition.

As I turn to walk away, he adds, 'Speaking of the blacks — they've been spotted over at South Direction. On the move again, evidently. They'll see us leave, you know. It'll be the perfect time for them to attack. You'd better make sure that *your* pet Chow knows how to shoot.'

'Thanks for the caring advice.'

He puts a sticky hand on my shoulder. 'I did warn you not to get so far into this.'

I brace myself to feel something, anything. But there's just annoyance at the tar he's leaving on my dress. I turn my head; look at his grimy hand until he removes it. Whatever half-baked childish infatuation I may once have had for him is dead. Stone dead.

50

From the secret diary of Mary Watson

22ND AUGUST 1881

'I think they should come with us,' Bob says.

His back is to me so I can't make out his expression. Percy's considering how much of his hand he should discard and doesn't answer. His face is underlit by lantern light. Shadows pull down the skin beneath his eyes, and age his cheeks with accentuated cracks and folds. This is how he will look as an old man. Better able to disguise his self-interest under deep-cut grooves of apparent wisdom. He's playing his cards well, and not just the ones on the table. If he speaks too eagerly now, he'll arouse Bob's suspicions.

'You could be right,' he says. He nods slowly and falls into silence.

'Ye know Miller's station at Flinders has been attacked.' Bob's back shifts under his shirt as he lays two cards face down and draws another two from the deck. After a moment, I hear the clink of pennies dropping into the pot.

No response for a few seconds. Night noises outside take over: the ocean's phlegmy lungs, the snare-drum hiss of wavelets petering out along the shore. Wind gently shakes the house's shoulders. There's a draught under the door, despite the cloth snake filled with sand that I've laid across it.

Percy raises one eyebrow. 'From what I heard, a few blacks came close to the homestead and took off when they were shot at. Hardly an attack. Miller had just been to Cooktown. They were probably after food and fishhooks.' He lays his cards down. 'Three aces.' The pennies jostle and tinkle on their way to his stack. 'My trick, I think, old boy.' Then, looking thoughtful, he adds, 'Could be more dangerous for them to come north. We don't know the currents or winds, and the reefs near Night are a bit of a mystery to us. Mary can't swim, and the baby would certainly perish if, say, the lugger were swamped. I suppose you'd just have to be particularly careful. Hove to at the first sign of foul weather, for instance, no matter how good the fishing. But it's none of my business. You'll do as you see fit. I'll be on *Petrel* so it won't be my problem.'

He yawns to emphasise his lack of concern. Downs the last sip of rum in his mug. 'Bedtime for me, I think.' He nods in my direction when he reaches the door, his pocket chinking with pennies.

I don't return the gesture.

I look back to the baby. He must be dreaming. His tiny, almost-transparent eyelids flinch and flutter. I study the intricate tributaries of fine blue veins. For some reason, my own eyelids feel hot and my forehead's aching.

Percy steps out and closes the door, but not before a cold rush of air threatens the flame at my elbow.

Bob turns to glance at me. He's clearly in two minds, and they're paired with the two sides of his face. The light from the lamp throws the ruined skin into relief.

'Do ye think ye could repulse the blacks if they came at the homestead?'

'I know how to shoot.' My teeth are chattering. Sudden pimples rise on my arms. 'There's a draught in here, Bob. I don't know where it's coming from.'

He pads across the floor to look closely into my face. He smells of fish, and of the whale grease used to lubricate the cleats on the luggers.

'There's no draught. Ye look sick. Go to bed.'

Now my bones are filled with lead filings.

'I haven't given Ferrier his last feed.'

The scar tightens on his cheek. 'Take him with ye, then. I'll sleep on yer sister's cot.'

My throat is dry when I wake in the morning, and my lips parched, but I feel better. Ferrier's staring at the ceiling, lost in some world of his own making. I reach over to feel his saturated napkin. When he sees my face, it's his cue to bellow. I slip my legs over the edge of the bed and stand experimentally. So far, so good. Just weak. And a little light-headed, as though the tether of my neck is not quite enough to keep me grounded. It's not the fever or I'd be lost to my bed for days, sweating and shivering.

'Missis, missis.' It's Darby's deep voice from the doorstep.

I hear Ah Sam answer him. 'Shoo, shoo. Missy sick.'

I move slowly into the main room. Ah Sam has all six household lanterns lined up in front of him on the table with the glass cases removed; the sheared beak of the wick trimmer in his hand. Darby's standing his ground.

'What is it, Darby?' I wrap my gown more tightly around me, pour myself a glass of water from the jug and take a sip. 'Quickly. I have to change the baby.'

Ferrier's still bawling in the bedroom. I look over to Ah Sam pleadingly. He sighs, puts down the trimmer and trots away to do my bidding. I hear his soothing voice from the bedroom. Darby pulls a hand from behind his back. Blood's dripping from a large gash in the palm.

'Me helpin boss chop up wood.'

I draw back a little. 'Strange-looking wood. Here.' I throw him a piece of rag. 'Wrap it up in this and then come in.'

Five minutes later, Ferrier's changed and quiet, and I'm washing my hands in potassium permanganate mixed with hot water from the pot Ah Sam's boiled for the morning's tea. The water is the pink of musk lozenges.

Darby perches on a crate. Once I've cleaned out the wound, I see the gash: two inches long, across the high part of his palm. It follows his lifeline. The skin is lumpy-looking at the edges and I'll have to trim it with scissors. Darby's looking grey now. I pour out a quarter cup of Bob's rum as anaesthesia. He swallows it with a shudder.

The flesh is thick, resists the blades. I have to stop when he tries to pull away.

'Just a bit longer, Darby. I'll have to stitch up the wound so your insides don't fall out.'

It's a joke but he nods seriously and grits his teeth. The skin is just as hard to get the needle through. It's the thick calluses on his hardworking hands. Despite the rum, Darby's eyes roll back in his head, reminding me of the morning I found him standing by my bedside, sleepwalking.

'All right. Done.' I give him a bit of a shake until his gaze clears, then wrap his wound in a bandage that I don't imagine will stay clean for more than a few minutes.

'Would you like a cup of tea to settle your nerves?'

He looks at the rum flagon.

'No more grog. What will the boss say if I send you back drunk?'

Still he hesitates.

'Is there something else?'

'This morning me and Charley Sandwich bin fishin.'

This is hardly news. The boys have a favourite cove on the south side where they go just after dawn. One or other of them is always turning up on the doorstep with fish, oysters or turtle eggs in exchange for tobacco.

'Yes?'

'We see canoe on beach. Wild-black canoe. We come back. No fish.'

'How many canoes?'

He holds up two of the fingers on his undamaged hand. I notice the skin's peeling off the pads, revealing paler flesh beneath.

'Did you see the blacks? How many? Do they have a camp there?'

He shrugs. 'Dunno, missis. We come back quick. No fish.'

The lack of fish is a recurring motif. I realise then he's on a different kind of angling expedition.

'Better than a spear in the belly though?'

'Too right.' He nods and his curls bounce.

'Almost a community service then, you keeping yourself alive ... Yes, all right, you can have a plug. But listen, did you tell the boss this story?'

He shakes his head.

'Well, don't. I'll tell him. You make sure Charley doesn't tell him either.' To emphasise the point, I go to the tobacco box, take two fibrous plugs and hold them out to him in a closed fist. 'Remember, Darby. Only I tell the boss.'

'Savvy, missis.'

My fingers uncurl. He takes the tobacco and disappears through the light of the doorway. When he thinks he's out of view, I see him picking at the end of the bandage to unravel it.

Three days later. When the luggers returned from the reef this morning, they brought back only two bags of slugs between them.

Now, mid-afternoon, Bob fills the doorway, his rifle in one hand and a dead goanna in the other. He holds it by its long tail. The flesh seems limp and wobbly inside its mottled skin, the dark tongue lolling. Its long, dirty claws drag on the gravel. Behind Bob's shoulder, woolly streaks of clouds spring loose from their bale. He hasn't shaved for a couple of days. With the scar, it gives him a wild look, like a pirate.

'Caught this bastard nosing around the chicken coop.'

I'm not moved to pity for the lizard. I've come to hate them for what they do to the poultry. Still, I've no wish to look revenge in the face.

'Good,' I say simply.

'If we do decide to build a homestead on Night and I take ye up there, ye'll like it. No lizards. Nothing but thousands of Strait pigeons.'

I nod, feigning anticipation. I'll never see Night Island. Never have to wade ankle-deep in pigeon guano. The Lizard will be my last lump of granite in the middle of the ocean, I swear.

I look at the dead lizard again. 'Do you believe in the afterlife, Bob?'

'Not for vermin like this. But I bide it. It bides me. Pity yer locked outside. Sure ye won't be turned?'

It's not the first time he's suggested I convert to Catholicism.

'Quite sure,' I say tightly. 'Eternal damnation will suit me well enough, I dare say.'

He frowns at the blasphemy, but doesn't scold me. Now Ferrier's taken care of, my soul's destination is only of academic interest to him.

Sluggish spring flies hover around the corpse. The sun sparkles on the grainy sand stuck to its patterned side. There is something slightly nauseating in the tiling of reptile skin. An ancient code that signals danger.

Charley Sandwich has moved up behind Bob and is hopping from foot to foot. 'Boss? Boss?'

Bob turns and flings the lizard. It does a leaden cartwheel in the air. Charley catches it with both arms and a grin. Blood from the goanna's mouth drips down his leg as he runs back to tell Darby of their sudden fortune.

51

From the secret diary of Mary Watson

1ST SEPTEMBER 1881

The luggers are loaded. Most of the crew is already on board. Bob pulls his hat down to secure it against a stiff onshore wind.

'Remember, now, if something goes awry, try to flag a passing ship.' He gives me an awkward smile, then pats Ferrier on the head. 'Be a good chappie for yer ma.' He turns to me. Speaks around a thick lump in his voice. 'Look after my boy.'

'I will, Bob. Thank you. For everything.' After all our differences, I can't bring myself to hate him.

Something softens to a wind-blown film in his eyes. He touches me on the cheek. 'Ye sound like I'll never see ye again.'

And then he's striding down the beach, stopping only to swear at one of the Kanakas who's dropped a box in the sand. I close my eyes in the warm morning sun. When I open them again, Percy's standing next to me.

'If there's a change in plans, I'll find a way to come back and alert you.' Ah Sam staggers past with a crate full of oranges. Percy waits until he's out of earshot before continuing. 'If you hear nothing, you'll know it's still on.'

'What if I need to make contact?'

'You can't. You're on your own. Look for the signal at 11 p.m. on the thirtieth at the co-ordinates I've given you. You have my position?'

'Yes. I've written it all down.'

'Good. I'll fetch you early in the morning of the first of October. Be ready. I'll have your money with me. There's a safe place down along the coast about fifty miles from Lookout Point. An armed outpost. A southbound bullock train passes through there every week, maybe oftener. *You* do the work of convincing Ah Sam. If he gives you any trouble ...'

He doesn't finish the sentence. He doesn't have to.

'I appreciate it.' I hold out my hand.

He takes it. His palm is cool. He drops it again. The way his glance skitters away from my eyes doesn't reassure me.

'What about Ah Leung? How will he get off the island?'

I can't help remembering what the Chinaman is here for: to clean up the mess should things go wrong. The exact nature of his cleaning activities is something I've tried not to dwell on. Nor his predilection for murder.

'I'll drop him off somewhere else.' But he still evades my gaze. An image comes to mind of an executioner wearing a black hood so he can keep his business impersonal.

I shift the baby slightly, so that he sits in the hollow of my waist. The wind has left a crack in my upper lip. My tongue seeks it out. I wince at the sting.

'It's been a long haul,' Percy says, looking to the ocean. 'No hard feelings?'

No hard feelings ... For what he's done? Or for what he's about to do?

This is my last chance.

'Percy ... I've held up my end of the bargain. Done what was asked of me, and it hasn't been easy. All I want now is what I've earned. After this last drop, I become Ferrier's mother. Nothing more.'

There, I've said it. Put all the cards I'll ever have on the table.

'None of us has a guarantee of safe passage.' He bends to pick up a bristly coil of rope. 'You can't say you weren't warned.'

I feel cold and rub my arms. There it is again: that something in the inflection of his voice that drags me back to the first time we met in Brisbane. The feeling there's a gap between the way he presents himself and the way he really is. I don't have the opportunity to interrogate him. He's gone: taking large steps towards *Petrel* and whatever new life he's chosen for himself. He doesn't look back.

52

'Alone' is a single word with two syllables.
Why, then, does it feel like a sentence?

From the secret diary of Mary Watson

The first night. Still life with squeaky rocking chair, sleeping baby and mosquito net. Ocean and wind conspire, as they always do, muttering about the next day's weather. The door is barred. There's a new dimension to the silence in the little limestone house.

For the last hour, on and off, I've listened to a curlew's heart-wringing wails from the darkness. It winds up and then falls in a sorrowful diminuendo. Seems to reach inside and squeeze my ribs. It's a death bird, or so Darby told me a few weeks ago when we found one under a bush near the farm, its eyes eaten out by ants.

The cries stop abruptly. The emptiness that's left behind is, in some ways, worse. I try to concentrate on the mending in my hands. There's something so sensible about thread and needle; the pact between the two to stitch up the holes of the world.

A single yelp from one of the two remaining dogs. The breeze catches the window frame, which in turn rattles the shutters. The lantern flares then settles.

Then I hear footsteps. Not measured enough for a goanna.

Two distinct thumps against the door.

I stand. Glance over at the cradle. The chair rocks for a few noisy arcs by itself before stopping. I fetch the rifle from the corner. Then return to the chair and sit. Feet square on the floor, ears strained to drum-skin tautness.

Nothing but the usual island noises. Ten minutes pass. Or twenty. It's hard to tell.

I go to the door and lift the bar. Pull it open. On the gravel path, two balls of feathers. Their necks broken.

My dead chickens come home to roost.

53

2ND SEPTEMBER 1881

The wind's from the southwest this morning, blowing hard and choppy like a series of slaps. It whines and whistles under and around the door. Puffs through the narrow gaps in the shutters.

'I go for water now, missy.'

Fear flutters softly at the base of Ah Sam's throat. I know what he's thinking. If we have water, we can barricade ourselves in the house.

He bustled over this morning, his usual cheerful self, but then I showed him the chickens and sent him to check on the dogs. He came back with the news that Rufus was dead, speared through the stomach. Bob's other cur, Sylvester, was whining and pacing miserably around the corpse.

'Untie him,' I told Ah Sam. 'Give the poor animal a chance to run and hide.'

Now, it's clear by the look on his face that he doesn't want to brave the heavily treed swamp to reach the clear spring beyond it.

'They realise the men have gone,' I say. 'They're just trying to frighten us into leaving.'

My words are empty. The blacks must know we have no seaworthy vessel to flee in. But what else can I tell him? That they are toying with us? That they will attack, in numbers, at a time and place of their own choosing?

I'm deliberately brisk, rushing around the house, rag in hand. Any cleanable surface gets polished to within an inch of its life. My eye catches the calendar hanging crooked on the nail. Only one day of solitude crossed off with a thick pencil. Twenty-nine to go until we're off the island.

I've brought the two shells that Porter gave me into the house. Placed them on the knick-knack shelf so that I can see them, with a twist of my head, from anywhere in the communal room. I walk over, run my fingers lightly over each, then look to where Ferrier sits on the floor, propped up by a blanket, a pillow on either side. His arms carve circles through the dusty sunlight seeping through thin cracks in the shutters. He chuckles in approval as the shadows swirl and loop. He doesn't realise he's responsible for the morning's entertainment. Doesn't know his own movements have conjured this image of a maypole, ribbons, young girls just out of sight, dancing.

'I won't let anything happen to my baby.'

I'm looking at Ferrier when I speak but talking to Ah Sam. When he doesn't answer, I turn to face him.

'Do you hear me? I'll shoot every native between here and Brisbane first.'

Two weeks on and now only fourteen days until the drop. The blacks have left us alone for over a fortnight. But that doesn't mean they're not bolder with every moment that passes. Ah Sam saw two canoes dragged up on the beach sixty yards to the south. No effort had been made to hide them. Fires are visible daily to the east, grey smoke spiralling up from behind Cook's Look.

Nights are the worst. For hours, I listen as they chant their songs near the house: nasal, repetitive. A concert just for me. The voices are insidious: words and melody together like an army crawling on its belly down my ear canals. Each night they make a bit more ground, getting closer to their target of my mind.

Coming on purple dusk. Standing at the ragged border where rough ground meets sand, I spot the steamer. Heading north. It's too far away to make out a name on the hull, and the looking glass is back in the house. I put a hand up to visor my eyes, squint out towards it. An unexpected wave of loneliness breaks over me.

I wonder what they're doing, the people on board. Playing games on deck; or chatting in the smoking room below. They would dress for dinner soon, of course. The women with buttoned-up, long silk gloves and soft, kid boots. The men in silk-lined twill suits, looking over the top of gilt snuffboxes. Gazing at the women. Imagining how it might be to open their mouths on those soft female throats, taste the perfume there. Nothing like what I remember of the journey from Cornwall: third-class steerage, smelly oil lamps, ticking stuffed with straw on a wooden stretcher for a bed. Fleas.

What is it that's caught me out like this? Is it only their money I'm envious of? The civilised life of the beautiful people? Or merely the ordered universe of wealth? Everything available at the drop of a hat. No centipedes under the table's oilcloth. No weevils in the flour. No amount of corruption festering at the core of things, that can't be bought off…

'What is it you want, Mary?'

I say it out loud. The same question Porter asked me. Back then, I could only pick at one ragged end of my dissatisfaction: the fact that I was worried about Carrie on the Lizard and wanted her safely away. I was hiding from the true and larger answer. But I've disciplined myself so well, and for so long, I wonder if I can even think beyond singular, immediate needs now.

'I want my baby to grow up happy and healthy.'

It's a given. Beyond that, my emotions seize on my restraint. I can hear Porter's voice in my head, nurturing, patient. *But what about you, Mary?*

It doesn't matter. Not here and now. Even if I had some epiphany, the smallness or hugeness of my desires are irrelevant when there's no one to hear. When the wind just takes my words like any other piece of detritus and carries them out to sea. I could talk to myself for days with no consequence but madness.

I feel an unamused smile lift the corners of my mouth. Now it's Mama's words whispering, telling me that all of my problems are of my own ambitious making. *You're more like your father than you think. Picking up an axe to split a toothpick.*

Ferrier's in his nightdress on a rug under a nearby tree. He's talking in a series of gurgles and grunts, addressing his commentary to the leaves of the pisonia as they rustle and flap above him. He seems so self-contained, amusing himself for hours on end. He knows nothing of the danger we're in. He doesn't understand that, if I fail, he will die. But I do. And I can't think of anything but what's at stake.

Ah Leung's further down the beach, casting a fishing line out beyond the crystalline break of the waves. Ah Sam's checking on the few remaining chickens. There'll be no eggs. Laying requires a settled life, not constant stress.

Over towards the swamp, a goanna heads leisurely for a tree. Its huge claws find purchase on the trunk. The long tongue flicks like a knife strap. They've grown insolent, the lizards, since the men have left. The last time I encountered one, instead of lumbering away, it turned and stared at me. Steadily, calculatingly, with cold, black eyes. I wonder if they're in league with the natives. And if they think they're winning.

54

From the secret diary of Mary Watson

25TH SEPTEMBER 1881

The last four nights, I've invited Ah Sam and his sleeping mat into the house. Neither of us thinks to suggest Ah Leung might be given the same treatment. Let his precious joss protect him.

Should anyone lift the roof at night and look down, we would appear like a couple. An odd one, but a couple nevertheless, caring for our child. They'd see Ah Sam change the baby's napkin, soak the soiled one in the bucket filled with water and a capful of Carbolacene. While I rinse the dishes in a shallow pan. Afterwards, they'd see me settle into the rocker with my knitting. Ah Sam sits cross-legged on the floor, the curved wooden box he uses as a pillow in front of him. He lifts the lid, takes out a few long sandalwood sticks. We argue briefly about whether or not he should burn them to keep evil away. My continued objection is that the smell makes the baby sneeze. But I give in, and he lights them by poking the tips through the top of the lantern. The prickly yellow smell creeps through the small room until we both grow sleepy, listening to the wheeze and stretch of the ocean on its rack. The night breeze licking at gaps in the roof.

Around nine o'clock, I ask him if he really believes there are bad spirits on the island.

'This very old place.'

I watch the thin, dirty smoke from the sticks curl as it rises to the ceiling. Wrap the wool around one finger and push the needle through the loop to begin a sleeve on Ferrier's new jumper. The men didn't think to fasten the loose sheet of tin on the smokehouse roof before they left. It gives a metallic twang as it lifts in the wind; a low creak as it falls back.

Ah Sam's face is oddly lit in the incense-soaked glow. I imagine an ivory statue left in the weather to gather moss. Once again I wonder at his age.

'Where are you from, Ah Sam? Which province in China?'

Sylvester barks outside. I can't tell from which direction. The ocean and breeze are up to their usual acoustic tricks.

'Kwangtung, missy,' he says.

'Do you have a wife … children?'

The baby snuffles. My foot goes out automatically to rock the cradle.

He nods but volunteers no details. Looks up at me. Straight through me, it seems. His eyes are bright. 'You go up again?' He points to where I know Cook's Look swells behind the house.

'One more time, Ah Sam.'

'Why?'

'Work for the Empire. That's all I can tell you.'

My eyes stray to the shelf that holds the lantern with its polygon reflector. I retrieved it from Percy's hut some time ago, after the incident with the dead chickens.

He leans back stubbornly on his haunches. 'I come with you.' His shaved forehead shines in the weak lantern light.

There's a sudden popping sound from outside. Did someone kick a steel bucket? No. Just an empty kerosene tin contracting in the cool night air.

'No. I need you to look after Ferrier.' It's time to tell him. 'When the next trip up the hill is over, Ah Sam, I'm leaving the island with the baby. Do you want to come with us? I don't want to leave you here.'

He nods, unsurprised. 'I go back to China soon. How you leave?'

I pause. Stop rocking. Gaze at him evenly. 'Ah Sam, you must promise me that you will never tell anyone about what has happened here. I need to know you won't betray me. It's terribly important that you say nothing. Important to us all.'

He gets up and walks over to the door to look through the peephole. Apparently seeing nothing untoward, he turns back, some private joke toying around the edges of his mouth.

'I very good at keeping quiet. How you leave?'

'Percy's coming back to fetch us.'

I don't know what I've said, but every muscle stiffens in his body.

'I not the one to betray you, missy.'

'Do you mean Ah Leung? It's all right. I know about him.'

He moves his mouth with his lips closed, as though tasting his next words before he spits them out. 'You don't know Mister Fuller.'

'Percy? What about him?'

A sudden prescience tightens in a band around my head.

'Mister Fuller, he work with Mister Boule. Both work for French government.'

I sink back in the chair. My shoulders drop. The knitting falls from my hands to my lap. Ferrier stares up at me from the cradle, his eyes big and wide, as if he too is listening.

'How could you know such a thing?' I ask.

Ah Sam takes up position again, cross-legged on the floor next to his wooden box. 'I work ASN Company's wharf in Cooktown. Sometimes, cargo come night-time. I unload, and hear things. From Mister Boule, Mister Fuller, French captain. I know they all work together.' He looks at me unsmiling, an old resentment in his eyes. 'White men not mind Chinese. Think we have no ears. Mister Fuller not remember me. Chinese all the same to him.'

A French spy. I start to shake. And if Ah Leung works for Percy, then he, too, works for the French.

'Do you think Ah Leung killed those prostitutes in Cooktown for some political reason?'

A quick nod. 'Maybe.'

And if Charley knew all along ... 'Perhaps Charley ordered it done?'

'Maybe those girls hear something they shouldn't,' he says.

The girls at Charley's are privy to all sorts of gossip from drunk and lusty clients. Easy to see now how a few of them — an unlucky few, whose only crime was talkativeness — had overheard something that sealed their death warrants.

'You need to watch out for Ah Leung, missy.'

It's all sinking in. Small discrepancies, signs I could have read differently. Charley getting me to deliver those notes. Was he using me to deliver misinformation to Roberts? Something he said in his office the last time I was there, when I mentioned he should go back to France: *A true Frenchman, he carries his country with him.* His total lack of concern about who had murdered his girls. And Percy's secrecies. That carefully coached English accent. His latest trip to Melbourne. The earlier disappearances that annoyed Bob so when I first came to Cooktown. The visit to the French man-o'-war immediately after the schooner had delivered the note from Roberts. Did he seduce me as an expedient way to keep me docile and incurious?

The most incredible thing is that all of this has been going on under Captain Roberts's nose. The man I thought invincible. The man I thought saw everything. And what about me — supposedly so good at reading people?

No time to wallow in my own humiliation now. I have to concentrate ... Ah Sam is right. Ah Leung is more dangerous than ever.

Then I see a small flaw in the narrative.

'You're mistaken, Ah Sam. You must be. Otherwise the last signalling wouldn't have gone smoothly. The French would have intervened to prevent the drop.'

But he's not moved to doubt. 'I tell you the truth.'

Am I grasping at straws? Perhaps. I know nothing about what really happened. I received and relayed a message I didn't even understand. In five days I'll do it again. This time, the message could be an order for my own execution and I'd never know. My clever plans all rest on the lies Percy and Charley used to groom me for their own purposes.

One of the sandalwood sticks has gone out. Ah Sam lifts it from the jar and relights it at the lantern. His fingernails extend beyond his fingertips, tapering slightly. But they're not claws like Ah Leung's. I watch him coldly. Can I even trust him? Who is he really working for? Who knows? Who knows with any of them? Maybe Ah Sam's just another murderous leopard, the island a pack of them. And I've let him into the house. Let him care for the baby. Maybe it's Ah Leung who has been most honest. He's never once attempted to camouflage his spots.

Ah Sam seems to feel the dark, impossible swirl of my thoughts. He looks me square in the eye.

'You have to trust someone, missy.'

Ah, but Captain Roberts told me to trust no one.

The baby whimpers. Automatically, I pull back the mosquito net. Lift him out of the cradle to put him to my breast. I've done this so many times in Ah Sam's presence, I never think to feel uncomfortable. Try as I might, I can't feel uncomfortable now. My mind won't rest, but my body responds to Ferrier's mouth. I feel the tug of his lips, then the tingle of my milk letting down. Just at the crucial moment he pulls away to look at my face. A squirt of milk hits him square in the eye. 'Silly!' I guide his mouth back to my nipple. He bucks then settles, kneads my breast with his tiny fist. I can smell the faint-vanilla scent of the milk flowing into him, making him strong. He's the light that I'll follow in the storm. The only light.

I gaze down at his perfectly formed face. Already his eyes are closing again. 'Little lighthouse.'

Ah Sam reaches into the wooden box for his opium pipe. The sickly sweetness soon fills the room. My nipple pops gently from Ferrier's mouth. He's too sleepy for the other side. I feel an uncomfortable tightness in the breast he hasn't suckled. Lift him back into the cradle, do up my blouse, then pick up my knitting.

The pragmatic side of me has the last few words: I have no choice. I have to proceed as though Ah Sam is on my side. I can't do this thing alone. But what now? If I don't go through with the signalling, Percy will know that something's wrong. If I do, he'll still be here just hours later to collect us. Or, more probably, to make sure Ah Leung has killed us. Unless, of course, by that time the blacks have saved him the trouble. Or maybe he won't come back at all, take my money and run, leave us to our fate.

'Oh, God. What do I do?'

When God doesn't answer, I turn to Ah Sam. But already his eyelids are drooping. The opium's kicking in. My own lips feel tingly from the borrowed air around the pipe. He takes another long drag.

'We can't win, Ah Sam. There's no way out.'

He just stares at me for a long moment. He's half-asleep, sitting up. The pipe falls from between his fingers to smoulder on the floor. His body lists slightly to the left. The faintest oriental snore.

55

*When you're stuck between a rock
and a hard place,
there's nothing to do but keep wriggling.*

From the secret diary of Mary Watson

30TH SEPTEMBER 1881

Ah Sam sprinkled some ground dragon bone and oyster shell into Ah Leung's opium pipe to make him sleep soundly. He's just come back from their hut to confirm Ah Leung is well and truly paralysed until morning. Now, he points with his head at the gun near the door. 'You take.'

'Yes, I will. Look after Ferrier for me.'

I've fed the baby and changed his napkin. He's drowsing now on Ah Sam's shoulder. With one finger, I wipe a thin worm of milk from his chin. The tendons in the Chinaman's wrist flex as he pats the baby's back.

'Bar the door behind me. I'll be back,' I say.

'You stay,' he says, his pale face obstinate. 'I go.'

'You don't know how. In any case, I started this. I have to finish it.'

The night outside is as cold as a reptilian eye. Cloud partially uncovers the quarter moon. The beach glows with an alien light. Stiff gusts from the southwest carry chilled hooks in them. I see the door close. Hear the bar come down.

Ferrier whimpers inside, sensing even in sleep that I've gone. Although my breasts seem empty, I feel the letdown reflex, then a leak of milk that almost immediately turns clammy and cool on my chest.

I start out towards Cook's Look, loaded rifle in my right hand, the handle of the covered signal lantern in the left. I trot through the open country near the house. The moonlight, though thin, is reliable enough to reveal anything untoward in the terrain I've become so familiar with. But if I can see, I can be seen. Branches rustle and click ahead. Air rushes too quickly out of my lungs; I make an involuntary noise. The clicking stops, but not the rustling. Something scurries past, inches from my feet. I yelp, then, too late, put a hand over my mouth. The night sky's a pour of treacle, that bright spoon-handle of the quarter moon dipping into it, flinging out bright filaments.

Clouds roll in as I reach the path and start to climb, then there's another blade of illumination from above. Last time the moon was more full, the sky clearer. I stumble and totter up the rough track. Tufts of knotty grass grab at my boots, threaten to trip me.

A twig-snapping noise to my left. I turn to see stunted trees, a few boulders big enough for someone to crouch behind. My finger moves down the barrel of the gun, rests for a moment on the trigger. I open my mouth. And close it. Why ask who's there? It's what every stupid heroine in every suspense story does. As if the blacks would answer. Or Ah Leung.

Instead, I stand still and listen. The ocean fizzes and rumbles in the distance. The cold wind rises and falls like a small boat in choppy water. My Cornish third eye knows well enough that they're watching me. What I don't understand is … what are they waiting for?

I put down the signal lantern and raise the rifle to my shoulder. I've no idea where to aim. The darkness around me writhes with observation, calculation, intention. I wait for five minutes. Maybe ten. Maybe only two. Nothing moves. When a curtain of cloud draws fully away from the moon, I pick up the lantern, turn and hurry up the path.

When I reach the summit, I'm panting too hard to stand. I sit with my back to the nearest boulder and struggle for air. Minutes pass before I can breathe with relative ease. Then all I can register is the cold and the fact that I'm still alive.

Alive and with a job to do.

I stand and begin by lighting the signal lamp. It's a struggle; the wind accelerates, unseasonably harsh and chill. My fingers are numb inside the gloves I've pulled on. I waste six matches before the wick catches. I warm my hands for a moment over the quickly heating metal, then unpack the compass, pencils and paper. My calves are about to cramp, so I cover the lantern, stand and stretch my legs.

The ocean's like a lamp itself; a floating shark-oil lamp, its wick lit by the moon. Veins spring high-pressure leaks beneath the surface in luminous trails of green. An occasional white flash near shore signals the spots where irresistible force meets an immovable reef and is transformed into fizz. A seductive voice in my head suggests that there are much worse places to die than this.

It would be so easy to lie down and wait, looking up at the stars, the distant, unflustered stars. It's been such a long journey. No one could say I didn't deserve a rest. I stand apart from myself for a few seconds, seriously considering this option. But then feel the wetness on my blouse, and remember Ferrier.

I set the signal lantern on the same flat rock I used last time. I've lost track of time, but the internal clock in my head tells me the first signal will come soon. I lift the cover off the lantern, check the compass, then align the light to the co-ordinates Percy passed on to me before he left. The wind drags the heat towards my face and I revel in the sensation. I don't remove my gloves, as cold fingers can still burn, but warm them again, as close as I dare. The remarkable lens captures my attention; the polygon reflector. It reminds me of the overlapping chambers of the nautilus shell Porter gave me, but made of glass. With that deep, bright eye of flame at its heart.

The sweat from the climb has dried and I have all over goosebumps when I see the first signal. One of the three pencils has blown off the rock; I pin the other two and the paper under my left arm. My gloved finger rests on the shutter.

I don't have to wait long. The little blinking dot of light seems familiar this time. I send the first password, and it's acknowledged. The message is long but I hardly notice. My writing jerks on the paper. Then it's time to reorient the signal lamp to relay the code I've transcribed.

I don't look around. Either the blacks have followed me up Cook's Look with their spears, or they haven't. Either Ah Leung is waiting for me at the bottom of the hill with a gun or a cane knife, or he's still lost in his opium dreams. Either I'll live or I'll die. I can't do anything yet about either, though it occurs to me that if I do survive this night I won't passively wait for Ah Leung or Percy to make the next move. I'll be ready for both of them. And not with tea and gingerbread.

When my relay is finally acknowledged, at first I feel nothing. Then I notice the snail trail of tears on my cheeks. It's not sadness, but anger. Anger at those who have stabbed me in the back. Anger at myself for this whole, self-serving mess.

I extinguish the lantern, pack it roughly into its box. Think about throwing it as far as I can down the slope, or just leaving it there on Cook's Look: a monument to greed. But I do neither of those things. Just dangle it from one hand, grab the rifle by its stock with the other. And set off down the path towards Ferrier.

I'm too tired to hurry and the wind has risen to a steady gale. Clouds still drag across the moon, and each time one obscures it altogether I go blind and must stand with my skirts billowing until it moves on. A wolf-howl of wind. A clatter of leaves. I imagine Ah Leung's outline in every stunted tree, blacks loitering in every shadow, but I'm too numb for fear.

The path begins to level. I know I'm almost home when I feel windblown sand prickle my calves and hear the *zizz-crash* of waves on shore, an undertone to the larger roaring. I can't quite make out the house, but I know now where it is.

Then I feel the air displaced around me. A long flexible spear trailing white feathers thunks into the ground a yard in front of my feet. A curdling cry behind me.

The next thing I'm aware of is banging on the door hysterically, the lantern dropped and forgotten. Ah Sam pulls me in so roughly, I feel a tearing pain in my shoulder. He slams the door shut. The blessed bar comes down. The forceful thwack of spears hitting the wood.

I can't fill my lungs. They're ten times too large for my chest. All I can do is keep pulling in air in small increments. It sounds to my ears like I'm sobbing.

Ferrier hasn't even woken in his cradle.

'They could have had me on the hill,' I manage. 'Don't you see?'

Ah Sam's face floats hazily above me. He doesn't seem to understand.

'They spared me, Ah Sam. I should be dead.'

56

*Even a third eye can close
when it's beyond exhaustion.*

From the secret diary of Mary Watson

1ST OCTOBER 1881

The next morning at eight, I stand outside with the rifle, swaying. Ferrier is asleep in the house. Ah Sam's gone with the revolver to find Ah Leung, who must have woken from his sedative by now.

My thoughts unfold, clunky as wooden letters spilled from a box. I'm beyond organised planning, almost beyond sense. The hollow ping of spears rebounded off the walls on and off all night. The eerie chants wormed through the shutters and under the door. I have to keep closing my red-peppered eyes against the crisp-biscuit light of morning. It feels as though my vision's attached to the lid of my head that's slightly ajar. The westerly breeze carries the whoosh and smell of the ocean into the gap, making the world blur and sting.

I must stay alert, somehow. When I braved outside at dawn, it was to see that the lantern I dropped on the way back from Cook's Look had disappeared. Four spears lay strewn on the ground to mark the spot where it had been. But there was no sign of the blacks. No sign of Ah Leung, either. And, so far, no sign of *Petrel*'s sail ballooning with air.

But wait. What's that? A small dot out in the bay moving towards shore. And a larger vessel behind it. I didn't bring the looking glass, but who else could it be but Percy? The bigger boat seems to be heading north. Odd. And the dimensions, now that I squint, seem like those of a ketch.

What of the smaller part of the puzzle. There's definitely something on the water headed this way. No sail. No mast. A rowboat then, bobbing unevenly towards the beach. Percy's come in a rowboat! Why? This temporarily defeats me and I lick my dry lips, try to order my dishevelled mind. To hide the evidence of his murderous intent from any passing ships? No. Percy knows this island better than anyone. If he didn't want to be seen, he could have simply anchored *Petrel* further around the bay, in one of the secluded coves the blacks found so convenient to hide their canoes in.

I aim the rifle at the black dot. Blink. Blink again. Now the detail's resolving. It's not Percy. It's no man. Glittery, watered sun drips off the oars as they rise and fall, pulled, haphazardly, by a woman in a bonnet. I must be hallucinating. Too tired. Too worn down. Is it Mama come to rescue me? Disobedient Carrie returning to the island?

I shake my head to dislodge the mirage. But it persists. There is still a woman in a rowboat, come from a ketch that's now sailing north in the distance, a single seagull keeping watch above it. I lower the gun. Hang it at my side.

I hear the rasp as the hull strikes sand. She — whoever she is — lifts something from between her legs. A loaf of bread? Then climbs out awkwardly, almost tumbling into the shallow water. Her skirt is drenched. She staggers up the beach towards me.

The closer she gets, the more familiar her clothing seems. I almost know her from the way she's holding her body. Not quite a swagger. Something's wrong with her. She's drunk, or ill. Maybe mad. She looks like a castaway who has neither eaten nor slept for days.

'Where is 'e?' Her rank breath hits me when she's three feet away. 'Where's Bob? I got somethin' for 'im.'

It's Laura from French Charley's but almost unrecognisable. She's gaunt, stretched. Her dress hangs from shoulders frail and sharp as twigs. Where once her bosom rose above her bodice, the bars of her ribs are now visible. Her skin's blotched with patches of red, some sort of rash. Her face is hollowed out at the cheeks, as though a spoon has scooped the flesh away. Only the eyes burn.

I step back. 'Who brought you here? You look like you've walked straight out of the pits of hell.'

She coughs and cracks out a laugh. 'And you strolled out o' heaven, I s'pose.' She lifts her head in a parody of flirtatiousness. 'I'm the pretty one. Remember, Mary Oxnam? The Devil's 'ad a 'and in you, not me. Though I must admit a few drunk Devils 'as been in me at times.' That cackle again, like autumn leaves underfoot. She finishes in a coughing fit that bends her almost double.

I still can't see what she has wrapped in her arms. She looks over her shoulder slowly at the ketch, just a jot in the distance now.

'That's Cap'n Levitt. I paid 'im to bring me 'ere. Saved me wages up for months, I did. Though 'e weren't real courteous. Made me stay down in the 'old.' Her eyes bore into me again. 'Where is 'e? Where's that dirty, two-timin' set o' scummy bagpipes?'

'Bob's not here. There's no one here but me and two Chinamen.'

She looks around. No luggers, no sign of activity. Looks back, her ruined face tilted upwards in suspicion.

'Out fishin' for 'is precious slugs, is 'e? Well, I'll just sit meself down and wait.'

She turns her back to me. Her legs give out and she collapses into a sitting position on the sand. She falls far too hard, but gives no sign of pain.

'Least an all 'is Majesty's bein' quiet … Lorry, it's cold in the breeze, ain't it?'

'Laura, what have you got there?' I step forward, try to look over her shoulder.

'It's me an' Bob's baby boy. Wilfred, I called 'im. Bob said 'e'd look after me with money and such, and 'e didn't. So I came over to make 'im take responsibility.'

I barely flinch at the news. It explains Charley's incredulous reaction when I told him I was pregnant. He knew that Laura was carrying Bob's child at the same time I was carrying Ferrier. That's why he sacked her. That's why I saw her scrubbing floors at the Federal Hotel.

'Can I see him? Your baby.'

I keep my voice low. Some slow stick is stirring my insides.

''E's asleep. You know that mongrel Charley Boule wanted me to get rid of 'im, don'cha? He sent me to Mrs Liggins on 'ope Street, but I didn't go. So then he made me swaller some pills, but I spat 'em out. I wanted me baby, y' see. 'E's the only thing I ever 'ad that's mine.'

She bundles the infant closer, but the faded piece of blanket comes away and I see part of one small, oozing, purplish foot. At the same time, a wave of decay rises up. I turn to vomit into the sand. Wipe my mouth on a dirty sleeve.

'Oh, Laura. Your baby's dead.'

I step away from the mess I've made, start backing up the beach away from her. I wonder how long she's been carrying the body around.

'No, 'e ain't. 'E's just sleepin'.' She stares out to sea, unperturbed. 'You always was a liar, and up yerself on account of yer fancy education. You're just sayin' it so I won't try to find Bob. But I'll just wait for him 'ere. Ain't nothin' you can do about it.'

'You're sick. What's the matter with you?'

I don't want her or her dead baby near me. I don't want them within a whole continent of Ferrier. As if there weren't already enough threats on the Lizard. Now Laura's brought typhoid!

Ah Sam staggers over from the clearing with the revolver hanging limp in his hand. His body is shaking: muscles twitching in his face.

I motion him over. 'What's the matter with you?' I whisper, out of Laura's earshot.

He blinks slowly. Looks down at this new development. His eyes widen just a little. 'What?'

'She's one of Charley's whores. I think she's got typhoid. Did you find Ah Leung?'

'Ah Leung dead,' he says. 'Speared at farm. I take him to our hut.' His eyes are suddenly frantic. 'I can't leave him there. They *eat* him!'

I nod slowly, but can't react. I'm so tired. Each new shock is part of one long dream. I sink back a little on my heels in the sand. Ah Leung killed by the blacks. But when? Last night, probably. He could have been hiding over near the farm, waiting for me to complete my signalling so that he could ambush and kill me when I was returning from Cook's Look. So much for Ah Sam's foolproof sedative.

Twice now, the blacks have saved my life. Though I can't count Ah Leung's slaying as a deliberate favour. They must have turned their attention back to me afterwards. That was when the spears landed at my feet. Perhaps they planned to collect Ah Leung's body this morning. But Ah Sam found it first. The Chinese are even more horrified than the Europeans at the idea of being cannibalised. Or, more precisely, at having their bones scattered unrecoverably after death. It means that their souls wander endlessly.

An important question occurs to me through the fug. I grab Ah Sam, one hand on each arm. 'Did you see any natives at the farm?'

He shakes his head, and I relax just a little.

'Good. They're still reluctant to attack during the day. We'll be safe until nightfall.' I keep my eyes pinned to his. 'Show Laura where Percy's hut is, but don't get too close to her. She can't stay here on the beach. Take her some food and a drink.'

Laura peers with that death's head over her shoulder. 'Oi. I know when I'm bein' talked about.'

'You must be tired,' I say, a bit louder. 'Ah Sam will show you a shack along the beach where you can rest. He'll bring you some food.'

'Don't want no food. Wouldn't mind a cuppa tea, though. I'm parched. An' a lie-down wouldn't go amiss.' She struggles to her feet. 'This shack. Does it face the sea? I don't want to miss Bob when 'e gets back.'

'Yes, it does. Would you like me to mind Wilfred while you sleep?'

I take a handkerchief out of my pocket and hold it over my mouth. I don't want to take the baby from her. But neither can I bear the thought of it rotting in her arms. I'm a mother too, after all.

'No, ya greedy piece. Ya got me man. Ya ain't gettin' me baby.'

She trudges off behind Ah Sam towards Percy's shack. I watch until she turns into a swaying stick insect in the distance.

By the time Ah Sam has taken a drink to her and come back to where I'm standing, I feel as though my legs are full of half-set jelly. He seems to have recovered from the shock of finding Ah Leung. He looks at my face and clicks his tongue at what he sees.

'I stand guard. You sleep ...'

He puts a hand out for the rifle and, after a second's hesitation, I hand it over. He gives me the revolver.

'Perhaps just for a little while,' I say. 'Will you wake me in a few hours?'

He nods, and I stagger towards the house. Ferrier still hasn't woken. He's breathing deeply as I pass the cradle. I look down at him for a moment. His fist is up against his mouth. His hair's so soft, it's like ducks' down. That poor wretch, Laura. Would I go mad too if my baby was dead? Yes. There would be no other state in which to live.

I put the bar down on the door. Don't even take off my boots in the bedroom. Just lay the revolver on the crate that passes for a bedside table and collapse on the bed.

It's noon when I open my eyes. Ferrier's bellowing. I hadn't meant to be out of commission so long. The wind is up outside. An offshore breeze from the east. There's a sound like someone thumping a rug against the back wall of the house. The twist and swish of pandanus leaves: a thousand noisy husks. The loose edge of tin on the smokehouse roof lifts with a series of screeches. The ocean is a nest of trapped snakes.

I stretch, taking a long inventory of my aches and pains. At least my head is clear.

'I'm coming, baby.'

By the time I reach the cradle, Ferrier hits his highest pitch. I change his napkin while he squeals and protests, his face tomato red. Then I sit in the rocking chair and feed him, humming a lullaby I remember from my own childhood. He looks up at me from under his long lashes, smiles around the nipple. All is forgiven. Finally, I got it right. Already, the tears have dried on his cheeks. I smile back. Offer my finger to his palm and he grasps it, like the mouth of a sea anemone closing over a morsel of food.

It's half an hour later when I can place him back in the cradle and brave the wind outside. Ah Sam, still on guard, is just holding his thin frame steady. The gusts are intent on bullying him out to sea. The white-spray of the waves near shore flies backwards in manes. Bob's sea kelpies returned for another gallop. I hold my hair back with one hand and approach Ah Sam. He mustn't hear me because, when I put a hand on his shoulder, he twirls around wild-eyed, his finger on the trigger.

I put both of my palms up. 'Steady! It's only me.'

He lowers the rifle again and takes a deep breath. 'You should not sneak up like that.'

'I wasn't sneaking. Percy hasn't come? No one's come?'

He shakes his head and I feel myself frowning. I was so sure he would be back, that there would be a confrontation. What if he doesn't come? The good news so far: we've survived being killed by a murderous Chinaman and a French spy. The bad news: we're still at the mercy of the blacks and stuck on the island.

Which tugs at the hem of another thought. Something's

missing on the shoreline. What is it? Scarves of sand blow off the beach and into the water.

'What happened to the rowboat Laura came in?'

Ah Sam's shoulders slump. He points to a dark spot in the distance, riding the waves and the troughs of the ocean, heading at a fast clip towards Brisbane.

'Oh, no! Why didn't you pull it ashore?'

'I did, missy! That wind too strong. I try to get it back. But then hear the woman cry out … I go to check … boat blow away.'

'Laura cried out? Why? The blacks?'

He shakes his head again. His queue rides the wind. 'She cry out once, then die. She too much sick.'

Laura. Dead. It occurs to me with a sickening jolt that, not counting the blacks, there's an even ratio of dead bodies to live people on the island.

I see, then, how exhausted Ah Sam is. Sand's blasted his face to pink. His eyes are two dark pits.

'It's your turn, Ah Sam. Go and have a sleep in the house. If you hear Ferrier stir, you can look after him. I'll yell loudly if I need you. Go. We both have to be as strong as possible.'

He looks nervously behind him.

'We'll be all right until night falls. Go on.'

We swap weapons again. I watch him stagger towards the house, pushing against the wind. Today, for the first time since I've known him, he well and truly looks his age.

When Ah Sam wakes it's three o'clock. No Percy. The wind's subsided to a few petulant gusts around the trees and the pinkish sun hangs lower in the sky.

'Is Ferrier all right?' I ask. 'He must need feeding.'

He nods and puts a hand out for the rifle. But I shake my head. Look at the position of the sun again. Time is of the essence as the afternoon wears down.

'You'd better fetch water,' I tell him. 'We're almost out … fill both buckets. Go now, before it gets dark.'

He doesn't need any further encouragement.

He's been gone half an hour when I feel the skin over my kidneys pull tight. I'm being watched. I whip my head around and over to the stand of pandanus that Ah Leung cleared of grass with his cane knife not so long ago. The black man stands next to the wall of the iron privy. He's tall and muscular with a loin-covering made of feathers; a cooking-pot belly. Strings of teeth around his neck. His chest is crisscrossed with some kind of branding that raises the surface of the skin like the ridges sandworms make on the beach. The spear by his side must be eight feet long. Vertical yellow stripes smear down either cheek. Even at this distance, his eyes glow with unwavering purpose. I know that my life was spared last night. But there's no pity in that gaze.

I bring the barrel of the rifle up and aim at his body. 'What do you want? We've done nothing to you.' My voice cracks. 'Go away or I'll shoot.'

I pull the butt of the rifle a little closer, line up the sight, so he knows I'm not bluffing. He disappears behind the privy and into the longer stand of trees on the way to the swamp. When my heart stops ricketting, I realise Ah Sam is over there collecting water, with only the revolver. I can't go to help him. I can't leave Ferrier on his own.

⁊

Ah Sam cries out and I throw open the door and pull him in. I fire the rifle three times, four, though there are no blacks to be seen. I slam the door shut and drop the bar. Ferrier wails.

The Chinaman buckles at the knees, holds onto the table. There's a spear protruding from his shoulder. He looks up at me, helpless. His breath comes in gasps.

I drag the mattress off Carrie's cot and throw it onto the floor. 'Lie down, Ah Sam. This way. On your stomach.'

He sinks face first. His eyes flicker, then close. I feel for his pulse at the wrist: fast, and weak. I fetch the sewing scissors and cut his pyjamas around the spear to get a clearer view of the wound. Something Inspector Fitzgerald said aeons ago comes back to me. How the blacks dip their spear tips in putrefying corpses. It's infection that kills, not the initial wound. I have to get the spearhead out and quickly. Ah Sam's eyelids are still fluttering. I wish he'd fall into a painless stupor.

Ferrier's given up crying, though my ears still ring with his distress. Only the odd, desolate little hiccough from the cradle. I grab a wad of cloth. Tear a sheet into strips. Mix up potassium permanganate and a bit of our precious remaining water in a mug, stirring with a spoon until the crystals dissolve.

The flesh puts up a sickening resistance when I try to pull out the spear. Ah Sam gives deep, quavering moans, gripping the edges of the mattress white-knuckled. I brace my foot and put my back into it. The spear comes out, and the momentum topples me onto the floor. The wound geysers blood. I scramble over with the cloth, press it down for perhaps five minutes until my fingers are numb and I sense the pulses slowing beneath. I pull the cloth away. Still bleeding but not profusely.

I turn my head to the side for a few seconds, dry-heaving at the warm, metallic stink of blood. It's everywhere. All over the mattress and floor. All over me. I leave the material in place. Dip my curved upholstery needle and lengths of coarse sail thread in what's left of the disinfected water. Then start stitching. Ah Sam's eyes spring open. He writhes in pain.

'You must stay still.'

Maybe I should fetch the rum. But I'm almost finished. He falls back into a quiet agony.

Finished. I ease him onto his side. Clear up the mess as best I can with rags and no water. Then I fetch Ah Sam's carved wooden box. I've watched him often enough, and follow the routine as I remember it. Pick up a small stick of opium, break it into shards, push them with one finger into the bowl of the pipe. Light it with a match and inhale on the stem. Now the smell, with a sickening poppy sweetness at the back of my throat.

'Ah Sam.'

His eyes are closed, but his mouth opens when I nudge the pipe stem against it. It occurs to me it's not much different to tempting a sleeping baby with a nipple. His first attempt to draw in is feeble, barely sparking the bowl, but the second is stronger. The opium spits and clicks. I hold the pipe as he inhales. Ease it slightly to the side of his mouth so the used smoke can escape.

'I not get water, missy.' His words are starting to slur already. 'Sorry, I drop the bucket.'

'It's all right, Ah Sam.'

But it's not all right. We have barely three inches of clean water left. And the afternoon is sinking fast.

'Sorry,' he says again.

'Don't talk now. I've taken out the spear. You rest.'

I ease the pipe back to the centre of his mouth. He sucks, but it's almost out. The opium is gone. I watch his shallow breathing until his muscles relax and he's finally fully asleep. A stray hair has escaped from his queue. I loop it away from his face with a finger, then stand.

Ferrier's fallen into a fitful sleep again. I pull up a crate to the table and sit staring at the limestone wall. It's quiet outside. Deathly quiet. What will we do without water?

Then I remember something. The slops basin under the bench. I grab it, careful not to spill a drop. Four inches at least: cloudy, and with a scum on top, but water nevertheless. I scoop a few spoonfuls of it into a clean pannikin. Pick up a pinch of potassium permanganate from the jar before sealing the lid. I drop the crystals into the pannikin and stir gently with my finger. If the water turns pink, it's safe to drink.

The water turns brown.

57

From the secret diary of Mary Watson

I wake with a start. The rocking chair quivers. Ferrier, dozing in my arms, frowns. From the light seeping through closed shutters, I can tell it's dusk. I hadn't meant to fall asleep.

Ah Sam hasn't moved from where I left him. I watch him breathing evenly. But all of a sudden, I'm tense, far too tight. Almost terrified.

Then I notice the voices. Outside, down at the beach. Not the blacks. More like the banter and catcalls of a lugger crew just landed on shore. Percy!

Do I wake Ah Sam? But to what use? There are too many voices. We're outnumbered. There's nowhere to hide. All bets have been placed and the pot's just right. Nothing to do but show our hands. Futility washes over me in one long wave.

I hear the cracking of a gun. Another shot, then another. High-pitched ululations. The now-familiar whistle-hiss of spears through air.

Then silence.

I take Ferrier over to the cradle and place him gently on the small mattress. I bend down and touch my lips to his forehead at the hairline. It's like kissing the softest peach down. 'I'm sorry, darling boy.'

I walk over to the peephole and look out. I can see three spears lying on the ground, and the lavish purples, pinks and oranges saturating the sky. The field of view is too small to see who was speaking. Whoever it is, I'm better off outside where I can see them, rather than hunkered down inside waiting for them to break down the door. Or shoot through it.

I take a deep breath. Pick up the rifle. Pull up the bar. Ferrier grumbles but doesn't wake.

Dark is falling quickly. I'm halfway down to the beach when I see a silhouette of a man walking towards me. He carries some kind of satchel over one shoulder. Behind him, three other men. I should be flattered, I suppose, if Percy thinks he'll need so many assassins to take care of me.

'Come one step further and you're dead,' I shout into the gloom, and lift the rifle.

I point it at the figure in front, but I can't seem to grip it properly. My hands are too tired from patching up Ah Sam. My arms feel weak. If I pull the trigger, the recoil is likely to tear my finger off. I don't care.

The silhouette in front seems larger than Percy, but the light is too poor to be sure. He stops. The men behind him stop. A few seconds pass before the big man speaks.

'That's hardly a fit way to greet your employer.'

Now it's my ears playing tricks as well. Roberts! But then his beard resolves in the darkness. I recognise the broad set of his shoulders. A cloud uncovers the last of the sun, lighting a fire behind him. I'm taken by surprise, but not reassured.

'Let me guess, Captain, you've come to kill me. I warn you, I'll put up a struggle.'

My voice doesn't sound like my own. Someone older. Someone harder. A rat, cornered and left with no option but to fight.

I hear a shuffling sound behind me. Ah Sam has dragged himself to his feet and is staggering towards the men.

'Ah Sam. No! Come back.'

He doesn't even have the revolver. I can do nothing but watch. He stumbles up to Roberts, mumbles a few words I can't hear, then collapses onto his chest.

'I have the ship's surgeon here,' Roberts says calmly, holding the unconscious Ah Sam erect with one burly arm. 'Let's get him into the house.' When I don't respond, he drawls, 'You'd rather he died, would you?'

I lower the gun a few inches. The group moves closer and I raise it again.

'Just you and the surgeon,' I tell him.

He's close enough now for me to see his eyes roll skywards in exasperation. He turns and mutters something to the men behind him. They wander back towards the rowboat pulled up on shore. Against the fading sunset, I can see their guns. One of them grabs something from between the seats. I point the rifle in his direction.

Roberts intervenes again. 'It's a medical bag, nothing more.'

Behind him, I notice for the first time the outline of what looks in the semi-darkness to be a Chinese junk moored a hundred yards out in the bay.

Roberts half-drags, half-carries Ah Sam towards the house. The other man with the bag follows. I'm determined to get there first. Ferrier's inside. By the time they walk over the threshold, I've lit a lamp and am standing guard next to the cradle.

'Just relax, will you?' Roberts throws his hat and satchel on the table.

The man with the medical bag has coaxed Ah Sam back down onto the mattress on his stomach and is rubbing something into his wound.

Roberts sits in my rocking chair, puts his boots on a nearby crate. 'This place smells like a cross between an opium den and an abattoir.'

'We've no water.' My throat is dry from just saying the words. 'I couldn't clean up.'

He looks at a blood-soaked rag on the floor, then cocks his head towards the door. 'You've had a spot of trouble with the blacks, I see.'

Some sound — a mangled laugh — escapes me. My tongue slips its harness. 'Ah Leung is dead. They killed him over at the farm.'

Roberts shrugs. 'Small loss.'

He seems so calm, so much himself. I rub my dry lips, suddenly uncertain. I'm thirsty. Very thirsty. I wonder if it's affecting my judgement.

'Where's Percy?'

'You needn't worry about him any more.' There's a lightness behind his deep voice, almost a chuckle.

'Are you working for the French, like he is?'

'No. And I wish you'd put that bloody rifle down. You're making Anderson nervous.'

Anderson must be the surgeon. He has large hands, I notice, and a bald spot in his brown hair on the crown of his head. He pinches the skin gently on the back of one of Ah Sam's hands and turns to Roberts.

'We need some fresh water. He's dehydrated, as well as everything else.'

Again, I lick my lips. Ferrier stirs behind me.

'Go and tell Davis and Green to fetch some,' Roberts says to Anderson.

'No,' I say quickly. 'The natives. That's where they hide. Over at the swamp.'

'We've water in the rowboat and on the junk. Plenty of it.' He eyes me steadily, his voice gentler this time. 'Put the gun down, Mary.'

I lay it carefully on the shelf, still within reach and put a hand on the cradle for support.

'Did you know Percy was working for the French?' I ask.

'Yes.'

'How long have you known?'

'All along.' He looks around. 'Do you have any food? The men will need to eat.'

It seems such an odd question under the circumstances ... like asking whether I have ever flown to the moon.

'Um. I don't know. I'll look. But I have to go into the bedroom and feed the baby first.'

I lift Ferrier out of his cradle. My hands are shaking so much, I almost drop him.

'You're thirsty too, aren't you?' Roberts comes over and holds out his arms. I pull Ferrier away from him, shield him with my body. But he brings my face around with one cupped hand. 'It won't do him any good if you drop him on the floor.'

I think about this. Roberts takes a step back, but makes a wriggling motion with his fingers. After a few agonising seconds of indecision, I hand Ferrier over. The comparison is comical. A creature so small up against one so big. A beetle on a cliff face.

Roberts rests the baby over his shoulder, pats him awkwardly but softly enough. The span of his hand reaches almost all the way across Ferrier's back. As for Ferrier, he's apparently forgotten his hunger and thirst. This new perch interests him, or rather the vegetation he's found on it. He tugs at the beard, fascinated. Roberts winces theatrically, which inspires Ferrier to repeat the experiment, this time with a larger handful, a more forceful pull.

'I might have to sign you up, you little blighter. Put you on torture duty.' Roberts catches my eye. 'Go to my satchel. There's a canteen of water in there. You'll pass out if you try to feed him without a drink.'

I find the canteen at the bottom of the bag. Under a looking glass, a book, a compass and a wad of cash. I unplug the cork and drink greedily. Then wipe my mouth with the back of my hand. There's still some left in the bottle.

'Ah Sam?' I offer.

Anderson looks up, gives a small nod. I hand him the bottle. He pours a little into his cupped palm, holds it to Ah Sam's lips. The Chinaman manages to swallow a little of it then turns his head away.

'A small amount is best for the moment,' Anderson says. 'Too much would just make him heave.'

'The child is getting more than enough liquid if this wet end is anything to go by,' Roberts says, holding Ferrier away from his body, his nose screwed up.

I go to retrieve him, but Ferrier doesn't want to let go of his new-found hairy toy. I have to peel back his tiny fingers one by one while Roberts grumbles like a deep earthquake. I take the baby into the bedroom, sit on the bed and give him the breast. By the time

I've changed him and gone back into the communal room, Ah Sam is sitting up on the mattress, pale, but looking much better. I place Ferrier in the cradle, passing him a wooden peg to play with and maul with his gums.

'You'll be all right now, Ah Sam,' Roberts says.

'Yes, boss.'

'Boss! Ah Sam?' I look down at the Chinaman, bemused and hurt.

He stares back at me, apology in his eyes.

Roberts is inspecting the last remaining box of ammunition on the shelf.

'How long has Ah Sam been one of your minions?' I ask.

'I mentioned back in Townsville that I used to work for the Chinese government all those years ago. Ah Sam was similarly employed. Our paths have crossed many times since then.'

A stocky crewman with wiry black hair brings a few more canteens of water into the house. His pants are tucked into boots that are cracked at the toe.

'Where do you want these, missus?'

'Over in the corner.' Roberts answers for me, pointing. He perches uncomfortably on a stool. None of our seats is large enough for him, except the rocking chair.

Before he leaves, the crewman turns back to the captain. 'The blacks' camp is behind the hill.' Threads of blood lust pull tight in his brown eyes.

'Leave them be,' Roberts says. 'We'll be off the island soon enough.'

The crewman mumbles something. Roberts's response is swift and cold. 'Keep your mouth shut, Henson, and people might not notice you're a fool. Exactly how do you reckon one woman and a wounded Chinaman could account for ... how many? Twenty blacks? You'd have us leave a massacre behind so blatant even incompetent idiots like Fitzgerald and Brooke would know we've passed through.'

Henson leaves, abashed. I go foraging for still-edible potatoes in the bin under the bench.

'Are you going to take us off the island, Captain?'

'Of course. I didn't come here for the balmy air and coconuts.'

While I was feeding the baby, he must have noticed Bob's rum and poured himself a slug. I watch as he downs what's left in the pannikin and pours in some more. I put the few potatoes that are passable in a dish, sit opposite him and start peeling. Part of me knows that I'm exhausted, that I desperately need sleep. But I'm even more desperate to know what's happening. Why Roberts is here. And what comes next.

'Where's Percy? You owe me an explanation.'

Roberts looks into the bowl. He turns to the surgeon. 'Rations are short here. Send the boat back to the junk for meat and bread. And make sure a proper watch is set on the beach. No fires, but ensure the blacks know we're armed and alert.'

It's clear he's sent the surgeon away so that we can talk. He gives me a candid look as soon as the other man has gone.

'Fuller's fine, I'm sure. Off to tell his Froggy friends where to find a catboat carrying a few dozen rifles bound for New Guinea.'

'No! You mean he'll get away with betraying you? I can't believe it.'

'He didn't betray me. On the contrary, he's been very helpful, albeit inadvertently. I wouldn't stop his quest for the world.'

'I wish you'd stop talking in circles. All I know is I risked my life going up that hill. And it seems it was all just a game. I've gone through all of this for nothing.'

'Oh, no. Not for nothing. That reminds me. The money in my satchel is yours. There's another packet in the front compartment for you, Ah Sam.'

The Chinaman looks up. His colour is better, and he's had more water to drink. I notice that my mouth is hanging open. I close it, but I can't take my eyes away from Roberts's smug face.

'You need more explanation, don't you?' he asks.

'I could have been killed. It doesn't matter so much for me, but the baby ...' I feel the emotion well up in my throat.

He takes another long sip of rum, then puts the pannikin down on the table with a thump. 'I assessed you carefully in Cooktown, when I last saw you. I knew that you were having a baby. Believe it or not, I'm not in the habit of putting a woman's life in danger, particularly one with a child. I knew Ah Sam's protection could only stretch so far.'

'So, the coded messages, the signalling — they were diversions. Let me guess. You had someone on another island sending and receiving the real signals?'

'No. Not exactly.' He's sick of the too-small stool and goes to sit in the rocking chair. Pulls a crate over and rests his boots on it. He stares into the middle distance. 'Do you remember me speaking back in Townsville about Britain's decoy ships? The political machinations over territory? Just five years ago, Disraeli spent four million pounds to buy the Suez Canal. He did so because Egypt was essentially bankrupt. If the hopeless government of Ismail Pasha had fallen, Grevy would have pounced. Even so, we still share financial administration of that bloody country with France. For the moment, at least.' He grunts and frowns. 'Forget I said that. That's another project, another time. Anyway, the French have invested a great deal in their network of spies. Now the Germans are getting involved. Bismarck thinks colonies a great waste of energy, but the captains of German industry would love to change his mind. They imagine colonies to be a bottomless trove of free resources ... though they're hopeless at colonial administration. Utterly hopeless. And they, too, have spies.'

I shake my head, bemused. 'What has any of this to do with Percy and Charley? Or with me, for that matter?'

'I'm getting to that. What we've done — no, what *you've* done — is give them exactly what they wanted: information on what measures Her Majesty has taken to protect the Empire's trade in the east. But, because we already know what they've learned, how they've learned it, and, often, whom they've told, we now have a very good idea of who their contacts are. The French think themselves very clever indeed, though all they're doing is wandering about inside the trap we've set. That boat that Fuller's intercepting is carrying forty-odd Gewehr 71 rifles, and the crew is Prussian. Now the French will be very peeved with the Germans, even though it's a perfectly reasonable shipment in support of Germany's trade mission in New Guinea. But the French know it's suspicious, because they learned of it by intercepting the message traffic of Her Majesty's Foreign Office.'

My head is whirring with the subterfuge of it all. 'Percy had no intention of coming back to take Ah Sam and me off the island, did he? He just thought to leave us here for Ah Leung to take care of, or the blacks?'

Roberts looks rueful. 'I'm sorry you've had to keep such bad company for so long.'

'So you intend to let Percy and Charley continue to do what they're doing?'

'Oh, they'll be dealt with when the conditions are right. When they are of no further use to us, or else the French have abandoned them.'

There's a sudden chill in the air. The old Roberts is back, complete with shards of obsidian in his gaze.

I finish peeling one potato and start on another. 'Why didn't Percy catch on sooner, after the first drop, that things weren't going to plan?'

'Because it *did* go to plan. As far as he could tell, anyhow. What I told you in Cooktown was the truth. There were delicate manoeuvres relating to French spies in Cairo. Boule and Fuller were told to cool their heels, play the game. Not to make a move until they had word to go.'

'You seem very sure I wasn't in league with them.'

A look passes between Roberts and Ah Sam. I feel anger flushing the skin on my neck.

'I see. Ah Sam was watching me all the time, wasn't he? Not looking after me so much as monitoring me.'

Ah Sam looks insulted. 'I look after you, missy.'

I push the finished potatoes aside, put my elbows on the table and rub my eyes. From what high moral ground can I fling my accusations? So they both lied to me. My whole life, since I met Percy in Brisbane, has been a lie. I look up dully.

Roberts glances over to the shelf in the corner, with its jars of fishhooks and insect-ridden flour, as though summing up what my life here has been like. 'How are you going to stop your husband looking for you and your son if the house is empty when he returns?'

I stand and walk over to the shuttered windows, rest my hands on the bench. 'I don't know.' I try for neutrality, but manage to sound resentful. I need time to think. Time to sleep.

'Be ready to leave at dark tomorrow night,' Roberts says. 'Until then, I'll get the men to take the junk up the coast. There's a cove half a mile north that's secluded enough.'

'Where's your steamer?' I ask.

He gives me a pitying look. 'I'd hardly advertise to all and sundry that I've set anchor off Lizard Island now, would I?' He glances at Ah Sam, who grins back. 'Ah Sam's connections come in handy sometimes. Though, no doubt, there are some disgruntled John Pigtails down the coast wondering what happened to their old junk.'

'Oh, I forgot.' I turn to face him. 'I have a surprise of my own. Then again, maybe you know about her too.'

'Her?'

'There's a dead woman and her baby in Percy's hut. The one just up the beach. Ah Leung's body is in the hut beyond it.'

He gives a low whistle. 'Starting a makeshift mausoleum, are we? Who is she, do you know?'

'One of Charley's girls. The baby is Bob's. She was sick when she arrived in a rowboat looking for him. Typhoid, I think. The baby was already ... gone. Ah Sam found her body this morning, after Ah Leung was killed.'

'It's a wonder the blacks didn't make off with her.'

'Maybe they knew what she died of and didn't want to catch it. As for Ah Leung, Ah Sam locked him in their hut so that they couldn't get at him.'

'Ah.' Something clears in the Captain's eyes.

'The bones. They need to be shipped back to China.'

Ah Sam nods solemnly, then looks at the floor. 'Very bad otherwise, boss. Spirit wander, always.'

58

*My best thoughts come to
me when I'm knitting.*

From the secret diary of Mary Watson

Strangely enough, I'm too exhausted to sleep. It's ten at night. Ah Sam seems to have roused himself. He's lit his opium pipe and he's sitting at the table with his mah jong tiles. The ivory blocks click as he uses the fingers of his good arm. He's playing an improvised game for one, based on the different suits: bamboo, character, honour, flower.

My knitting needles clack: plain two, purl two.

After I fed the crew a stew of potatoes and carrots, some meat and bread, all but half-a-dozen armed men rowed back to the junk and sailed north to the secluded hiding spot. Captain Roberts is here in the house, with his gun, asleep in the rocking chair. Ferrier's in his cradle, snoozing. Purl one, plain two. A branch is scratching on the roof: the sound of someone trying to strike the same match over and over. And, in the distance, the boom of the reef, like my own pulse to me now. But no stealthy tread of the blacks. No singing. With so many guns around, they seem to have withdrawn.

Ah Sam mumbles something to himself in Mandarin. Captain Roberts shifts his weight and the rocking chair squeaks.

If Ferrier and I did disappear from the island, how would the world see it? As Bob's fault? Would they imagine him absent-minded at best, cruelly careless at worst, to leave his young wife alone with a baby, two Chinamen, no boat and cantankerous blacks just over the hill?

Plain one, purl one.

How would Fitzgerald and his incompetent crew determine what had happened to us?

I remember something then: the diary I bought in Cooktown, as any young pioneer wife should. In dutiful fashion I've written in it regularly since I've been on the Lizard. It is an alibi of sorts, for public consumption: full of boring whiffs of authenticity; domestic trivia by the pint. A litany of poultry: deaths, eggs and hatchings. Ginger cakes. Wind directions. Passing boats and newly dug privies.

Ah Sam looks up from his tiles, the opium pipe in the corner of his mouth. And, just like that — call it inspiration or my Cornish third eye — the pieces start to fall into place.

Ah Sam, the baby and I could escape in the tank used for boiling the sea slugs. The stirring paddles would suffice for oars. We would take what water we had, which would not be enough unless we made landfall and found more.

I think of the small period of thirst that Ah Sam and I have just experienced. What if that sensation of dry mouth and dizzy head grew worse for days and days until finally we succumbed?

Dying of thirst. What a terrible, epic way to go.

Plain one, purl two.

It's the next day and I've been listening to the bird sounds of dawn for a while before Roberts wakes. Finches with their fussy calls, pecking the morning open. The deep half-grunts of gannets out to sea. I will miss the birds.

I've fed the baby and am in the main room when Roberts opens his eyes. His beard has a life of its own, poking out like a chimney brush.

Ah Sam, much recovered, is rubbing tea leaves together in his palms to release their aroma. He scatters them from his closed fist into the boiling billy on top of the kerosene stove he's set up on the table. Gives them a few minutes at a rolling boil, then lifts the billy off with a piece of cloth wrapped around the handle. He rotates it three times on the table to brew.

Roberts takes a sip of the tea Ah Sam hands him, wincing at its bitterness, while I pace the room, trying to keep up with my thoughts.

After I tell him, Roberts sits scowling and thinking, blowing occasionally on the surface of the tea. Naturally enough, I suppose, he isn't keen on my idea. But I feel he has a debt to me. I'm owed something more than money for my trouble. I would do it all alone, but I need help with the details. Specifically: his nautical knowledge. Where would our journey in the slug tank take us, given the currents and likely wind directions at this time of year? Where might we make landfall? What might be our final resting place if we failed in our mission to reach the mainland?

Ah Sam nearly has a fit. The old horror rises up in his eyes, even though I've explained the necessities of the situation.

Roberts finally comes down on my side. He fishes a gnat from his pannikin with a finger and observes evenly, 'Ah Sam's right. It's not wise to interfere with Chinese customs. Maybe you could just leave him on the island — with a note pinned to his pyjamas for the blacks, asking nicely if they'll leave his bones in a pile when they're done.'

This more immediate threat chases away the old one in Ah Sam who gives a rough shudder of resignation and I know that it will be done. Roberts's crew can do the preparations. I'll advise them on what is needed.

We spend the morning planning the details.

Roberts only once tries to stop me. He looks up from under his brows. 'Are you sure you won't just come with us without all of this folderol? I can arrange for a new identity for you and the baby.'

'Yes, I'm sure. If Bob even imagines we're still alive, he won't rest until he finds us.'

He nods. 'I'll tell the men to help you, then. But be careful. Take a gun. The blacks haven't quite given up and gone away. Have you seen your smoking shed lately?'

I shake my head.

'They've drawn their witchcraft all over it,' Roberts says. 'And decorated the ground in front with a dead dog.'

With all that's been going on, I haven't spared Sylvester a thought.

'What do you think they'll do when we've gone?' I ask.

Roberts gets to his feet and reaches for his cap on the table. 'Loot the place. If you're leaving anything you want found in the house, you'd better put it somewhere out of the way, where it won't be destroyed.'

*

I arrived on the island in the dark, and I'm leaving the same way.

I have such a feeling of *déjà vu*. I remember the night when Carrie and I first landed on the Lizard; the strange thought that came to me when I saw the slug tank squatting over its cold firepit: the Owl and the Pussycat and how they went to sea in their beautiful pea-green boat. Both Carrie and Bob scoffed at me then. But now, as the slug tank bobs in the water on a gentle swell, it all seems so right — inevitable, even.

Night's fallen softly and the sky above is heavy with the anchor of the Southern Cross. Phosphorescence sparks moss-green under the water. A new moon hangs like a bauble of pale resin in a dark hive. The horseshoe of beach glows as we move away from shore, but already the little limestone house I've lived in for sixteen months is just a shadow. I can just make out the smokehouse, with its eerie artwork, an insignificant smudge. Only Cook's Look still seems real, looming above the island like a single overwhelming idea none of us has quite deciphered.

Hard to make out from here, but I think I see two black men standing at the water's edge at the northern tip of the beach. Watching.

They make no attempt to follow in their canoes. Which answers the question that tormented me for so many weeks and months. It was never my death that they wanted. They could easily have killed me that last night I climbed Cook's Look.

All they ever wanted was their island full of lizards.

We reach No. 5 Howick at about midnight. I let Ah Sam and Roberts's crew arrange the scene by lantern light. Ah Sam, thank goodness, has been helpful. He alone knows the etiquette of how a Chinaman takes himself away to die. The head resting on the small wooden box. The quilt pulled up neatly to the throat. As though the body, he told me, the fear still in his eyes, is just asleep and waiting to be woken in the flowery land.

I stand at the railing of the anchored junk, swatting mosquitos, watching the lights of the bobbing fireflies on shore. I go through the tank's contents in my mind. The revolver, the baby's things, an umbrella to keep the sun off through the day, our few tins of remaining food. In a small box: my clothes, jewellery, watch and piddling amount of money Bob left me. Most importantly, a record of our imaginary journey: a diary written in pencil, wrapped in waterproof cloth.

Captain Roberts invites me to come ashore and inspect the handiwork, but I decline. Call me superstitious, but I want to stay safely away from my own death. From Ferrier's death (he's tucked up in a crate made into a makeshift cradle below deck). From Ah Sam's. I feel afraid. Strangely empty and afraid. Those bodies — Ah Leung's, Laura's and her baby's — could have so easily been ours.

I do not want to see our epitaphs made flesh.

In a small time-stopped moment, like a photograph, I visualise Ah Sam lying on a small beach, his head resting on the wooden opium box, his quilt pulled neatly up to his chin. And there I am, in a green-tinged open coffin in the mangroves, the box at my left elbow; and, inside the box, my diary of our last days. I'm not yet lifeless but I'm terribly thirsty. The sun is hot. My baby's dying of dehydration on my chest.

I make an involuntary noise and come back to the present with a jolt. I tell myself, it didn't happen that way.

I'm not ungrateful to Laura and Ah Leung. Though both past redemption in their respective ways, they've given Ah Sam and me the future. It's only Wilfred I feel a pang for. So small and innocent. Just like Ferrier. There, but for the grace of God, goes my own baby.

I rub my ring finger, feeling the slight indentation where my wedding ring once circled it. When I handed it to Roberts to put on Laura's finger, I'd noticed the white worm of skin beneath it and thought to myself, 'Soon enough it will fade.' And so will Mary Watson. She's there in the tank, wearing her brown dress, her belt, her wedding ring. Her much beloved child, asleep forever on her chest.

59

From the secret diary of Mary Watson

3RD OCTOBER 1881

It's a beautiful morning, the sky a lapis-lazuli blue, like some Renaissance religious painting; not a single blot of sin to mar it. It's almost as if the universe is co-operating in my plan. The rainless sky matching up with accounts of no rain in the tank-diary entries.

I've been standing at the rail almost since dawn, just watching. Ferrier's snoozing in my arms. Roberts came by twenty minutes ago and pointed out a small dark spot on the horizon, *Blackbird*, waiting for us. We should reach it by noon. Soon it will be time for me to go below. Push my hair under a sailor's cap. Dress in the ragged pants and shirt that is uniform for the rest of the crew. Just until we've passed the danger of encounter with other boats. Until we reach Sydney, where no one knows me. Where Ferrier and I can disappear into the crowd.

Ferrier wakes and starts squirming. I hold him up to my face in the sunshine, blow gently on his belly where his nightdress has bunched up. I'm letting the sunlight bathe his skin as long as possible. Soon enough he'll have to stay below deck until the danger of us being recognised has passed. The water cleaves beneath us in a series of smooth, clean swishes. We're making good time.

Ah Sam approaches and stands next to me, smiling with his eyes. We both look out to sea.

'After we dock, Ah Sam, will you go back to China?'

He nods and adjusts a grimy sailor's cap with one of those hardworking hands.

'I'll miss you,' I say. And I will. 'You've been a good friend.'

'Will you go to Mister Green?' he asks.

I think of the address in my pocket. The two shells carefully wrapped and packed away. 'Yes. If he'll have me.'

Captain Roberts has offered me work. A more sedate job, encoding and decoding messages. He thinks I'll be good at it. But the work's in Sydney. That's not quite where I want to make a new start. And, in any case, I've had enough. Ferrier's growing fast. He's survived the Lizard, small thanks to his mother. I need to settle somewhere, somehow, where he'll be safe and happy.

My arms ache from holding him close for so long.

'Here, will you take him?' I say to Ah Sam.

Ah Sam holds Ferrier with the ease of long practice. His shoulder doesn't appear to bother him as he holds the baby out and over the rail. Ferrier squeals with delight at the sparkling water rushing by, the foam flying from the hull. I notice then just how far the baby is from safety. Just one slip. One cramp in

Ah Sam's hand. One stab of pain in his sore shoulder and he might inadvertently let go. Ferrier's blowing bubbles above the churning water, his chubby legs riding a bicycle of air.

My voice is shrill. 'Don't do that, Ah Sam! I'll die a thousand deaths!'

He's never laughed before in my presence. There's an alarming shriek in it, his eyes close tight and his whole face twitches. Then I'm laughing myself, realising what I've said.

When he recovers himself, he pulls Ferrier back in and hands him over. The baby squirms in my arms and starts to cry. His little arms are reaching for the Chinaman. He wants to do it all over again.

The last words Roberts said to me as we boarded the junk still linger. 'You know you'll be remembered as the brave heroine of Lizard Island. *She fought off the blacks and took to sea, indomitable, undefeated. Only to die of thirst.* They'll say it with great solemnity.'

'A pity I won't be around to enjoy the celebrity,' I'd said dryly.

Truth is, I don't want to be a symbol of the struggle between black and white. I don't think the natives should be punished for what they haven't done. But I could think of no other scenario. No other way.

One day, however, I might tell the real story.

Later, when I lie on my small berth staring at the overhead, I realise I may, unwittingly, have begun already to tell the truth. I made a mistake in the tank diary entries: I've prefaced them with September dates when it is in fact October. Why? Tiredness perhaps? Not carelessness, surely, after all that I've been through? Will any harm come of such a small act of self-sabotage?

Perhaps I secretly want someone — fifty years, or a hundred years from now — to look more closely at the evidence and to wonder.

Maybe some part of me wants the truth to be known.

AUTHOR'S NOTE

According to the accepted historical record, Mary Watson, aged twenty-one, had been married less than eighteen months when she died of thirst. Mainland Aboriginals attacked the two Chinese workmen at her absent husband's *bêche-de-mer* station on Lizard Island: Ah Leung died in the vegetable garden; Ah Sam suffered spear wounds. With her four-month-old baby, Ferrier, and the injured Ah Sam, Mary put to sea in a smoke-blackened, cut-down ship's tank used for boiling sea-slugs. They drifted for eight days and forty miles, making landfall in several places without finding water.

Their remains, identified by Mary's husband, Robert Watson, were found some months later, in January 1882, on No. 5 Island in the Howick Group off the Cape York Peninsula. Still in the iron tank, now resting in the mangroves, their bones were immersed in fresh rain from a recent tropical downpour. The baby's skull rested on his mother's breast. The skeleton of a Chinese man lay on a woven mat in the shade of a tree a little way from the tank, his head on a wooden box used as a pillow, a quilt pulled neatly up to his throat.

In the tank, investigators found a small wooden box containing clothing, jewellery, a small amount of money, and a diary in Mary's hand, carefully preserved in waterproof cloth, describing their last days.

Much of the evidence supporting this version of events is equivocal, reliant on Mary's diary entries. A copy of the diary found with the bodies in the tank appears at the start of the novel. The original diary is held in the John Oxley Library in Brisbane.

Robert Watson's deposition after the bodies were discovered is also part of the public record and is also reproduced at the start of the novel.

My version of events is fictional speculation, transforming the real people involved in Mary's story into characters. In no way do I propose their actions or personalities to be a true and accurate account of their lives. I have attempted , nevertheless, to respect historical accuracy while imposing my own interpretative slant on what is known. This interpretation maintains, as far as possible, consistency with the public record: newspaper reports, official documentation, and preserved sentiment on the events surrounding Mary's demise.

At the time, what happened to Mary and her baby threw fuel on an already incendiary debate regarding white and black collisions in Far North Queensland. Punitive expeditions against indigenous tribes in the area were carried out regardless of a lack of evidence.

The references made by the characters to cannibalistic practices of the indigenous people around Cooktown and the Palmer River reflect a widely held, though wholly unsubstantiated, belief of the time. These rumours were no doubt a useful psychological lever to justify harsh retaliation against tribal groups in the area.

The references to 'Myalls', 'Merkins' etc do not reflect true indigenous groups. The nomenclature was merely a convenient way for Europeans to divide different tribes according to locality, appearance and perceived customs.

The patronising attitude of Mary towards the indigenous boys on Lizard Island, and the disrespectful approach of all characters to the Chinese, though totally unacceptable to our contemporary sensibilities, were nevertheless commonplace at the time.

ACKNOWLEDGEMENTS

Creating a novel is never a one-person exercise. My deepest debt is to Rob Riel who has offered support, both editorial and emotional, throughout the whole writing process. Huge thanks go to my agent Selwa Anthony for her belief, loyalty and, last but not least, her love of dogs. Thanks to Amanda O'Connell, Jo Butler and the team at Harper Collins for making the editorial process a nurturing experience instead of a fraught one. The John Oxley Library in Brisbane was an invaluable resource in the writing of this novel. The work has also been informed by several books: *Lizard Island: The Journey of Mary Watson* by Suzanne Falkiner and Alan Oldfield; *Lizard Island: A Reconstruction of the Life of Mrs Watson* by Jillian Robertson; and *River of Gold* by Hector Holthouse. And finally, thanks to Mary Watson, whatever her fate, for her undeniable strength and courage.